LORD JOHNNIE

LESLIE TURNER WHITE

LORD JOHNNIE

CROWN PUBLISHERS • New York

To My Good Friends
Paul R. Reynolds
and
Paul D. Conover
Godfathers to Lord Johnnie

LORD JOHNNIE

PART
ONE

1

ON THE 18TH OF MARCH, 1756, LONDON WAS AGOG WITH EXCITEMENT. From the Court of St. James to the dives of Whitefriars, two portentous events were under discussion—the inevitability of war with France and the hanging of Lord Johnnie on the morrow.

There was no connection between the two events. War would be a grim catastrophe, but the hanging of such a popular hero was a holiday affair, and Johnnie the Rogue was the idol of London's lowly, as well as a sliver under the toenail of London's gentry. Yet now that he was gallows-bound, rich and poor willingly turned out to do him honor, and everybody in the city who could possibly manage it would be at Tyburn in the morning to cheer him on to glory.

The day itself was gray and cold, and the rawness penetrated into the prison office of old Newgate where huddled the two officials responsible for Johnnie's fate. Mr. Goad, the hangman, through whose calloused hands Lord Johnnie would pass to eternity, resembled an unhappy mastiff; a large, scarred man with a dirty leather jacket, and hair cut short enough to make poor hiding ground for lice. Mr. Muggins, Newgate's Chief Gaoler, was gaunt and sallow, and looked as if he himself had been hanged the week before.

The little office was not a cheerful place. The furnishings were sparse, and it had but two small barred windows on either side of the room, one of which gave a view of the prison press-yard, where at the moment Lord Johnnie was holding court at a drunken banquet to celebrate his departure into the unknown. The opposite window looked down upon the street in front of the prison, which, since daylight, had been jammed with people hoping for a glimpse of the condemned. Unable to see their hero, they were enjoying a vicarious thrill from the snatches of song and squeals of happy laughter which came over the gray walls.

An exceptionally wild gust of shrieking from the press-yard brought Mr. Goad to his feet. He crossed to the courtyard window, and what he saw made him wince. Even the thought of Lord Johnnie's elegant garments, which as the hangman's rightful perquisites he would inherit, failed to buoy him.

"'E shouldn't have allowed the brawl, Muggins," he grumbled, turning away. "H'it'll breed trouble, mark 'e!"

"H'allowed h'it? Ha! Bleedin' little I 'ad to say about h'it!" The Chief Gaoler laughed without mirth. "The ruddy bastard's the most popular knave we've ever 'ad in Newgate in my time. 'Appy 'tis I'll be to see the last o' 'im."

"Aye," agreed Goad. "A regular Devil 'e is, wi' more lives than a cat."

"Than a bloody 'ole litter o' cats."

"'E ought to be drawn an' quartered," reasoned Mr. Goad. "Then we'd be certain 'e was dead."

Muggins nodded. "I've h'arranged for six h'extra guards."

"Six? *Six?*" Mr. Goad sniffed. "'Tis said before 'e left France, 'e single-'andedly out-fought a baker's dozen o' the King's Guardsmen 'oo tried to h'arrest 'im!"

"Rumor," mumbled Mr. Muggins. "H'idle rumor."

Mr. Goad ran a horny hand over the stubble of his pate and walked to the street window. Avoiding looking at the sea of morbid faces below, he scanned the low-hung clouds.

"H'I don't like it," he reiterated. "If there's a fog tomorrer—!" The very thought sickened him, and he slumped into a chair.

Mr. Muggins cherished the same unspoken fear. Not in a generation had gallows-conscious London been so excited over an execution. In the coffee-houses and grog-shops, wagers were being laid on the length of time Lord Johnnie would dance at the rope's end. Street urchins erected miniature gallows and played at hanging dolls; eel-criers sold more rumors than fish to eager ladies of quality; chambermaids discussed with lords, Lord Johnnie's alleged amours, and coyly claimed impossible intimacies; and for once thieves and bailiffs met on common ground. And even now, nearly twenty-four hours before the appointed time, the people were trekking out to Tyburn—bucks on horseback, ladies of fashion in carriages, lackeys representing their lords and ladies—all seeking to engage the choicest seats in the galleries, erected permanently around the gallows, from old Mammy Douglas, the female pew-opener who kept the key to them. Most of the poor would follow the prisoner's cart from Newgate in the morning, but the less hardy of these were now tramping out to Tyburn on foot, carrying a crust of bread and just enough gin to warm them during the cold night's wait.

"Well, 'e h'ain't no cat, an' 'e h'ain't no Devil; 'e's h'only a bloody scoundrel," said Mr. Muggins determinedly. "H'an' w'at's more—" He paused as the door opened and a smirking turnkey ushered a young woman into the office.

She was a tiny thing, gowned in black silk, and though heavily veiled, had about her an air of distinction. There was a pleasing sensuousness in the rustle of her costume and in the furtive bird-like way she moved into the room, but Mr. Muggins recognized quality when he saw it, so he stumbled erect and groped behind him for his wig. When a gale of laughter, shrill and obscene, swept into the room from the press-yard, the woman shuddered and appeared to wither. Muggins gallantly closed the window, and in the operation managed with a look to convey to Mr. Goad that his absence was more to be desired than his company. Mr. Goad took the hint.

With the door and windows closed, Mr. Muggins enjoyed a titillating sense of isolation. He bowed the visitor into the chair so recently vacated by the hangman.

"Your servant, m'lady?" he said tentatively.

She perched stiffly on the edge of the rough seat, silent, regal somehow, yet not quite at ease. Muggins was uncomfortable, as he always was in the presence of the highborn; a squirmy sense of inferiority which even his powerful position as Chief Gaoler failed to dispel. His sallow face puckered warily, and he reflected, logically enough, that though highborn this creature might be, she wanted something of *him,* else she would never have come to Newgate in this clandestine fashion. This knowledge acted as a leveler.

"Now, m'lady?" he urged confidentially.

She seemed about to resent the intimate tone, but a perceptible flutter of her tiny hands was the only outward indication. Yet Muggins caught the gesture, slight as it was, and waited patiently.

"I understand," she began in a low controlled voice, "that it is possible for a lady . . . for a woman plagued by debts to, er, marry a condemned felon and thus be cleared of her indebtedness in secret."

"H'mmn!" Muggins perceived the slip about "a lady," and realized that he had a neat profit in the offing, if handled properly. She was obviously in deep trouble, but her genteel poise had not yet cracked, so he let her simmer a few moments longer while he carefully examined a broken fingernail. ·

"Aye, m'lady," he conceded finally, "it 'as been done in the past, but 'tis now a practice frowned upon. Laws are bein' planned to prohibit it."

She swayed slightly. "If it is a question of money, I can pay you well!"

"Ah-h!" Muggins' frown of concentration melted into a conspiratorial smile. "In that event, it just might be arranged, m'lady." He moved as close to her as he deemed safe and lowered his voice. "The procedure is simple enough: ye marry a condemned rascal, who as yer 'usband becomes legally responsible fer yer debts. We promptly 'angs 'im, leavin' ye a pretty little widow, free as a bird o' both 'usban' *an'* debts."

"But how do we prevent everyone in London from knowing about it?"

Muggins winked. "Ah, m'lady, we keeps the records safe 'ere in Newgate. Ye gets a marriage certificate, w'ich ye shows to yer creditors. Since by that time, yer dearie is removed from this vale o' sorrow, there's precious little the money-lenders can do but gnash their teeth."

"Yet won't the truth get around?"

Muggins shrugged. "Per'aps a bit o' gossip may leak out, 'tis true, but as the money-lenders, w'ich I presumes ye fear, don't sit in the parlors o' the gentry, such as ye plainly be, m'lady, ye'll 'ave naught to worry about fer a long time."

"This, er, wedding? Does it have to be, well, consummated?"

He permitted himself a smirk. "Not unless ye wishes to bed the scoundrel, m'lady. Of course if ye did—"

She said with asperity, "Prithee don't jest, sir!"

"No offense, m'lady!" Muggins took a slow turn around the office to cool off. "Now," he said crisply, "'twill cost ye fifty guineas fer me; the risk is great, y'understand. Five guineas fer a Bishop, an' a proper High Church cleric I can promise ye, an' mebbe a tenner fer the lucky bridegroom hisself." He noted her reaction with a practiced eye, and though she wavered slightly, she finally nodded.

"Methinks I can manage that, if you're sure everything will be all right. But, oh merciful God, it must never be known!"

"A fiver fer the clerk will guarantee secrecy, m'lady. Ye can safely leave all arrangements in me capable 'ands." He felt his fever overcoming his natural caution and he hovered close above her. "Surely, 'tis cheap enough fer a great lady, such as 'tis plain ye be, to escape the debtors' prison?"

She cut off his familiarity with a tart question. "Have you a felon *now?*"

Muggins gave a flustered chuckle. "Aye, more'n enough an' some to spare, m'lady. There's Conkey Cobb, due to dance Monday week, an' Punch Conover—a likely lad is Punch, if I may be so bold to say so—the followin' Friday."

"That's too late! Good Lord, I must be free before this week is out! I must, I *must!*"

"Ah-h! Another marriage, m'lady?"

She was cracking under the strain and some of the starch melted from her backbone, leaving her very tiny, very feminine and very desirable. Mr. Muggins felt his lips go dry with desire, and the thought crossed his mind that perhaps, just possibly, *he* might find some way to enjoy this tiny "bit of fluff." But on the other hand that might jeopardize the financial arrangements, so he magnanimously pushed desire aside. A sudden burst of hilarity from the press-yard forced his mind into another channel.

" 'Od's blood! Methinks I 'ave it, m'lady!" he exclaimed. "There's one tomorrer, Tyburn-bound. The one they calls Johnnie Rogue, or Lord Johnnie, of 'oom ye've no doubts 'eard."

She seemed to be crying softly behind her veil, but she managed to nod her head. Muggins cackled.

"Oh, 'e'd make an 'andsome 'usband, deed 'e would, m'lady. 'Tis said that any female in the kingdom would be 'appy to bed the scamp, an' most 'ave. Be that as it may, 'e's an arrant knave an' 'ard to 'andle. 'E'd not be bought fer no paltry ten guineas, I can tell ye that, m'lady, but 'e's all we 'ave goin' to glory this week."

That wrenched a sob out of her. "I . . . I couldn't go much higher," she whispered. "Perhaps twenty guineas, if this . . . if he is the only chance, but that is absolutely all I could stand."

Mr. Muggins knew when a limit had been reached. "H'mmn! Well, m'lady, twenty *might* do it. 'Tis true that Lord Johnnie cares naught fer man nor devil, but 'e's a gallant laddie, an' fer a pretty wench—beggin' yer ladyship's pardon—'e just might oblige. Of course, 'e ain't no *regular* lord; 'tis but a nyme given 'im because o' 'is 'igh an' mighty airs. Yet 'tis plain to see 'e's well-born, like yer ownself, m'lady, if I might speak bold. Some as believe 'e's a bastard sired by a Scottish laird turned ship captain, out o' an English lydy-in-waitin' to the French court. 'Tis known 'e was eddicated in that country an' much traveled on land an' sea, but 'e skipped out o' France some five years ago, one jump ahead o' the King's Guardsmen. Since that time 'e's been a road-agent an' dandy-dan fer a gang o' London thieves w'at preys on the gentry—God bless 'em! But 'e's caught now, an' by the grace o' God, tomorrer we stretch 'is bloody—"

"Spare me the details!" she interrupted. "Can I marry this wretch at once?"

Mr. Muggins' silence was eloquent. The woman took the hint, opened her purse and counted out a stack of coins. Muggins sat down opposite her and picked up each coin separately, dropping it into a leather pouch like a squirrel stowing nuts. After that, he excused himself and left the office to issue the necessary instructions.

He was in high good humor when he returned, and offered to open a bottle of French wine, but the girl haughtily refused. Nettled, Muggins dropped into a chair and stared as boldly as he dared. He wished that he had the courage to tear aside her veil. A faint glimmer of sunlight eluded the clouds and slanted through the high window, illumining her figure. She was beautifully proportioned and every line of her, from her exquisitely held hands to the carriage of her body, showed breeding. The gaoler was impressed, but he was also irritated. Since he couldn't have her, he wanted to hurt her.

"After ye set yer eyes on Lord Johnnie," he baited her, "ye might want to *consummate* this 'ere marriage, m'lady."

She ignored the thrust, but he could hear her breathing. He sniffed the air like an old hound, and found it scented with perfume. He moistened his lips and sighed resignedly; he'd keep his place, for such as this was not for him.

In a suspiciously short space of time, a clergyman and his clerk bustled in as if, perhaps, they had been waiting around the corner for just such a call as this. The clerk, a callow one-eyed youth who looked more like a tavern potboy than an ecclesiastic assistant, produced cushions and other accouterments and began silently to rearrange the office.

Mr. Muggins rose and made a show of respect.

"M'lady, 'is Worship, the Reverend Adam Wryneck!"

The reverend started to bend his knee, after the manner of a peasant, then caught himself in time and bowed awkwardly. He was a shapeless flabby creature, like an oat-sack tied around the middle with twine, and his flushed moon-face was scarred by pox. Under a mop-like black wig, his watery eyes suggested two open sores. In his hairy paws, he clasped a large Book of Common Prayer. His great carcass was arrayed in frowsy canonicals which, though orthodox enough, seemed incongruous, for he exuded a distinctive odor customarily associated with the goat-yard.

"Yer 'umble servant, ma'am," he purred. "I didn't catch yer nyme?"

The girl hesitated and waved a heavily scented handkerchief before her nose. Mr. Muggins smirked.

"Now, now, yer Worship, 'tis to be a *secret* weddin'," he explained, and tossed five guineas on the desk to substantiate it.

The cleric snatched at the gold like a cock at a worm. "'Pon my oath, 'twill be so. Yet, ah, we must 'ave at least a Christian nyme to embellish the marriage certificate, m'lydy?"

"For that purpose you may put down the name Leanna," whispered the girl. "I can . . . well, fill in the rest later."

"Aye, t'be sure, t'be sure," soothed Muggins. "Now fer the lucky 'usband." He winked broadly at the cleric and stepped out of the office.

The Reverend Wryneck carefully fitted his bulk into a chair and placed the prayer book on the ledge of his belly. "Prithee, dearie, don't be nervous," he soothed.

Though Leanna held her head high, her voice quavered slightly. "I am not nervous, only . . . well, are you positive this is all *legal?*"

Wryneck gave his eyes a pious roll. "I wean 'tis so, 'pon my honor. You 'ave nothin' to fear, my child—trust Father Adam." He leaned over as if to pat her hands, but she drew back. "Oh, 'tis true the Church tries to anathematize such marriages, insisting they be solemnized *in facie ecclesiae,* but legally, dearie, 'tis sufficient that a man an' woman contract to marry *per verbe de praesenti,* or as it is called, *per verba de futuro,* to be properly acknowledged in the eyes o' the law." He beamed toothily. "Ye see 'ow ridiculously simple it all be?"

The girl nodded dully, and grasped her purse. Wryneck smiled, treated himself to a pinch of snuff, and wondered how he could squeeze an extra shilling or two for himself. The noise in the press-yard outside the window had gone strangely quiet.

Abruptly the office door banged open as Mr. Muggins returned, followed by a young giant in chains. Two burly keepers guarded the door, but the girl had eyes only for the prisoner.

Apparently Mr. Muggins had encountered some difficulties, for he was damp with sweat and groveled as if presenting the Lord High Commissioner of the realm.

"M'lady," he announced unctuously, "'ere's the celerbrated Lord Johnnie!"

The prisoner gave her a courtly bow. "Your servant, my lady," he said in a rich voice tinged with mockery.

Lady Leanna was too startled to move. Lord Johnnie was an impressive figure, with shoulders, wide and straight as a bullock's yoke, that tapered smartly down to a slim waist and slimmer ankles. Under a clean white wig which contrasted vividly with his tanned skin and black brows, was the face of an eagle, save for a full sensuous mouth. He had a wide sloping forehead, a long curved nose that seemed to quiver like an excited stallion's, and penetrating eyes twinkling with mischief. His large wedge-shaped body was encased in a rich suit of white and silver cloth. Leanna noticed particularly his hands, for the ill-born had warped, claw-like talons or bloated paws. Lord Johnnie's were strong and well kept, the fingers long and supple as a swordsman's. Although heavily manacled, he wore his chains with a debonair indifference, almost, she thought breathlessly, with distinction, as if they might be small silver bracelets such as dandies sported.

"Johnnie," babbled the Chief Gaoler, "'er ladyship 'as consented to pay ye, er, ten guineas to marry up with 'er. I assured 'er ye'd be 'appy to oblige."

"Blood and fury!" roared Johnnie. "*You* assured her! Why you puling catch-thief, by what God damned right—"

"Now 'ere, 'ere!" interposed the clergyman. "We shan't tyke the Lord's nyme in vyne, young 'un!"

Lord Johnnie paused, glancing at the reverend as if seeing him for the first time. Then he lay back his head and howled. "Stab me, if it isn't our old goat-herd the ordinary, all masqueraded as the Bishop of Hell!"

"Come now, Johnnie boy," pleaded Mr. Muggins, his face scarlet. "We'll make it twenty guineas!"

"*Twenty!*" trumpeted Johnnie indignantly. "'Od's fish, you whoreson, the ghoulish surgeons offered fifty guineas for my carcass *dead!* Why, damne, am I not worth as much *alive?*"

The girl leaned over and whispered something to Mr. Muggins. He shuddered slightly, and croaked: "Thirty guineas, Johnnie Rogue, an' a pox on ye fer blackmailin' a poor lady o' quality!"

Johnnie laughed and turned the full power of his gaze on Leanna. She bent before it, like a reed in a gale. Johnnie's smile twisted.

"Do I understand her ladyship is *proposing?* If so, then 'tis strange business that the offer must come through a swineherd like you, gaoler!" He made a leg to the girl. "Your servant, my lady."

She came slowly, majestically, to her tiny feet. She stood looking up at him like a diminutive queen.

"Prithee do not mock me, sir," she said coolly. "What do you demand?"

"Why, my lady, I demand nothing, save to return to my friends. May I ask what *you* demand?"

"Won't you marry me?"

Johnnie smiled. "Bless you, you haven't asked me!"

She steadied herself against the desk. "Oh, this is humiliating!" she cried impatiently. "Must I abase myself by begging in my own words? If that be your wish, then here it is: Will you be charitable enough to marry me . . . for a price?"

He stripped her with his piercing eyes until she shrank back.

"That was genuinely touching, ma'am," he said dryly. "I confess the proposal sounds much sweeter from your lovely lips than the cackle of this grave-snatcher. Especially the mention of *price.*"

She was crushed. "Don't taunt me, sir," she whispered. "I haven't much to offer, but—" She backed against the desk and covered her face with her hands.

"Stab me, my lady!" laughed Johnnie. "But you have more than enough to offer! 'Tis my misfortune to have so little. I unblushingly regret your proposal comes so late, for a husband should spend the nuptial night with his bride, but, unfortunately, I have other plans for the evening."

"Now, now, Johnnie, don't be obscene!" growled Mr. Muggins. "Set your blackmailin' price an' 'ave over."

Johnnie favored him with a look of scorn. "So be it. I shan't be unreasonable. 'Tis obvious some other knave has bedded her already, else she'd not come to this stinking hole for succor, but I'll not mind being cuckold if we put in the marriage contract that the child be named after me. 'Twould be a shame for my name to die along with me tomorrow."

The girl was shaking her head and crying softly.

" 'Tis an ill time for jest," Wryneck observed.

Leanna pushed away from the desk. "Oh, pray get on with it!" she snapped. "I can't stand more of this ghastly mockery. I agree! I agree . . . to *anything!* There is no child, but if 'tis your wish, sir, then upon my oath, my first-born son shall be named . . . John! Now in God's good name, let us have done with this bestial farce!"

Johnnie slapped his thigh. "So be it, my lady! Come now, you weavely ghouls, let the play start as her ladyship suggests. And you, Wryneck, seal well these sacred bonds of matrimony, for 'pon my honor, 'tis the first time I've been wed, and no doubt 'twill be the last." He bowed to the girl. "You'll excuse me if I wed and run, my lady? My friends await me in the press-yard, and if you'll pardon my mentioning it—time is scarce."

The one-eyed clerk, having slipped into his priest's orders, took his place beside the Reverend Wryneck. Lord Johnnie moved close to Leanna who stood braced against the desk, and Muggins hulked somewhere in the background.

And so the ceremony began.

Lady Leanna seemed dazed, for she stood with her head bowed numbly, oblivious to the mumbling responses of the rite of matrimony. Johnnie towered above her, steadying her with his strong arm. Of all those in the room, only the one-eyed clerk saw Lord Johnnie's slender fingers dip into her ladyship's purse, but as that youth had long since learned the virtue of tending strictly to his own business, he said nothing. *Virtus Laudatur et Alget,* as the Reverend Wryneck would have phrased it.

When at long last it was over, Wryneck seated himself at the gaoler's desk and began to fill in the ornate certificate of marriage. In a flourishing script he wrote the name Leanna, leaving sufficient space for her to insert her family name. Then he glanced up.

"Now, Johnnie, w'at's yer last nyme?"

"Stab me!" laughed Johnnie. "Is there a knave in all London who doesn't know my name?"

"Aye, 'tis Johnnie Rogue, shortened from Johnnie *the* Rogue," grumbled the cleric. "But that's no legal nyme for a certificate o' marriage."

Johnnie's eyes glowed—a danger signal which Mr. Muggins recognized. "If it's legal enough to be hanged by, it's legal enough for wedding! If not, then leave space for my wife to place a name of her own choosing!"

"Oh, yes, yes, yes!" cried the girl. "Only do stop this incessant quibbling! I'm going mad!"

Mr. Muggins moved out of the shadow. "Aye," he agreed, " 'tis enough. Ye can go back to yer friends now, Johnnie." He nodded at the guards.

But Johnnie continued to stare at the girl. "Thank you, sir," she murmured with an effort. "I shall pay you now."

Johnnie laughed. "Aye, that you will!" He started to bow, then before she could defend herself, he whipped aside the veil!

Even the one-eyed clerk gasped aloud in admiration.

From under a tiny French cap cascaded soft ringlets of hair, black as a crow's wing moistened with dew. These framed a small heart-shaped face with features of the exquisite delicacy of Flanders' lace; the type of face an artist would paint for glory. The eyes were large and vaguely slanted, and of such a deep blue they now seemed black in their anger. Her full lips, half-opened in surprise, disclosed perfect teeth. Though she was startled, her breeding gave her dignity.

Not so Johnnie. "By the powers, my lady, you are more beautiful than even I believed! Can it be that you are an angel, or are you mortal, too? I swear I must find out—!" And seizing her so as to prevent a struggle, he possessed her lips with his own.

She did not resist, but lay cold and stiff in his embrace. In sudden anger he shoved her away.

"By my troth, madame!" he growled. " 'Tis a poor showing of affection for your lawful spouse. I regret now that I lack time to melt your frigidity in a more convincing fashion!"

She regarded him with loathing. "Will you leave, sir?"

"Gladly!" snapped Johnnie, his face reddening. He turned to the door, trying to recover his swagger, and as he passed into the corridor he blew her an insolent kiss. But Lady Leanna had already turned her back on him.

Though the wedding might be kept a secret from the rest of London, there were no secrets in old Newgate. Marriages between felons and ladies of quality, while not common, were far from rare; they were matters of convenience, and except for death itself, the only avenue of escape for ladies facing imprisonment for debt, or big with child from an indiscretion and therefore in need of a husband's name. And so, through devious channels of communication, the news of the wedding had seeped into the darkest dungeon almost as soon as Lord Johnnie himself had returned to the press-yard.

He was quivering with rage as he tramped through the dank corridors. The guards sensed the change in him, and they edged warily beside him as though he were a tiger, but Johnnie walked mechanically, hardly aware of their company. He had been profoundly stirred by what had taken place in the gaoler's office, yet for the life of him, he could not reason why. He reviewed the experience step by step, but that told him nothing; he had merely wedded a strange woman in a law-cheating marriage, kissed the wench, and left. For Johnnie, such trifles were of passing moment. Nevertheless, his blood seemed on fire, an unfamiliar ache haunted his diaphragm, and a touch of perfume clung to his mouth.

A door clanged, and before he realized he had come so far, the guards ushered him into the press-yard, where he was promptly surrounded by a ribald and admiring mob who pressed him with food, drink, and banter.

"'Ow was she, Johnnie? . . . Did 'e bed the bitch, Johnnie boy? . . . Aye, don't be no snob, Lor' Johnnie; let wifey meet yer ol' frien's!"

Johnnie opened his mouth to retort, then checking himself, paused to look them over. In the months of his incarceration he had grown accustomed to them, yet now, after his brief glimpse of the outside world, they seemed strangers. Their collective skins were gray and lifeless as the prison walls; their eyes sunken and lusterless even under the impetus of gin. Were these his kind—ugly, brutal, scarred by pox and gaol-fever; all in rags, all stinking worse than the open sewers in the dungeons below?

He forced himself to laugh away their maudlin queries and walked off by himself to a quiet corner of the yard. Brash as they were, their affection for him was tempered with awe, and for a few moments he was left alone. He took from his pocket the pilfered stuff—a wispy handkerchief of Holland lace, a small pot of rouge, and a tiny notebook. Inside the latter he found an inscription written in a precise feminine hand:

> *Lady Leanna Somerset,*
> *St. James Park, London.*

The ache in his stomach sharpened. He read the name again, then dropped the notebook down a sewer. The fragment of lace, he passed under his nose, but as that seemed only to irritate him, he shoved it up his sleeve. Beauty and cleanliness and perfume were not for the likes of him, yet above all else, he hated poverty and sordidness. Abruptly he was seized with an almost overwhelming sense of aloneness. He glanced up in a panic as a drunken slut came reeling across the cobbles toward him, shouting his name.

"Johnnie darlin'! Wassa matter wi' 'e, Johnnie? 'Ave a swig o' gin an' be merry. We 'uns all loves 'e, an' tomorrer—"

He stared at the coarse flat-nosed face, the lank hair, the purple-veined breast which flopped out of her dress as she staggered. His quivering nostrils picked up the stench of her. A moment only he hesitated, then with a mirthless laugh he sprang to meet her and jerked the bottle from her hand.

"Aye, we'll drink!" he bellowed, holding the bottle high. "A toast it will be! Damn you, drink up, drink up, you rotting progeny of whores! You thieving dregs of London's sewers, you spawn of rats and swine. You are my friends, my *only* friends! Aye, I'm one of you! So drink, I charge you, to the day we'll all meet again in hell!"

2

LONG ERE DAYLIGHT, THE STREETS SURROUNDING NEWGATE WERE jammed solid with an eager mob, and the noise of them, an ever-increasing roar as from an approaching storm, carried through the barred window into Lord Johnnie's cell. It blew against him like a fetid wind, but he ignored it. He was alone. Earlier, he had thrown out the unctuous Wryneck, rather than listen to his pious exhortations, for the mere sight and smell of the old fraud had started again the chain of thought that Johnnie wanted to forget. Yet somehow the damage had been done, and now he stood by the window fingering the wisp of Holland lace, only half hearing the howls of the human pack below.

He was the star of the hour. The audience was all for him as they crowded and jostled in the streets, shrieking his name, begging a glimpse of his lean, dark face, wishing him luck and Godspeed. Few of them had ever seen him; to the masses he was a legend, a phantom centaur, cloaked and masked, who haunted lonely roads to prey upon the rich. But whether the mob remained for him depended to a large measure on how successfully he could perpetuate the illusion. He had dressed meticulously for the role. His pockets were full of alms to distribute to the poor along the route, and his gallows' speech had been rehearsed in solitude. Aye, he had laid his plans carefully and he was ready for the show, yet in some strange manner he could not understand, the whole thing had soured.

He wondered, as he stood waiting, how much the girl had had to do with his reaction. Women had heretofore played a minor part in Lord Johnnie's life; coming under the classification of amusement only, they had never touched him emotionally. He cursed the impulse which had made him look upon Leanna's face. The clean lushness of her lips, the scent of her, the pliant indifference of her body—these things haunted him, and for the first time, he found himself unable to relegate them to the background where he felt they belonged.

The jangle of a key in the lock jerked him back to the present. He shoved the handkerchief up his sleeve, and by the time the door had opened, he had a grin for the turnkey.

"Be 'e ready, Johnnie?"

"Aye, ready as I'll ever be."

The turnkey furtively whisked a small flask from the tail of his coat.

" 'Ere's a wee nip for 'e, lad. 'Twill cheer 'e along the road."

Johnnie laughed. "Drink it yourself, man! From the sickly look of you, it's you who need cheer."

The turnkey swallowed the drink and wiped his mouth with the back of his hand.

"We uns 'ates to see 'e go, laddie, damme if else!"

"You have my sympathy," Johnnie said dryly.

He picked up his chains as a woman would lift her skirts, and sauntered out of the cell. The sniveling turnkey had revived his humor, and his passage through the dim stone corridors was a march of triumph. The convicts in the adjacent cells set up a howl, until in a short time the entire prison was in an uproar. As Johnnie swaggered between the cages, men reached taloned hands through the bars to shake his hand, and women blew him kisses.

"Courage, Laddie!"

"Luck, Johnnie Rogue!"

"We'll see 'e in 'ell, Lor' Johnnie!"

Like the consummate actor he was, Johnnie fell into the part. Waving and bowing, he had for each a ready quip.

"I'll put in a good word to the Devil for you, Alf! . . . Bless you, Annie my bitch; you'll share my bed in hell! . . . Stop blubbering, Conkey! . . . Aye, Blacky, I'll give 'em a lively dance, don't fret!"

They met the extra guards just inside the main gate, and when they stepped into the street, the crowd went wild. The bailiffs were forced to use their staves to clear a path to the waiting cart, where the officials waited nervously: Muggins, Goad, the hangman, Wryneck, and the High Sheriff of London. By this time, Johnnie was beginning to enjoy the excitement, but he knew the mob was as dangerous as a powderkeg so he resisted the impulse to taunt the officials, and climbed quietly into the cart. When he shook his clasped hands above his head, the crowd gave him an ovation that shook the ground and echoed like thunder off the prison walls.

The High Sheriff frowned bleakly. He was a heavy gross man, not lacking in courage, but it was a long ride through the narrow London streets to Tyburn, and slowed by such a stinking herd as this, it might

take a good three hours. He leaned forward and spoke in Mr. Muggins'
ear. Muggins winced and whispered to the driver. That worthy, terrified by now, clucked loudly and flopped his reins. The draft horses put
their weight against the traces and, with a jolt, the venerable cart
creaked into motion.

The crowd cheered again, and surged forward in a solid mass.

Mr. Goad's apprehensions about fog were groundless. This was one
of those rare spring days favored with a cloudless sky and a soft west
wind. A wan sun peered shyly through a haze of dust and soot.
Johnnie braced himself sailor-fashion against the jerky roll of the cart
and took an appraising look at London town. During his months in
prison, he had remembered it with affection. Now, to his surprise, he
found it incredibly dirty. Filth and rubbish which had been thrown
from the windows into the street lay there until ground into dust, and
the ancient houses appeared to lean wearily against each other. Some,
having given up the struggle, had fallen into decay, while others were
but shells, gutted long ago by fire. Where the pavement had sunk were
slimy holes full of stagnant water, and whenever the cart wheels
dropped into one of these, Johnnie was thrown against either the
hangman or the gaoler.

As the High Sheriff had anticipated, it was slow going. The holiday
throng surged along before and behind the cart, jamming the twisting
thoroughfares until the bailiffs had to precede the horses to force a path.
They in turn fell into the ruts, tripped over carelessly left-open cellar
doors, or the stone steps which occasionally projected across the footpaths.

Watching it all, Johnnie felt one of his black moods coming on, but
remembering his stellar role, fought it off. The mob was a fickle organ-
ism. If it turned against the condemned, its viciousness and brutality
were more to be dreaded than the gallows. Studying the sea of upturned faces, he became aware that there were more women than men.
He wondered in passing how the fiction of the so-called gentler sex
had started. These were the faces of beasts—sodden, starved and
lustful. They held their scrawny brats atop their shoulders, the better
to view the man who was about to die. Johnnie understood them only
too well: they would tramp for miles like this, strange dark emotions
stirring in their pent-up organs. At Tyburn, they would lick their lips
and revel in his death, and after it was over, would take home their
aroused passions to squander in bed when night came down.

Off on the fringe of the mob, Johnnie could see the more daring young bucks struggling to protect their mistresses from contamination with the lowly. Theirs was the same impulse and would engender the same result. It was not difficult to identify them, for the line of demarcation was plainly defined. The London poor were stamped, not only by their rags and smell, but by the coarseness of their features, their stunted bodies and labor-gnarled hands.

They jostled around the cart, offering Johnnie drinks and tossing nosegays. He caught the flowers until his shackled arms were full and let the rest bedeck the cart. He played his part, grinning and nodding like a triumphant Caesar, until he noticed a dozen or more black-garbed men who had appeared mysteriously behind the cart.

"By my troth!" he remarked to Mr. Muggins. "Where did those ghoulish vultures come from? Are they the surgeon's *beadles?*"

The gaoler mopped his damp face. "Nay, worse luck!" he grumbled. "They be professional mourners, 'ired by yer bloody friends!"

Johnnie laughed. "That was damned considerate of my friends!"

As the cart jolted around a corner, the bell in the churchyard of St. Sepulchre's tolled for Johnnie the Rogue. The doleful clanging laid a momentary pall on the mob, for it symbolized the reproach of God, the stern relentless Deity of the Church. Even after the peals died away, there remained a period of awed silence.

Johnnie caught the eye of one of the mourners and winked. The man quickly turned his face away. Inwardly, Johnnie cursed the changed mood of the throng and sought to recover the former lightness of the occasion. He burst out laughing, and dumping the flowers to those around the cart, began scattering coins.

"Here—drink to me, lads and lassies!" he shouted.

The chill left by St. Sepulchre's bell was forgotten, and with shrieks of delight, the mob fought for souvenir flowers and money. The cart was rocked in the excitement and the officials shortened their necks like nervous turtles. When the Reverend Wryneck started to expostulate, Johnnie rammed a nosegay into his open mouth.

Mr. Muggins wagged his head. "Fer God's syke, don't rile 'em, Johnnie. 'Tis a powder keg wi' a very short fuse!"

The High Sheriff, seeking to divert Johnnie, laid a hand on his arm.

"Come, lad—tell us where you hid that six hundred quid from your last stage robbery?"

Johnnie wrenched his arm free and appealed to the mob.

"Hear him, my friends!" howled Johnnie. "His nibs wants to know what I did with the six hundred quid!"

"Ho, wouldn't we all!" bellowed a man close by. "Tell us uns, Lord Johnnie! We'll colleck it an' syve 'is bloody nibs the trouble!"

"Aye! 'Tain't no good to 'e in 'ell, Johnnie!" a woman screamed.

"So reasons his honor," laughed Johnnie.

The Reverend Wryneck rolled his eyes; his one pious gesture. "May the Lord 'ave mercy on yer black soul, Johnnie Rogue!"

"I've bought mercy for a lot less than six hundred quid!" Johnnie retorted.

The High Sheriff bit his lip and edged over to a far corner of the cart. It was apparent he regretted opening the subject of Johnnie's last escapade.

Like slow-moving lava, the procession poured through Snow Hill, then Holborne, and as far as Furnival's Inn the route was fenced with spectators, and the old prison cart bobbled along, a tiny raft swept by the turbulent current. Johnnie laughed softly. This was the famous London rabble—the terror of despots. They were the foundation of old England, for there was nothing comparable to them in all Christendom. Individually they might be cringing serfs but, massed, they could strike terror into a regiment. No king could long suppress them and, ill-born, lowly, thieves and bastards though they might be, yet at this moment they were all for him.

But he could not depend on it too long. Under the hot sky, the little knot of men in the cart grew tired and sweaty, and the rabble, too, were beginning to weary of the long march. Soon they would crave stronger fare than Lord Johnnie's witticisms. He sighed with relief when, about noon, the cart was trundled into the grounds known as "Tyburn Fair."

If the gallows were not a new sight to Johnnie, at least he regarded them now with a new interest. He appraised the three tall upright timbers which were connected by spars at the top to form a triangle, known facetiously as the "hangman's couch." It was Mr. Goad's callous practice to stretch out comfortably on this perch, smoking his pipe while his victim kicked out his life below; Mr. Goad also had a touch of showman in him. Surrounding the gallows were a number of boxes, familiarly dubbed "Mother Douglas's Pews," after the cowkeeper's widow on whose grounds they were erected. These favored vantage points were occupied by the lords and their ladies, for the price came high.

Johnnie gave the boxes a sweeping glance to see if Lady Leanna might be present. The thought irked him. If she had come at all, it would be only to make certain that he died and that she was free of him.

His face must have reflected his feelings, for a man shouted: "Keep yer courage, Laddie!"

Johnnie caught himself and laughed. "Stab me, man, I was just thinking of the six hundred quid!"

"Lor' blime, Johnnie, h'ain't we all!" shrieked a woman, and the crowd roared with merriment.

Johnnie glanced down sharply at the woman who had spoken. She gave him a knowing smile and wriggled up close to the cart as it lumbered to a stop beneath the gibbet. Though Johnnie made no sign of recognition, he was surprised. Certainly he had not expected to see Moll Coppinger standing under the very shadow of the High Sheriff who would cheerfully have paid a sack of gold to grab her. For Moll was gallows-bait herself—when they caught her; Moll, with her sharp tongue, her swaying willing hips and funny little broken nose, who could lift a poke or slit a throat with equal facility.

Yet there she was! In a way he was pleased to see her again, though he had long since grown weary of her tantrums. He shook his head, but she only risked another wink and inclined her saucy head toward the professional mourners now faithfully clustered close around the cart. Johnnie bit his lip; so she knew about that, too, did she? He tried to scowl her away, but she ignored the warning and, drawing her shawl over her features, screamed: "A speech, yer lordship! Gi' us a fine speech!"

A gallows' speech was an accepted preliminary to a public execution, but Mr. Goad, not wanting to be kept so long out of the limelight, marched over determinedly with the halter. Johnnie shoved him away, and such a roar went up from the assemblage that Mr. Goad took the hint and restrained himself.

"Fer the love o' 'eaven, Johnnie, myke h'it brief!" begged Mr. Muggins. "We don't want to stand 'ere in the 'ot sun all d'y!"

"I've nothing better to do," jeered Johnnie, and hobbled over to the tail-gate of the cart.

By now the cry had become a chant. "Speech, speech, speech, speech—"

Johnnie nodded and held up his manacled hands for silence. While waiting for the tumult to subside, he surveyed the scene.

Fully twenty thousand people were gathered for the festive occasion, and Johnnie Rogue was the cynosure of forty thousand eyes. Piemen and vendors of gingerbread nuts wormed through the throng, hawking their wares. Beyond the boxes, carts, drays and carriages served as vantage points for those neither rich nor lucky enough to gain the boxes. The poor stood or squatted, gaping while gnawing crusts of bread or drinking from pots of beer. Some of the more credulous had hopefully brought along scrofulous children, for it was believed that the hands of a hanged criminal, if stroked nine times over the affected parts of the body, provided a cure for the dread disease. The gentry sat aloof, daintily holding split oranges or flowers under their noses to counteract the stench of rabble.

Finally the noise faded to an expectant hush. Johnnie smiled whimsically. These people had come to see a show. Well, he was going to give them one they'd long remember.

"Friends," he called out in the mocking tone which had become part of his legend, "the gaoler urges me to hurry, and I know you are all impatient for the fun to begin; especially those of you who have parted with a shilling to balance on the wheel of a cart."

The mob loved it! Cheering enthusiastically, they pressed forward to catch his words. With a fine sense of timing, Johnnie paused, grinning confidently as the bailiffs tried vainly to control the crowd. Near the tiers was a squad of soldiers to protect the gentry, but these, Johnnie noticed, were being fast jammed into impotency.

"Come now, good people," he laughed. "Move aside and permit my dear mourners to gather about me. Strangers though they be—for my friends cannot stand the sight of the gibbet—a hired mourner is better than no mourner at all!"

Despite the bawling of the bailiffs, the twelve garbed figures were jostled forward by the good-natured crowd until they completely surrounded the back of the Newgate cart.

"This has gone too far!" complained the High Sheriff. "Here, hangman, do your duty!"

Mr. Goad fumbled with his halter but stopped short of touching Johnnie.

"Yer speech, Lord Johnnie!" bellowed a man. "Gi' us yer speech!"

As Johnnie stared out at the mass, something snapped inside him. Though he had carefully prepared a mocking address, he knew he could never deliver it now. He took another look at the smirking lords and ladies; another look at the gaping, morbid poor, and the smile went out of his face. He was reminded of a gaunt wolf he had once seen caught in a trap, who waited coolly and defiantly for death, too proud to let his killers see him cringe. Abruptly, he realized that he despised them all—rich and poor alike. Like the remembered wolf, his lips curled back in a snarl.

"So *this* is England!" At the cold fibre of his voice, the amused smiles wilted. "The England which boasts of liberty and justice! What a two-faced slut she is! You"—he pointed an accusing finger at the lords in their boxes—"she suckles generously on gold and fame, while the rest of you, groveling and starved, can have her left breast which is a cancer that gives off nothing but gall and wormwood!"

In the startled silence, Johnnie sneered, "Aye, she's a proud and selfish bitch, fawning on a few mincing lick-spittles while the bulk of you wail with hunger! Your heads rot on London Bridge and stink in chains at every crossroad. Yet this great England hasn't enough manhood left to produce a king of her own, but had to import that dull-witted German, George!"

"*Treason!*" cried a young buck in one of the boxes. "Run him through!"

An angry muttering came from the crowd, but subsided quickly when Lord Johnnie wheeled around and glared at the boxes.

"*Who* said that?" he challenged. "Is there one man here today who would dare step up here and cross blades with me? Are there *two?*" On receiving no answer, he spat in disgust.

"I thought not!" he taunted them. "Yet tonight a dozen or so of you Roaring Boys will beat up some aged and hapless watchman. Scurvy cowards, all of you!"

A wizened old crone shook her fist at him and screamed: "We uns didn't come out 'ere to 'ear 'e preach, yer bloody lor'ship! Syve it fer Saint Peter!"

Johnnie glanced down at her. "Hold your tongue, old mother, for if you steal a loaf of bread to feed that starving brat you're holding, they'll hang you from this same gibbet!"

"Damme, 'e speaks the God's own trufe!" snarled a man. "There h'ain't no ruddy justice 'ere!"

"You are just a thief!" shrieked a young girl in a box.

Johnnie laughed at her. "Aye, and a good one, too!" he shot back. "We're all thieves, my lady—you, I, all of us! With this difference—I never stole the food out of the mouths of babes, nor a husband from his wife. And for my part, I'd rather burn in eternal hell than have to live with the consciences of you perfumed harlots!"

The rabble went berserk! Howling delightedly, they threw their hats in the air, while coins and flowers fell over the cart like snow. The High Sheriff bellowed orders but his voice was a sigh in the gale. Mr. Goad sprang forward and tried to throw the halter around Johnnie's neck. . . .

A well-directed rock caught Mr. Goad flush in the face, and as he sank into the arms of the Chief Gaoler, the sheriff drew his pistol. But with the famous signaling cry of Whitefriars, *"Rescue! Rescue!"* Moll Coppinger leapt onto a wheel hub and felled him with a cudgel.

The cry touched off the explosion! The unsuspected dam broke, carrying everything before it. The bailiffs disappeared under milling boots; the soldiers found themselves cunningly immunized. Some of the younger gentry afoot drew swords, only to have the weapons snatched away and turned against them. A hundred fights broke out simultaneously like incendiary fires. For years afterwards, witnesses were to argue over exactly what *had* happened at the hanging-match of Johnnie the Rogue.

The shower of nosegays had been but the forerunner of a hail of rocks and mud. Knowing it was coming, Johnnie had thrown himself flat in the cart, leaving the terrified officials to take the barrage.

As they went down like ninepins, the tail-gate was ripped open and strong hands seized Johnnie. With the "mourners" clearing a path with drawn knives, Johnnie was carried horizontally, a swirling eddy through an ocean of humanity.

Cursing the chains that prevented him from using his feet, Johnnie shouted encouragement to his deliverers. While the uproar about them was almost deafening, above it he could hear the plaintive commands of the officers, and twice a musket exploded uncomfortably close. Occasionally his bearers stumbled and Johnnie felt the pressure of the crowd.

"Steady, lads, steady!" he cautioned. "Slip me a knife if we're stopped."

The thunder of the mob sounded like heavy surf battering a rocky shore, and the rescuers panted and swore to cover up their mounting terror. This wasn't the first time a condemned man had been snatched from the gallows, yet all too often it was to meet a worse fate—to be torn to pieces by the rabble! But for his own part, Johnnie felt a singing sense of exultation. The only death he dreaded was a drab one, and here was excitement in the essence, heady stuff.

He savored the drama as they swirled around the boxes. Sometimes the crowd gave willingly, but more often the rescuers had to fight inch by inch. And all through the tumult Johnnie could hear the shrill yelps of Moll leading the pack like a faithful hound bitch.

It was hard to lie supine and miss the fun, so Johnnie lashed out with his chains until one of his bearers panted: "Fer the love o' God, 'old still, Johnnie, else we'll all be crow-bait 'ere night!"

So Johnnie controlled himself and spurred them on with words. They started another good run through a corridor of faces that flowed past like gray pickets on a fence. Then suddenly the running ceased, and Johnnie was thrown head first into a coach. Moll and a couple of men leaped in behind him, and the next instant the vehicle careened across the fields.

Johnnie banged around the floor of the coach until strong hands lifted him onto a wooden seat. It was hardly more comfortable, for the rough ground set the springless coach to bouncing until Johnnie's spine went numb. But he braced himself as well as his chains would permit, and grinned into the flushed pug-nosed face of the girl.

"Bless you, Moll! It was a surprise to see *you* here!"

She was breathless. "Aye, you arrant rakehell!" she panted. "W'en I 'eard about the plan, I came along to make sure I'd get 'e back!"

"She didn't hear about it from me, Johnnie," grunted the ghoulish man who had waited in the coach for them. "But I had no peace until I let her come along. 'Twas a close shave, I noticed?"

" 'Tis still close!" growled a black-bearded giant hunched opposite Johnnie. "The whoresons be givin' chase!" He glanced apprehensively out the rear glass. " 'Twas a mad scheme, I fear!"

Johnnie laughed, and the men looked sour. The last speaker had been Bagnigge Blackie, a Darby Captain, or gaming-house bully from Bagnigge Wells, chosen for his strength. One-Ear Strube, a purse-snatcher of doubtful fame, but fast on his feet, guarded the right-hand door. He made a ludicrous picture dressed as a mechanic, in a worn waistcoat, worsted stockings, and a tri-cornered hat sloped to conceal his missing ear. The third man, and leader of the expedition, was a quack known as "Doc Yarrow," who made a living selling drugs and profit selling corpses, many whom were killed by his prescriptions. He tried to emulate a dandy, but his face was as sallow and cadaverous as the corpses he peddled to the surgeons.

Of them all, only Moll Coppinger looked completely human. She was wearing a waist of flowered silk and a cream-colored skirt secured around her slim young body by a bright green sash. Atop a mass of coppery hair, she sported a gay straw hat decorated with flowers. Her puggy face was streaked with sweat, yet her green-gray eyes sparkled with excitement.

"'Pon my soul, Moll!" teased Johnnie. "You look like an apple blossom!"

Though pleased, she only puckered her broken nose. "'Tis no time fer yer grand manners now, Lord Johnnie! 'E better stop showin' off 'till we're syfe!"

Johnnie stopped smiling. "Showing off?"

"Aye!" she scolded. "'E nearly spoilt the plan wi' that crazy speech about feedin' folks wi' lef' breasts an' right. I swear, Johnnie, 'e sounded like a bloody traitor!"

"Damme, so 'e did!" grumbled Blackie. "'Tis one thing to 'eckle the gentry, but 'e near got the rest to mob 'e wi' that talk o' treason!"

Johnnie sneered. "Blackie the *patriot,* is it now?" He was about to enlarge on his thesis when One-Ear groaned: "'Od's blood! We're bein' fast o'ertaken!"

Johnnie jerked around for a look, then before any of them guessed his intent, he opened the door of the swaying coach and grasped the luggage rail above. On the next roll of the vehicle, he swung out into space and hauled himself on top.

"Johnnie! Johnnie!" screamed Moll. "Be 'e crazy?"

Johnnie crawled onto the seat beside the startled coachman. "You're driving to your own funeral!" he barked at him. "Give me those reins!" He seized the lines of the four horses in his own hands, and took one more backward glance.

A score of carriages and coaches had taken up the chase, and came sweeping across the open fields. Then through the clouds of dust, he glimpsed a group of horsemen surging ahead of the chariots.

"Your pistol!" he ordered the deposed driver. "Lay out on top and slow them with a ball or two! They want a race, do they!"

He lashed the horses and the coach picked up speed, rolling like a pinnace in a seaway.

"Y're gainin', 'e crazy devil!" he heard Moll cry.

"Why not? I've got an assignation tonight in London Town!"

It seemed incredible that the aged vehicle could stand the insane pace, but miraculously it held together, and soon they struck a dirt road where the going was easier. As they galloped through Marylebone, Moll herself monkey-climbed up beside him.

"Oh, 'e fool, 'e fool!" she sobbed. "I swear 'e love it!"

Johnnie laughed, and ricocheted the coach off a mile-post as they swept into London. The coach groaned and clattered, and the slap of harness and the rhythmic beat of hooves created a mad symphony that was music to Johnnie's ears.

"Aye, Moll! It's better than French wine, I vow!"

By now the streets were partially paved. Dogs darted out at the horses, only to be sent ki-yi-ing out of the way. The iron tires gave off a shower of sparks as from a grindstone, and the coach lurched sickeningly whenever the hubs crashed against the row of posts which guarded the footpath from the carriageway.

"Easy, Johnnie!" begged Moll, hanging onto the grip-rail for her very life. "We 'ave to myke a sudden turn ere long."

"Did Doc Yarrow make the arrangements according to my plan?"

"Aye, 'tis as 'e ordered, Johnnie!"

They rocketed through Aldersgate and when opposite Bull and Mouth Street, Moll screamed: "Now, Johnnie! *Now!*"

She had expected him to slow for the turn, but Johnnie kept her going full-tilt. He leaned sideways and shot the coach into St. Anne's Lane. The maneuver threw Moll against him, and he kissed her lightly on the cheek. Moll wept, and turned around.

"The *Dragoons!* They gain!"

"Oh, to hell with the Dragoons!" laughed Johnnie. "If you're born to swing on the gallows, you'll never drown in the sea!"

Moll gripped his arm, pointing ahead. A heavy dray could be seen nosing out of Monger Lane. Moll screamed and covered her face with one hand but Johnnie careened the coach past the dray, and a moment later it had lumbered into the intersection, for the moment blocking pursuit.

"Dear God!" moaned Moll. "'E even thought 'o *that?*"

"You have to think to stay alive," chuckled Johnnie. "Now if Doc carried out the rest of my plan—!"

Johnnie guided the now-exhausted horses into Old Jewry and fought them to a shuddering stop. The coach doors flew open and the men jumped into the street. Johnnie automatically waited for Moll to dismount, but she gave him a shove that toppled him into the waiting arms of Bagnigge Blackie, then scrambled down beside them.

"No hoity-toity airs, Johnnie!" she snapped.

Doc Yarrow was lashing the horses to continue their unguided run, and Moll was leading the way to a big wagon heaped with hay. Blackie offered to carry Johnnie, but he picked up his own chains and hobbled after the others. The coachman had disappeared on his own tack.

Strube and Blackie had already burrowed out of sight in the hay, and Yarrow was following suit. Moll urged Johnnie to hurry.

" 'Urry!" she pleaded. "The Dragoons won't be long delayed."

Johnnie dove into the hay and a moment later Moll wriggled in beside him. The wagon had barely groaned into motion when the horsemen pounded past in pursuit of the coach, which by this time was racing for Cheapside.

Johnnie shut his eyes and relaxed. After the wild ride on the coach, the gentle pace of the haywagon was soothing. He lay still, listening to the weary whine of the axles. He could see nothing, yet from the sounds of excited voices, he knew the footpaths must be lined with people. He chuckled softly, but when a small hand tightened possessively over one of his, he stopped smiling. Its touch portended the kind of trouble Lord Johnnie did not enjoy.

3

ON THE NORTH SIDE OF THE STRAND WAS A NARROW PASSAGE KNOWN as "Butcher's Row." It was not much more than a gloomy corridor formed by wretched wooden houses, whose each succeeding story overhung the one below it until their roof-peaks almost touched those of their neighbors across the street, like tired stags with interlocking horns. A miry ditch, called the "kennel," flowed like an open sewer along its length, in which hogs and children wallowed indiscriminately. At the mouth of Butcher's Row stood Doctor Yarrow's apothecary shop.

This location afforded the old quack a deal of cynical amusement. Not only was it convenient to St. Giles and Whitefriars—two of the worst crime-breeding sores in all London, and thereby an excellent source for corpses—but it was also directly across the Strand from Temple Bar. For a ha'penny, Yarrow rented spy-glasses to the curious so they might stand in the doorway of his establishment and view the row of bleached skulls which were set atop the "City Golgotha," as the Bar was dubbed.

So it was to Butcher's Row the haywagon creaked this afternoon. Too wide to enter the dank thoroughfare, it halted briefly at the entrance while Johnnie was whisked into the backroom of the apothecary shop.

Though the room was dark and chilled, he surveyed it with the affection of a traveler home from a distant journey. Despite the dirt and grime, he had always found it a fascinating place, but never more so than now. Dust-covered shelves lined the walls from floor to beamed ceiling, all filled with a wondrous array of jars and bottles: drugs and mysterious potions, powders and sweetmeats, washes for the complexion and highly scented pomades, Italian sleeping-masks and love charms. Wonderful, it was!

Johnnie spread his shackled arms and breathed deeply of the blended odors.

"Damme!" he laughed. "It's good to see this hell-hole again!"

The others ringed the room, glumly silent. Moll stood hugging herself against the cold, her full young breasts pressed together. The diffused light slanting through a window set high in the wall shimmered in her hair. Bagnigge Blackie, ever the gaming-house bully, characteristically leaned his back against the street door. Yarrow had perched himself vulture-like on a high stool, his pale face blank. One-Ear Strube, having produced a file from a hidden source, stood slapping it nervously against his leg.

All this, Johnnie absorbed in one quick glance. It was so typical of them he wanted to laugh in their faces. Instead, he moved casually into a corner among the bottles and lolled against the shelves.

"Well, what are you waiting for, One-Ear," he challenged softly. "Come—file off these damn chains!"

The purse-snatcher hesitated, then started for him, but Yarrow stopped him.

"Hold, One-Ear! Those bracelets stay on you, Johnnie, until we reach an understanding."

Johnnie raised his eyebrows and appraised each of them in turn. Moll took a nervous turn around the room, and Strube looked the other way. Blackie tried to meet Johnnie's eyes but couldn't manage it. Only Yarrow's gaze held steady. But even he winced when Johnnie smiled.

"So?" observed Johnnie. "Let's hear about it?"

Blackie spraddled his legs. "H'it be the gold," he rumbled aggressively. "We uns want the six 'undred quid 'e stole off'n the flyin' stage!"

"Do you now?"

Yarrow nodded. "I would have preferred a more delicate approach, Johnnie, but Blackie's bluntness expresses the thought in a nut-shell. It is a small enough price for bringing you back from the grave, so to speak."

"We had a clear understanding about payment," Johnnie returned contemptuously. "Do you scurvy whoresons think you can gull *me*?"

Blackie growled like an angry mastiff. " 'Ere now, enough o' 'at guff, yer ruddy *lordship*. Save yer mighty airs fer 'em as likes 'em! We uns h'ain't fergot we can colleck some 'undred quid bounty from the law fer 'e. Live an' let live be our motto, but—"

Johnnie tilted his head back and guffawed. "Hear the crow cackle!" he jeered. "By my troth, who slit your tongue?"

Doc Yarrow banged the ferrule of his cane on the floor. "Stop that superior sneering!" he cried angrily. "You are no longer the top-dog around here, Johnnie Rogue, and just remember you are still in chains. We didn't risk our necks for the fun of it!"

"I agreed to give you three hundred quid," Johnnie reminded him. "You fell all over yourself at the time."

Yarrow shrugged his bony shoulders. "When you were in Newgate was a poor time to argue terms. But we're not servants, to be ordered about by your whims. We know what we want and how to get it. Do you want to be sent back to Tyburn? The decision rests with you. We demand all, or nothing!"

"Aye!" sputtered Blackie. "Six 'undred quid, er back 'e go!"

Johnnie grinned. "Just what do you three puling dogs think you can do about it?"

Blackie pulled a knife and moved slowly across the room. At the same time, Yarrow slipped off his stool and started to bare the blade of his sword-cane. Strube came edging along the wall.

Hardly had they begun to converge, when Johnnie reached back, grabbed a long-necked bottle and smashed the end against the stone wall. Then before Yarrow could clear his blade, Johnnie seized him by the throat, yanked him in front of him to form a shield, and laid the jagged half of the bottle against his face.

"Back!" he warned the others softly. "Back, or I'll spoon this quack's eyes out of his skull!"

"Mercy!" bleated Yarrow. "Mercy, Johnnie lad!"

Bagnigge Blackie paused like a confused bear, then slowly retreated. Strube scuttled for the door, poised for flight. Moll stood regarding the affair with detached interest.

"Tyke h'it easy, Johnnie!" mumbled Blackie. "H'easy does h'it!"

Johnnie chuckled and balanced the bottle against Yarrow's cheeks. "What was it you said, Doc?" he taunted. "All . . . or *what?*"

"Nothing, Johnnie!" whined the quack. *"Nothing,* in Christ's own name!"

Johnnie winked at Moll and she gave him a twisted little smile.

"The same old hellion," she laughed ruefully. "I warned these carrion 'e was too smart fer 'em, but they insisted they could gull 'e. What now, Johnnie?"

"Gather their toys," he told her. "An idiot like Blackie and an old fool like Doc shouldn't play with naked steel."

Moll sniffed, then relieved Blackie of his knife and picked up the fallen sword-cane. She sauntered over to look coldly at Yarrow, still trembling in the grip of Johnnie.

" 'E greedy grave-snatcher!" she spat, in an I-told-you-so voice. "I ought to carve yer nuggets off! All er nothin' it 'ad ter be, instead o' arf, like Johnnie promised 'e!"

Johnnie howled and slapped his thigh. "Why, so I did, Moll, so I did! And half it will be."

Yarrow took a new lease on life. "You mean it Johnnie? You are not jesting?"

Moll stared in amazement. " 'E can't mean it, Johnnie? Not after w'at these whoresons tried to do!"

"Bah, they were only teasing, Moll!" Johnnie said sarcastically. "A great hulking toad like Blackie and a half-dead cadaver such as poor old Doc here would know better than to fight with *me!* Isn't that right, my hearties?"

Yarrow flushed under the lash, but nodded. Blackie fairly groveled. " 'S God's own trufe! I swear h'it! 'Twas but a bit of fun, yer lordship!"

Moll flounced away in disgust. "Y'er an arrant show-off, Johnnie!"

Johnnie stopped smiling. "A promise is sacred, Moll, even when made to scum like these." He laughed again. "Now, One-Ear, stop trembling long enough to strike off these fetters. You'll get three hundred quid to divide amongst you all."

As Strube filed nervously on the chains, Blackie commenced squirming like a nervous puppy.

"No 'ard feelin's, eh, Johnnie boy? We uns all love 'e, 'pon me honor."

Johnnie looked at him with unsmiling deliberation. "Sometimes, I think you could stand to lose a little blood, Blackie."

Moll stamped her foot in exasperation. "Johnnie! Stop terrifyin' these yellow-bellies, else One-Ear never will saw through that shackle. An' we've got to get away, fer there's a great party planned fer 'e this night at Mother Trull's to celebrate. So 'ave at it, One-Ear, an' stop shakin' like a bloody leaf, else I'll lay this cane across yer blind cheeks!"

From Fleet Street south to the Thames, bounded on the west by London's jurisprudence and on the east by the great mart of English trade, sprawled the festering abomination that was the district of Whitefriars. Once the haven of the white-frocked Carmelite Friars, this labyrinth of mouldy rookeries and dilapidated dens had become the Alsatia of criminals, and every one of the tottering hovels was packed from cellar to cockloft with desperate outcasts. Debtors in terror of bailiffs, footpads, forgers, highwaymen, harlots bright with paint, and witnesses who carried a straw in their shoes to inform those interested where a false oath might be obtained for a few shillings— all these, and more, crowded into Whitefriars in one hideous chaos of crime, disease and gin, and found sanctuary from the law.

Though this was common knowledge, no peace officer dared enter these swarming alleyways, for if recognized, the cry of *"Rescue! Rescue!"* would immediately go ringing through the district. Then the rabble would debouch from every hole, bullies with swords, termagant hags with cudgels, until the unfortunate bailiff would be indeed lucky to escape with his life. Nothing less than a company of Foot Guards could penetrate this civic cancer, and on the rare occasion that had happened, a riot had ensued.

Mother Trull's establishment was located in the very bowels of Whitefriars, halfway up Doxy Lane, a crooked alley that squirmed off Water Street, and because of its impregnable position, was the popular rendezvous of the criminal elite. Originally erected for a French nobleman, the four-storied building had a secret egress to the river Thames which washed its back. Through this entered the goods of smugglers and the choicest of rare wines. The street level was given over to a tavern and kitchens, which lent a legitimate excuse for its existence. The second floor harbored the most celebrated brothel outside the Continent where the connoisseur of lechery could gratify the most extravagant sensuality with girls of any race, size or color. Mother Trull was credited with having imported the first Chinese harlot into England.

But profitable as these sidelines were, the good madame derived the major portion of her income from the two top floors which she had cannily reserved for the criminal aristocracy. And the finest suite of all belonged to Johnnie the Rogue.

Tonight, even the tavern was closed to the public, and the dining room glittered with silverware against a background of snowy linen. No noble in all England could set a more lavish table than Mother Trull, for her service had been stolen from their own homes. It was a common jest that the crests of her service read like the roll of the House of Lords. To spice the celebration, her winsomest harlots had been selected to act as serving girls, a task they were delighted to do, for Lord Johnnie was a favorite with them all. Like the perfect hostess she was, Mother Trull herself supervised every infinite detail. She was a stately female of mysterious age and origin who invariably dressed in simple black.

At the moment, in his private parlor on the top floor, the guest of honor sat hunched up in a huge wooden tub of soapy water, grinning contentedly while Moll Coppinger scrubbed his back.

"Oh, Johnnie, 'e handsome devil! H'it fair cozens me 'ead to 'ave 'e back home again!"

"Scratch a bit harder between the shoulders, Moll," urged Johnnie. "I'll swear those Newgate lice bite worse than rats!"

"Can't 'e say somethin' nice?" she cried, eyes abrim. His quick indifferent laughter stung her, so she said with hurt: "I laid out yer favorite suit; the scarlet one wi' the gold an' lace. I' faith, 'twas so beautiful I almost feared to touch it."

"It should be beautiful," Johnnie conceded. "I stole it from the best fop-maker in all London town. I want my red wig to match."

" 'Tis on yer wig-stand, lover."

"And my jeweled sword?"

"Aye, 'tis ready, darlin', an' I greased yer best boots."

"Bless you!" grunted Johnnie. He stood erect, dripping, and after a hungry glance at his gleaming body, Moll handed him a rough towel. Her thoughts were plainly readable in her eyes. He was handsome; there wasn't an ounce of surplus fat on his clean limbs. The hair on his head was crow-wing black, like his brows, but the triangular mat on his chest had a reddish cast.

Johnnie caught her look, and when she flushed, he chuckled lightly. "Hadn't you better go and get dressed yourself?"

She smiled knowingly. "There's still a deal o' time, sweet'eart, so-o-o, w'en 'e dry off, do come acrost the 'all to me room. I . . . I . . ."

He understood, but he didn't commit himself. When she ran out of the room, he shook his head grimly and stepped out onto the mat. Rubbing his body exhilarated him, and he began to sing:

"Oh, and Johnnie shall have a new bonnet
And Johnnie shall go to the fair,
And Johnnie shall have a blue ribbon
To tie up his bonnie brown hair."

He dressed without haste, picking and choosing as fussily as a king's mistress. First he doused himself with perfumery—oil of Venus, *eau-de-luce,* and attar of roses—after which he sprinkled them on his attire; drawers of silk, white satin breeches, and long silk stockings. He put on gold-buckled shoes, a tight-fitting flowered waistcoat, then wrapping a towel around his neck to protect his clothes, he daubed his face with scented powder and plastered his hair with pomatum. That accomplished, he tied his cravat, slipped into his scarlet coat and adjusted his periwig.

Stepping back to admire himself in a tall mirror, he set the jeweled rapier against the elegance of his coat, and deemed it too ornate. He chose instead from his collection, a Spanish blade of beautiful simplicity. He was perfuming his pocket handkerchief, the final touch, when Moll called from across the hall.

"Sweet'eart! W'at's keepin' 'e?"

"Coming!" he shouted back. He sighed, hating to do what had to be done, but he had plotted his course now and he meant to stick to it. With a flourish of bravado, he clapped the gold-laced hat on his head, and once more checked his mirror-image. Aye, by God! He was as much a gentleman as any cursed lick-spittle who ever drooled over a fat king's hand!

Now for it! He picked up a small though heavy leather handbag, and with a last farewell glance around the room that had once been home to him, snuffed out the candles.

Crossing the corridor, he entered Moll's room, and paused with his back against the door. She lay propped up against a pile of silk-covered pillows on one side of her bed, and the sheets on the opposite side were turned down invitingly.

For an instant, Johnnie wavered in his resolve. She made an entrancing picture, in all truth! A short blue velvet jacket trimmed with white fur, left her eager body partially naked, and the firm tips of her breasts were rouged, after the fashion of the French courtesans. With a fine dramatic flair, she had strategically placed candles on either side of the bed, so that her hair appeared on fire.

Her eyes, which had been full of delight when he walked in, quickly faded into dismay.

"Lover! Yer *dressed!*"

"'Pon my oath," chuckled Johnnie. "It's downstairs I believed the party to be!"

Her hurt turned to a swift anger he had long since learned to recognize in the offing.

"'Tis a full hour an' more till the party, Johnnie Rogue, as 'e damn well know." She sat bolt upright, forgetting her coy pose. "Where be 'e goin'?"

His fixed smile warped a trifle at the corners. He knew her too well to take a soft approach. "Since when have I had to account for my movements, Moll?"

With a sob, she flung herself out of the bed and into his arms.

"Johnnie! Johnnie! W'at's 'appened to 'e? Yer not yoursel', Johnnie! Don't 'e love yer Mollie-girl no more?"

Tears streaked her make-up, and Johnnie hated tears. He had been through sessions like this before, and they angered and disgusted him.

"Oh, don't start that all over again!"

She clung to him with a desperate urgency, her fingers biting into his arms, her body pressed hard against the length of him, as if hoping by her own warmth to melt away the coldness she dreaded.

"Yer runnin' away . . . *fer good!* I can see h'it in yer eyes, Johnnie! Swear on yer sacred oath 'e mean to come back to me?"

Johnnie sighed and dropped his bag to the floor. He firmly disengaged her arms from around his neck, and still holding her hands pushed her onto the bed and sat down beside her.

"I won't lie to you, Moll; I never have. Yes, I'm going away. No— don't argue; just listen to what I'm going to say."

He felt her body go stiff. She seized her lower lip between her teeth, her eyes rigid on his face, but she controlled her tongue.

"Moll," he said patiently, choosing his words with slow deliberation, "you can't fan cold ashes into a flame. I'm sorry if you're hurt, but in all honesty, there's nothing I can do about it. I warned you from the first that I'd have no strings attached to me. I'm restless, Moll, and I'm not the faithful kind."

"Don't 'e love me a little, Johnnie?" she whimpered plaintively.

Johnnie frowned. "I'm fond of you, yes, but love is something youngsters talk about, I suppose. I don't know. There was no talk of love when we met, Moll; you wanted a good time, and so did I. Well, we've had our fling, so why not call it quits and part good friends."

"*Friends?* Oh, Johnnie, after I helped—"

He cut her short. "I know—you helped save my neck. For that, I'll always cherish the thought of you. But for God's sake, don't spoil everything by reminding me of it!"

She flushed scarlet, but held her peace. Johnnie let go her hands and folded his own in his lap.

"I'm going away," he continued, "because there is no chance for me in London. I'm weary of being a hunted, penny-grabbing thief, living in a whorehouse and associating with swine like Yarrow and Blackie. Perhaps somewhere else, with all I've learned, I can make something of myself. Maybe I'm chasing a vision, but I've got to seek my fortune as I see it."

"But . . . but w'at will 'appen to me?"

That surprised him. "Why, the same as if you had never met me, I suppose. I'm going to leave you a deal of gold, also all the stuff in my rooms. My clothes, swords and the other stuff will bring you several hundred quid. With such a dowry, a smart wench like you will be able to marry a steady mechanic, possibly even a merchant."

Moll burst into tears. "I don't want no bloody merchant! I want 'e, Johnnie! Tyke me wi' 'e, lover! I'll work for 'e; I'll steal. I'll do anythin', jus' to be wi' 'e!"

"That's impossible!" he said flatly. He opened the satchel, blessing the foresight that had made him lay out her share of gold in advance. Lifting the leather sack, he dropped it onto the bed beside her.

She stared at it, stunned by his earnestness.

"No, Johnnie, *no!* 'E can't buy me off like a tu'p'ny whore!" Her voice rose to a scream. "So-o? I h'ain't good enough for the magnificent Lord Johnnie, eh?"

He was tired of the whole business and her voice grated on his nerves.

"For God's sake, stop acting like a silly bitch!"

"Bitch? *Bitch,* am I?" He knew her shrieks must be carrying all over the house and he had an impulse to slap her. "H'it was Molly-me-angel w'en I 'elped syve yer bloody neck. *Now,* 'tis Molly-me-bitch!"

He clapped his hands to his knees and stood up. "I was a damned fool to think you might understand. I told you I was grateful for your voluntary services today, and I've tried to repay you as best I could. But you knew long ago that I wouldn't marry—"

"—a slut like me, eh? Don't pull yer 'igh-an'-mighty airs on me, Johnnie the thief! Aye, I'm just a rotten little gutter-brat, but y'er no better, me uppity rakehell. 'E got big notions o' bein' a gent'men an' risin' out o' yer class, but 'e can't do h'it! Gent'men don't come out o' Whitefriars an' Newgate, as 'e'll soon fin' out! An' y'r just a low-born common bastard like the rest o'—*Johnnie, come back!* Come back, darlin'! I didn't mean h'it, afore God! Johnnie—!"

But Lord Johnnie was gone.

4

AS LORD JOHNNIE, COMFORTABLY ENSCONCED AMIDST THE CRIMSON velvet cushions of a sedan chair, was trundled past Charing Cross into Pall Mall, he heard the familiar call of the watch: "Pa-a-st twelve o'clo-o-ck, an' a foo-ggy mo-o-ornin'!" Johnnie pushed aside the damask curtains and peered out. Long feelers of mist groped exploratively through the deserted streets so that the flambeaus of his link-bearers cast but a feeble though comforting light. Dimly across the Mall, he could distinguish the ancient watchman, wrapped in his great-coat, scuttle away with his pole, rattles and lantern. London streets were dangerous at midnight even for the old watchman, yet they held no terrors for Lord Johnnie. This was not unwarranted conceit, for he was a consummate swordsman, having learned the skill on the Continent, and he made no secret of it. Thus no footpad in the land would dare attack him, knowingly, and for the young bloods of the gentry who terrorized honest citizens for sport, he had only contempt. So he let the curtains fall back in place and relaxed, lulled by the rhythmic lurch of the leather shoulder straps of his sturdy Irish chairmen.

At the moment, he was mighty pleased with himself. It was a long, long journey he was taking. In actual miles, Whitefriars was quite close to St. James Park, but socially it was as far distant as a Mongolian cowherd's tent is from Versailles. Johnnie liked metaphors, and this one delighted him. Since he was planning a new life for himself, could he have chosen a better time? His escape had been, in effect, a re-birth, or better yet, a resurrection, for he had been able to carry over from his own life into the new some of his possessions. A sizable satchel of gold rested between his legs and he had a wife of quality—a pleasurable birthright, that! From his pocket, he plucked the scented wisp of lace and waved it gently back and forth under his nose. The perfume tantalized him exquisitely.

He was tantalized, too, by the knowledge that his name was on everybody's lips this night; he was the talk of London town. Every law officer in the Kingdom would have been alerted. Even these husky chairmen would have dropped the chair and fled into the darkness had they known the identity of their debonair passenger. The thought amused him. Few men became legends while still in their prime.

He chuckled softly, wondering how Lady Leanna Somerset would receive him. He tried to visualize the coming scene. Doubtless, she would weep and tremble; perhaps try to buy him off. There was some risk that she might go into hysterics, but remembering her cool poise, he felt inclined to discount the possibility. True, he had had scant experience with ladies of quality, but he reasoned that a female was a female, rich or poor, and he was confident he could handle the situation.

Admittedly, it was a late hour to call upon a lady, but when the lady in question was his lawful wife, time should not matter. Quite likely her ladyship would be abed. Well, that would not be inappropriate. A quiet talk should make it clear that Lord Johnnie had come to stay.

Nor would her ladyship be the only surprised person in London. By this time, the celebrants assembled at Mother Trull's would have been made aware that their guest of honor had flown. And how they would revile him! And Moll? Despite the fact that he was still irritated by her shrewish possessiveness, he felt sorry for her. Bagnigge Blackie and Doc Yarrow would heckle her cruelly, but Johnnie was satisfied she could more than hold her own against those knaves. However, she should have known better than to have fallen in love with him. His own conscience was clear in the matter, for he had done his best to discourage her. It was one thing to gambol in a bit of dalliance, but to take it seriously was something else again. He shrugged the thought aside. She would soon get over it, he assured himself; a lusty wench like Moll Coppinger would never lack for swains.

His reverie was broken when the chairmen came to an abrupt halt and lowered their burden. Johnnie straightened his wig, picked up his precious bag, and stepped out into the street. The fog had settled, lending an aura of mystery and enchantment to the scene which matched his mood.

Across the Mall stood the great house he sought, lighted windows shimmering in the mist. For a transient moment, Johnnie was nonplused. In actuality the three-story stone building was simple and unpretentious, but to Johnnie Rogue of Whitefriars, it loomed magnificent as a palace. Across the whole front was spun a web of wrought ironwork, silhouetted against the windows. Twin lantern-holders stood as sentinels on the front railings.

He frowned impatiently at the sight of a fine coach-and-four standing near the gate. Then his sense of humor brought a sardonic smile. After all, he chuckled, since his charming wife was not expecting him, why shouldn't she have company?

He paid off his chairmen and linkbearers, and strode over to where the coachman and footman were huddled out of the dampness. He noted the gilded crest on the coach door, but in the gloom it was indistinguishable. The lackeys stiffened nervously at his approach, for of late the blooded young bucks had adopted the habit of trouncing servants and watchmen for sport, but Johnnie dispelled their fears with a friendly grin.

"Is this my Lady Somerset's residence?" he asked.

The coachman knuckled his forehead. "Aye, sire, that it be."

"And whose coach is this?"

" 'Tis 'is lordship Colonel Laughton's, sire." He coughed discreetly. " 'Er lovely ladyship's betrothed, if I may say so, sire."

Johnnie laughed and gave them each a shilling. "Stab me! Laughton's, of course! I should have recognized the crest." He readjusted his costume, making sure that his sword was loose in its scabbard, and sauntered up to the massive oak door. As he waited an answer to his knock, he studied the beautiful fanlight overhead. His heart thumped unnaturally.

The aged manservant who answered his summons looked embarrassed when Johnnie demanded to see his mistress.

"But, sire, the hour's late," he stammered, "and—"

Johnnie brushed him aside and stalked into the high-domed hallway.

"Come, come, my man!" he scolded imperiously. "Where are your manners? Announce me to your lady immediately, else, by God, I'll see you whipped!"

"The name, sire?"

Johnnie had not anticipated that question, and he was taken back momentarily. "Tell her," he said, after a short hesitation, "tell her Lord John . . . er . . . Ballantyne, her estimable cousin, has arrived from France."

The old lackey bowed. "At once, sire! And may I beg your lordship's pardon!" He moved resignedly down the corridor. Under the deference of his tone had been a slight suggestion of scorn that shook Johnnie's confidence.

"H'mmn! Surly dog!" Johnnie grumbled, then he set down his bag and preened himself before a full-length mirror. The reflection revived his cockiness, and he chuckled at the thought of the coach-and-four. Her ladyship's betrothed, eh? Zounds, it was a fine state of affairs when the lawful spouse of the great Lord Johnnie had a *betrothed!*

At sound of a step behind him, he turned to see Leanna moving toward him. He made her his grandest bow as she pulled up short, frowning in puzzled impatience.

"Your servant, my lady," he said, with a trace of mockery. When she continued to stare, he prodded: "Can it be you fail to remember me, my dear?"

Despite his raillery, his pulse raced. He began to feel uneasy. She was standing under a twelve-pronged candelabra which filled the hallway with a golden light that endowed her skin with the texture of ivory. She wore a gown of rose-colored satin, trimmed with black fur, and in keeping with the mode of the period, the bodice was cut so low that the points of her firm young breasts seemed all that held it in place.

"I fear, sir, there is some mistake," she said frigidly. "I recall no cousin who—"

Abruptly her eyes widened. She opened her mouth to scream, then stifled the outburst with her fan.

"Control yourself, madame!" warned Johnnie. "A scene will be fatal!" He stopped talking as a tall, stout man walked out of the parlor.

The latter was richly attired in the dress uniform of an officer of a Scottish Highland regiment, and large though he was, he moved with easy arrogance. His ruddy, pouty face, topped by a white tie-wig, held small suspicious eyes. He stared at Johnnie, and Johnnie stared back.

"Your pardon, my dear," he rumbled. "Is something amiss?"

Not trusting the girl in her shock, Johnnie bowed. "I fear my unannounced arrival has unduly startled my fair cousin," he offered suavely. "The fault is entirely mine, for I should have sent word of my coming in advance. I am quite contrite."

Leanna miraculously recovered her poise. "You most assuredly should have warned me, my lord," she snapped with asperity. "I certainly was not expecting you." She hesitated. "You gave me a start, sir. You had been reported dead!"

Johnnie laughed delightedly. Here, by the grace of God, was a woman of wit!

"The report was a gross understatement, cousin, inspired I doubt not, by the wishful thinking of my enemies. 'Pon my honor, I never felt more alive and vital that at this moment, especially when I find myself in the bosom of the family, so to speak!"

She had the grace to color at this thrust, but still loath to rely on her, Johnnie turned again to the grim-faced soldier.

"I believe, sir, you are Sir Clarence Laughton? If memory serves me, I have seen you at Court."

Laughton bowed stiffly. "Your servant, sir. You will forgive me if I fail to remember *you!*"

"A normal oversight," laughed Johnnie. "As my dear cousin will no doubt confide in you, I have been considered something of a black sheep, which accounts for the family reticence in speaking freely of me. However, I intend to change my mode of life, which should delight our ladyship."

A silence descended on the hallway. The girl gave him a hard stare.

"You have a most unenviable reputation, I confess, but this is not the time to discuss it. Since you are here, shall we return to the parlor, my lords?"

Laughton was plainly provoked, and made no attempt to conceal it. "I must beg to be excused," he said ill-temperedly. "The hour is late, and it is obvious you two cousins have family problems to discuss."

"I trust I'm not interrupting a tête-à-tête," remarked Johnnie.

Leanna threw him a glance like acid, then slipped her arm through Laughton's.

"Oh, please, Sir Clarence! Must you go?"

"I must, my lady," he said bluntly, and firmly disengaged her arm. He bowed to Johnnie.

"I bid you good night, sir!"

Johnnie returned the cold courtesy, and watched Leanna accompany the officer to the front door. He was reluctant to let her out of his sight, but then he decided that her betrothed would be the last person she would dare confide in. So he swaggered into the parlor to await her return. He heard her whispered entreaties followed by the opening and closing of the street door. It was evident the Colonel's farewell had been unconscionably brief.

There were sparks in the girl's eyes when she came back. Sheer temper enhanced her beauty and gave her face new vitality and spirit.

"You!" she exploded. "How dare you come here!"

Johnnie grinned, and inclined his head in the direction of the man-servant hovering in the background. Leanna caught herself.

"You may retire, Roberts," she said peremptorily. "I shan't need you further."

"Hold a moment!" interposed Johnnie. "What manner of hospitality is this for the prodigal, er, *cousin?* In my anxiety to reach your side, my lady, I've neglected to sup since breakfast. 'Pon my oath, this has been an arduous day!"

Leanna needed all her training to maintain her poise. Save for a tightness around the mouth, she gave no outward sign of her distress.

"Forgive me," she murmured. "Roberts, lay out a cold supper in the ‚dining room. After you have done that, you may go to bed."

Roberts coughed behind his hand. "Beggin' your ladyship's pardon, but will 'is lordship be staying the night?"

"Of course not!"

"Oh, but on the contrary," insisted Johnnie. "I shall be!"

The old servant was embarrassed. "In that event, my lady, which room—?"

"The green room!" Leanna said impatiently. "Now begone!"

As the lackey sidled out of the parlor, the girl closed the tall doors.

"Now!" she challenged furiously. "Be good enough to explain this obnoxious intrusion!"

He gave her a Frenchman's shrug. "Zounds, my lady, it should be self-evident. The haunting memory of your charms infatuated me to the point where I decided not to hang—though to speak true, I disappointed fully half of London by my decision."

"You mean . . . you *escaped?* Grammercy! I was assured such a thing was impossible!"

"I specialize in the impossible, my lady. If proof be needed, come into my arms and you'll find me very much alive."

She crossed to a bell-cord. "You won't be alive long!" she retorted grimly. "I'll have the servants turn you over to the watch!"

Johnnie laughed and sprawled lazily in a brocaded chair.

"It will make a luscious scandal," he observed. "I can imagine how your pompous Laughton will regard the recapture of your *husband.*"

She paused with her hand on the cord. A flush pointed up her high cheek bones.

"Just what *is* your game, sir?"

He slapped his leg with his scabbard. *"Game,* madame? 'Pon my oath, I fail to understand such talk! Here am I, your legal husband, home to claim his marital rights—and you speak of game. Doubtless you jest, or"—his eyes twinkled mischievously—"is it a game of dalliance you have in mind?"

She went white. "Stop this mockery!"

"I mean no mockery. You married me, did you not?"

That took the starch out of her legs, if not her backbone. She let go the bell-cord and sank unsteadily into a gilded chair. Yet for all her confusion, her little chin was firm and proudly held.

Johnnie laughed admiringly. "You are a cool one, my dear! I swear I find you more attractive by the minute."

She entwined her slender hands to stop their trembling. "You impertinent swine! How can a vulgar gallows-bird sit there and address a lady in such fashion?"

His dark face sobered. "Madame, watch your tongue! Do you deny being my wife?"

"Oh, fiddle-faddle!" she cried, stamping her tiny foot. "That was a mere . . . well, it was a convenience!"

"I find it so."

She rose and paced the room to pause, finally, and lean on the back of a chair.

"See here, I've had enough of this arrant nonsense! How you found me matters not. What is it you want? If it is money—?"

"Bless you, wife, I have plenty of money. Not a great fortune, but ample for a honeymoon."

She threw up her hands. "Merciful God, this is impossible!"

A timid rap on the door interrupted them. Leanna's eyes widened, but almost instantly she recovered her superb poise. It was the man-servant announcing supper.

She gestured him away. "Very well, Roberts. Make certain the servants are in their quarters. That is all."

When the lackey had retired, she looked scornfully at Johnnie.

"Is it possible you can eat now?"

"Ho! Can I?" he exclaimed, bounding out of his chair.

She led the way into a great dining hall, and they sat at opposite ends of the long table. For a moment Johnnie was awed by the setting, but the reaction passed quickly at the sight of food, and he began to eat. Meanwhile, Leanna sat erect and haughty at the far end of the board.

To a hungry man, it was a sumptuous repast. There was cold roast duckling, cold veal and roast beef, warmed-over bean tansy, stripped with bacon, and excellent burgundy. Johnnie's spirits soared and he began cracking oysters.

She made a *moue* of disgust. "You swill food like a swine!" she observed contemptuously.

His smile vanished and a deep flush spread over his features. Without replying, he reached for another bottle of wine. Leanna, shrewdly sensing she had found the weak chink in his armor, pressed her advantage.

"I'm astounded," she goaded him, drumming her fingers on the table, "that a gutter-rat of your stripe had the temerity to come *here!*"

"Madame," grated Johnnie. "Remember, you speak of your husband!"

"Stop saying that!"

He sneered, and cut himself a chunk of beef. "Ah, it hurts, does it? Well, let me remind you also that it was your doing, not mine. You may have married me solely to rid yourself of debts, but in accepting that responsibility, I acquired you in body and possession. That is the law."

"Fie! *You,* a condemned felon, dare to talk of *law!*"

He smiled disarmingly. "Aye, it is a trifle ludicrous."

She sucked air through clenched teeth. "O-o-oh! I could kill you!" she exclaimed with such quiet intensity that Johnnie felt the hair rise on his nape.

"A solution," he admitted dryly, "but very risky, my dear. I don't kill easily, as London knows this night, and furthermore, the murder of a husband, even such as me, would mean the gallows for you. I'm sure you will find our marriage preferable to *that.*"

She was stricken wordless by his logic, so he finished his meal in silence. He also finished three bottles of wine. When he could eat no more, he picked up a decanter of brandy.

"Shall we retire, wife?"

She winced. "Come into the parlor, sir," she said firmly. "We must reach an understanding at once."

He followed her into the other room, and she closed and locked the doors. For the first time, he noticed that there was a lack of personal knick-knacks in the room; and several packing cases stacked in a corner suggested that she was moving out of the house. Meanwhile, Leanna had taken her place in a tall-backed chair and was gesturing him into another near by. He dropped casually into the proffered seat and set the decanter on a table within easy reach.

"At your service, my lady," he prompted.

She methodically folded her hands in her lap and studied him intently. It seemed to him the slant of her dark eyes grew more and more pronounced until it altered the character of her face. Then she began to speak in a low, controlled voice.

"Now let us stop this farce. Your name is Johnnie, I believe? Well, Johnnie, since we are alone, I confess I am your wife legally. But you must realize it was an accident."

"The accident is that I'm alive."

She said, with impatience, "Don't fence. This is no time for humor. The most incredible circumstances have tangled our lives. Why did you come here, Johnnie? What do you want of me?"

The excitement of the first encounter had worn off, and Johnnie was tired. In addition, the wine and brandy had numbed his senses. He stretched out his long legs and stared back at her.

"Very well," he agreed shortly. "Just drop your high-and-mighty posing, my girl." He frowned, wondering how much he should confide in her. She was not quite what he had expected her to be. Blended in with her obvious gentility was a predatory hardness that warned him she might be difficult to handle, but whether it was a temporary condition, born of desperation, he had no way of knowing.

She must have had some intimation of his thoughts from the silence of hesitation.

"Let's be honest, Johnnie!" she urged.

His bitterness overflowed. "All right—I'll be honest. I'll tell you something I never spoke aloud before, because, until the moment you walked into Newgate, it was nothing but a vain, silly, hopeless wish." He talked rapidly, as if trying to keep ahead of the restraint of reason. "I have always wanted to be a gentleman! I've hated sordidness and poverty, hated coarseness and vulgarity. Then, miraculously, you came into that hell-hole and married me. In that I saw the hand of Providence. I would have been a fool to have thrown the opportunity away."

He saw her eyes widen, and then to his surprise, she laughed.

"Merciful heaven!" she cried. "Did you expect to move in here with *me?*"

"May I remind you I *have* moved in!"

She drew a hand across her eyes, as if to wipe away a vision. She had difficulty keeping her voice steady.

"Johnnie, you are a man of some intelligence. You should realize that marrying me does not of itself make you a *gentleman*. Good Lord, gentlemen are *born!*"

His features darkened under a flood of color, as he recalled Moll Coppinger's denunciation: *Gent'men don't come out o' Whitefriars an' Newgate, as 'e'll soon fin' out!*

"You asked me what *I* wanted," he said, scowling. "Now, as one thief to another, madame, let's hear what *you* hope to do about it?"

She steadied her back against the chair and toyed with a large diamond on the third finger of her left hand.

"That was a brutal thrust," she whispered after a pause. "But let it pass. I'll be equally candid with you, Johnnie. As you can well imagine, only the most desperate straits drove me to do what I did yesterday. I had been gambling heavily on the future, but time was against me and I went deeply in debt. After several extensions, my creditors became impatient and began threatening me with prison. I needed only a few more weeks. . . ." She stopped, finding it increasingly difficult to hold her feelings in check. He did nothing to encourage her, so after a moment, she forced herself to go on.

"I was trapped, I had to do something! Then I remembered gossip about other ladies marrying fe— well, I mean, men in your position. It seemed the only possible way out of my predicament, so—" She made a fluttering motion of helplessness with her hands. "So, I married you!"

He chuckled harshly. "Expecting, of course, that I would hang, leaving you free to marry Laughton?"

She could contain herself no longer. "But I had nothing to do with your conviction!" she sobbed. "Under the circumstances, I was prepared to marry *any* felon. It just happened to be you!" She gripped the arms of her chair. "Yes, it is true I hope to marry Sir Clarence!"

"*Hoped,*" he jeered, stressing the past tense.

She sprang to her feet. "You can't mean that! You can't! You have to give me my freedom!"

Johnnie slumped lower in his chair. "*Have to?* Why? You wanted a husband. Now you have one. What's wrong with me?"

She made a grimace of distaste. "Don't be ridiculous!"

"Damme, you're Lucifer-proud for a wife, my dear!"

"Stop mocking me! You . . . you ill-bred knave!"

Johnnie snorted. "What a rotten temper! I confess, madame, you sorely disillusion me."

"Disillusion? Oh, how dare you!"

"Aye. I expected something more of a lady of quality, but it is quite apparent you have less morals or scruples than the tawdriest whore in Whitefriars!"

Her knees buckled and she sank into the chair, staring at him.

"If I am so low and disappointing to you," she whispered, "why not release me?"

"Release you—*how?* Divorce, if not impossible, is obviously impractical. Do you expect me to kill myself, madame?"

"You could go away. After I marry Sir Clarence, I'll have money, and I could send—"

"I'm not a pimp, Leanna," declared Johnnie. "No matter where I might go, you would still be my lawful wife. If you marry that fat capon, Laughton, you will be guilty of bigamy—a serious offense, I might add."

Her eyes were startled circles. "Father in Heaven! What *do* you want?"

Johnnie hesitated. He was overwhelmed with a sense of frustration. Like his dream, the fire in the hearth had gone out and the long room had grown cold. She had bested him and he knew it. He studied her moodily, and despite his hurt, the modeling of her body stirred desire. He reached for the decanter and drank deeply. The brandy warmed his blood and rang in his head.

"You have done me an inestimable service, my lady," he snorted, "in proving that the gentry are not worth striving for; a lesson I sorely needed. For that, I am in your debt. In the morning, I shall leave for the coast and take passage out of the country. After that, what you do with your miserable little existence will be no concern of mine."

She leaned forward eagerly. "You mean it, Johnnie?" When he did not answer immediately, her eyes darkened in suspicion. "Or is this a trick to blackmail me if I do marry Sir Clarence?"

Johnnie's voice dripped scorn. "You should associate with other thieves, madame, to learn something of their code. We do not poach on one another's preserves. Have no fear, my dear wife; after I'm gone, you'll hear of me no more."

"I wish I could believe that," she muttered sulkily.

He remembered Moll as he had last seen her, warm and hungry in her bed. And he had left her for this scheming shrew? What a fool he had been! Well, he had closed that door behind him, and there was no turning back. What he would do after tomorrow, he did not know, but he had no intention of letting this wench dismiss him without payment. He shoved to his feet, and found them a trifle unsteady.

"You can believe it," he assured her coldly. "Meanwhile, there's tonight. Let us retire to bed, spouse."

"*To bed?*"

The horror he read in her eyes pleased him, and restored his ego. The old mockery crept into his tone.

"Must I remind you, madame, of your marital duty? To lie with your lawful husband for just one night seems a cheap enough price to pay for freedom. Mine came higher, I can assure you. Don't be squeamish at this belated hour. It is perfectly legal, you know!"

She drew a sharp breath, quite audible in the silence. "You incredible beast!"

For the first time since they were alone, he was enjoying himself. "Passion enhances your beauty, my love!" he laughed. "Come, I grow impatient. If I am to leave the country tomorrow, we must have at it."

"I'd die first!"

He shrugged, and stumbled back into his chair. "As you wish. I'm quite content to stay here. In the morning, I'll help you unpack your boxes. A few knick-knacks will make the place more homey, I'm sure."

As he reached again for the brandy, he felt her eyes boring into his face. He raised the decanter to his lips, but she stopped him.

"Don't drink any more!" she cried. "We must discuss this sanely!"

"The choice rests with you, madame."

She was so filled with resentment she found it difficult to speak. "Are those your *only* terms? If I don't . . . don't sell myself, you won't leave?"

"You've already *sold* yourself, madame. I'm your husband. If I go, you'll sell yourself to Laughton." He uttered a brittle laugh. "You drive a hard bargain, my lady."

She closed her eyes. "Dear God! I am actually married to this creature!" she muttered to herself.

"Aye. You took good care of that, madame."

Leanna didn't seem to hear him. Though her eyes remained closed, he saw a change come over her features. Some of the hardness melted away, leaving her face soft and frightened.

"What can I do?" she whispered. "I'll eternally despise myself if I do this awful thing, yet if I don't—?" She shuddered convulsively. "Oh, Lord, if I could only be certain it would end . . . afterwards!"

Johnnie was thrown into confusion. "I'm a thief, yes; a bastard, true!" he exclaimed angrily. "But, by Heaven, madame, there is one thing no man has ever disputed—my oath! You've had it!"

"May God forgive me!" she said bitterly, and with a firm hand, snuffed out the candles.

5

WHEN LORD JOHNNIE FOLLOWED LEANNA ACROSS THE THRESHOLD of her boudoir, his first glimpse left him speechless. Here was no mere sleeping chamber, rather it was an Eden plucked from a lover's dream. The ceiling was a domed sky where against a background of summer blue was inlaid a myriad of golden stars. Where the ceiling met the walls stretched a broad border of painted cupids and cherubs who appeared to frolic in the flickering candlelight. A huge four-posted bed, large enough to sleep four people, was set into an alcove lined with mirrors, and above it an oval glass had been set up under the brocaded canopy. Crystal globes hung in each corner of the room and by their swaying motion warmed the setting in a shimmering glow. Beside the bed stood a tripodal frame on which rested an oriental urn filled with exotic perfume.

Johnnie moved hesitantly across a carpet, soft as an ancient lawn.

"'Pon my oath!" he exclaimed, in the tone of awe one might use on viewing a great cathedral. "It's magnificent!"

Leanna had paused to close and bolt the door, and when he turned she was standing with her head bent against the panel, watching him. He started to speak, then decided against it. His self-assurance had deserted him, and he felt out of place. He set the bag of gold down carefully and put the decanter on a table.

After what seemed to him an uncomfortably long time, she spoke, her voice strangely quiet.

"Johnnie, are you very drunk?"

Somewhat to his own surprise, he found himself completely sober. He told her so.

"I'm glad of that," she went on. "We've made a bargain, and there is nothing to do but see it through. However, it would be intolerable to continue our bitterness. I couldn't stand that. Suppose we agree to forget what passed between us downstairs? Tomorrow, you will go away and we shall never meet again, yet for this one night—I am your lawful wife. What is to be, will be, so let us not cheapen it."

Johnnie was a trifle bewildered. "I confess I do not fully understand, my lady!"

Her eyes had misted. "You have doubtless known many women, yet I wonder if you *know* women, Johnnie. What I am trying to ask you, is that regardless of our stations, or what we privately think of each other, let us push it aside and at least pretend sincerity. Only a whore would lie with a man she did not love, or who had no legal right, and I'm not a whore, believe me. Through a twist of fate, you are my husband, and while I grant I had dreams of a very different bridal night, maybe pretending will make it seem more real."

He wondered if she were becoming hysterical. He had not foreseen anything like this, and his confusion increased.

"I . . . I think I understand," he said uncertainly.

"Oh, please try to, Johnnie, please! I don't want to be raped, nor do I want to feel I'm paying cash for a blunder. It may sound utterly silly to a man, but . . . well, possibly I have too much imagination, Johnnie."

"I've had day-dreams myself, my lady."

"I thought perhaps you had." She gave him a wan smile. "Then will you dream with me now, Johnnie? We are husband and wife snatching this one night out of a lifetime. Perhaps this can be beautiful if we make it so."

An unfamiliar humbleness gripped him. Even though he could not follow the reasoning of her words, he sensed the gist of it.

"In all truth, I would it should be so, Leanna!"

She crossed to him with a steady step. "Then kiss me again, Johnnie!"

For the life of him, he couldn't stop the trembling of his hands as he took her into his arms. This time her hands crept up around his neck to cup the back of his head and draw it down. There was none of the animal passion he was accustomed to, but a strange tenderness. With a feeling of awe, he took her mouth, and his head swam giddily at the aliveness of her lips.

She stepped back. "You *can* be gentle, Johnnie!"

His devastation was complete. He felt cloddish and out of his element, and only his pride kept him from leaving. For the first time in his life, he saw himself as he really was—a knave trying to ape a gentleman. The realization sickened him.

Yet when she moved to enter a curtained dressing room, the wariness that for so long had been second nature returned.

"Play fair, my lady!" he warned. "You must stay here!"

Instead of malice, she stared at him with compassion. "You don't trust anyone, do you?"

"I have never been able to," he said bitterly. He threw off his coat, his wig and sword, and dropped into a chair to watch her undress.

She accomplished this with a naturalness which astounded him; not brazenly, nor coyly, rather as if she were alone. In all truth, she was acting as if he was her husband. Abruptly the realization hit him with full force: *she was his wife*.

The implications staggered him. Up to this moment, he had regarded it as something of a joke; now it was no longer humorous. He watched the loveliness of her emerge from the cocoon of clothing, and instead of unbridled pleasure, he was touched with a sense of sadness. He had no right to be here. She was unattainable perfection, and as she stood revealed, he was struck with the difference between her and the trollops he had known. It was a gutter vulgarism that all women were alike in the flesh; now he knew this was not true. Even Leanna's body reflected an indefinable quality of breeding that was as obvious as the difference between a high-bred race horse and a fish-peddler's nag. In the golden candlelight, she moved like a queen.

"You are more beautiful than I could have dreamed possible!" he breathed reverently.

She made no reply, but went about cleansing her face. Without the paint, patches and powder, her skin had the texture of velvet. She took down her hair, and brushed it until it fell in soft tumultuous waves around her bare shoulders. At long last, she put down her brush and with complete assurance circled the bed and slipped demurely under the silken covers. Then she met his eyes.

He rose as if hypnotized and sat down on the opposite side of the bed. Her expression puzzled him; he could not be certain whether she was eager or frightened, but suspected that the truth lay somewhere in between. The shifting candlelight left her eyes sultry, almost smoky.

Tentatively, he leaned down to possess her lips. He felt her tremble and press away from him into the pillow. His hand found her breast. Unexpectedly, she returned his kiss, hesitantly, then ardently.

A long half-sigh, half-moan escaped her. "Johnnie! Johnnie! Oh, merciful God!"

Later, it was like resting on a cloud. At Leanna's suggestion, Johnnie had snuffed out all but one of the candelabras and the light was soft as moonglow. Luxuriously weary, she lay snuggled against him, her head tilted back so she could study him with lazy-lidded eyes. Flat on his back, Johnnie stared up at the mirror built into the canopy above, hardly able to believe the vision he saw reflected there. An incredible moment of ecstasy snatched out of time.

"A penny for your thoughts, Johnnie?" she whispered.

He pondered. "I was thinking," he mused slowly, "that you cannot put a bubble into a cage."

She turned onto her stomach and looked down into his eyes.

"Why, that's poetic!"

"So are you, my lady."

"Your wife, Johnnie. Remember?"

He regarded her with surprise, and she dropped her face against his great chest. The touch of her skin had a quality that was utterly new to him; a peculiar ebb and flow that seemed to pass rhythmically from the contact, yet was not entirely physical. He did not attempt to put a name to it; all he knew was that it transcended anything he had ever experienced before.

"Johnnie," she asked abruptly, "why did you become a thief?"

The bubble exploded, and he was back on earth again.

"To get what I want."

"But aren't there other ways?"

He smiled. "You couldn't find another way, could you?"

The dream evaporated for her, too. She twisted onto her back, and flung a small hand across her forehead to shield her eyes as if, perhaps, she did not want to see the truth.

"At least you were not a *common* thief," she murmured. "I've heard people gossiping about you—how you used to appear suddenly on the lonely post-roads; a phantom in a black cape and mask, riding like a centaur! You were always courteous and romantic!"

Once, such talk would have pleased him, now he felt embarrassed. Was she trying to justify him?

"It was but an identifying trade-mark, Leanna. And I suppose it amused me."

When she made no comment, he prompted: "Turn about is only fair. Tell me what you are thinking?"

She stretched, cat-like. "You would be surprised, really you would," she said softly. "Yet I'm not sure I can phrase my thoughts accurately. You are, well, you are not quite what I expected. I don't know just how to say it, for I find myself confused. Earlier this evening, you confided that you had always wanted to be a gentleman, and I was vulgar enough to laugh at you. I was wrong. You could pass for a gentleman."

"Thanks," he said dryly. "I have, on several occasions, and not in bed, either."

"Don't spoil it!" she pleaded sharply, then after a pause: "That name you sent in by Roberts—*Ballantyne*. Is that your family name?"

Her question knocked on a long-locked door. He was silent for several minutes, wondering whether to open the door or refuse. While he hesitated, she said gently, "Don't tell me, if you would rather not."

"It was my father's name," he admitted finally.

She tested it on her lips. "John Ballantyne. John Ballantyne. Why, it's a noble-sounding name, Johnnie!"

"My father was a noble, Leanna."

She propped up on her elbows. "Would you care to tell me about it?"

He folded his hands behind his head. "I don't know; I've never told anyone before." She touched his arm, and the understanding pressure urged him on.

"Well, my father was a Scottish laird who loved the sea, so I've heard. He built a great ship at his own expense and put it in the service of the King of England, with himself as Captain. It was said he was well known in all the ports. About thirty years ago, he was sent to France on a diplomatic mission, and while in Paris, met my mother, an English girl of gentle birth, who acted as a lady-in-waiting to the Empress.

"They fell in love, but the idyll was shattered when war broke unexpectedly, and Father was recalled to his ship. He wanted to marry at once, but mother held out for a great wedding, so as not to offend her family. Of course, they didn't know I was on the way. So my father sailed, and was reported lost at sea off Trafalgar. My mother died in childbirth, though it was told to me she did not want to live without him." Johnnie sighed wearily. "So—I am just a bastard!"

"Have you ever sought to trace your father? To make certain he died?"

He shrugged. "I've been much too busy keeping alive. Anyway, what good would it do?" He turned to look into her eyes, misty now and very blue. "Can you believe the story, Leanna?"

"Oh, yes, yes! *Lord Johnnie!* Why, I declare, the title fits you like a crown!"

He grunted, but he was pleased. "It's but a false crown of tinsel and glass; the title a nickname given in jest because . . . well, to be truthful, I don't just know. Some say I'm a snob who puts on lordly airs. Others say I am different—"

"Oh, but you are different, Johnnie! You are! You are! Tell me about yourself—your life, your schooling, everything! Please, Johnnie? I've never met anyone like you!"

He laughed bitterly. "Schooling, did you say? I had none, and perhaps I'm better off. Your schools are just big stables where a spirited colt is gelded and broken to be ridden at the pleasure of the gentry. For my own part, I'd rather be a young stallion ranging free than a drudge bent to the whim of the lords of the realm."

She lay quiet against him, like a child listening to a fairy tale.

"Yet you speak as an educated man," she mused. "Somehow, you must have learned."

"Aye, I've learned aplenty, Leanna—mainly to look out for Johnnie the Rogue. You see, I was brought up by friends of my mother and sedulously tutored. But they never forgot that I was a bastard, nor let me forget it. I soon got a crawful of that, so I ran away to sea, and served my time before the mast. A brutal life it is, in God's truth! I killed a man in a fair fight, but in France that meant death for a foreigner. As a consequence, I was shoved onto the other side of the fence, the criminal side. I learned things they don't teach in schools—to duel, not from your fancy fencing master, but on the field where you either won or died. I learned to ride, not *to* hounds, but *from* the hounds— the King's own Guards thundering at my tail. When France became too hot, I fled to England, only to find that even here, for such as me, there remain only the quick or the dead."

She lay silent, and he could feel the beating of her heart. He was filled with a sense of inadequacy, as if there was something more he should say, yet he didn't know quite what. So he put an arm about her and tried to imprison the tenderness of the moment.

She snuggled close, sighing wistfully. "It's passing strange," she whispered finally, "I find myself wishing—" She jerked abruptly out of his arms and crouched on her knees above him. Her eyes flamed ferociously.

"I hate you! *I hate you!*"

He gaped in amazement. "Hate me—*why?* Because I'm just a thief and a bastard?"

"No, no, no! I care naught for that! But you have upset the whole plan of my life! Why did you have to come here tonight? Why did you touch—" She covered her face with her hands and cried in anguish: "Oh, Father in heaven! I loathe myself!"

"Damme, you're a changeable wench!" He laughed nervously, and tried to take her in his arms. "Here, kiss me and you'll get over it."

She was really in a temper and fought to get away, but in the tussle, their bodies met. Suddenly she lay still, quivering, her head thrown far back to avoid his lips. Murmuring endearments, he smothered her arched neck with kisses, until she broke into sobs.

"Oh, Johnnie, Johnnie—!"

Seizing his hair, she hauled up his head and pressed her mouth hungrily, demandingly, to his.

Lord Johnnie had not meant to fall asleep, yet it seemed that one minute the room was bathed in dreamy candlelight, and the next, the windows sparkled with sunshine. On the instant of awakening, he could not remember where he was, then when it came to him abruptly, he jerked up out of the deep feather mattress and looked for Leanna. She was gone!

Cursing himself, he sprang out of bed. That sort of carelessness would get him hanged! It was some satisfaction to find his sword still hanging on the back of the chair with his clothes. He saw, too, Leanna's garments lying where she had dropped them on undressing. However, that meant only that she had left precipitously.

He stifled a weary yawn. God's blood! It would almost be worth hanging to get another hour's sleep! The rumpled bed, so soft he could still see the twin hollows where their bodies had lain, resembled a cozy bird's nest. His head ached and his tongue, as he phrased it to himself, tasted like a swineherd's stocking. Fuming, he drew his sword from its scabbard and placed it naked on the bed close to hand. Then he began to dress hurriedly.

He was just pulling on his tight-fitting breeches, when the door opened. Caught like a hobbled-horse, he grabbed for his blade, but it was only Leanna.

She burst out laughing at the sight of him standing there with his breeches tangled around his knees and a black scowl of suspicion on his face.

"Where in black hell have you been?" he stormed. "On my oath, woman, if you've betrayed me, I'll—"

She smiled enigmatically. "Why, Johnnie Ballantyne! How you carry on!"

He tried to read her eyes, but they were veiled with mockery. She stood with her hands folded behind her on the knob, her head tilted back against the door. Despite his quick anger, he was conscious of the picture she made. Her body was sheathed in a green velvet negligee, and her long black hair tumbled in provocative confusion about her shoulders.

"Oh, for heaven's sake, stop glowering and pull up your breeches! You look ridiculous!" She giggled as Johnnie dropped his sword and hastily complied.

"I merely ordered breakfast for us," she assured him. "After all, my dear knight, I could hardly permit you to leave on an empty belly! Now could I?"

Distrust kept him silent as she walked daintily around the bed and climbed in, heaping pillows behind her back. When he continued to stare, she made a face at him.

"Well?"

Johnnie exhaled slowly. "You're a bewitching minx!" he grunted ruefully. "I confess I hate to leave."

Her eyes turned smoky. "You made a bargain!"

"Aye, and I'll go through with it. Have no fear about that, my pet."

She luxuriated there, soft as a contented kitten, and watched him dress. Her hair was still rumpled from the madness of the night, and her scarlet lips were parted. He was tempted to kiss her, but knowing what that would inevitably lead to, he resisted the impulse. A long, hard day's march lay ahead of him, and he was tired already.

He was buttoning his shirt when there came a discreet knock on the door. Johnnie automatically started for his sword, but Leanna gestured him away.

"Come in, Roberts!"

The old lackey wheeled in a small serving table and, moving it close to the bed side, began fussing with the silver plate covers. Leanna dismissed him.

"That will be all, Roberts."

"H'mmn!" observed Johnnie, as the door closed behind the servant. "Old Roberts didn't appear unduly perturbed. Can it be that my good wife is accustomed to breakfasting with gentlemen in bed?"

"Fie! Don't be a vulgar lout!" she snapped. "It is quite the custom for a lady to have a gentleman to breakfast in her room."

Johnnie sniffed disdainfully. The illusion which had made the night so beautiful was gone; this was the morning after. *Pretending,* Leanna had said then, would make it seem real, but it was obvious the pretense was over. Well, that had been the bargain. He shrugged the memory aside, and without putting on his cravat or wig, kicked his chair up close to the bed and sat down facing her.

Yet as he watched her heaping shirred eggs and bacon onto a plate for him, the old bitterness crept back. What a damned fool he had been to trade his legal prerogatives for one night of pretense? By that bartered glimpse of what might have been, Leanna had managed to hurt him more than he had ever been hurt before.

Suddenly he knew that he hated her, and that he hated England— the England which decreed that there should be a social abyss no ill-born man could hope to bridge. But England was not the whole world, thank God!

Leanna passed him a plate. "From the way you have been scowling and muttering to yourself, Johnnie, you must be making plans."

"I am," he said curtly.

"You mentioned going abroad. What will you do, for heaven's sake?"

"For my own sake, not heaven's, I'll buy a sloop and seek my fortune."

She laughed. "La! A *pirate*, Johnnie?"

"It's preferable to bigamy, at least." She winced at the thrust, and he went on savagely: "There is only one real crime, madame—getting caught. While it is true that an unsuccessful pirate meets his end on Execution Dock, it is equally true that the successful ones sometimes get a seat in the House of Lords. I might remind you, my aristocratic spouse, that some of the greatest fortunes in England today were originally founded upon piracy."

She avoided his eyes. "Oh, I suppose that's true."

He smiled crookedly. "As I see it, we are two of a kind—a couple of unscrupulous thieves trying to lift ourselves by the bootstraps."

A flush spread over her features. "That's not fair, Johnnie! I am no different from any other lady in England!"

"Aye, that I grant you! Nor am I different from any lord. We all seek power, wealth and position, each in our own peculiar fashion. Unfortunately, I got away to a bad start, and therefore must do my stealing in the open, but you, my lady, should be able to afford the luxury of subtlety."

Her lower lip edged out sulkily. "You don't know anything about my personal problem."

"True, you've told me little, but I'm not blind. Despite all that virtuous prattle you gave me last night about not lying with a man you did not love, or who had no legal right, it's obvious you've had affairs before this."

Her color mounted. "I spoke the truth," she whispered. "There was one I loved greatly."

"Not that paunchy Laughton, I'll wager. You couldn't love him."

"No, it was not Sir Clarence!" She raised her eyes to his, and he was startled by the desperation he saw in them.

"Love does not enter into the question of marriage for a woman of my position," she said recklessly. "Once upon a time, I had ideals and romantic dreams, but that's over. I've got to have security, and that means *wealth*. Love has nothing to do with it. My parents died leaving me nothing but a good name—not much of a dowry in these competitive times. I'm twenty-three now, and Sir Clarence is my last chance. I'm going to get him regardless of obstacles."

"You consider me an obstacle?"

"No longer," she said grimly.

He realized that her superb self-assurance was an armor his shafts of sarcasm could not penetrate. Aye, he could make her flush, but he could not hurt her as he had been able to hurt Moll Coppinger. Moll used to fly into screaming tantrums, but Leanna simply withdrew into her impervious shell of superiority. He gave up the attempt, and began to eat.

His appetite surprised him, and he ate greedily in silence. Little patches of brilliance moved across the lush carpeting to remind him the sun was climbing. He grew anxious to be gone.

"Tell me," she asked abruptly, "how you intend to reach the coast?"

"Walk. I can reach Portsmouth in two or three days."

"Portsmouth?" She seemed startled.

He nodded. "Aye, Portsmouth. Why does that surprise you?"

"Oh, stop acting like a cornered fox! I had assumed you'd head for Dover. Anyway, I was about to offer you a coach."

"Thanks. I prefer to foot it."

"Won't they be watching all roads for you?"

"Undoubtedly. That's why I deem it best to trust my legs."

She toyed nervously with her fork. "What will happen if they catch you, Johnnie?" she asked, after a long pause.

"If they catch me, I'll hang, of course."

"I mean—" She colored prettily. "I mean—what about *us?*"

Johnnie laughed mirthlessly. "I thought that was what you were sneaking up to. But a good thief doesn't betray his fellows, so rest your mind about it, my lady."

She took her lower lip between her teeth. The peculiar arch of her brows gave her face an oriental look he had not noticed before.

"Forgive me," she murmured. "I should have known you are much too fine to do such a thing. I'm not myself, Johnnie."

"You're an excellent likeness."

"Please don't be cruel. Look—if you take the *old* Portsmouth road, I know of a tiny inn on the bank of a river—I forget which one—but the inn is called the *Blue Boar*. I've stopped there several times, and I know that the old clod who runs the place is very discreet."

"H'mmn!"

"Father in heaven, can't you stop that ill-bred sneering?" she flared. "Yes, if you get any satisfaction out of the knowledge, I went there with my lover! I'm not ashamed, either; it was one of the few lovely things in my life!" Her eyes welled over, and she cried at him: "Oh, can't you see I'm only trying to help you? Believe me, Johnnie, I'm just as much interested in getting you safely out of the country as you are!"

"I doubt that, but go on with your story."

"The place is about a third of the way to Portsmouth, and I have reason to know you would be safe from the law. If you care to muzzle your fox-like distrust, you may use my name to Mr. Barnaby, the publican."

Her intensity made him a trifle ashamed. "The *Blue Boar,* eh? Very well, I'll remember that."

He wiped his mouth on a napkin, then rose and finished dressing. Ready at last, he strolled over to the bedside and looked down at her.

"This is farewell, my charming little wife. We'll never meet again unless you communicate with me."

"For God's sake, stop calling me your wife! That's over! Good-bye!"

Johnnie raised his brows in feigned surprise. "Why, the wench is angry! I wanted merely to finish our brief honeymoon on a note of sincerity!"

While she glared up at him, he bent swiftly and kissed her mouth. At first she was coldly passive, but as his lips lingered, she capitulated and threw her arms around his neck. At that he disentangled himself and stood erect.

"Bah! You can't make up your silly little mind just what you do want, can you?" he taunted.

She buried her face into the pillows. "Get out!" she wailed. "Get out of here!"

Smug in the knowledge that at long last he had wounded her, Johnnie buckled on his sword, picked up his bag, and sauntered out of the room.

Despite the brilliance of the sun, the day was cold, and a raw wind lashed up the Mall with furious determination. Johnnie clutched his hat in his free hand, and bowing his head against the wind, walked across the street, to pause in the lee of a tall hedge for a last look at the great house. The clean invigorating air purged him of most of his bitterness, leaving his resolve intact. *Aye, Johnnie my lad, you'll have as fine a mansion as that, perhaps finer!* he assured himself. The prophecy buoyed him, and squaring his shoulders, he struck out across St. James Park toward Birdcage Walk.

He had barely entered the grounds, when a voice called: *"Johnnie Rogue!"*

His hand moved swiftly to his sword hilt as he spun around. For a troubled moment he saw no one. His first thought had been of the watchmen, but they were creatures of the night. Far more dangerous were the savage Bow Street Runners, the nearest thing London had to a police force. But now Moll Coppinger stepped out from behind a hedge, and he knew he was due for a different sort of unpleasantness. She was blue with cold, despite a heavy linsey-woolsey cloak, and the dark circles under her swollen eyes bespoke a tearful, sleepless night.

Johnnie groaned inwardly and released his sword hilt. " 'Od's blood, Moll!" he said with forced cheerfulness. "Where did you pop from?"

She stood with her back hunched against the wind which teased and tormented her skirts. "I been watchin' 'ere as long as 'e was *there!*" she grated between her teeth, tilting her head toward the Somerset house. "So-o, 'e've already started gettin' up in the worl', 'e rakehell?"

The smile left his face. "You dared to follow me?"

"Dared? Bah! Now I see why I wasn't good enough fer 'e. My fine cock 'ad to find 'imself a quality 'ore to bed, didn't 'e, 'e ambitious bastard?"

Her voice had risen to the raucous screaming of a petulant macaw, and Johnnie glanced apprehensively around to see if anyone was within earshot. Fortunately the beaus and belles who would soon be strolling in the park were now either breakfasting or in bed.

"Are you deliberately trying to rouse up a Runner?" he demanded.

She gave a harsh vindictive snort. "Aye, an' I wish't one was in hailin' distance now! Y're not runnin' out on Moll so easy's this. I found a few choice tidbits on me own, me brave buck. A kiss er two can loosen the tongue o' more'n a coachman. I learned 'oo 'e was joustin' wi', an' I'm a-warning 'e, Johnnie Rogue, no fancy slut like Lady Somerset can steal *my* man!" She thrust her contorted little face close to his. "Surprised 'e, didn't I?"

Johnnie flexed the fingers of his empty hand. "If you so much as breathe her name to a living soul, Moll Coppinger"—he measured out each word as if it was deadly poison—"I'll carve out your vicious tongue!"

"Oh-ho! So *that's* 'ow it be, eh? Well, hark to this, me uppity bastard —belike w'en the Scottish Colonel 'ears 'ow 'is coy betrothed bedded the great Lord Johnnie Rogue, 'e'll tyke steps—"

Johnnie's open hand caught her flush on the mouth, knocking her upside down in the bushes. She teetered there, skirts awry and the wind bluing her bare thighs, while she stared up at him in shocked amazement.

"On my oath, I've a mind to run you through!" His voice was so jerky from rage, he had to pause to control it. Yet when she opened her mouth to speak, his scowl silenced her.

"Keep your whining mouth shut and listen!" he snarled. "If any harm comes to the lady in question, *any* harm whatever, I swear now before Almighty God, I'll come back from the ends of the earth to slit your throat myself! Do you understand that?"

She groveled against the ground, completely cowed. Johnnie finally got his temper in leash and concluded coldly: "Now—follow me again at your peril!"

Satisfied she would trouble him no more, he turned on his heel and strode across the park.

6

THE JOURNEY CONSUMED MORE TIME THAN LORD JOHNNIE HAD ANTICI-
pated, and as he plodded along the miserably rutted road, he regretted
he had not accepted Leanna's offer of a coach. Fast horses could make
the trip in one full day; afoot, it might take him three or four. Even
now, he was not certain exactly why he had refused. He had acted
intuitively, and he seldom questioned his intuition. He shook his head
regretfully. His brain felt addled, and he found it difficult to believe
that only yesterday at this time—a bare four-and-twenty hours ago—
he had been riding in the prison cart to Tyburn. Somehow, it seemed
merely a bad dream. At the moment, he was exhausted beyond all
reason and suspected that in some unaccountable fashion he had left
a goodly portion of his spirit as well as his strength with Lady Leanna.

By midday, the weather turned against him. The sun disappeared,
leaving a sky that resembled a dirty slate roof. After an hour of this,
the wind veered skittishly, bringing rain, monotonous, inexorable, as if
it meant to go on forever. Yet, paradoxically, the rain helped, for, as he
surmised, the roads were guarded and the guards, being human, kept
within the keepers' huts at the turnpikes, or huddled around their
bivouacs at the open intersections. Whenever he neared one of these
possible ambuscades, Johnnie dodged behind the hedgerows or took
a by-pass through the heaths. But all this tedious circumventing used
up time so that it was dusk when finally he reached the little thatch-
covered hostelry at the sign of the *Blue Boar*.

Even then, had it not been for the downpour and the lassitude of his
body, Johnnie would not have tarried, for an inner voice urged him
to continue. Yet common sense bade him pause. He was long since
drenched to the skin and his aching feet were lost in huge clumps of
English clay. He knew, too, that local foot-pads would be haunting the
roads on such a night, and while he held the breed in contempt, the
satchel of gold had grown intolerably heavy, and for one of the few
times in his life he lacked the zest for combat. So, almost against his
will, he plodded up the lane toward the inn.

A pair of snarling mongrels charged him as he entered the inn yard, but he sent them yelping with a cut of his sword. To the sullen hostler who came out to see what the trouble was, Johnnie tossed his bag.

"Here! Take me to your master at once!"

The fellow gawked uncertainly. Foot travelers at night were of necessity regarded with distrust, and Lord Johnnie's appearance was anything but prepossessing.

"The Devil take it!" roared Johnnie. "Are you rooted? Isn't it enough to lose one's horse and have to tramp two leagues through this accursed mud without having a dog of a hostler turn insolent? Move, you stupid oaf, or I'll lay this sword across your buttocks!"

This typically grandiose approach overawed the man. "Yer pardon, sire, yer pardon!" he mumbled and scuttled ahead of Johnnie into the inn.

In the kitchen they were greeted by Mr. Barnaby, the publican— a most peculiar fellow, pot-bellied, with thin spindly legs and a massive head. He kept prancing around as if the floor was too hot underfoot, until he put Johnnie in mind of a nervous pixie.

Johnnie glared around him with lordly disdain. "You were strongly recommended to me by my Lady Somerset," he declared, "else I'd not have patronized this kennel!"

"Thank 'e, thank 'e, sir!" burbled the innkeeper, hopping from one foot to the other. "God bless 'er ladyship, sir!"

In spite of his obsequiousness, there was avarice in Mr. Barnaby's eyes. Johnnie tossed him a gold coin.

"I demand peace and privacy, a front room facing the inn yard, dinner served in my parlor—and take heed that it's edible—four bottles of your best wine, and a pipe. I'll tolerate neither questions nor insolence! Hear me, fellow?"

Mr. Barnaby was duly impressed. "Aye, aye, yer ludship! The best 'twill be!"

"In the morning, I'll require a mount. Not crow-bait, but a horse fit for a gentleman!"

"Indeed, sire! We keeps a fine stable, me lud!"

"Good enough! Be off with you and prepare my rooms. Meanwhile, I'll warm my backside by the fire. No—leave my bag here! I'll take care of it."

"Yer 'umble servant, sire!" muttered the publican, and danced off to do his bidding.

Left alone, Johnnie stomped the worst of the mud from his shoes, then backed over to the hearth and spread his coat-tails. The warmth soothed the vague restlessness which had at first disturbed him, and he looked about him with increasing satisfaction. The place seemed ideally suited for his purpose, being small, discreet and pleasingly clandestine. In addition, it was clean, and Lord Johnnie had a fetish about cleanliness. The kitchen was paved with well-scrubbed brick and furnished with a stout table and a few Windsor chairs. There was evidence of prosperity of a sort, yet, strangely enough, no sign of other guests. Johnnie chuckled softly. Being reasonably close to London, no doubt Mr. Barnaby's cozy little retreat was a popular rendezvous for the young bloods and belles. He wondered how Leanna had learned about the place. From her lover, probably. Well, it was no business of his.

In the warm airless atmosphere of the kitchen, weariness caught up with him. He cast off his coat and sprawled drowsily on the settle by the fire. Steam rose from his sodden clothing and the mud fell into growing puddles under his shoes. As if angry at being thwarted, the rain drummed against the windowpanes, spattering like tiny eggs to the murmuring accompaniment of the kettle singing on the hearth.

When the landlord came back, Johnnie was nodding sleepily.

"All ready, me lud!"

Johnnie jerked erect, feeling the fool. "Damme, I must have dozed!" he grumbled. "Come, host—two pints of your best ale at once, and join me in a drink. By me troth, I came close to falling in the fire!"

Barnaby produced the ale with alacrity, and Johnnie gestured him into the opposite settle. Even seated, the publican couldn't keep his feet still.

"Tell me, host—have you any other guests this night?"

"Nay, me lud. This bloody rain ha' stopped all travel, worse luck!"

"It's the roads that stop travel," growled Johnnie. "I swear England has the worst roads in the world. They remain just as God left them after the flood. Now the roads in France—" He caught himself; he would have to muzzle his tongue.

"Ah-h! Then ye've been lately in France, sire? What thinks the people there of war? Will it come soon, as rumor 'as it?"

Johnnie shrugged and quaffed his ale. Lacking any particular love for England, he did not share the average Englishman's ardent patriotism and martial zeal. He found his own reckless existence sufficiently exciting without the stimulus of war. But in the publican's eagerness he recognized a reflection of the tradesmen to whom war brought prosperity and expansion.

"To be honest," countered Johnnie, "I gave it no attention. Are the English talking of war?"

"Zounds, me lud, they talk of naught else!" exclaimed the landlord, patting his feet on the floor. "Actually, sire, 'tis said we've been at war these past two years in the Americas, but the formal declaration will come soon. Scuttle me, sire, it fair galls me pride to consider that stinkin' treaty of Aix-la-Chapelle. Imagine, me lud, imagine *England* havin' to surrender Cape Breton to them Popish frogs! Fair mykes me blood boil, so h'it does!"

"No doubt," grunted Johnnie disinterestedly. "Yet, I've troubles aplenty without concerning myself about war." He downed the last of his ale, and stood up. "Now, fellow, be good enough to light me to my quarters."

The host popped to his feet. "Yer 'umble servant, sire. I meant no offense."

"No offense taken, man. I'm merely weary unto death."

Mr. Barnaby lighted the way upstairs, and Johnnie was well content with the room. It was rough, but spacious and clean, with a small fireplace and ample windows on the front and side. He kneaded the bed experimentally and found it to his liking.

When the publican minced off to fetch his dinner, Johnnie hung his coat and wig on a chair backed up to the blaze. After that, he explored the room with a wariness born of long experience. A few minutes later, Mr. Barnaby brought up a tray of food.

"Ye can rest 'ere syfe an' sound, me lud," he said ingratiatingly, and skipped away.

Johnnie kicked off his shoes and attacked the meal. The mutton was tough, but the wine helped it down, and there was plenty of both. When he had finished, he was overcome with a delightful lassitude, quite apart from sleepiness, so he snuffed out all but one candle and stretched full length on the bed with his pipe to dream awhile before undressing.

Without conscious direction, the events of the previous night floated back and forth across the surface of his mind. What a strange creature she was, this Lady Leanna. He wished he understood her better. Her talk and action indicated an unscrupulous hardness, but he was inclined to suspect that was merely a crust born of desperation. Again he cursed the impulse that had made him agree to leave her. Lord Johnnie's folly! He laughed aloud. Imagine the notorious Johnnie Rogue of Whitefriars married, and to a noble lady at that? A joke of the Devil! He wished he had told Moll Coppinger about it, just to see her rage!

He sobered, thinking of Moll. He regretted having struck her. While he had always been aware of a dark strain of violence hidden inside of him, he had never before experienced such a whiplash reaction as Moll had engendered by her verbal assault on Leanna's name. The riddle of that tormented him.

You have doubtless known many women, Leanna had observed, *yet I wonder if you know women.* A point to be considered, Johnnie conceded; he was beginning to wonder about it, too. Their range of emotional instability bewildered him. One moment they claimed to love a man so madly they would willingly risk their lives and reputations for him; the next, they could with equal zest see him hanged, drawn and quartered. How could a mere male hope to understand them?

Moll, he imagined, was furious enough right now to turn him over to the High Sheriff, even it it meant hanging for her as well. He thanked God she didn't know where he was. Leanna knew, yet she would not dare betray him. She was gambling for larger stakes.

He frowned, exploring that angle. True, she might not run the risk of an open betrayal, yet there were other methods, and who would profit more from his death? It came to him abruptly that it had been Leanna who had urged him to stop at this very inn.

Damning his gullibility, he stood up, nerves on edge. What had happened to his native caution? Twice now, in the same day, he had ignored that inner voice. He paced the room, fuming angrily, then little by little his rage petered out.

"Bah, the devil take it!" he grumbled at length. "You're wuzzling like a pregnant bride!"

Undressing rapidly, he snuffed out the remaining candle and slid naked between the cool sheets. The miracle of sleep would restore his spirits. He closed his eyes.

But it was useless; sleep would not come. The blinking embers in the hearth cast nervous shadows on the ceiling, while outside, the crickets commenced their nightly orchestration. In this peculiar half-silence, he could hear the horses stomping in the stables. When a dog barked, he almost sprang out of bed.

Time passed, and the shadows quieted. Still, he had the sensation of waiting. His muscles grew tense, and all his senses were awake and vibrant. His nostrils filled with the lush fragrance of damp earth, his ears noted the slightest change in the insect's song, and his eyes followed every flicker of the coals. In vain he sought to reassure himself all this was but a combination of fatigue and an unfamiliar countryside, yet a small voice whispered: *Beware, Johnnie! Beware!*

He did not know when he fell asleep, for even when he did, he dreamed he was awake, yet an alien drumming sound brought him bounding out of bed. For a space of minutes, he stood alert and puzzled. Then a handful of pebbles rattled on the side window. He sprang across the room and threw open the sash.

"*Johnnie!*"

He leaned over the sill and stared down into Moll Coppinger's face.

"By God!" he seethed. "Didn't I tell—"

She laid a warning finger across her lips. "Fer the love o' 'eaven, 'ear me!" she gasped pleadingly. "They be comin' arter 'e, Johnnie! They're near the lane right now!"

"Who's coming?"

She was breathless from running. "Four armed ruffians! I spotted 'em followin' 'e acrost the park right arter 'e left me this mornin'!" She threw a terrified glance over her shoulder. "Run, Johnnie, run! I beg 'e!"

He was familiar with her tricks, and he cursed the darkness that hid her eyes.

"If you are lying, Moll!"

"I ain't, I swear 'efore God! I followed 'em all the way! They seemed to know w'ere 'e was 'eadin'! *Oh, Johnnie—*"

He was no longer listening to her. Staring down the shaded lane which led to the road, he could just make out several figures moving toward the inn.

"Go around back to the stables, Moll, and get us horses!" he called softly. "I'll dress and join you." As she melted into the darkness, he ducked back into the room.

Although bitterly angry with himself, he felt a fine sense of relief. His doubts had been resolved, and he knew how to cope with men. Laying his bare sword close to hand, he drew on his breeches, but before he could squeeze his feet into the soggy shoes he heard footsteps creaking in the corridor.

He grabbed his blade and padded across to the open window. His eyes, accustomed now to the darkness, marked shadows skulking on the fringe of the yard. When he caught the glint of pistols, he realized escape that way was blocked.

Johnnie smiled without mirth. He had thrust himself into a well-spun web which would require all his wits if he hoped to save his skin. Tiptoeing over to the door, he set his ear against the panel. He heard voices and one of them was the nasal whine of the landlord. The treacherous dog! Small wonder the kennel stank of intrigue. He backed away and flexed his sword wrist. A thin sliver of light appeared beneath the door.

With sardonic eagerness, Johnnie prepared for the reception. He seized a throw-rug from the floor, and wadded it under the sheets to resemble a sleeper. Then as the knob turned slowly, he sprang behind the door and flattened himself against the wall.

Guarded light from a candle laid a pale rectangle across the bed as the door was eased open. Johnnie held his breath. The shadow of a moving man stretched along the floor. Between the hinges, Johnnie glimpsed Mr. Barnaby prancing nervously while shielding the candle with a trembling hand.

The other man came into Johnnie's line of vision; a burly ruffian armed with a short, straight-bladed sword. He edged warily toward the bed, then, with a bound, plunged the blade into the mound beneath the sheets.

That was Johnnie's cue. With one stockinged foot, he slammed the door shut in the landlord's face and, almost in the same movement, brought his own sword-hilt down on the head of his would-be assassin. As the rogue crumpled, Johnnie jerked open the door, but Mr. Barnaby had already gained the stairs and was bellowing lustily for help.

Johnnie re-entered the room and bolted the door. His victim was bowed on hands and knees, wagging his head like a stunned bullock. Johnnie kicked him over onto his back and laid the point of his blade on the fellow's throat.

"Quick! Who sent you?" He gave him a prick to encourage an honest answer. "Talk fast, else I'll spit you to the floor!"

" 'Ave mercy, me lud!" gagged the man.

Johnnie skewered the point. "Answer, you dog! *Who sent you?*"

The man screamed. "My Lydy Somerset! Oh, pity me, sire! I'm only a poor lackey w'at—"

Johnnie laughed, and rapped him on the skull again to quiet him.

"Out of those clothes and into mine!" he roared.

The lackey obeyed as in a trance. It took but a moment to exchange outer garments, and as the lout was fumbling into Johnnie's scarlet coat, he whined again: "Prithee, good marster, let me fly!"

"I'll let you fly," cried Johnnie, slapping his sodden wig on the fellow's pate. "Like this—!"

Dropping his sword, he seized the other by the scruff of his neck and the seat of his breeches, and ran him across the room. With a great heave, he tossed him through the front window, taking both glass and casing.

"Now *fly*, you whoreson!"

The man wailed in terror as he toppled through space. Johnnie leaned out the shattered casement and watched him crash in the mud below. Then as the fellow staggered drunkenly to his feet, Johnnie shouted, "There 'e goes! There 'e goes!"

The waiting confederates moved out from the trees. The groggy lackey must have sensed his danger, for with a frightened bleat he started to run toward the hedge. A pistol exploded. The runner stumbled. On the second shot, he slid on his chest and lay still.

Johnnie pulled back into the room. The shooting had stirred up a hornet's nest, and there was a deal of shouting below. Johnnie buckled his belt-scabbard over the lackey's coarse ill-fitting coat and unbolted the door. The hallway was empty, and from the clamor he knew everyone was running toward the front of the building.

He was about to leave when an idea came to him. He crossed the room and scooped up a shovelful of glowing goals from the hearth and dumped them onto the bed. As the sheets caught, Johnnie piled a couple of chairs on the flame. Then with his sword in one hand and his precious bag of gold in the other, he ran down the backstairs and gained the kitchen.

Outside, someone was shouting: *"Fire! Fire! Fire!"*

Johnnie's heart beat high. This was like old times. He paused sufficiently to shove a loaf of bread and a bottle of Rhenish wine into his tunic before slipping out into the friendly darkness.

Emerging into the rear courtyard, he found Moll waiting with a pair of saddled horses.

"'Urry, Johnnie! 'Urry!" she cried.

But Lord Johnnie was enjoying himself much too thoroughly for haste.

"Bless you, Moll! Saddled, no less!"

Her face glistened with sweat. "A knife to the ribs o' the 'ostler done it. Don't tarry, Johnnie!" Her voice rose to a scream. "For the love o' God—*'ere they come now!*"

Johnnie turned his head. A group of men came running around the corner of the inn. Johnnie was tempted to stand his ground and fight the lot of them, but Moll had already scrambled onto one horse, so with a laugh he leaped onto the other.

"Away we go, Moll!"

He hit the big gelding a slap across the rump with his sword that lifted him into a gallop, then leaning out of the saddle, holding his blade low like a lance, he charged the crowd. The men scattered, and with Moll's mare pounding close behind, Johnnie headed down the lane and swung south on the main road.

They maintained the mad pace for a mile or so before Johnnie raised his hand in signal and fought the gelding to a halt. Then he swung sideways in the saddle to watch the road behind.

Moll finally found her breath. "They won't be comin'!" she gasped. "I 'ad the 'ostler turn all the other nags loose!"

Johnnie howled with laughter. "Burn me, you're a cunning wench!" He sprang to the ground and caught the halter of her plunging mare. Tethering both steeds to a tree, he reached up to help her dismount.

"Now, by heaven, we'll split a bottle of Mr. Barnaby's best wine!"

Moll limped around in a circle, massaging her buttocks. "Gor' blime!" she moaned. "Me poor arse aches like I'd 'ad the cat!"

Johnnie laughed until the tears came. "'Pon my honor, Moll, you look like a drowned cat!"

"*Cat*, is it?" she shrieked, shaking a fist under his arched nose. "'E don't look like no 'igh-blooded court fop yer ownsel'!"

"I own that's true, but these clothes were all the knave had to offer, save his life."

"Ah, 'e killed the dog? Good enough!"

"His friends did a neater job," chuckled Johnnie. "They thought he was me."

Her anxiety appeased, Moll grew sentimental. She moved up close to him.

"Did 'e learn 'oo sent 'em to kill 'e, sweet'eart?"

Johnnie edged away, ostensibly to draw the cork. "There was no time for chit-chat," he lied glibly. "Come—have a drink!"

She knew he was avoiding her caresses, so with an angry oath she snatched the bottle from his hand and drank deeply. The strong wine warmed her enough to bring a wry smile.

"How did you find out about them?" he asked, to forestall any further demonstrations.

Moll wiped her mouth with a damp sleeve. "I tolt 'e that!" she said snappishly. "W'ilest I lay arsy-turvy in the bushes w'ere 'e knocked me, I spotted 'em come pussy-footin' arter 'e. At the time, I 'oped they'd kill 'e, as 'twas plain from their manner such they meant. So I follered 'em to see the fun. Aye, 'e high-toned bastard! I 'oped they'd slit yer gullet!"

"Bless your kind heart, Moll!" he teased.

"More fool I," she sniffed, and went on with her story. "The dogs seemed in no 'urry, as if they knew w'ere 'e was 'eaded. All day I follered in the rain. But I couldn't 'ate 'e long as that, so soon I began to worry w'at was brewin'. W'en late in the arternoon, they paused at a tavern fer a nip, I went in an flirted wi' 'em w'ilest their wine was bein' mulled. They said they couldn't tarry then fer an assignation, but if I'd meet 'em this night at the *Blue Boar,* w'ere they 'ad business, they'd pay me a shillin' apiece to lay wi' 'em." She made a wry grimace. "That tolt me all I needed to know. I ran pell-mell a'ead to warn 'e."

"And I thank you for it, Moll," said Johnnie. "On my oath, if I'd known about all that, I'd have slain the other three as well. Imagine the dogs offering but a mere shilling for a lusty wench like you!"

She let her head droop onto his shoulder. "Don't tease me, Johnnie, please! I'm done in. 'Tis more than a month since I've rested me 'ead, I vow!"

Johnnie sighed and put his arm around her. "We can't rest along this road, Moll. They'll soon raise the hue and cry. Pull yourself together for a few hours more while we ride for Portsmouth. Once there, you can sleep safely for a month."

Nodding, she stumbled toward her mare, and Johnnie gave her a comradely slap on the backside as she hauled herself into the saddle. Then he mounted the gelding and turned toward the Channel.

7

IF EVERYTHING HAD GONE WELL, MOLL AND JOHNNIE MIGHT HAVE reached Portsmouth by mid-morning. As it turned out, they did not reach the ancient naval base until late afternoon. The journey had been a veritable nightmare. Twice during the hours of darkness they had escaped traps more by sheer luck than by intelligence, and on the second occasion, while galloping madly over the heath, Moll had been thrown into a spinney. She had been badly scratched and shaken, but otherwise unhurt. However, there had been no time to search for her mare, so Johnnie had yanked her up behind him on the gelding, and in the darkness had eluded their pursuers.

With the immediate danger over, reaction set in, and by the time they entered the town, Johnnie was depressed and irritable, while Moll, utterly exhausted, slept heavily against his back. The weather had changed from the storm of yesterday to the serenity of summer, and the sun blazed with unseasonable warmth. Not having shaved since the morning he had set out for the gallows, Johnnie felt dirty and unkempt, and the rough wool of his purloined garments added to his general discomfort.

Although he had visited Portsmouth before, he was amazed at the change. Here, war was an actuality and the town seemed crowded and confused. The narrow streets were thronged with soldiers awaiting transportation to the Colonies, and with the wind-bitten seamen who manned the ships which would carry them. As the fugitives jogged down the cobbled thoroughfare, the gelding was forced into the kennel by a company of Highlanders. The wild skirl of the bagpipes set the country-bred horse to plunging, and Moll awakened.

"Why, look, Johnnie!" she gasped. " 'Tis the same sort o' female skirt I saw on Lady Somerset's betrothed!"

"It's not a female skirt," Johnnie grunted. "It is the kilt of the Highland Scots."

He steadied the jittery gelding as the soldiers marched past, and despite a contempt for all military pomp Johnnie thrilled to the spectacle. Giant fellows all, brilliant as tropic birds in their plaided kilts, scarlet tunics and half-savage bonnets jauntily cocked. The weird pibroch of the pipes stirred up a strange response in Johnnie to remind him that his own father was a Scot.

The thought of his father invariably disturbed him. He seemed to epitomize a pinnacle which Johnnie could never hope to reach. No matter how high he might climb, there would always remain a gap no ladder could scale—that stain of illegitimacy.

Moll was giggling. "Methinks they 'ave the look o' savages!"

"Hold your tongue!" he snapped, and guided the horse up an alley.

Moll lapsed into a hurt silence, and Johnnie forced his troubled mind to consider their immediate problem—to find lodgings. The town being jammed with strangers, that might be difficult. Then, too, there was another danger, as yet unmentioned, that heightened his wariness and caused him to thread through a labyrinth of back alleyways.

Finally Moll sensed it. "Be 'e afeared o' the law 'ere? 'Od's fish, no King's officer would guess such a scarecrow to be the great Lord Johnnie!"

"I'm not worried about the law," he told her grumpily. "It's the press."

"The w'at?"

"Press—press gangs. They comb these seaports in search of likely hands to impress into the naval service."

"I declare! I never 'eard o' 'em!"

Johnnie growled in his throat. "The whoresons never come to London, where the recruiting is handled by my Lord Mayor, who gives common criminals the alternative of hanging or entering the service. We sent the Navy a deal of that ilk from Newgate. It's the coastal towns where the press gangs thrive, snatching any yokel they can lay their filthy hands on, even paying blood-money to crimps and publicans for information."

"W'at an evil practice!"

"Aye, it is that. Yet with war coming, the press will be hot after all able-bodied men, especially one as lowly-looking as I am at the moment. I'm taking no chances, my girl."

They wound their devious way down to the waterfront. It was a sight to quicken the pulse. The Spithead channel appeared almost decked-over solid with ships, their tarred hulls glowering in the late afternoon sunlight, while tall gaunt masts and cockbilled yards stood etched against the sky, resembling a burned-over forest. The air was pungent with the odors of boiling pitch and oakum and, on the wharves, sheets and hawsers lay snaked out in the sun.

Moll was enchanted. "'Tis wondrous, darlin'!"

As he anticipated, it was not easy to find lodgings. He stopped at five different taverns, without success, before a friendly seaman directed him to a small harbor-front hostelry at the sign of the *Crown and Anchor*. In accordance with the business boom, there was scant hospitality in Portsmouth, and the hostess they encountered in the *Crown and Anchor* was a blowzy, suspicious female who eyed them sullenly. Perhaps she recognized the difference between the two, for after a shrewd appraisal she asked, "Ye'll be wantin' two rooms?"

Before Johnnie could reply, Moll pushed ahead of him and looked the old shrew coolly in the eye.

"Keep yer peepers off'n my man, else I'll scratch 'em out o' yer 'ead!" she said waspishly. "We'll want *one* room an' *one* bed. Just 'e rustle that up, me good woman, an' I'll 'andle things from there!"

Johnnie burst out laughing and hastily salved the woman's temper with gold. The jingle of coins melted her hauteur and she grudgingly ushered them upstairs to a dingy room overlooking the harbor. To offset Moll's outburst, Johnnie put on his grandest manner and ordered a tub of hot water to be followed by food and wine. A few extra shillings reduced the hostess to groveling servility, and she backed out curtsying.

When the door closed behind her, Johnnie scowled at Moll. "Well, you damn near lost us this room!" he chided.

She collapsed on the bed in a paroxysm of merriment. "Lor' bless me, but y're the dashing scalawag! 'E 'ad that ol' termagant's 'eart goin' a-pitter-patterin', I vow! 'Tis a way wi' wimmen 'e 'ave, me 'oity-toity rake!"

Johnny grimaced. Unbuckling his sword-belt, and shoving his bag of gold out of sight, he stretched into a chair.

"Though it often galls me, there are times, Moll, when you can catch more flies with sugar than with vinegar."

"So I've 'eard," she retorted pointedly. "Yet it don't always work, I've found." She sat up straight and eyed him. "Tell me true—did 'e mean to get us *separate* rooms, Johnnie?"

It was a question he preferred to leave unanswered, even to himself. As a matter of fact, he *had* considered the advisability earlier in the day, but in the anxiety to get located, had forgotten it. His mind was in a turmoil, most of which he attributed to fatigue, and he wanted rest to soothe it before reaching any major decisions. However, Moll demanded a reply, so he temporized: "Would I have brought you here if I had wanted separate rooms?"

She accepted that as an affirmative, and squealing her delight, she hurled herself off the bed and into his lap. There was an impulsive madness about her which he found dismaying. Purring like a contented kitten, she snuggled so as to fit the contours of her rounded body to his. She fingered his features with a tremulous delicacy, as if unable to believe he was real. Through her breasts pressed hard against his chest, he felt the heavy beating of her heart. The response was inevitable; his own pulse quickened, and when she puckered up his mouth with her hands and laid her lips against it, he was suffused with warmth and passion. He folded his arms about her possessively, and whimpering in ecstasy, she twisted around to be flat against him.

The timely arrival of two servants laboring under the tub brought their passions under momentary control. Johnnie unceremoniously plumped Moll onto her feet and gave the men a shilling each. The instant they were out of the room, Moll flew at him again, but he laughingly evaded her.

"'Pon my oath, you're a lustful wench! Here, we're filthy as hogs and we haven't eaten for a day!"

She sucked in her breath, her eyes devouring him hungrily. "Aye, but we 'aven't *loved* for longer still, darlin'!"

"Well, the world isn't going to end in the next hour, so behave yourself, Moll. I'm famished."

For answer, she walked to the door. Locking it, she removed the key and dangled it before him.

"'E'll not run out on me *this* time," she said archly and, with elaborate show, slipped the key into her bodice between her breasts. "'E'll 'ave to work fer it, me 'andsome buck!"

Somewhat to his surprise, Johnnie discovered that he was thoroughly enjoying himself. He ejected everything save Moll out of his mind, with the result his sense of indebtedness turned to desire. A phrase he had once heard came back to him as he watched her: *She had all the virtues save virtue.* How aptly that fitted Moll Coppinger!

"Come, let's get these baths over," he suggested. "They'll be back here with dinner before we get out of the tub."

Moll sang with happiness and fairly tore off her clothes, flinging them about the room in wild abandon. For all her one and twenty

years, her body was firm and solid, with a vague olive tint that supported her claim to gypsy blood. She plopped into the tub, like a
happy child, throwing water all over the floor. Watching him out of
the corner of her eye, she soaped her body with such deliberate
provocativeness, that Johnnie fell laughing on the bed.

"Moll, you're the most brazen hussy I've ever seen! You're enough
to frighten a man!"

She hurled the soap at him and hopped out of the tub. " 'E shouldn't
have made me wait so long fer me man!"

Johnnie rolled off the far side of the bed and warded her off.

"Wait, you crazy hoyden!" he protested. "I'm going to bathe and
eat first!"

Pouting, she slipped into her outer dress, and while he completed
his toilet, explored the room in detail. She had, he knew, never been
outside of London, rarely beyond the limits of Whitefriars in fact, so
she found everything new and exciting. The battered provincial furni-
ture fascinated her and she giggled delightedly at the crude obscenities
sketched on the walls. The clear cold note of a bugle sent her rushing
to the front windows, where in the street below, a company of marines
went strutting by.

"Lor' blime, Johnnie! 'Tis 'eavenly!"

Having caught some of her contagion, Johnnie agreed it was. The
bath had revived his spirits, and by the time he had finished dressing,
their meal was carried in by a jolly little serving maid. Johnnie pinched
her bottom (because he knew she would expect it) and sent her out
happy, richer by two shillings.

"Stab me!" he chuckled. "Why, it's repast fit for the King—damn
his German soul!"

Bowing with courtly grace, Johnnie held a chair out for Moll, as
she came mincing across the room, swaying her hips in exaggerated
imitation of a lady of quality. A shadow of irritation marred the moment, though he didn't know just why, but once seated, the mood
passed quickly. The food, though in all truth plain enough, was better
than they had a right to expect in such a hovel, while the wine, doubtless smuggled in from France, was excellent. Johnnie imbibed heavily,
and under its mellowing influence, his vivacity soared.

Studying Moll across the table, Johnnie suddenly decided what was
wrong with himself. He was like the Persian who had sold his farm to
travel far in search of diamonds, only to discover, too late, there had

been diamonds in his own backyard. But it was not too late for
Johnnie Rogue; he had realized his mistake. Moll was his kind; he
was a fool not to have recognized it before.

He opened a fresh bottle of wine. Aye, Moll was the woman for
him! He would take her abroad somewhere—he was still a trifle vague
as to his plans—but they'd go together, and between them, well, the
possibilities were limitless.

He opened his mouth to tell her his decision, but it was plain that
she was not in the mood for talk. Physical love (and it was the only
kind either of them recognized) was Moll's panacea for all differences.
He grinned inwardly; conversation would come in its proper order.

Yet without knowing why, he lingered over his wine. Disturbing
thoughts kept knocking at the door of his mind, demanding a hearing,
but he resolutely kept them out. The die was cast. When the voices
grew insistent, he rose quickly and walked around the table. As he
lifted Moll into his arms and carried her to the bed, her passionate
fervor routed the strange ghosts.

Afterwards, Johnnie lay on his back, his hands locked behind his
head, and stared moodily at the beamed ceiling. The moon had risen
above the grove of masts out in the harbor and filled the room with a
delicate, somehow haunting light. Moll lay curled in a contented knot
on the far side of the bed. But past experience had taught him she was
not so easily satisfied, and he found himself braced against her inevitable demands.

As he anticipated, after a few moments she flounced around and
began kissing his face and neck.

"Oh darlin', darlin', 'tis been 'ell wi'out 'e!" she crooned. "'E'll
never leave me again—promise, lover?"

Johnnie squirmed. This was the time to tell her of his decision, but
he only muttered evasively, "You're an unquenchable vixen! Give me
a chance to catch my breath."

But it was more than breath he lacked, and he knew it now. Where
once Moll had been able to transport him, the talent was dead; he
could no longed deny it to himself. Beyond that point, he refused to
go. No matter the cause, the old fire he had attempted to re-kindle
was cold. He felt guilty and restless, and hard-put to restrain his impatience with her determination to hold him against his will.

Perhaps Moll sensed the change in him, for she started babbling effusively with the humiliating gratitude of a woman who has obtained from her lover an unwilling sacrifice. He was revolted. The ghost came back. He tried desperately to block out the truth, but there it was: *Leanna Somerset had entered the room!*

In vain he sought to exorcise her, yet she remained, growing into substance. Her dark, slanted eyes mocked him in the half-light; the perfume of her tortured his senses. Almost in terror, he turned to Moll. She was peering intently into his eyes, as if seeking what lay behind his passiveness. Then he held out his arms for her, but she drew back.

"Do 'e love 'er so much, Johnnie?"

His quick understanding of her question betrayed him. "Bah! Love a bitch who sent lackeys to kill me?" he snorted. "You must be crazy!"

Moll reared back on her haunches, just out of reach.

"So-o? *'Twas* 'er w'at hired the assassins?"

"Aye, if you want the truth! Now, damn it, let us have no more foolish prattle about love!"

His vehemence fell flat. "Don't lie to me, Johnnie," she said slowly. "I can forgive 'e layin' with 'er, yet"—she studied him, her green eyes glowing—"yet love you she must."

"For God's sake, stop crying about *love, love, love!* I don't love any-body!"

Though she flinched at that, her pensiveness remained. He became increasingly uncomfortable. He wished she would explode into anger; he could handle her tantrums, but this quiet desperation was strange, and he didn't know how to cope with it.

"She must love 'e out of all reason," Moll reiterated, "for only a woman deeply in love would be so wrought-up as to want 'e dead, rather than lose 'e. 'Tis gospel, Johnnie!"

In a burst of temper, he tried to rise out of bed, but she threw her body across his and forced him back.

"No, lover, no!" she wailed. "I won't mention 'er again, ever! I swear it, Johnnie! We'll go away together, me'n 'e, an'—"

He was cold and angry. *"No!* I'm leaving England and all she stands for, and I'm going alone. *Alone,* understand?"

Her mouth formed a startled O, but the expected tirade did not follow.

" 'E can't! 'E simply can't!" It was a calm assertion of fact, not a challenge. "Last week I visited an astrologer, an' she tolt me w'at the stars said."

"Hell and damnation!" stormed Johnnie. "If you would spend less time on foolish nostrums and more on getting a husband, you'd be a deal better off."

" 'Tis one an' the same thing. The stars made it very clear: 'e are goin' to marry me."

He had not meant to tell her, but his truculence made him incautious.

"Stars, blah! I couldn't marry you if I wanted to; I'm married already!"

She shrank back as if he had struck her. "No, Johnnie! Oh, *no!* Y're jes' teasin' me!"

"It's the God's truth! I was married in Newgate." The stricken expression on her face made him ashamed of his harshness, so he added gently: "I'm sorry it came out this way, Moll. It was a marriage of convenience." He found it difficult to talk about the matter, so he lapsed into silence.

" 'E married that Somerset *bitch?*"

"Hold your tongue!" he growled defensively.

The news seemed to have paralyzed her. She continued to stare at him until Johnnie decided finally that she was not seeing him at all. It was like meeting the eyes of a corpse. The sensation was distinctly unpleasant, and he oscillated between resentment and compassion. To break the spell, he reached out and patted her arm.

"Come, old girl," he said. "You'll do all right."

She wrenched away from his touch, and getting up, walked over to the window. For a long time, he watched her, silhouetted against the sky, but the manifold drain on his emotions had exhausted him, and when he drifted off to sleep, she was still standing there, staring bleakly out at the harbor.

Sunlight in his face awakened Johnnie. He sat up, clear-headed and alert, eager for whatever adventures the day would bring. It was that zest for living which made him beloved by his friends and hated by his enemies. He glanced down at Moll, his rancor gone. She was flat on her back, her gaze focused on infinity, and he knew intuitively she had not slept. In a playful mood, he rumpled her coppery hair. At first, she did not respond, but when he leaned over and kissed her on the mouth, she looked at him and smiled a twisted little smile. Satisfied she was now reconciled to the inevitable, he laughed his pleasure.

"Wake up, Mollie my girl!"

He half expected her to hurl herself into his arms, as had been her morning custom in the past, but instead she lay inert, toying idly with the mat of hair on his chest.

"W'at's yer plans, Johnnie?"

He braced himself on one elbow. "First I'll give you gold enough to take the best stage back to London, and—"

"Gold! Gold! 'E thinks gold can do anythin'!"

"Can't it?"

She sighed and took her hand away from his body. "Aye, belike it can," she admitted listlessly. "An' 'e, Johnnie? 'Ow soon do 'e expect to leave England?"

"As soon as humanly posible. Portsmouth is a dangerous place to tarry."

She threw her legs over the side of the bed and sat up, her back to him.

"Then 'e'd better get started," she advised.

He had never seen her act this way and it puzzled him. When they were dressed, he had breakfast brought up. Moll sat opposite, keeping her eyes on her plate. He began to be plagued with doubts. It disturbed him to recall how adroitly Moll had been able to read his mind the evening just past. She had been wrong, of course, about his loving Leanna, and it was equally preposterous to imagine that Leanna loved him. Nevertheless, Moll *had* divined, in that half-gypsy way of hers, that it was Leanna who had come between them. Or was it so? Had not the flame flickered out before? Reflection only made him restless, so he volunteered: "I'll send you a pretty gift from Spain, Moll."

She glanced at him through her long lashes. "If 'e ever get to Spain," she muttered.

"Oh, I'll get there," he laughed, glad the tension was broken. "And someday I'll come back to England in style." He talked rapidly, thoughtlessly, merely to fill up the silence he dreaded. "By my troth, they'll sing a different tune about me then! I'll be rich and famous, and it will be *Whitehall* I'll visit, not *Whitefriars*."

"Yet Whitefriars is w'ere yer friends be, Johnnie."

He shook his head. "There is only one friend a man can depend on, Moll—*gold!* Without it, you are either kicked around and starved, or marked for gallows-bait. But with it—ah! The world's your oyster, my girl! Gold can buy position, respect, a great mansion, a beautiful wife, anything!"

"Tell me—w'at kind o' shop sells 'appiness, Johnnie?"

He stared at her in amazement. In all the years of their association, he had never heard her make such a comment.

She avoided his eyes. "An' 'e'll doubtless 'urt a lot o' little folk on yer selfish climb to the top, methinks," she remarked in the same strained unnatural tone.

"Damme, you sound like a Puritan!" he snapped, provoked. "If I don't stand on somebody's neck, another will stand on mine. There is scant room for sentiment in this life!"

"Aye, I believe that now. Sentiment be only fer fools like *me*."

He rose abruptly, anxious to be gone, for he knew if he tarried there would be another quarrel.

"I'll be back in a few hours," he said brusquely. "Why don't you take a nap? A little sleep will make you less gloomy."

" 'E need worry about me no longer, Johnnie. 'Tis over an' done wi'."

He wished he had not agreed to return, but it would be foolish to relinquish the room until he had secured passage out of the country. He pondered the advisability of offering her money now, in the hope she would leave at once, but that, too, might precipitate a scene, so he decided to let her cool off in her own good time.

Rising, he circled the table and brushed her forehead with his lips. She did not move. He buckled on his sword, then stared at the satchel of gold. It would be a chore to tote it around the waterfront, and yet . . . Moll was a creature of unpredictable impulses, and distrust was as characteristic of Lord Johnnie as recklessness and daring. He picked up the bag.

She was still sitting there when he left the room.

8

THE IMMINENCE OF WAR HAD BROUGHT A BOOM TO PORTSMOUTH. THE narrow streets were thronged as on a holiday, and the din was even worse than that of London. Here, the shopkeepers maintained the old custom of stationing an apprentice outside to bawl the familiar invitation: *"Rally up, lydies! Rally up!"* The carriageways were snarled for blocks with rumbling carts, brewers' sledges, rattling chariots, and the inevitable foul-mouthed chairmen. It appeared to Johnnie as if every peddler and charlatan in the south of England had congregated here. There were hawkers selling almanacs, pewter pots, Holland socks, flint-and-steel; or things to eat and drink—saloop, Shrewsbury cakes, furmity, Chaney oranges, hot codlins, and a hundred other such tidbits. And mixed among these, were tinkers offering to mend chairs, solder pots, grind knives, or else pleading to buy old clothes, old wigs, old swords, old anything.

It was like a gigantic carnival and Johnnie loved it. His sharp eyes spotted a few pickpockets plying their trade and he was minded to fork a poke or two himself, just for devilment. He restrained the impulse, however, and shouldered his way through the crowds toward the merchant ships berthed at the far end of the waterfront.

Having reached a decision, his mind was at peace. But it had not been easy, especially with regard to Moll. He felt sorry for her, yet he reasoned that to leave her now was the kindest thing, for he knew that pity and gratitude alone would not satisfy her for long. She would demand more, and he had nothing more to give her.

As for Leanna, his feelings were confused. For some illogical reason, he had an almost overpowering desire to see her again. According to his lights, she had broken their pact when she sent her lackeys after him, yet to go back to London was to court disaster and avail him nothing. So he had brushed the thought of her aside and decided to continue with his plan. When he was rich and powerful, he'd find another woman to his liking.

He quickened his stride, and though he kept a wary eye out for
bailiffs or pressmen, he missed none of the bustle and excitement. There
was a sufficiency of both. A myriad of quacks had set up their shops
in old buildings, and in front of these consulting rooms had been
erected stages on which montebanks tumbled, troupes of trained dogs
did their pathetic little acts, or girls danced on tightropes to the tune
of pipe and drum. It was the same old story: everything was baited
to lure the gullible country yokel or the lonely sailor home from the
sea. Strolling ballad-singers chanted on almost every corner, and at one
intersection, Johnnie had to wait while the bear-ward paraded past,
with his animals, his dogs and his drum, all followed by a howling
procession of urchins.

Out on the quay, the scene was just as chaotic. Jolly-boats shuttled
back and forth like huge water-bugs, ferrying soldiers and seamen out
to the waiting ships, while barges and lighters dotted the channel like
crawling ants. Beyond and above all these towered the grand fleet, the
proud dowagers of the seas. The wharves were a colorful bedlam of
sobbing wives and jaded harlots, where somber merchants jostled with
stevedores and sailors in blue and soldiers in scarlet. Long-bearded
peddlers scuttled through the mob, hawking shoddy wares to drunken
seamen. Aye, thought Johnnie cynically, prosperity rode the vanguard
of war, yet how few of the masses remembered that famine also followed in the train.

He spent some time asking questions before he learned of a brig that
was sailing for Spain. Eventually he found her berthed alongside an
ancient wharf where she was taking on stores for the voyage. She was
anything but prepossessing—a grimy jade with a foul bottom—but
since she was going his way, he meant to court her.

As he strode toward her gangplank, he had to stand aside to let a
sweating porter trundle his load aboard, then he followed, and bribed
a hand to escort him to the captain, a black-bearded bull of a man
hunched over a table in the cabin aft.

"I've been informed you're bound for Spain," Johnnie began without preliminaries. "I desire to go there."

The captain regarded him speculatively, as if trying to reconcile the
cheap lackey clothing with Johnnie's lordly deportment.

"Do ye now? Suppose I got a full crew?"

Standing erect, Johnnie eyed the captain along the lean ridge of his
nose as though sighting a double-barreled musket.

"Do I look like a lout seeking work?" he snapped, tossing a few golden guineas on the table between them. "It is a cabin I want, and a good one. Now to what port in Spain are you bound?"

The captain weighed the gold with his eyes, and then weighed Johnnie.

"Devil take it, lad, mebbe I misjudged ye," he conceded, "an' again, mebbe I didn't." He groped for a pipe and shoved it cold between his teeth. "These be treacherous times, matey, an' 'tis wise to watch the tongue. Howbeit, since ye arsk me blunt, I'll answer blunt—mebbe I do be bound for Cadiz, then again, mebbe I ain't. Depends."

Johnnie grinned. "Depends—on what?"

The captain worked his pipe to the opposite corner of his mouth, and one eye drooped into what might have been meant for a wink.

"Let's put it this way, matey," he said tentatively. "Ye don't know *my* business, nor I *your'n*. Nor do I arsk, mind ye! Nay, nay, I ain't a nosy man. Howbeit, if I was a lusty young cock, out to seek me a quick fortune, say, an' mebbe a sleek craft in w'ich to seek 'er in, methinks I'd 'ead for Tangiers, in Morocco. You arsk why Tangiers? That's a fair question, I'd answer, an' I'd tell ye true. There's a heap o' piracy operatin' out o' that 'eathen port, an' a shrewd young buck, such as I used to be, might pick up a prize real cheap." He shrugged indifferently and avoided Johnnie's twinkling eyes.

"O' course I *could* be wrong, matey. Mebbe ye ain't interested in the brotherhood; mebbe you're a missionary out to carry the gospel." He raised one eye and looked at Johnnie.

Johnnie roared with laughter. "Stab me, Captain, your name should be Captain 'Mebbe.' I swear I've never met a more discerning man. And *mebbe* there's a chance you just might be touching Tangiers this voyage?"

The other raised his hands in protest. "Now, now, friend, don't rush me. I'm a cautious man, I am, an' wi' war clouds makin' 'tis 'ard tellin' w'ere I'll go." He dribbled the coins on the table.

Lord Johnnie knew a horse-trader when he saw one. "I believe we can strike a fair bargain, Captain," he countered.

"To that I'll naught say nay," admitted the other and, reaching under the table, produced a demijohn. " 'Twon't 'urt none to talk a bit, an' belike this'll myke it easier."

Chuckling, Johnnie dropped into a chair. When he rose from it an hour later, he was a trifle poorer and a trifle drunk. But he was content, for he had secured passage for Morocco.

The captain accompanied him to the head of the gangway, and as

Johnnie navigated his way ashore, bellowed: "Hark ye, matey—ye'd better be aboard tonight, fer we leave on the early mornin' tide!"

Johnnie doffed his hat. "Aye, Captain Mebbe, and, God willing, I'll be aboard!"

Though he retraced his steps over the same route by which he had come, everything looked different. The afternoon sun burnished the ships and wrapped them in an aura of glamor sadly lacking in actuality. Now they resembled noble ladies curtsying to the gentle swells, and he bowed mockingly in return. The strutting officers, whom an hour before Johnnie had considered pompous dolts, were cloaked in dignity. It was a wondrous sensation to be treading on the clouds, and his humor seemed to permeate the entire carnival. People smiled and gave way before him as if, in all truth, he was a lord. The wise doxies and Lovely Nans (waterfront harlots) glanced wistfully at his eagle's face and bullock's shoulders, sensing shrewdly he was too content for their services. Certainly the beggars caught his mood, for they hobbled into his path, whining, "Yer ludship! Yer ludship!" He repaid them handsomely with shillings, though he realized his stock of wealth was dwindling. The brig's master had driven a hard bargain, and Johnnie still had to give Moll enough to get her safely back to London town. Yet now that he was started on the way to fame and fortune, he felt he could afford to be generous.

The remembrance of Moll dulled the keen edge of his glow, for he dreaded to face her again. By the time he returned to their room, she would have forgotten her pique and the whole weary argument would have to be thrashed out again, to the tiresome accompaniment of tears and wailing. He cursed himself for not having taken his leave once and for all. As it was now, she would be waiting, anxious and penniless, but the least he could do was to play fair. However, he had the whole afternoon and evening free, so he decided to postpone the ordeal until the last possible minute.

Strolling aimlessly along the quay, his eye caught the office of the Port Captain. Acting on impulse, he strode inside and asked to see that official.

To his disappointment, the Port Captain was a comparatively young man, not ten years older than himself, yet now that he was here, he put the question he had come to ask.

"Have you any records or information about a Lord John Ballantyne, a Scot who commanded a King's ship some thirty odd years ago?"

The man's eyes faded to the inverted dullness of remembrance.

"Aye, I've heard the name," he acknowledged. "But it was long before my tenure." He regarded Johnnie. "What did you want to know about him?"

An emptiness descended on Johnnie. "What he looked like, the manner of man he was—that sort of thing. You see he was . . . he was a relative of mine, so to speak."

The Port Captain shrugged. "My Lord Ballantyne entered this port many times, that I know. Look—why don't you enquire among the old ship chandlers and the like? Some ancient will doubtless recall the information you seek."

Johnnie emerged into the street, feeling the fool. He wondered what had prompted him to learn about his father, then with a jolt, he remembered: *Leanna!* When he had told her about his background, she had asked: *Have you ever sought to trace your father, Johnnie? To make certain that he died?*

He was furious with himself, and with her. He swore she would never interfere in his actions again. His father was dead, and he was a bastard. Nothing could alter that fact. Nevertheless, when he passed a ship chandler's a few squares down the street, curiosity goaded him inside.

The results were similar to what he had gleaned from the Captain of the Port: Lord Ballantyne's name was familiar, yet none of the present employees remembered him personally. But a great seaman, aye; a true laird and fighting man! Perhaps if Johnnie cared to try the chandler down the block . . . ?

Somewhat to his surprise, Johnnie discovered that he did care. With that tenacity which was such an integral trait of his character, he visited shop after shop until finally he wandered into an old sail-making establishment, and his search was ended. The proprietor took him upstairs to a sail loft where they found a wizened gnome of a man plying his needle.

"Ames," the proprietor asked of the old fellow, "haven't I heard you speak of Lord John Ballantyne?"

The ancient raised a pair of watery eyes to look owlishly first at his employer, then at Johnnie. He smiled, and the solitary tooth in the front of his mouth glinted like bronze.

"Aye, sir, ye've 'eard me speak o' 'im times aplenty, an' a grand man 'e was. Served me apprenticeship under Cap'n John five an' forty years ago."

The proprietor inclined his head toward Johnnie. "This man would

ask you some questions, Ames. He is a distant relative of Lord Ballantyne."

The old sail-maker made no comment until the proprietor took his
leave, then he came erect like a spider standing on his hind legs.

"Distant relative, me arse!" he cackled slyly. "Ye're the bloody
spittin' image o' ol' Cap'n John. Give me a start to see ye come
marchin' in 'ere, so it did."

Johnnie laughed and proffered a guinea, but the ancient glowered
at him and waved it away.

"Satan's backside! No son o' Cap'n John pays me to talk about him;
scuttle me if else!" He cocked his head and surveyed Johnnie from
head to foot. "Aye, ye've the same cut to yer jib, but a wee bit on the
small side, I ken."

Johnnie grinned. "Damme, old one, nobody has ever called me *small*
before."

"Then they ain't seen yer pa, youngster. Aye, I grant ye're a strappin'
lad, bigger'n most, no doubt, but ye don't bulk like Cap'n John. By
damn, ye don't!"

"Tell me what he looked like?"

Old Ames stared into the past. "Well, sir, 'e was 'arf an' 'ead taller
than ye an' some wider. Built like a tun, 'e was, mebbe not so graceful
as ye, laddie, but stronger, I wean. By God, 'e was strong, yet kindly,
mind ye; the blessed kindness w'at comes from confidence an' strength.
Laird 'e was, every well-born inch o' 'im, yet none too proud to 'ale an'
draw wi' the 'ands w'en goin' was bad. An' *fight?* Arsk any Spaniard!
They know! Why, I mind the time back in seventeen ten, w'en we—"
He paused. "Be ye in an 'urry, young un?"

"No, no!" protested Johnnie. "I want to hear everything."

Old Ames snorted. "Everythin'? Damme, 'twould tyke me a year o'
Sundays to tell yer just *'arf* w'at I recollecks. But o' this particular
fight I speak, we come upon a whole covey of Spaniards an'—"

He rambled on, and the lowering sun stretched lengthening shadows
over a half-sewn royal. Rats scurried out of hiding and seemed surprised
to find men still in the loft. The light waned, and somewhere in the
distance rang the scream of a hunting cat. Johnnie dreaded to break
the spell, but time was running out.

"Look, Ames, I have to go aboard my ship," he broke in reluctantly.
"But come with me to the tavern, and we'll continue this over a tot of
port."

"Satan's backside! If ye ain't the spit o' yer pa!" exclaimed the old man. "Not that Cap'n John ever arsked me to drink wi' 'im. Nay, not that, fer 'e was a laird to the core. But 'e'd talk, 'e would! 'Ow 'e loved to gam!" He wagged his head and reached for a battered hat on a nail. "Bless ye, lad, I'll be right 'appy to drink wi' the son of Cap'n John!"

For all his age—and Johnnie judged him to be five and sixty—Ames moved rapidly in a queer crab-wise gait. He was small, yet leathery and wiry, and he kept pace with Johnnie. He continued to chatter with the eagerness of old men reliving their youth, and for an illiterate man, or perhaps because of it, he had a gift of imagery which brought the past into focus with the present.

Tramping along, old Ames asked suddenly, "Ye mentioned a ship, lad; be ye a captain, too?"

"Not yet," grinned Johnnie. "I'm taking passage to—" He hesitated, then knowing instinctively he could trust the old man, went on: "—Morocco, where I hope to purchase a sloop and seek my fortune."

Old Ames gave him a sharp sidelong glance, then chuckled. "Aye, an' why not? Ye'll do it, too, an' if I was a mite younger, go wi' ye I would, scuttle me if else!"

"And I'd be proud to have you," added Johnnie.

The sail-maker returned to his favorite topic, but suddenly Johnnie wasn't listening. His roving eyes had spotted a stooped familiar figure moving through the crowd.

With a curt, "Follow me, ancient!" he plowed a furrow through the mob and grabbed the arm of Roberts, Leanna's aged manservant.

"Hold on, fellow!" he growled, jerking the lackey to a halt. "What are you doing in Portsmouth?"

The servant gawked in startled confusion before recognition finally came into his eyes.

"Why, yer lordship—I brought me lydy 'ere!"

"Here? *She* is here in Portsmouth?" He couldn't believe it. "Take me to her at once, Roberts, and if you're lying—!"

Roberts' manner implied surprise that Johnnie hadn't known about it.

"Beg pardon, sire, but 'er lydyship 'as just departed. Not five minutes past, I 'anded 'er aboard the shore-boat of 'Is Majesty's transport."

"Then she married Laughton already?"

"No, sire. Sir Clarence 'ad to leave promptly wi' 'is troops. Me lydy follows in the transport to New York, sire—a town in the Colonies— w'ere they'll be wed."

Cold hands seemed to be holding Johnnie's heart. "Tell me—has the shore-boat left? Where is it?"

Roberts pointed a quaking finger at a wharf a block away. "The h'officers' wives an' families are embarkin' there, me lord, but per'aps Sir Clarence might not like—"

"To hell with Sir Clarence!" snapped Johnnie. "Come on, Ames!"

He left Roberts, and went off on a run. He did not pause to examine his motives; it was enough to know that Leanna was here; he had to see her. He shoved and elbowed his way out onto a wharf packed with excited women, caterwauling children and weary porters. Pyramids of luggage and queues of sedan chairs added to the confusion, as leather-lunged sailors tried to herd the women and children into the proper shore-boats.

As Johnnie reached the embarking stage, he saw her, seated in the after end of a boat just pulling away. She was wrapped in a blue velvet cape, with the fur-trimmed hood framing her face. In that brief instant, she seemed alone, for he had eyes for none other, but as his focus widened he saw the heavy shape of Colonel Laughton beside her.

He opened his mouth to shout her name then snapped it shut. He stood, angry and impotent, and watched the gap between them widen. Then suddenly, by chance or premonition she looked up and saw him. Her eyes went wide. She clutched at her throat and half rose from the thwart, but her legs crumpled, and she fainted away.

Sir Clarence caught her in his arms, and scowled up to see what had affected her. But all he saw were milling women, children and porters—for Lord Johnnie was gone.

When they emerged into the comparative calmness of the street, Johnnie slowed for the old man to catch up with him. They marched along in silence for a block and a half before Old Ames chuckled softly.

"Y're one up on yer pa, I reckon," he remarked slyly. "I never seen him do *that.*"

Johnnie was abstracted. "Do what?" he muttered.

"Cap'n John 'ad a way wi' wimmen, I won't deny. They'd eye 'im like sick calfs, an' simper an' giggle an' blush, but scuttle me deep if I ever seen one knocked down on 'er beam's end at the mere sight o' 'im. 'E weren't *that* potent, bless 'im!"

"She was just a friend," grunted Johnnie, and because he didn't want to sound curt, added: "She hired three knaves to kill me, so I imagine she was shocked to find me still alive."

Old Ames gave him a dry smile. "Friend, ye say? Hummnn! Wi' friends like that, lad, ye don't need no enemies!"

Johnnie ignored the jibe; he was thinking about Leanna. He recalled the packed crates, and how startled she had been when he announced he was coming to Portsmouth. She had known then that she, too, was coming here. Possibly that explained the assassins? Perhaps she had hired them in desperation?

What he could not fathom was his own reaction to the sight of her. He had been drawn toward her as surely as a piece of iron to a magnet. The argument that he had wanted merely to denounce her for attempting to have him murdered was invalid; he couldn't delude himself with it any longer. The truth rose to mock him; he dreaded to face it, yet there it was: *He wanted his wife!*

For a moment he was startled, then he firmly disowned the notion and closed his mind to it. He realized suddenly they were nearing their destination, and his thoughts jumped ahead to Moll. He debated the wisdom of taking Old Ames up to the room. Moll might make another scene, yet, on the other hand, the presence of a stranger might dissuade her. Johnnie shrugged. If she didn't behave herself, he'd simply walk out and close the door.

As they came in sight of the *Crown and Anchor,* he glanced up at the jutting bay window, half expecting to see her standing there. He was relieved to find she was not. He led Old Ames into the taproom and purchased two bottles of wine. The room was crowded with seamen and soldiers, trying valiantly to soak up enough liquor to last them two months at sea. It was no place for talk. The air was foul with stale tobacco smoke and they couldn't find a private table. Yet somehow, a premonition of impending trouble made Johnnie tarry. They drank a bumper of ale apiece in the taproom, then because time was short, took the wine and climbed the stairs.

But moving down the hallway, Johnnie felt he had to offer some explanation.

"I've got a wench here, ancient, who—" But the old man cut him short.

"Be damned strange if ye didn't," he said matter-of-factly.

Johnnie grinned his appreciation. To his surprise, he found the door of their room bolted on the inside. Slightly puzzled, he drummed their private signal on the panel.

Moll's voice, strained and tense, called, *"Who is it?"*

He was relieved to know she was all right. Winking at the old man, he roared, " 'Od's blood, who else were you expecting? Open up, my girl—it's your own Johnnie!"

After an uncomfortable pause, the bolt creaked. So Moll *was* going to be difficult, he thought bitterly. But he set his smile in advance, kicked the door wide and strode inside waving the wine bottle, closely followed by Old Ames.

Moll was half crouched on the far side of the bed, her face rigid as a mask. Johnnie tried to humor her.

"Come, sweetheart!" he shouted boisterously. "I brought company, and something to celebrate with." He pretended not to notice her obvious stiffness. "I've got passage, my girl!"

"Aye, 'e've got passage!" Moll rasped, then cried loudly, *"Seize 'im, lads! Seize 'im!"*

A swift scuttle of feet brought Johnnie around. Three burly men, who must have been hiding behind the door, closed in on him. Though taken unawares, Johnnie felled the foremost with a wine bottle, and tried to spring backwards for space in which to draw his blade. But the bed blocked him, and while one man dove for his legs another hurled himself at Johnnie's throat.

In the tumult, more men crowded into the room. Old Ames had hopped onto the back of one assailant and was riding him like an angry cat on a dog, and though he was clubbed twice to the floor, he rose again and again.

Johnnie fought savagely. A product of the toughest brawling school in the world—Whitefriars—he crippled two more of the gang before he was finally overwhelmed by sheer numbers. Even then he surged back and forth, like a bear with mastiffs clinging to him. The bed collapsed, every chair was shattered, and not one pane of glass remained intact.

At last, a blow on the temple sagged him to his hands and knees. Clubs beat on his head and neck until the next thing he knew he was flat on his back, his hands bound behind him.

His first coherent thought was of Ames. After the beating, he feared the ancient might be dead. But Old Ames was very much alive, though lashed securely to the remains of the bed. His face was bloody and battered out of recognition, but the water in his rheumy eyes seemed to boil with indignation.

The leader of the gang, a keg-shaped giant in striped shirt and baggy blues, looked glumly at Johnnie, and then at the three inert figures on the floor.

"W'at a goddam stinkin' business!" he complained. "Fer three o' me best buckos, I get a mad bullock an' an ol' piss-ant sparrow!"

"Piss-ant sparrow!" shrilled Old Ames, tugging at his bonds. "Why, ye yellow-bellied bastard, gi' me five minutes wi' yer two brawniest, an' I'll splice their bleedin' gullets together! An' ye thrown in fer good measure, ye speckled whoreson! Sparrow, be I?"

The leader hit him a back-handed swipe across the mouth that only increased the old man's flow of imprecations. Ignoring Ames, the man turned to Moll, standing flat against the wall.

"W'y in 'ell didn't ye warn me there was *two* o' 'em?" he growled.

"I didn't know," Moll muttered. " 'Twas 'im I 'ad in mind!"

Her eyes met Johnnie's, and he was startled by the cold hatred on her face. He had seen her furious a score of times, but this was something new—an iceberg of hate that would never melt.

He said bitterly, "So! This was your doing, Moll?"

She flew across the room and thrust her pudgy face close to his.

"Aye, 'twas my doin'—every last bit o' it!" she shrieked. "An' w'at did 'e expec'? My blessin' mebbe, w'en 'e sneaked off to marry another?" She gave her head a defiant toss. " 'E wanted passage, so I got it fer 'e . . . *free!* Aye, yer lordship, I got 'e passage to the Colonies, so 'e'll be close to yer favorite 'ore, yer 'igh-toned *wife!*" She spat in his face to punctuate her words.

Johnnie shook his head to clear it. He didn't quite comprehend what she was talking about, but Old Ames did.

"A press gang!" he yelped. "Satan's backside! A press gang!"

The men laughed sourly, and the leader poked Ames in the chest with his club.

"Hear 'im mates? The ol' codger knows the ropes. Sink me, belike 'e's got another voyage left in 'im yet!"

Johnnie's stomach turned over. *Impressment!* God in heaven—that was worse than hanging!

"You treacherous bitch!" he roared, and tried to rear off the floor, but the leader rapped him on the head and he sank back, twitching.

Yet it was Moll's betrayal that sickened him more than the blows. Spots wheeled before his eyes and he came closer to fainting than ever before.

Then he heard a man bellow. " 'Ere, mates, look w'at I've found?"

"No, no! That's mine!" Moll was screaming. "Gi' it 'ere!"

Johnnie forced his head up. The leader was holding Johnnie's satchel of gold in one hand while he fought off Moll with the other.

"Ho, me 'earts! We've struck it rich!"

" 'E can't 'ave h'it!" wailed Moll, clawing at him. "I tolt 'e I'd arsk no blood-money fer this man, but the gold's mine by rights!"

The giant laughed, and imprisoned Moll in his free arm. "Tyke 'em out, lads," he ordered his companions. "I'll quiet the wench an' foller 'e!"

A half-dozen pressmen jerked Johnnie to his feet. He tried to resist, but it was futile.

"I'll kill every French-pocked whoreson of you!" he raged hysterically.

The leader spat at him. "Out wi' 'im, me bully boys! Let the nyvy tyme 'im!"

Moll had taken another tack. Instead of struggling, she had relaxed against the giant's shoulder and was smiling into his battered face.

"We shan't quarrel about h'it," she purred.

Johnnie was sick enough to vomit. "You faithless slut!" he grated between his teeth.

But Moll didn't even glance his way. As the pressmen dragged him from the room, the last he saw of her, she was in the leader's arms.

9

THE PRESS GANG ROUGHHOUSED JOHNNIE AND AMES DOWN THROUGH the crowded tavern and into the street. Their arms were bound and their legs hobbled, and the pressmen formed a cordon around them to ward off a rescue by friends or sympathizers. Johnnie stumbled along, too numbed by Moll's betrayal to offer further resistance, and Old Ames realized the futility of it. But the ancient's tongue was free, and his vocabulary uninhibited. His fiery denunciations bit as deep as the knouts of a cat, and though the pressmen cuffed him as much as they dared in public, the old man continued to play his profane lash to the delight of the throngs along the footpaths.

To Johnnie it was all a nightmare from which he expected to awaken. Even the jeers of the crowd seemed to come from a great distance, somehow detached from reality. As he struggled up from the suffocating depths, he paused, like a diver, to equalize the pressure, yet this was a level of humiliation that seemed but another phase of his dream. On the occasions of his few previous arrests, he had been treated with the awe-tinged respect due his notoriety, but now he was being dragged through the streets like a common criminal.

His pride thus pricked, Johnnie was jerked abruptly into the present. Physical pain he could endure, but not abasement. He stared at the press-bullies, as if seeing them for the first time. This *couldn't* be real; it must be a grisly jest!

But he knew now that it was real, and all he had ever heard about impressment swept through his mind. With the imminence of war, the navy needed pawns to man her rotten hulks, and while in legal theory only seamen could be impressed, in actual practice all fish that came into the net were devoured and forced to submit to a discipline compared to which the tyranny of an oriental despot was almost tender.

Johnnie went berserk. Bellowing defiance, he butted the nearest bully in the face and felt the nose bones crunch. A blow on the head felled him, but he rolled onto his back and lashed out with his tethered feet.

The pressmen converged on him, but when the leader jumped with his knees on Johnnie's chest and tried to throttle him into submission, Johnnie sank his teeth in the man's arm until he tasted blood.

Left to his own devices, Old Ames hopped up and down screaming, "Don't fight the bloody swine, lad, else they'll kill ye! Bide yer time!"

But Johnnie was beyond the power to reason. Madness had given him a strength that neither blows nor kicks could subdue. This was too much for the old sail-maker, and with a shrill blast of obscenity, he threw himself into the melee. But he was quickly battered into impotency, and the gang concentrated on Johnnie.

For a few minutes, the crowd merely jeered and hooted, but as the press-bullies seemed intent on killing Johnnie, a determined knot of men moved forward to interfere. Fearing a full-blown riot, the pressmen turned from their victim and with club and pistol cleared a path through the angry mob. Johnnie was picked up bodily and hustled off to prison.

Along with Old Ames, he was flung into a cell already occupied by two other dupes of the net. For a long time, he lay where he had been thrown, on a tick-ridden pallet of straw, while the fire of his rage burned down. Wisely, no one spoke to him, not even Old Ames; he endured his ordeal in silence until at last he emerged from the ashes with his pride sustained by a cold unrelenting hatred.

Finally, he propped himself up against the wall and looked about him. They had not been trusted with a candle, for in the past hysterical prisoners had attempted to set the place on fire, but a lanthorn had been hung in the corridor just outside the door so that its feeble light filtered into the cell.

Old Ames sat opposite, his arms folded on drawn-up knees, his head bowed dejectedly. Johnnie felt a pang of guilt.

"I'm sorry I got you into this, ancient," he apologized.

The old man lifted his head. Though his features were battered out of shape, his eyes blazed with indignation.

"Ye're sorry!" he shrilled. "Did ye make the Recruitin' Act? Did ye sick the press gang on't us? If not, then syve yer bloody pity fer them goddam swine w'at did!" The edge went out of his voice and he cackled mirthlessly. "It don't myke no difference to me, matey; I'll be shark-bait afore one voyage's o'er." He dropped his head onto his arms again, and withdrew into the solitude of his thoughts.

Johnnie appraised the other occupants of the cell. The youngest, crouched in a sobbing knot by the door, was plainly a country bumpkin.

Not over fourteen, he had the look of a crazed ewe, and every sound in the prison set his thin body to quaking. Johnnie sensed that a word would send him into hysterics, so he turned his attention to the fourth man.

The latter was a shaggy bear of a man, well over a fathom tall, who resembled a ship's figurehead clumsily cut from teak. His hair was a blazing red mop, and his eyes, now focused quizzically on Johnnie, seemed peculiarly out of place in the truculent face. They were a very pale blue, with the mischievous sparkle of a child's. Under a broken, lop-sided nose, was a wide, sensuous mouth. He exuded the smell of a hostler. Johnnie guessed his age at six and twenty.

"Suit ye?" the fellow demanded, at the conclusion of Johnnie's examination.

Johnnie grinned. "You should suit them. You're big enough."

"Me name's Ben Bottle," announced the other, in a strident voice that seemed to echo all over the prison. "Benjamin Bottle, o' Belfast, Ireland, an' I'm 'ere to state that I ain't fightin' fer no goddam English king, an' ye can lay to that!"

Old Ames glanced up. "Pipe down, Mick," he cautioned, "else they'll flea the 'ide off'n ye! Any'ow, from the cut o' yer jib, methinks ye've already served in 'Is Majesty's nyvy."

"A pox on yer English King! May 'e die o' the bloody flux!" raged Ben Bottle, but this time his voice was lowered perceptibly. "Aye, ancient, 'tis true I served in the nyvy, but through no fault o' me own, b'Jesus!" He turned back to Johnnie.

"Ye've an air o' quality, friend," he observed admiringly. "How come the varmints got the like o' ye?"

Johnnie grimaced. "A slight miscalculation, Ben."

"Ho! The word I don't ken, but the meanin', aye! Can be but one thing—a *woman!* Let me tell ye, friend—wimmen are the spawn o' hell!"

"You got it hind-end-foremost," contradicted Ames, without troubling to lift his head. "The only hell is that spawned by a jealous woman."

The Irishman guffawed boisterously, slapping his thigh and repeating the witticism over and over to himself. Johnnie found the merriment contagious, and though he had little enough to laugh about, he couldn't help grinning.

But the country boy was not amused by this brutal humor, and he began sobbing aloud. Old Ames edged over and patted his shoulder.

" 'Ere, 'ere now, matey, batten down yer lip," he advised with gruff kindliness. "W'at's done's done, an' snivelin' 'll only get ye the cat."

"I don't want to go!" wailed the lad. "I don't want to go!"

"Holy Mither!" snorted Ben Bottle. " 'Oo does?"

"That's so, lad," Johnnie counselled. "We're all in the same pot and we all feel the same about it. Yet there is nothing we can do at the moment. But I can promise you this, for what it's worth—it won't seem so bleak tomorrow!"

The boy was panting heavily. "I can't stand it! I want to go home!"

A guard thrust his face against the wicket. "Belay that gab in there an' get some sleep. Y're sailin' early."

"Ye kiss me regal Irish arse!" shouted Ben Bottle, but the guard had wandered away, taking the lanthorn with him.

"It was sage advice," conceded Johnnie, in the darkness.

" 'Oo's?" asked Old Ames.

"I meant the turnkey's," chuckled Johnny, "though I grant you, friend Benjamin had a point."

The boy cried a long time, but eventually he stopped, and the cell went quiet. Yet for Johnnie, stretched on the straw pallet, sleep would not come, and in the silence of the ancient prison, imagination began to work on him. Despite his realistic counsel to the country lad, he, too, suffered a twitch of panic. He tossed and squirmed, wishing there was some way to work off his nerves; a walk, a fight, anything except to have to lie here and think. But there was no escape from his conscience. In vain he sought to project the responsibility for his plight onto Moll, but his inner voice argued that he had invited it. As Moll herself had execrated him, *W'at did 'e expeck? . . . My blessin' mebbe?*

The outward anger which had up to now sustained him turned inward, and he writhed in self-reproach. He had been trapped by his own overweening ambitions. Even the actions of Moll and Leanna had been engendered by his selfishness.

Yet, admitting all that, he remained bewildered. What other course could he have taken? True, he might have stayed away from Leanna, and perhaps even married Moll. But what of his hopes and aspirations? Without them, his existence would have been intolerable! He turned over and buried his face in the straw. There was no point in torturing himself further. He had cast the dice with Destiny, and lost. Instead of a quick, dramatic death at a rope's end, the great Lord Johnnie, the terror of London, was to be a galley slave!

He must have fallen asleep, for the next thing he knew, a bugle was blowing, and the cell was filled with eerie light. Sleepily, he raised his head—then sat up with a jerk.

The body of the country boy dangled from the window. One end of his belt was attached to the bars, the other to his twisted neck.

Ben Bottle and Ames were also awake. The big Irishman was softly mixing oaths with prayers, but Old Ames accepted it philosophically.

"Well, bless 'im, the wee laddie won't go arter all!"

10

ALTHOUGH THERE COULD BE NO MORAL JUSTIFICATION FOR THE SYSTEM of impressment, there was a plausible excuse. Harassed and schemed against by her jealous enemies, England required a mighty fleet to protect her shores and maintain the web of lifelines to her far-flung colonies. Ships necessitated crews, and due to the incredible privations of life at sea—made even more unbearable by stupid regulations and the brutality of many of the officers who enforced them—no Englishman in his right mind would enter the service of his own accord. Hence, a desperate Parliament had sanctioned the Recruiting Act in a vain effort to amend one abuse by adding another.

However, the knowledge that his plight was shared by uncounted thousands did not lessen Johnnie's resentment. He did not belong to the herd, and he accepted no responsibility for their laws or their mistakes. And though he was prodded to the landing in company with a score of others, in spirit he walked alone. Yet for all his indifference, the memory of this sailing day would never be erased from his mind.

The waterfront was a bedlam wherein fifes and bugles and boatswain's pipes vied with wailing women, the bawling of drunken seamen and the shrill cries of the bum-boatmen. The channel swarmed with shore-boats shuttling to and from the gloomy transports. It seemed impossible there could be any order in the chaos.

"Fools!" muttered Old Ames, waving his arm in an all-inclusive arc. "Look 'ow 'ard they work to kill themselves."

" 'Tis the way o' English oxen!" offered Ben Bottle. "Now in Ireland—"

But Johnnie paid no attention. He was less concerned about the problem of nationalities than he was with this indignity to which England was submitting him. He thought regretfully of Captain "Mebbe," who at this moment was comfortably headed for Spain.

After a long wait in the broiling sun, Johnnie and his companions were packed in a cutter and ferried out to an ancient East Indiaman, anchored on the fringe of the Grand Fleet. The coxswain of the boat remarked that she was named the *Eagle,* which brought a hoot of derision from the Irishman.

"*Eagle* they calls 'er now!" he jeered. "Fair turns me gorge to see 'er agin!"

Old Ames glanced at him. "So—ye know 'er, Mick?"

"*Know* 'er? B'Jesus, she's older'n ye be, ancient, an' a bloody sight more rickety. I'll wager a shillin' to a maiden'ead she won't hold together 'till we get round the Lizard! Why, man, look at 'er full belly, them flat floors an' them 'ard turns to 'er bilger! Look at 'em, an' then arsk if she ain't a wallowin' ol' sea bitch! Aye, I knows 'er only too well. She's the ol' *Merchant Maid,* condemned an' on the beach these five years past."

Old Ames chuckled good-naturedly. He seemed to regard his plight with a calm and philosophy which most people reserve for the misfortunes of others.

"Methinks the government's 'ard put w'en she 'as to impress ol' ships as well as ol' men, an' like as not, I won't last around the Lizard either." He winked at Johnnie. "Well, w'at think ye o' 'er, lad?"

Johnnie grinned. "Her old name seems more descriptive than her new, ancient. It's plain she's no eagle, yet she does put me in mind of a fat spouse of some paunchy merchant. Ben's right, I suspect. She'll be a capricious sea bitch."

The cutter maneuvered alongside, and Johnnie mounted to the *Eagle's* deck, followed by the other impressed men. He found the ship in an uproar. Petty officers were trying to round up the Lovely Nans and bundle them into the returning shore-boats, and the more robust seamen resisted their efforts. Obviously, plenty of liquor had been smuggled abroad, for some of the waisters were strutting around like admirals. Several fights were in progress amidships, and limp bodies were trampled underfoot.

Hardly had they stepped aboard, when Ben Bottle got into a brawl with a marine, but Johnnie and Old Ames edged over behind a gun-carriage to watch the fun. If the waist was chaotic, the usually sacrosanct quarter-deck was nearly as bad. Up there, peddlers haggled with the lieutenants over monies due them, drunken women sobbed for permission to sail with their lovers, who in turn sobbed that they might. The harassed officers tried to keep their tempers, for though things would be different once the ship cleared port, this last day was traditionally one of tolerance.

Old Ames summarized it succinctly: "The dolts'll 'ave their fun today, an' tomorrer they'll be grovelin' on their bellies." He nudged Johnnie and pointed at Ben Bottle who at the moment was all snarled up in the arms of a drunken harlot.

"W'at think ye o' the Mick, Johnnie?"

"Crazy as a stallion, and young."

"Aye, an' methinks he's stayed young too long. Oh-oh! There's the cap'n!"

Johnnie's attention was thus drawn to the quarter-deck, where a large man came out of the companionway in pot-bellied majesty. He paused a moment, fingering a gold-headed cane, while he surveyed the scene. Although well out of earshot, Old Ames dropped his voice to a mere whisper: "Satan's backside, I know that un! 'E's an 'ard case. Cap'n Bloodsmythe's 'is nyme, though 'tween decks they calls 'im *Ol' Bloody!* Damme, Johnnie, this'll be an 'ell-ship fer fair!"

Johnnie shrugged, and studied the captain with a calculating eye. Bloodsmythe was a large-torsoed man with slim bandy legs which gave him a top-heavy look. Under a tri-cornered hat trimmed with gold lace, his powdered hair was worn in a long queue tied with a black ribbon. His simian face was bloated smooth of all wrinkles, and contrary to the popular supposition that a seaman's hide necessarily becomes leathery from wind and sea, his skin was as pink and transparent as a child's. He had a protruding lower lip that gave him a perpetual pout. A flat nose and small, shot-hard eyes completed the unpleasant ensemble.

After a few moments of portentous silence, the captain began suddenly to lay about him with his cane.

"Get off my deck! Get off my deck!" he shrieked, in a high-pitched lisping tone.

He lashed out indiscriminately at women and seamen alike until the drunk and the sober fled before his unbridled temper. Soon the quarter-deck was cleared, and while Bloodsmythe stood haughtily at the head of the quarter-deck ladder, the officers charged down into the waist to aid the petty officers round up the harlots.

"We'd better get below," advised Old Ames.

Johnnie snorted. "Would you run like a mouse, old one?"

"Exactly! W'en I run wi' the lions, I roar, but w'en wi' mice, I sneaks into a good syfe 'ole. Gi' me a score o' bully-boys, an' I'll seize this tub, but since I can't I'll do w'at I'm tolt, an' . . . so will ye, Johnnie, if y're smart!"

It was sage counsel, and Johnnie knew it. The officers were having trouble aplenty and things were getting dangerous on deck. A Lovely Nan tore past Johnnie, leapt into the rigging and went screaming aloft, stripping off her clothing enroute to the delight of the crowd.

"After the slut!" shrilled the captain. "Throw her overboard! Throw any of them overboard who aren't in the boats in five minutes!"

Near by, a frantic boatswain's mate struck Ben Bottle across the face with a knout, knocking him against the bulwark. Ben seized a belaying pin and laid the bully cold. Johnnie realized it was time to move along. With a nod to Ames, he collared the happy Irishman and dragged him away. At the head of the foc'sle hatch, Ben resisted so stoutly, Johnnie was forced to drive his fist into the Irishman's midsection. Ben passed out, and with the sail-maker's help, Johnnie lowered him into the unsavory darkness below.

The foul air made Johnnie retch, and he was tempted to go back on deck. But Old Ames argued that unless they secured a decent place in which to swing their hammocks, the trip would be unendurable. So towing the unconscious Irishman, Johnnie followed Old Ames to a vantage spot amidships where the pitch and roll of the vessel would be least obnoxious, and claimed three hammocks for their own.

Despite Ben Bottle's pessimistic prediction, the ancient East Indiaman held together around Lizard Head and bunted her bluff bows into the Atlantic swells. But if the Irishman's prophecy of her sudden demise had been premature, his opinion had not. The *Eagle* was in all truth a "wallowin' ol' sea bitch!"

Though originally well armed against the normal hazards of pirates and minor marauders, since her recent entry into government service, she had been pierced for additional cannon. These massive guns, for which she had not been designed, altered her trim and made her even more top-heavy and cumbersome. The exigencies of war required more men than she was fitted to accommodate, and the crowding below decks was intolerable.

Active discontent began to fester before they cleared the English Channel when word had got around that the *Eagle* was unseaworthy and only expected to last this one voyage. As Ben Bottle had stated, she had lain rotting on the beach for several years until the demand for bottoms became acute. Whereupon she had been hauled out of her grave by ghoulish borough-mongers, patched sufficiently to float, and

leased to the government at a vast profit to carry supplies to the troops
in America. The food, supplied by corrupt contractors, was rotten and
inedible, and the discipline unreasonably harsh.

Of her officers, only Rodney Yew, the first lieutenant, had experienced naval service. Captain Bloodsmythe and the second officer,
Lieutenant Shad, were products of the old East India Company, and
the added authority granted them by the *Articles of War* was abused
from the start. Unfortunately for Lord Johnnie, he and Old Ames
were assigned to the starboard watch under the second officer.

This despot was as big a man as Johnnie, and heavier, with thick
legs that had the appearance of tree stumps growing out of the deck.
His arms were abnormally long, as if stretched from years of hauling
line, and his fists were large mauls hardened on the skulls of recalcitrant
seamen. He had a voice a lion might envy and the disposition of a
mongrel with rabies. 'Tween decks gossip had it that a lack of common
intelligence had prevented him from ever hoping to rise above his
present station, which frustration accounted for his savagery toward
the unfortunates beneath him. Be that as it may, he was the second
lieutenant, and as such, his tyranny had the backing, even the encouragement, of the master.

Ben Bottle fared better. He was put in the larboard watch under
Rodney Yew. The first was the oldest of the after-guard, being somewhere in his fifties; a stolid, leathery man who though small in build
somehow created the impression of being much larger than he was. He
was stern without being cruel, and if he possessed any nerves, he failed
to display them. If the hands did not like him, they at least respected
him. It was rumored that Yew and the captain were not on friendly
terms, but whether this was true or not the men soon learned that no
advantage could be gained by it.

The first open trouble started over the "salt horse," as the beef was
dubbed. It had long been the custom to eat the "old meat" first, that is,
meat which had been returned from a former voyage, but on opening
one of these venerable casks, the stench flooded the space between decks
and hung in the air like smoke. When the cook retorted to the voluble
complaint by saying the men would eat it or go without, a seaman
named Quinn fished out an unsavory chunk the color of mahogany and
carried it aft on the point of his knife to show the watch officers.

Johnnie was on deck when the incident occurred. He watched
Quinn, a large, emotional Bristolman, walk up to Lieutenant Shad,
who was lolling near the wheel.

"Beggin' yer pardon, sor," Quinn began humbly enough, although his voice shook with feeling. "I'll arsk ye to tyke a w'iff o' this putrid offal!"

Shad's eyes brightened. "What's wrong with it?"

"Can't ye smell?" cried Quinn. "'Tis poison, unfit fer a jackal, sor! We 'ands can't work on such swill—"

That was as far as he got when Shad kneed him in the groin. Quinn screamed and fell into a groaning convulsive knot on the deck.

Captain Bloodsmythe chose that particular moment to appear at the rail of the quarter-deck, just above them. He stared down at the squirming seaman with studied indifference.

"What's the trouble down there, Mister?" he lisped.

The lieutenant knuckled his forelock. "This man's a troublemaker, sir. Told me the men refused to work on the food. Belike they expect rare roast beef, from the cheek of him."

At this deliberate mishandling of the truth, Johnnie raised an eyebrow, but the rest of the watch grumbled audibly. This demonstration merely increased the captain's wrath.

"Damn the mutinous hounds!" he shouted, waving his arms excitedly. "Am I to be annoyed by the insolence of these prison sweepings? Refuses to work, does he? What is his name?"

Shad barked a question at a man close by, and on receiving a grudging answer, passed it along to the captain.

"Quinn, sir!"

"Very well! If Quinn demands rare meat, by God, he shall have it aplenty! Seize him up!"

At a gesture from Shad, two pigtailed old tars reluctantly lifted the still-moaning Quinn to his feet. By this time, the watch began to suspect what was coming, and grumbled resentfully. Captain Bloodsmythe beat a noisy tattoo on the deck with the ferrule of his cane, as if to drown out the muttering of the men.

"Pipe all hands on deck, Mister Shad, and rig the gratings!" he trumpeted. "By God, I'll teach these people who's captain of *this* ship! Rare meat, eh?"

As the order for all hands was piped, Captain Bloodsmythe turned on his heel and stalked below. Meanwhile, the carpenter and his mates dragged two ponderous wooden hatch covers over to the lee bulwarks and secured them; one flat on the deck to form a platform, the other standing on end and lashed to the shrouds like a back-drop. By the time these preparations were completed, the sleepy-eyed watch below had gathered on deck in sullen surprise.

Johnnie, leaning against a gun-carriage with Old Ames, viewed the proceedings with cynical detachment. He felt no compassion for Quinn; the fool should have known better than to attempt reason with a bully like Shad. But the sail-maker seethed with righteous wrath.

" 'E lied! The dirty bastard lied!" he grumbled.

Johnnie shrugged. "Quinn asked for it. There's better uses for a knife than balancing a piece of dead meat on the end, ancient. He should have buried it in Shad's ribs."

"Quinn was tryin' to 'elp us all," snapped Old Ames.

"He wasn't helping me," Johnnie grunted. "I don't need a blunderer like Quinn to handle my quarrels."

Old Ames looked him in the eye. "I don't know nuthin' about yer past, lad, but ye 'ave the bleat of a ram w'at's tryin' to play tiger. Mebbe y're used to 'untin' alone, but now y're just one more lamb in the flock, an' w'at 'urts one, 'urts all."

Johnnie started to laugh, then changed his mind. There was a modicum of truth in what the old man had said; it was a point Johnnie had not considered. He had been a lone hunting tiger for so long, he had forgotten his own youthful days in the foc's'le.

Further discussion was halted by a stir in the crowd, and all eyes turned to the quarter-deck, where Captain Bloodsmythe had returned, bringing his wife. Johnnie had heard she was aboard, but this was her first appearance on deck. He regarded her with interest.

She could not have been over five and twenty—slightly more than half the age of her husband. She had bright golden hair, worn in long plaits, and her features were well formed; but these natural attributes were marred by a drab gray gown that concealed any shapeliness of body and by an utter blankness of expression. She moved up to the quarter-deck rail beside her pompous spouse with the curious listlessness of a sleepwalker.

Bloodsmythe had put on his dress coat for the ceremony, a blue coat with Mechlin lace at the throat, white cuffs and small flat buttons, and he had exchanged his cane for a dress sword. Yet watching him tower there above his diminutive wife, Johnnie was reminded of Ben Bottle's comment: Old Bloody *did* resemble a large toad on his hind legs.

Quinn knew what to expect, yet with the peculiar perversity of the

British tar, seemed to take a certain pride in it. He stripped off his coat and shirt and, bared to the waist, stood waiting for sentence.

Captain Bloodsmythe leaned his hands on the rail. "There appears to be some doubts as to who is the captain of this ship!" he lectured them, in a high-pitched voice which he controlled with difficulty. "That doubt is going to be cleared up right now, and the next man who questions authority will not get off so lightly, I promise you! Seize him up!"

Two quartermasters marched Quinn onto the platform and secured his outspread arms to the vertical grating with lengths of spun-yarn. Then they reported: "Seized up, sor!"

Bloodsmythe moistened his liver-colored lips. "Two dozen!" he barked.

A powerful boatswain's mate strode forward carrying a red baize bag from which he extracted the cat-o'-nine-tails, a short wooden stick with tails of knotted cord about two feet in length. He drew the cattails affectionately through his fingers and glanced at the master.

"Do your duty!" ordered Captain Bloodsmythe. "And see that you lay it on!"

The boatswain's mate took his stance against the roll of the vessel, drew back his arm, and struck. Johnnie heard the whistle of the lash through the air, the involuntary sob it wrung from the victim, then saw the series of scarlet welts appear on the white skin.

As the blows quickened, Johnnie turned his attention to the audience. The people (as the common seamen were termed) viewed it with the muteness of cattle. Lieutenant Shad, standing near the mainmast, wore an expression of smug satisfaction. Johnnie's gaze roved to the quarter-deck. Captain Bloodsmythe leaned over the rail, his ponderous lower lip twitching as his button eyes followed every movement of the whip. His wife's face was vapid as before, but Johnnie noticed that each time the lash struck flesh, her eyes closed momentarily.

On the lee, opposite the Bloodsmythes, stood Rodney Yew. Although he exhibited no emotion, his stern, wind-burned face lacked the emptiness of the woman's. Johnnie attempted to read something of the man's thoughts, but failed.

Save for an occasional sob, by the tenth blow, Quinn had made no outcry. This lack seemed to incite the captain, for he bellowed: "Stop shirking there! Lay into it, I tell you! Let's see the dog's backbone, by God!"

The boatswain's mate paused to wipe the sweat away from his eyes before changing his position so that the whip would criss-cross the now-bleeding welts. Quinn endured one more blow in silence, but the twelfth drew a shriek of agony that seemed to permeate every corner of the ship.

"That's better!" lisped Captain Bloodsmythe, folding his arms. "See that you keep it up!"

At each stroke now, Quinn screamed and beat his forehead against the grating.

"Oh-o, Jesus Christ! O-o-oh!"

Johnnie Rogue was inured to violence, yet the utter unreasonableness of this incensed him. The victim's cries made him restless, and he marveled that Englishmen could submit to the spectacle with such bovine passivity. He looked again at the quarter-deck. Rodney Yew had not moved, but his mouth seemed a trifle thinner. All color had drained from the woman's face, and as he watched, Johnnie saw her take a step from the rail and turn away. Captain Bloodsmythe reached out and yanked her back, snarling something under his breath. She flushed, and until the end of the torture, kept her gaze fixedly on Quinn's raw back.

On the twenty-first blow, Quinn fainted. His body sagged grotesquely against the grating, and his head rolled with each motion of the ship. An involuntary sigh came from the crowd, followed by a silence broken only by the swish of the cut-water and the whimper of wind in the shrouds. The boatswain's mate paused to flip the blood and small pieces of flesh from his whip, for it was pointless to flog an unconscious man.

But Captain Bloodsmythe was unsatisfied. "What are you waiting for?" he shouted violently. "Lay onto your task, or, by God, I'll have *you* flogged!"

"Aye, aye, sir!" muttered the boatswain's mate, and finished the sentence.

When Quinn's lacerated body had been cut down and carried below to be doused with brine, Bloodsmythe straightened from the rail.

"Let that be a warning to you, men! I'm a lamb of kindness if you behave yourselves. But, give me any further insolence and, by God, you'll find me a *rogue!* Now back to your duties!"

As the men sullenly dispersed, Johnnie watched the Bloodsmythes leave the rail. The captain tried to take his wife's arm, but she wrenched away from his touch. For a transient moment there was a loathing on her face such as Johnnie had rarely witnessed, but it vanished instantly to be replaced by her habitual blankness. Then they went below.

The wind had increased, and Yew bellowed an order to take in the topgallants. The activity was a welcome diversion; the men monkey-handed up the ratlines with a will.

11

THE *Eagle,* TOO SLOW AND UNWIELDY TO KEEP UP WITH THE REST OF the convoy sailing for America, stood off on her own tack to seek a helpful tradewind for the west. This was not unusual, for in these times, each ship was deemed to be a "navy unto herself." But the antiquated East Indiaman was rife with dry rot, and both the officers and men cursed the extra armament foisted upon her, not only for the way it affected her trim and sailing qualities, but because of the ever-present danger of a heavy gun breaking adrift from its fastenings. A loose cannon at sea was a nightmare, for the two or more tons of iron, charging about the rolling decks like a rogue elephant, could easily tear such a hole through her rotten timbers that might sink her.

On the third day after the flogging of Quinn, the forward breeching of a twenty-four pound cannon did let go in a bad seaway. The entire ship was thrown into an uproar, and Captain Bloodsmythe himself came panting to the scene. For nearly a quarter of an hour, the gun plunged around the pitching deck with what appeared to be a devilish intelligence. Finally, by heeling the vessel sharply, the runaway monster was trapped in a corner where hammocks were flung under the chocks and it was brought under control. Captain Bloodsmythe tried to find a scapegoat, but when it was proved that the hemp fastenings had been rotten, he issued orders for all the gun tackles and breeching to be doubled, and dropped the matter.

However, the fears of the seamen were not so easily allayed. By this time, they hated the ship as much as they hated the officers, and had equal confidence in neither. Quinn, whom they would ordinarily have thought a fool, was elevated to the status of a martyr. Less than half the ship's complement had ever been to sea before, and at times fully two thirds of the crew was desperately seasick. Unfortunately, the captain chose to regard sickness as an attempt to shirk duty, and floggings became commonplace.

Off the Bay of Biscay, the weather worsened. The people prayed for the customary order to shorten sail, but Bloodsmythe elected to drive her. Seams opened, and the pumps were manned day and night; the decks leaked until there wasn't a dry piece of clothing below. In addition, the sloshing bilges churned up nauseous fumes that made sleep impossible. The *Eagle* was a fertile womb for trouble.

Lord Johnnie endured it all with haughty disdain. He remained aloof from both the mutterings of the men and the tirades of the agitators, for he was concerned solely with his own problem of escape. Being a powerful swimmer, he toyed with the notion of slipping overboard some night when they passed close to Spanish territory. The only thing that troubled him was the knowledge that he was, indirectly at least, responsible for the plight of Old Ames.

It was a novel experience. Never before had he concerned himself about the safety of another; his code had always been "let the Devil take the hindmost." Yet in some strange fashion he could not quite define, the old man seemed irrevocably linked to his background. The reaction made him impatient, yet he was unable to shake it. So he tried to concoct some scheme of escape that would include the old man. Meanwhile, the *Eagle* wallowed south.

After the softening influence of Newgate, the work hardened him, and if he did not enjoy it, he considered it in the light of training that would condition him for the moment of escape.

But Old Ames was not equal to it. After a decade of squatting in a sail-loft, his legs refused to accommodate to the corkscrew motion of the ship. On the twelfth morning at sea, he was too sick and battered to crawl out of his hammock. When he tried, he crumpled instantly to the deck, and Johnnie had to lift him back.

"You stay in that hammock," Johnnie told him.

"They'll come arter me!" whimpered the old man. "They'll flog me!"

Johnnie patted his arm reassuringly. "Nobody will flog you, old one."

Ben Bottle, who had just come off watch, heard this. "B'Jesus, ancient, me'n Johnnie'll see 'to it nobody lays an 'and on ye!"

Old Ames writhed in misery. "Reckon it don't matter. May's well die a sheep as a lamb."

As the shrill squeak of the boatswain's pipe sent the men scurrying for the ladderway, Ben drew Johnnie aside.

"This be a taut ship," he growled anxiously. "Belike they'll put a knout to the ol' coot."

Johnnie frowned. "It would mean the death of him," he reasoned. "And while I grant this is a hell-ship, I doubt Bloodsmythe would deliberately murder an old man."

Ben shook his head worriedly. "Ol' Bloody's a killer. 'Tis said that arter each floggin', 'e lays 'is wife in lust." He spat in disgust. "It fair makes me puke to set eyes on 'im!"

Johnnie promised to do what he could, and hurried on deck. Despite the southerly latitude, the wind was cold and piercing. The *Eagle* scudded along to a quartering breeze and her topmasts made wide circles against the blue sky. But Johnnie was disturbed as he came into the waist. So far on the voyage, he had managed to keep clear of the churlish petty officers who went about goading seamen with their *starters*—short, knotted ropes wielded like whips to "start" the hands to their tasks. Though it galled him to speak to one of them, he could not stand aside and see Old Ames abused without reason.

Lieutenant Shad was bawling to have the topsails reefed, and the hands were scrambling aloft. Crossing toward the windward shrouds, Johnnie passed a boatswain's mate by the main fife rail. Muzzling his pride, he paused. "That old man in this watch is very sick," he reported.

The petty officer looked blank. "Didn't 'e 'ear the pipe?"

Johnnie kept his voice respectful. "Aye, but when he tried to get out of his hammock, he collapsed. I had to lift him back into it."

The boatswain's mate gave him a shove. "Get aloft where 'e belong!" he snarled. He drew back his starter arm, but when his eyes met Johnnie's, he let it drop. Johnnie turned without a word and sprang into the rigging.

Once above the scant shelter of the bulwarks, the wind bit through his sodden clothing, and by the time he had worked out onto the arcing yard, his hands were blue with cold. The rotten canvas was stiff and unmanageable, and most of the men were untrained. Time after time the wind whipped the almost-muffled sail out of their bleeding hands and the work had to be redone endlessly.

Johnnie was so busy he had not glanced below until the man next to him on the yard burst out: "Oh, God A'mighty! Look at that son o' hell maul the ol' one!"

Johnnie, balanced precariously on a foot-rope, looked down. Far below, the boatswain's mate to whom he had reported the sickness of Old Ames had dragged the aged sail-maker onto the upper deck and was trying to beat him to his feet.

Johnnie's stomach contracted into a hard knot. The other men crowded onto the swaying yard were watching, too, and hurled obscene oaths which were safely carried to leeward by the squall. On the

quarter-deck aft, Lieutenant Shad stood viewing the brutality
with serene indifference. Three times in succession, the old man
staggered erect under the blows, only to have his legs jackknife under
him.

"The filthy bastard'll kill 'im!' growled the man to windward of
Johnnie.

Glancing at the speaker, Johnnie felt strangely alone. This was not
an alien sensation—he usually felt alone—but of a sudden, he grasped
the significance behind it. These sodden creatures were without initia-
tive; blindly they subscribed to the old rule of the sea: *Grumble you
may, obey you must.* Without leadership, they were helpless, and thus
it was possible that a mere handful of arrogant bullies could keep five
score of them in abject submission to a point where they could meekly
watch while one of their own number was being beaten to death without cause.

He forced his eyes downward again. Now the boatswain's mate was
using his heavy boots on the old man. Ames was squirming on the deck,
trying to protect his face and stomach with his feeble arms. A few more
minutes of this would kill him.

Perhaps it was better so, Johnnie tried to tell himself. He knew the
futility of single-handed interference and there was no time to plan
concerted action. All his experience and instinct warned him to mind
his own business. Yet some stronger emotions blacked-out reason, and
without conscious premeditation, he dove suddenly for a brace and
went hurtling down the line to the deck.

As he shot from the bulwarks, he jerked a belaying pin from the rail.
The boatswain's mate heard him coming, and swung around with
starter raised. But Johnnie jabbed him in the belly with the pin, and as
the bully doubled, lashed him over the head.

Old Ames was sobbing: "No, lad, fer God's syke, *no!*"

The boatswain's mate had slid into the position of a Mohammedan
at prayer. Now that he had committed himself, Johnnie's temper, too-
long repressed, exploded. He kicked the man onto his back and ground
his heel into his face.

"Johnnie! Look out be'ind!"

Johnny pirouetted. Shad, followed by the boatswain, came charging
toward him. Johnnie flung the heavy pin into the latter's face, breaking his nose, and closed with the officer.

Shad tried to use his knee—a tactical error, for Johnnie squirmed
aside, caught the half-bent leg, and heaved Shad onto his back. Other

petty officers were running to get into the fight, and Johnny realized it was but minutes before he would be either killed or captured. He was past caring now, and his hate was implemented by an obsession to kill Shad before he himself was downed.

He knocked an over-eager gun-captain aside and jumped with both feet on Shad's chest. He tried to grab the lieutenant's pistol, then somebody hit him at the base of the skull with a marlin spike. The blow left him half-blinded, but he distinguished the fuzzy outline of a man and seized him by the throat. The ship heeled sharply and they were thrown across the deck to come up with a crash against a gun carriage. The squall had broken!

Still Johnnie hung on. He felt the rain come, cool and sweet. The blows he felt no longer. As from a distance, he heard a voice shout that the captain had come on deck, and the wish filtered into his mind that it was Captain Bloodsmythe he was choking. The thought fathered strength. But another heave of the ship flung them away from the gun carriage and into the pump. Then something exploded in Lord Johnnie's head, and he knew no more.

His return to consciousness was an ascent from a deep and lonely well. Time out of number, he tortuously dragged himself out of the darkness toward the light only to lose his grip and crash back into oblivion. During these intervals of half-awareness, he imagined himself strapped to the back of a great winged stallion that dipped and soared through space, but whenever this phantom steed stumbled, the blackness closed in again. Flying through this swale of shadows, he could see nothing, yet there were vaguely familiar sounds which he sensed he should recognize but could not; a weird orchestration of murmuring strings, of whistling lutes, and of deep booming drums that somehow always died away in gurgling laughter.

After interminable effort, he finally struggled over the rim of the pit, to lie aching on the borderline of comprehension. Piece by piece he fitted the fragments of the puzzle into place until the chimera evaporated into reality. The bald truth shocked him completely awake.

He found himself spread-eagled on his back, his hands and feet secured to iron rings in the deck. From the labored rise and fall of the ship, he knew he was confined up forward near the stem. What had sounded like laughter was but the tumble of seas past the cutwater, the harp music but the whine of wind in the rigging.

It all came back: the beating of Old Ames, and the fight on the deck. Oh, what a bloody fool he had been! It had been so pointless, so futile. No doubt old Ames was dead anyway, and whether so or not, why, raged Johnnie, had he elected to be "his brother's keeper"?

Yet as he reviewed the happening, the injustice fired him, and his whole being was ablaze once more. Logic, no; he had been motivated by something far more potent. His action had been inevitable.

Craning his head forward, he stared at the pale rectangle of dimness that was the wicket in the door of his cuddy, occasionally blurred by the movement of the guard stationed outside. He tested his fetters, but they were secure.

It was manifest that he would never again have the opportunity of repeating his action. His was the unforgivable sin, the most heinous offense that could be perpetrated by a seaman. He had mutinously struck an officer; worse, he had struck several of them. The punishment was certain death; he would be hanged from the starboard yardarm of the *Eagle*.

He composed himself to face the inevitable with fortitude, and his thoughts turned back to Leanna. What a start his sudden appearance on the wharf at Portsmouth had given her! Knowing he was alive, would she dare marry Laughton?

Destiny was playing a macabre jest. Johnnie the Rogue would hang, yet nobody save Johnnie himself would know it. The stage-drivers on the London roads would continue to glance apprehensively over the lonely heaths, and Lady Somerset would live in terror of his reappearance. There would be no record; his only obituary would be a brief notation in the *Eagle's* log-book stating that an impressed mutineer had been hanged at sea.

Yet withal, he would like to see her again. He remembered the tender moments, and minimized her treachery. She had been desperate, and he had provoked her. . . .

Sometime later, he heard the chime of six bells. In what watch, he wondered? The ship was riding more comfortably, so he decided it must be night. Another hour slipped away before a blur of increasing light at the wicket indicated that the guard was relieved. When the lanthorn was held up to the square hole, he closed his eyes.

"H'ain't dead, be 'e?" growled the relief.

The guard grunted. "Not 'im. 'Eard 'im thrashin' around a w'ile back. An 'ard case, 'at un."

The relief moved away with his lanthorn. "Ol Bloody'll 'ate to lose 'im." He chuckled. " 'E's goin' to give 'im six dozen lashes—"

"*Six* dozen!"

"Aye. Crisscrossed, by God, then 'ang w'at's left o' 'im!"

"Ol' Bloody must h'enjoy it!" grumbled the other without enthusiasm, and stomped away.

When Lord Johnnie hated, he hated well, and his helplessness made him seethe. Once again he examined the possibilities of escape and found them nil. He took solace in one thought—Captain Bloodsmythe would never hear a single cry from his lips!

He heard the watch strike eight bells, then a step on the ladder, followed by a grumbling challenge from the guard. Muted words came indistinctly, so he concluded it was merely another change of sentry. He raised his head. There was an oath, a blow, then the wicket was blotted by the head of a man.

"*Johnnie!* Johnnie, me b'y! Are ye alive?"

A trick of the mind! Johnnie shook his head to clear it. The bolts creaked before he could reply and the door opened to admit the body of a man holding a hooded hurricane lamp.

"Ben Bottle! How in God's name—?"

The Irishman set the light on the floor and drew his knife.

"Quiet!" he cautioned. "I'll 'ave ye free in a trice." He began groping for the hempen fetters.

"Wait!" gasped Johnnie. "That will do no good, Mick!"

Ben reared back in surprise. "No good? D'ye want the meat flayed from yer spine an' then 'ung? That's w'at's awaitin' ye, lad!" He made another start at the thongs, but Johnnie stopped him.

"You forget I'll still be aboard this damned ship at sea!"

"B'Jesus, ye'll be better off to jump overboard, damme if else!"

"No, just a minute!" pleaded Johnnie. "Let me think!"

It was difficult to think clearly with his heart hammering against his ribs. Having resigned himself to his fate, he wasted precious moments in readjustment. Ben's nervousness high-lighted the need for speed, so when the plan did come, it came full-blossomed.

"First—how is Old Ames?" he demanded.

Ben squirmed impatiently. "Hell, 'e's all right. But you—"

"Now listen," Johnnie cut him off. "I have an idea. It's a long chance, I grant, but if you and Ames will help—"

The Irishman gave him a reassuring growl. "Me'n the ol' one will do anythin' ye say, Johnnie, an' ye can lay to that."

"Good! Then hear me. . . ." Swiftly he outlined the idea that had been born in his mind, supplementing it as he went along. Ben Bottle sighed, grunted, nodded, slowly picking up enthusiasm as the scheme unfolded.

"Holy Mither!" he swore at the conclusion. " 'Tis just crazy enough to succeed!"

"If it doesn't," Johnnie said grimly, "I'll never forgive myself for involving you, my friend."

Ben gave him a clout of rough affection. "Friend, there's just one thing *I'll* not forgive ye—lettin' that whoreson second live." He chortled savagely. "Howbeit, mebbe I can do somethin' about that me ownsel'!"

Johnnie laughed softly. "Easy, Mick! One thing at a time. Now get out of here before you spoil the show!"

When the big Irishman sidled out with the lamp, Johnnie relaxed in the darkness. The fog which had obscured the future was rising, and Lord Johnnie began to look ahead.

12

SHORTLY AFTER SIX BELLS IN THE FORENOON WATCH, LORD JOHNNIE was brought on deck, closely guarded by two brawny boatswain's mates who barely came up to his shoulders. He carried himself boldly erect as always, a hint of a sneer on his mouth as he absorbed the scene.

The *Eagle* seemed to have found her meter in the light northwest breeze, for she glided along on the starboard tack, curtsying to the long rollers with all sails drawing. Captain Bloodsmythe and his wife, flanked by his officers, stood on the weather quarter-deck, directly above the already lashed-up gratings. Johnnie smiled inwardly at sight of Lieutenant Shad, whose left eye was swollen tight and whose nose resembled a mangled apple.

The boatswain with his mates and a few other petty officers huddled together under the break of the quarter-deck. They wore cutlasses with the tension of men anticipating trouble. The people crowded into all other available space: on the booms, the boats, and the leeside of the waist. Of the hundred odd members of the ship's company, only the steersman at the helm was excused by virtue of his duties; everybody else had been turned out to witness the punishment.

Prominent in the foreground loomed Ben Bottle, his great bulk accentuated by the lateral stripes of his sweater. His folded arms looked like twin hams and his tarred pigtail jutted out at an aggressive angle. Johnnie risked a surreptitious wink and looked around for Old Ames. He sighted the old sail-maker poised at the head of the forward hatch opening.

In the brilliance of daylight, the plan conceived in the dark bowels of the ship now seemed fantastic. The hands looked cowed and dull, the officers wary. The sudden silence that had descended on the gathering became oppressive. The contrast with Tyburn swept across Johnnie's mind. Then he had been a great personality; he recalled the fervor and emotionalism of the crowds, and the obvious nervousness of the officials. This was startlingly different. Not a face in this audience reflected a trace of expression.

Captain Bloodsmythe broke the quiet. "Bring the prisoner forward!"
The guards shoved Johnnie to a position below the captain.

"You are charged with mutiny and the striking of an officer!" roared
Captain Bloodsmythe. "You know the penalty?"

"Aye," conceded Johnnie.

"Say *sir*, when you address the captain!" snarled one of the guards
in an undertone.

"Hold your puling tongue!" barked Johnnie, in a voice that carried
over the deck. "I need no advice from a bully's bully!"

Captain Bloodsmythe reddened, and while he chose to ignore the
outburst, the rasp in his tone grew more pronounced.

"Have you anything to say?"

Johnnie smiled slightly. "Only this—I'd like thirty seconds of sword
play with you to relieve the gas in that fat paunch!"

"Seize him up!" shrieked the captain. "Seize him up!"

The boatswain's mates rushed Johnnie onto the grating and secured
him in place, but he noted with satisfaction that his calculated defiance had set their hands to fumbling.

"Seized up, sir!" one reported.

"The prisoner," thundered Captain Bloodsmythe, "shall receive eight
dozen lashes, after which he will be taken to the cathead and hanged
from the yardarm! Every hand present will man the yardrope, and the
officers will stand by with cutlasses to cut down anyone who shirks the
duty!"

After a grim pause, Bloodsmythe produced a copy of the *Articles of
War*, and in a squeaky, breaking voice, read the Article which dealt
with the offense. As he began, he removed his hat, and every man
present solemnly followed suit. Johnnie sneered. He thought: *they act
as if God himself was reading them the Ten Commandments!* His
glance wandered up to meet the large, bewildered eyes of Mrs. Bloodsmythe. When Johnnie gave her a curious half-smile, she turned hastily
away.

The reading droned to a conclusion. Captain Bloodsmythe shoved
the *Articles* behind him and scowled down at the boatswain's mate who
waited with the cat.

"Do your duty!" he commanded.

The boatswain's mate tested the cat-tails and met Johnnie's eye.
Johnnie gave him a direct I'll-see-you-later look, then turned his face
to the grating. The lashings on his wrists brought back the sensation
of helplessness he had endured the night before, but they bolstered

his determination to let no scream pass his lips. Then came a sharp whistling sound and the first blow fell. . . .

It felt to Johnnie as though he had been struck by a bolt of lightning which, entering between his shoulder blades, shattered to send electric slivers throughout every portion of his body. The surprise was as great as the pain. Though he had been hurt many times in his checkered career, he had not known such agony was possible. It took all his will-power to keep from gasping.

But though he thought he knew what to expect now, the second blow, laid a few inches lower, made the former seem a gentle caress. Every nerve was filled to the bursting point with a shock that seared to the fingertips, to the balls of his feet, and burned his eyes from the inside. When the whip was withdrawn, it seemed to tear the flesh from his back. His whole being quivered like a struck bell.

The blows came faster, building up pressure inside him until he had to bite down on his tongue to stem involuntary cries. His only antidote was rage.

"Lay into it!" bellowed Captain Bloodsmythe. "Make the dog sing!"

Johnnie tried to keep track of the blows, but the agony had grown so constant that somewhere after the sixth, he lost count. He wanted to turn his head for a bit of reassurance from Ben Bottle, but his eyes were blinded by sweat. He kept his forehead braced hard against the grating and clenched his teeth.

Then at long last it came—a thundering crash that sent a shudder throughout the ship!

The flogging stopped, and in the abrupt stillness, a man screamed: *"God 'elp us! A gun's loose below!"*

The men began to shout and mill about. Ben Bottle's brogue roared loudest of all.

"B'Jesus, she'll sink us! We're lost, we're lost!"

"Silence down there!" cried the captain. "Mister Yew, take a gang below and secure that gun! Mister Shad, seize the next man who opens his mouth!"

Lieutenant Yew came briskly down the ladderway, and beckoning the petty officers from the shelter of the poop, headed for the hatch-way. Shad limped down painfully. As he reached the waist, the *Eagle* rolled heavily to another swell, and an instant later there came a rumbling roar, like the crazed bellow of a charging bull, that ter-minated in a timber-shaking crash as the two-ton cannon struck the opposite side of the ship.

"Fall off the wind!" Captain Bloodsmythe shrilled at the helmsman. "Keep her heeled over, on your life!"

For the moment, the prisoner seemed forgotten. Fully half the seamen had followed the first lieutenant below to try to trip the runaway gun, and the remainder were stampeding about the decks like terrified cattle. Shad, flanked by three brawny quartermasters, tried to awe them into order, but Ben Bottle was carrying out Johnnie's plans with masterly precision.

"The ol' scow's sinkin'!" the Irishman yelled excitedly. "To the boats, b'ys, to the boats! Syve yersel's!"

"Seize that trouble-maker!" shouted Captain Bloodsmythe.

Johnnie twisted his sore neck around to watch this, for it was the crux of his scheme. But Ben had placed his few cohorts well; they formed a human funnel with himself at the far end. Shad blindly led his quartermasters into this trap, and the funnel closed. Johnnie lost sight of them, but he heard a scream, then Quinn broke from the mob and came running over to him, knife in hand.

"Be ye all right, Johnnie?" he panted.

"Aye! Cut me down—*quick!*"

Quinn wasted no more words. With four strokes, he freed Johnnie's ankles and wrists. As Johnnie reeled back dizzily, he heard Bloodsmythe's piping voice.

"Good God! It's *mutiny!*"

The cry acted on Johnnie as a powerful stimulant. The faintness passed, and he was himself again—the old Lord Johnnie. He wiped the sweat from his eyes and glanced up.

"Aye, you fat swine—it's mutiny!" He swung to the Irishman standing guard over the hatch. "Are your men at their stations, Mick?"

"Aye, aye, b'y!"

Johnnie grinned. "Where's Old Ames?"

The sail-maker came scuttling out of the passage under the poop to answer for himself.

"'Ere I be, Johnnie!"

"Good!" Johnnie appraised the situation. Captain Bloodsmythe had drawn his sword and was guarding the head of the ladderway, while his wife crouched in terror against the weather rail. The startled helmsman at the wheel was trying to hold the *Eagle* canted sufficiently on her lee to trap the runaway gun.

Johnnie backed up to the fife rail, chose a sturdy belaying pin and hefted it tentatively.

"Quinn," he called, "guard the ladderway. Let no man up or down. You, Ames—have you a knife?"

"Aye, long an' sharp she be, Johnnie!"

"Then induce that helmsman to keep this old tub *rolling* until I settle an *affaire d'honneur* with Ol' Bloody!" He rubbed the soles of his shoes on the deck to clear off the blood. Then with a "Here we go!" he made a run for the quarter-deck.

Captain Bloodsmythe expected Johnnie to ascend the ladderway, thereby making a fatal mistake. For Johnnie shot up the latticed grating and gained the quarter-deck before the captain divined his intention.

"On guard, you pot-bellied murderer!" Johnnie invited.

Captain Bloodsmythe needed no urging. To his credit, he showed no fear, only an overbearing rage. Though a mediocre swordsman, he did have a good blade in his hand, and he made it apparent that he regarded Johnnie a mere fool armed with nothing but a wooden stick. Bellowing in temper, he charged forward to cut him down.

Using the pin like a rapier, Johnnie deftly parried the blow and took the wind out of the captain by a sharp riposte to the stomach. Bloodsmythe paused in bewilderment, and in that moment of indecision, Johnnie could have knocked him down. But Johnnie wanted more than that, so he slashed the captain across the face with his club, and sprang back to permit him to recover.

Captain Bloodsmythe was too bull-headed for caution. He trumpetted like a mad elephant and attacked again, slashing, slashing. Taunting him, Johnnie gave ground, edging along the lee rail. Old Ames had carried out his chore! The *Eagle* lurched suddenly, throwing the combatants across the quarter-deck to the weatherside. Again from between decks came that rumbling crash as the runaway cannon swapped sides, and the thud of it was punctuated by a wild scream of pain.

" 'Urry it up, Johnnie!" shouted Old Ames from below. " 'Urry it!"

Johnnie was in no mood to hurry. He had a debt to pay, and he meant to settle it in full, so he gave himself over to the sheer ecstasy of the fight. He jeered and mocked his man, blocking the savage cuts, thrusting him in the paunch or face at will. He saw the arrogance in the piggy eyes turn to perplexity, then to something akin to terror as the realization was driven home to the bully that the advantage was no longer his.

On the next roll of the *Eagle*, Johnnie listened for the reassuring crash of the gun. It did not come. They all realized what that meant: the gun had been tripped. Certain that help would soon be coming, Captain Bloodsmythe's battered lips curled into a sneer.

"Now, you damned blackguard!" he squeaked, rushing in again.

Johnnie knew his fun was almost over. He parried the next cut, then slashed the captain over the sword wrist. The blade clattered to the deck and slid into the scuppers while Captain Bloodsmythe stared unbelievingly at his broken arm.

"Strike 'im dead, lad!" bawled Old Ames.

Johnnie had other plans. Casting aside the pin, he threw the captain onto his back, then sitting on his face, went through his pockets until he found a ring of keys. These he tossed to the old sail-maker, who had mounted the quarter-deck.

"Here, ancient! Go down to the cabin and bring up pistols and shot for us. Quick!"

As the old man scurried below, Johnnie hauled the captain erect. The arrogance was gone, and he put Johnnie in mind of a great, slobbering jellyfish.

"Mercy! Mercy!" sobbed Bloodsmythe. "Give up this madness and I'll forgive and forget. Before God, I will!"

"*You'll* forgive and forget?" jeered Johnnie. "Well, 'pon my soul, if that's not generous!" He spun the wailing captain around, caught him by the collar and the seat of his breeches, and lifted him into the air.

Quinn, seeing this, shouted frantically, "Syve 'im fer me, Johnnie! I got a score to even wi' the slimy hog!"

"So have we all!" retorted Johnnie, and heaved. Bloodsmythe's long scream of terror ended in a splash.

Johnnie turned in time to see the woman dart aft. Fearing she meant to follow her husband, he started after her. But she pulled up short at the taffrail, and braced there, mutely watched the bobbing figure dissolve in the white wake astern.

Though he felt compassion for her, there was nothing he could say, so he was grateful for the sudden reappearance of Old Ames, staggering under a load of armament.

Followed by Ames, Johnnie strode to the head of the ladderway.

"Get back on your course!" he barked at the trembling helmsman. "And keep her steady if you value your life!"

Ben Bottle and Quinn were guarding the main hatchway with cutlasses taken from Shad and his bullies.

"How many trustworthy lads have you, Mick?" called Johnnie.

Ben waved his blade like a happy urchin. "A baker's dozen!" he roared cheerfully. "An' every damn openin' 's covered, Johnnie me b'y! We got 'em sealed below. W'at now?"

"I'll pass out pistols and ball to all your men," said Johnnie. "Have Quinn relieve you, then bring up the officers."

"Aye, aye, matey!"

He distributed the guns, but the raw wind tortured his mangled back, so he sent Ames back to the cabin for a shirt and coat. By the time he had donned them, Ben Bottle and two of his supporters marched the first lieutenant onto the quarter-deck.

Rodney Yew resembled a rock more than ever. Whatever his thoughts may have been, he gave no sign. His pale gray eyes held unwaveringly on Johnnie's own.

Johnnie glanced at the Irishman. "I told you to bring up Shad as well!"

Ben chortled. "'Ow'll ye 'ave him, friend—in a 'ammock or a bucket?"

"Dead?"

"Aye, worse luck! One of me b'ys dropped 'im down the 'atch an' 'e fell 'tween the gun-carriage an' the timbers. 'E'll 'ave to be scooped up wi' a spoon."

"Lieutenant Shad was foully murdered!" Yew put in firmly.

Ben roared angrily and laid the muzzle of his pistol against the lieutenant's head.

"An' so'll ye be, ye cold-blooded whoreson!"

Johnnie said sharply, "Put down that pistol!"

Ben hesitated. "B'Jesus, I got me rights!" he growled.

"Put down that pistol!" repeated Johnnie.

The Irishman sullenly lowered the cocked weapon. "Now don't get too 'igh-'anded, matey! I done most o' the work, but I ain't 'ad no fun. Ye got Ol' Bloody, an' the b'ys got Shad. W'at do I get out o' it?"

He was pouting like a spoiled child, and Johnnie burst out laughing.

"Stab me, Mick, you look ready to blubber! But use your head, man —we need him to navigate the ship."

Yew looked him in the eye. "You are a mutinous, treasonous hound!" he said coldly. "I'll work no ship for the likes of you!"

Johnnie smiled thinly. "Mutinous, aye; treasonous, perhaps; yet do you worship that bestial murderer enough to follow him overside?"

"My feelings for Captain Bloodsmythe are no concern of yours," retorted Rodney Yew. "He was captain of the King's ship!"

The little knot of men were eyeing them closely, and time was passing. Johnnie raised the point of the captain's sword and placed it against the lieutenant's throat.

"*Mister* Yew, I am now the captain of this ship," he said. "How I became so is not your responsibility. The decision from here on rests with you. You do not need to join the mutiny, and your opinions shall be entered in the log. But you *will* navigate this ship to a port of my choosing, where I give you my word you will be set ashore. If you refuse, I'l be forced to run you through. Now—your answer?"

Yew never batted an eye. "What of the other loyal men aboard?"

"We'll throw the bloody swine to the sharks, rape me if else!" snarled Ben, angered at the delay.

He was ignored. "They'll be given the same choice," promised Johnnie. "But they'll be carefully watched, and the first man who starts trouble will go overboard!"

"If this vessel is retaken by one of His Majesty's ships," Yew warned, "I shall testify against you."

"We'll chance that," Johnnie said, grinning. "Your answer?"

"Let the log show I submit under duress," said Lieutenant Yew. "I'll navigate to a port of your choosing."

"Make 'im swear 't on the Bible!" suggested a seaman.

Johnnie lowered his blade. "Rodney Yew's word is sufficient," he said tartly. "He continues as first officer. Ben, you'll replace Shad as second. Now station the men you can trust along the bulwarks and in the shrouds with loaded muskets. After that, herd up those below into the waist."

As the men hurried to their stations, Lieutenant Yew walked coolly below to the wheel and glanced at the compass. He looked up at the set of the canvas, then in a voice as calm as if nothing had happened, said, "Keep her off a point!"

"Off a point she is, sir!" whimpered the terrified steersman.

Rodney Yew climbed back to the quarter-deck to stand by the lee rail, his hands folded behind his back. Johnnie took a position at the weather rail.

The Irishman, having covered the decks well with his "baker's dozen," was letting the men come up from below in single file. As each man mounted the deck, Ben bawled out: "Them as wants to be free men an' seek their fortunes, line up to starboard. Them as is satisfied to be slaves, form on the larboard. Step lively, me 'earts! Lively does it!"

The seamen, dazed and surprised by the sudden turn of events, slowly filled the waist.

"That's all o' 'em, Johnnie b'y!" reported Ben Bottle.

Johnnie walked to the head of the ladderway amidships. His back stuck to the shirt, and the pain of it sharpened his awareness.

"Men," he told them bluntly, "we've taken this ship. It was my life or Ol' Bloody's, and I preferred my own. Some may call it mutiny or treason, but like most of you, I am here through no choice of mine. I owe no allegiance to that pompous German George, so 'tis my plan to seek my fortune like a free man. Those of you who desire can sail with me." He paused to gauge the effect of his words.

"W'at 'appens to 'em as don't?" asked an old tar.

Ben opened his mouth to answer, but Johnnie gestured him silent.

"Those who don't will be put ashore at the first available port. However, until that time, you will swear on your oaths to offer no resistance and will obey orders. Now—any more questions?"

The one-legged carpenter limped out of the crowd. "W'at about the lef'tenant? Is 'e wi' you?"

Johnnie glanced across the deck. "Lieutenant Yew will answer that himself, Chips."

Rodney Yew regarded the crowd steadily. "This is an English ship," he said in evenly clipped words. "I am an Englishman; I intend to remain so. The log will bear me witness that I have not taken, nor will I take, part in this mutiny. Having no alternative but death, I have accepted the same terms offered to you. What each man does now is a matter he must settle with his own conscience." He turned on his heel and strode aft.

Johnnie bit his lip. He found himself envying Yew's unruffled dignity. He brushed aside the reaction and turned his attention to the waist where the confused seamen were trying to reach a decision. Theirs was a bitter choice. Many of them had been torn from the arms of wives and children whom, if they joined the mutineers, they would never see again. Yet if they elected to remain loyal, their future was equally uncertain. In desperation, they turned to each other, seeking guidance; yet as every man was faced with the identical problem, he could ill advise his neighbor.

"Yer pardon, sir," begged a big Lancastershireman. "Think ye we'll e'er see England again?"

A hush settled over the waist.

"I doubt it," Johnnie said at last. "For my own part, I care naught for England. She's given me prison, impressment, flogging and promise of death. What the future holds, I do not know, save only that it can be no worse than the past." His voice grew crisp. "Now, men, make up your minds, but remember this—once made there will be no turning back. You'll have a half hour to decide. That is all."

He called Ben Bottle over. "Don't try to influence them, Mick. I want no malcontents."

"But sink me, Johnnie! We needs 'ands to run this tub!"

"We'll have enough. Just keep the guards posted until they make up their minds. In the meantime, I'm going below. Yew will be in charge."

Ben scowled. "Ye trust 'im?"

Johnnie nodded. "Aye, but you keep a weather eye on the mob and call me if anything goes wrong."

He left Ben grumbling, and looked for the woman. She was not on deck. Seeing Old Ames hovering near the taffrail, he beckoned him.

"Where's Mrs. Bloodsmythe?"

Old Ames shrugged. "She went below. Said nary a word, did she."

Johnnie grimaced. "Go down and ease her out of the cabin, ancient. Move her things in Shad's cuddy. The Mick will have to swing his hammock somewhere else."

"Aye, aye, sir." Ames hesitated. " 'Ow's yer back, lad? Methinks it should be washed wi' brine to lull the poisons."

"I know, I know," Johnnie said impatiently. "But get rid of the woman first. I'll stay up here until she's gone."

When the old man had scuttled off on his errand, Johnnie joined Rodney Yew on the lee rail.

"Where are the charts, Lieutenant?" he demanded, more sharply than he had intended.

"In the cabin."

"I understand we're bound for New York. By what route?"

"Southerly," snapped the lieutenant. "We're standing on a course to clear the Azores and pick up the trades."

Johnnie stroked his unshaven jaw. "I'll leave the deck in your charge. Will you have dinner with me? There are some matters to discuss."

Yew looked at him icily. "Is that an order?"

Johnnie felt the flush mount his face. "Damn it, what difference does that make?" he challenged.

"Just this," retorted Yew. "I'll have nothing to do with you except under specific command!"

Old Ames bobbed on deck just as Johnnie was balling his fists, so he said grimly, "I'll settle with you later!" and turned away.

"She's gone!" piped the old man. "An' the cook's sendin' hot water fer yer back." He grinned toothily. "Satan's backside, 'tis a royal cabin, Johnnie!"

"We'll have a look," Johnnie grunted, and went below.

It was a royal cabin! Running the entire width of the vessel, and built outboard so that it appeared suspended over the rudder, like a great gilded excrescence, it was spacious in the extreme. There were glazed ports on either side, and the stern was pierced for five windows, also glazed. Under the ports were settees, and at the forward end was a massive double bed. The bulkheads were elm—it being less liable to splinter if struck by shot—and ornately carved. A large fixed table marked the center of the cabin, with heavy chairs to match.

Old Ames seemed to regard the place as a private discovery. "Look 'ere, lad!" he crowed, opening a small door that led out onto the ginger-bread sternwalk. "A bleedin' piazza, I'll swear!"

Johnnie laughed, and continued his survey of the more practical aspects of the cabin. There was a wardrobe filled with dress uniforms, and the captain's foul-weather gear hung from a peg on the forward bulkhead. He noted with satisfaction that there was a goodly supply of small arms—swords, cutlasses, pistols and muskets—set in neat racks about the mizzen mast. The charts were all in place, a telescope in its bracket, and a good tell-tale compass within sight of the bed.

He pulled a cherry-colored coat out of the wardrobe and held it up.

"By my troth!" he laughed. "These rags have the belly of a blown-out mains'l. Can you re-cut them to fit me, ancient?"

Old Ames myopically examined the coat. "Aye, methinks 'tis possible to snip enough from the paunch to patch out fer them ox-like shoulders of your'n, though in all truth, 'twould be simpler to put 'em on upside down." He tossed the coat onto the table. "Now, laddie, lemme see yer back."

Johnnie peeled off his coat with difficulty, but the shirt was glued by blood to his skin. He would have jerked it away, but the old man stopped him.

" 'Ere, 'ere! None o' that!"

So Johnnie straddled a chair while Ames went at the mess with his knife, wielded with paternal gentleness. Before he had finished, two seamen brought in a tub of hot water, and a bucket of warm brine. The salt renewed the agony of the flogging, but it passed and was forgotten in the pleasure of the tub.

Cleanliness, though not a prerequisite of the times, was essential to Johnnie. Grime and filth embittered him as symbolic of his degradation, but a clean body and fine clothes encouraged the *sang-froid* for which he was famous. He went into the tub an angry, resentful seaman; he came out of it, *Lord Johnnie.*

Old Ames was picking lice out of Johnnie's hair when, without bothering to knock, Ben Bottle and Quinn swaggered into the cabin lugging a small cask of rum. From their manner, it was plain they had already sampled the liquor. They stood the cask on the table, and as Quinn started to fill some flagons he had brought along, Ben sprawled casually on a settee.

"B'Jesus, Johnnie, b'y!" he crowed. "We done it! The ship's ours!"

"A neat haul," agreed Johnnie, grinning. "You timed it well, Mick. I saw how you boys trapped Shad."

The Irishman scratched his jowls. He was growing a beard which had reached the itchy stage.

"Aye, but I'd like to 'a seen 'is end, the dirty whoreson!"

Quinn plumped an overflowing flagon in front of Johnnie.

"Drink up, matey!" he urged. "'Appy cruisin'!"

Johnnie hesitated. Old Ames hadn't touched his flagon, and was scowling resentfully, but Quinn and Ben Bottle were happily swilling the stuff. Johnnie chuckled, and took a drink.

Ben banged his flagon on the table. "W'en Ol' Ames cut that gun loose, 'twas a sight to see, say the b'ys w'at was there. Better'n a baited bull, fer the damn thing seemed to 'ave a strange cunnin'! First it would charge one gang, then sheer off an' run another."

"You can thank Old Ames and the helmsman for that, too," laughed Johnnie. "They kept the tub rolling from gunnel to gunnel. Now, Mick, how about the men?"

Ben made a broad gesture with his arm. "'Appy as clams! We 'ave three an' seventy fine, upstandin' lads wi' us, leavin' only two an' thirty sons o' bitches w'at want to kiss the King's arse some more."

"Did any of the petty officers and idlers join us?"

Ben snorted. "A few; mebbe 'arf. The sailin'-master, the purser, the master-at-arms an' 'is mates, an' that stripe is goin', though I'd rather throw the bastards overboard! Rape me, Johnnie, that goddam bos'n's mate w'at flogged 'e 'ad the gall to want to jine us. I tolt him nay!'"

"Go back and tell him *aye*," snapped Johnnie. "He's an experienced man, and we need all of those we can get."

Ben sputtered and buried his face in the flagon. Quinn peered owlishly at Johnnie.

"That bugger flogged us!" he protested.

"Aye, and a thorough job he did, too. Quite possibly we'll have need of the cat before this voyage is over."

Quinn lurched angrily to his feet. Ben lowered his flagon.

"The *cat?*" growled Ben, scowling. "I'd like to see anybody order *me* whipped! B'Jesus, we're free men now an'—"

"On the contrary," Johnnie interrupted him, "we are *not* free men; we're hunted men. We have the hand of every government in the world against us. In addition to that, we have the sea and the wind to buck. No man on a ship is free, Mick."

"Then why'd we take the ship?" shouted Quinn.

Staring at them, Johnnie was reminded of his session with Bagnigge Blackie and Doc Yarrow in the old apothecary shop in Butcher's Row. He restrained his temper with difficulty.

"To better our lot," he answered Quinn. "But whether we actually better it depends on how well we work together."

Quinn leaned his knuckles on the table and faced down at Johnnie.

"We'll work wi' 'e, but don't get no big ideers o' yer own h'importance, mister! Nobody'll gi' me the cat again, an' ye can lay to that!" He turned on his heel and stalked out of the cabin.

Ben sighed. "Ye shouldn't ha' angered 'im, Johnnie!"

"'Twould have been better to cut 'is bloody throat!" piped Old Ames, shaking a gnarled finger in the Irishman's face. "Even a pirate 'as to 'ave discipline, else 'ang they will, every mother's son o' 'em!"

"The ancient is right," agreed Johnnie. "Now, answer frankly— are you with me, or against me, Mick?"

"Holy Mither! I'm wi' ye, matey, to the last, but Johnnie b'y—"

"*Captain*," corrected Johnnie. "This is a ship, *Mister* Bottle, and if we're going to have discipline, it must start at the top. Mark that?"

Ben's loose-lipped mouth sagged open. He blinked stupidly at Old Ames. The old man's watery eyes were bright.

"Ye heard the cap'n, *Mister* Bottle?"

Ben gulped and mechanically moved a fist to his forelock. "Aye, aye, Jo—I mean, *sir!*"

Johnnie suppressed a smile. "Just one thing more. Pass the word to all hands that the first man who insults or molests Mrs. Bloodsmythe will be keel-hauled."

"God A'mighty!" gasped Ben, reeling to his feet. He started to pick up the rum, but Johnnie motioned him away.

"You've had more than enough of that already, Mister Bottle. Now get on deck and see if you can act like an officer."

"Aye, aye, sir!" stammered Ben, and walked out in a trance.

Old Ames wagged his head as the door closed. "Ye 'ad me worried fer a w'ile. Your daddy would 'a spitted them varmints to the deck at the first sign o' lip."

"My daddy wasn't a mutineer, ancient."

"True. Yet 'e was a cap'n, an' so be ye. A cap'n 'as to be supreme, else 'e'll not stay cap'n long."

"I'm beginning to realize that," conceded Johnnie wearily.

"But ye 'andled it proper," chuckled the old man, "onc't ye got under weigh. 'Tis a rare gift to lead men, an' make 'em like it. Never let go the reins, lad, *never*."

"Was my father a Tartar?"

Old Ames grinned. "Aye, an' nay. 'E kept a shell around 'imself like a turtle, but ye couldn't see it; ye just knew 'twas there. 'E'd talk pleasant an' soft on occasion, yet w'en the time came fer toughness, my God, 'e was tough! But 'e was allus the gentleman, come shot or storm. Polished 'e was, an' wi'out fear." The old man cocked his head and appraised Johnnie closely.

"Aye," he mused sagely, "y're to the manner born. 'Pon my oath, the rank fits ye like yer skin. Why not tyke yer rightful nyme now, laddie? *Captain Ballantyne!*"

"No!" said Johnnie sharply. "That is the name of an honest gentleman, not a bastard and a mutineer! I'll draw your tongue, old one, if you betray my secret!"

Old Ames grinned and went back to his task on Johnnie's scalp.

" 'Tis not me who'll betray ye, lad, but y're own sel'. Blood will tell." He popped another louse between his thumbnails.

13

"To the manner born." JOHNNIE TURNED THE PAT PHRASE OVER AND
over in his mind as he completed his toilet and dressed in the late
captain's elaborate, if ill-fitting, clothes. Paradoxically, it both pleased
and disconcerted him. He stretched out on the settee and watched
Old Ames tidy up the cabin. Two seamen idled in and whisked the
tub away. Though for the week past they had slept with Johnnie in
adjacent hammocks, they now acted as diffident as if Ol' Bloody himself was seated there.

Intellectually, Johnnie could understand their attitude better than
his own. To them, the captain was absolute, and they preferred him
that way, for the British tar despised a slack hand at the reins. Though
they loathed a "rogue," they respected one who, in the vernacular,
was "a bit of a Tartar." What did surprise Johnnie, however, was the
strange naturalness of his present role. True, he had spent several of
his crowded years at sea, but never in command. Yet sitting here in this
ostentatious cabin, he had the peculiar sensation of having done this
thing before.

"The rank fits ye like yer skin," Old Ames had observed. Johnnie
wondered about that. Was it just his natural conceit, his trait of aping
the manners of his betters, or did he inherit some of his father's qualities of leadership? He brushed the thought aside with impatience. Lord
Ballantyne had faithfully served his king and his country, whereas his
son—his bastard—was a mutineer. Any comparison was odious, and
even their problems were entirely different.

The magnitude of the thing he was attempting came home to him.
Difficult though it might be, the responsibility of a regularly com-
missioned captain was established by precedent and tradition; by such
rote as the *Articles of War*. The entire ship's company, from cabin
boy to first lieutenant, was adjusted to this authority, and had accepted
the fact that strict obedience was necessary. Johnnie's problem was
the antithesis of this. He had soared to his present eminence on a wave
of excitement, and when it subsided, he would be dashed to destruction

—unless he managed to hold up his weight by substitute means. It was a dangerous game. His followers had risked their lives in the mutiny, and they would demand an equal share in the results. Having thrown off all restraint, they would not easily submit to it again, particularly from one of their own number.

Yet their success, even their very lives, depended on Johnnie alone; he knew it, if they did not. If he could maintain the fervor of excitement, and keep them so continually busy they would have no time for reflection, he might hold them together. But it was a tenuous position and would require all his skill and decisiveness.

The great cabin had grown dark and Old Ames, having lighted the lamp hung in gimbals over the table, now looked to Johnnie.

Johnnie grinned. "Ancient, tell me true—do you think me a fool?"

The old man chuckled. "W'en a man fails 'tis considered folly, but 'tis genius if 'e succeeds."

"Aye, but when an ambitious knave commits a folly, it is never a small one." He rose briskly. "Well, see if you can find some decent food aboard this hell-ship, then present my compliments to Rodney Yew and inform him I desire his company for supper."

"Aye, aye, sir."

"And Ames, pass the word to the cook that unless the food served to the men is better prepared, I'll have him flogged."

"Aye, *aye,* sir!"

As the old one hurried away, Johnnie strolled out into the stern-walk. He felt very much alone, yet it was not unpleasant; his was the solitude of command, and he could not share it. He stared at the wake, stretching like a great white scar across the deep blue of the sea. The western horizon was a ruddy glow, and the sky was laced with feathery transparent clouds, known as "mares' tails," while under these lay a bank of creeping mist, or "mackerel sky." Somewhere out of memory, he recalled an old rhyme:

> *"Mackerels' scales and mares' tails,*
> *Make lofty ships carry low sails."*

Aye, he brooded, it was all coming back, and he realized of a sudden why he felt so different: for the first time in his lonely existence, he was totally responsible for the lives of others. A short time ago, he had been depressed because he had Old Ames on his conscience; now that sensation was magnified a hundred fold. The knowledge appalled him, so he turned and walked back into the cabin.

He had been out on the sternwalk longer than he had suspected, for now the table was laid, and Rodney Yew had just arrived. The lieutenant was dressed formally in a long coat of somber blue, white breeches and white stockings, much mended.

Johnnie nodded. "It appears we're in for more wind, Mister Yew," he remarked.

"Aye, sir, so it does," Yew agreed stiffly.

Johnnie pretended not to notice the rebuff. He took the chair held out by Old Ames and gestured Yew into the opposite seat. The clean white table cloth and the heavy silver brought to mind the wondrous night he had supped at Leanna's home, but he quickly downed the memory and turned his attention to the fare.

Although the best on board, it was meager enough. The ship's beef, more aptly described as "salt junk," was tough and unappetizing, even when supplemented by suet pudding. But for a change there was plenty of it, and the good French wine, doubtless seized from a prize, was excellent.

Rodney Yew ate in silence, as if alone. Johnnie left him in peace while he studied him, seeking a chink in his armor. When the food was gone, and Old Ames had whisked the empty plates away and disappeared, Johnnie refilled the glasses with wine and leaned back.

"As I understand it, Mister Yew, it is traditional that when a captain dines with his officers, the formalities of the quarter-deck are dispensed with. Correct me if I am wrong."

Only the quickness of his glance indicated that Yew was surprised. He looked steadily at Johnnie a moment before acknowledging: "That is correct, sir."

Johnnie revolved the long-stemmed glass between his fingers. "You conceded that I am the captain?"

"Self-appointed," the lieutenant corrected coldly. "You are a mutinous scoundrel, sir!"

The stem snapped in Johnnie's hand. He flung the fragments aside and gripped the arms of his chair. Yew didn't move a hair. Finally Johnnie relaxed.

" 'Pon my oath, you're a man of courage, Rodney Yew!" he said grimly. "I can't quite fathom you."

"Nor I you, sir!" snapped the lieutenant. "You have the appearance of a gentleman, yet no Englishman of good birth would seize a King's ship, especially in time of war!"

"Not even to save his own life?" mocked Johnnie.

"Not even to save his own life," Yew reiterated. "There are worse things than death."

"Aye, slavery and torture!" Johnnie was disturbed as always when he found himself unable to cope with a situation. He continued irritably: "Nor can I understand how an honorable man can remain loyal to a brutal monster like Bloodsmythe!"

"Captain Bloodsmythe was captain of this ship," retorted Rodney Yew. "As such he received my obedience. My loyalty is to England, sir! At the moment, she is desperate for cargo-carriers, and this vessel carries supplies for the troops in the Americas. Englishmen perchance will perish in the wilderness for want of the stuff we carry."

"Very touching," sneered Johnnie. "Do you suggest we retrace our course and fish for Old Bloody?"

"I suggest, since you ask for it, that you take this ship back to England!"

Johnnie laughed mirthlessly. "You must be crazy!"

"A personal risk, I grant you," Yew said with a shrug. "However, at your trial I would testify to the abuse of power and the bestiality of Captain Bloodsmythe."

Johnnie shoved back his chair and rose angrily. After a nervous turn around the cabin, he stopped before Yew.

"We'll have no more of that kind of talk!" he snapped. He cleared the table and spread out a chart, weighting it flat with glass and bottle. "Come now—point out the course."

Rodney Yew indicated their position with the tip of the dividers. "We're standing, roughly, southwest," he said.

Johnnie bent over the chart. Taking the dividers from the lieutenant, he spanned the distance to the most northerly island of the Azores group.

"What's our speed, Mister Yew?"

"Five knots and a mite over, sir," Yew reported. "I've had the log heaved every hour. But the glass is still dropping, so I suspect the wind will veer nor'easterly tomorrow."

Johnnie made some calculations in his head. "With a fair breeze, we should raise Graciosa Island about sunset, three days hence." The sharp, sidelong glance of the lieutenant was gratifying. "The islands are neutral, at the moment, so it should be a good spot to drop the men who have chosen to leave us."

"*Drop?*"

Johnnie straightened. "I have no intention of sticking my head in the lion's mouth, Mister Yew. They can row to the town of Guadalupe, or, if the wind shifts, to Santa Cruz. Will you see to it that a boat is made ready for them?"

Rodney Yew considered himself dismissed. He said, "Aye, aye, sir!" and picked up his tri-cornered hat. Just then, the *Eagle* rolled gunwale-under to a swell and Yew had to grab the table to keep from falling.

"England's precious cargo-carriers!" snorted Johnnie, hanging onto the other side of the table.

"She's better than nothing," Yew retorted.

"Aye, my own thought," laughed Johnnie. "However, tomorrow dress her trim. We won't need all those cumbersome guns. Jettison a few of the larger ones. I want her lightened."

"May I remind you those cannon are the King's property?"

"You may, but since I have appropriated them, you'll carry out your orders."

"As you wish it!" snapped Yew, and stalked out.

Johnnie flung himself on the bed, boiling inwardly. Though he'd had his way, he felt that Yew had bested him. He toyed with the idea of going ashore himself at the Azores and leaving the whole rotten mess to shift for itself. He was still fretting, when Old Ames eased into the cabin.

"'Ow's the back, lad? Want I should dress it ag'in?"

"To hell with my back!" snarled Johnnie, then pulled his wits together and sat up. "How was the grub forward, old one?"

"Salt junk be still salt junk," observed Ames, "yet enough o' it lines the belly."

"Was the woman fed?"

"Aye, sir. I 'anded it into 'er cuddy, but didn't see 'er."

Johnnie shrugged. Leaving the old man turning down his bed, he went up on deck.

Ben Bottle had the watch, and was enjoying it. He strutted up and down the weather rail, obviously more concerned with his own position than the ship's. Johnnie chuckled to himself, but when Ben saw him and came smiling over, he merely nodded his head and strode to the quarter-deck rail.

The wind had increased, and though the foresail had been reefed, the aged *Eagle* was plunging into the seas with a recklessness that made her tremble from stem to counter. It provoked Johnnie that Yew had done nothing about her condition, then he remembered suddenly that *he,* not Rodney Yew, was in command. He watched the foremast bend under the pressure of the wind, then in a voice so loud that even the Irishman jumped, he roared, "Man the fore-clew garnets!"

The shadows in the waist sprang into action, and within the minute, the sail rose gradually on the yard. Almost at once the relieved ship stopped groaning. Johnnie ordered the headsails trimmed to ease her further, and that done, walked down to the wheel. The steersman was plainly nervous under the scrutiny, so Johnnie eased him also.

"Good work," he told the man. "You hold her as if the compass card was nailed to the binnacle."

"Thankee, sor!" muttered the startled helmsman, who probably never before had elicited a compliment from a captain.

Johnnie mounted the quarter-deck. "Mister Bottle!"

The Irishman hurried over. "Aye, Jo—*sir?*"

"Station some of your best men at the mastheads. Keep a sharp lookout, and call me if there's a suspicion of a sail."

"Aye, aye, sir!" Ben stood shifting nervously from one foot to the other.

"Well, out with it, Mick."

"Kin I arsk some'n?"

"Certainly."

"D'ya know w'ere we're goin'?" whispered Ben.

"I haven't decided."

Ben spread his big paws in a hopeless gesture. "God A'mighty, Johnnie—" he gulped to a stop.

"Say it, Mick."

"Ye've changed!" stammered Ben. " 'Tain't like ol' times, Johnnie, if I may say so."

"You may," Johnnie said dryly. "I might add that you had better change, too. You are now second officer on a vessel manned by mutineers and soon to be hunted by every ship in the King's navy. If we're taken, we'll all dance on Execution Dock. *That* is a point to bear in mind, *Mister* Bottle."

"B'Jesus, ain't it now!" Ben recovered himself. "Aye, aye, sir."

"Then get your lookouts posted."

When Ben Bottle scurried off on his duty, Johnnie took another look around. The old scow was acting more comfortable, and the glass had steadied. Unless the wind veered again, she'd lie on this same tack until daybreak. There was nothing more he could do here, yet he tarried, dreading somehow to go below. Strange emotions were playing through him—the thrill of his first command, his distrust of the men, the unfamiliar sense of responsibility, and the knowledge that the next moment might bring a sail over the horizon. But he was fatigued, spiritually as well as physically, and he needed sleep, so making the effort he forced himself to go below.

The cabin was darkened, save for a tiny candle-lanthorn above the bed. Old Ames had put perfume to burning in a silver censer, designed to offset the stench of the bilge. Johnnie grinned sourly, surmising the old rascal had lit the stuff in jest. Nevertheless, it served to remind him of the abyss which separated the luxurious state of the captain's quarters from the stinking hole left to the seamen. That was the way of the sea, he reassured himself, and there was nothing he could do about it. However, the incense irked him, so he stubbed it out and opened the glass doors of the sternwalk to clear the air.

Staring out at the silvery wake, he was reminded of Captain Bloodsmythe's wife. Doubtless, her normal grief would be heightened by worry about her own predicament. At least he could spare her that. He pondered the wisdom of sending Old Ames, or even Rodney Yew, to reassure her, but it would be an unpleasant ordeal to inflict on either of them and an admission of his own cowardice. So acting on the principle that he would not ask another to do something he himself would not do, he strode out into the passageway.

There was a thin line of light beneath the door of her quarters, so bracing himself against the expected bitterness, he knocked. On the strained command to "Come in!" he opened the door and entered the tiny cuddy.

She was half seated in her bunk, propped up by pillows, and by the light of the lanthorn, much better-looking than he had remembered her. Her hair tumbled over her shoulders, and her hands were folded limply in her lap. There was a peculiar fey quality about her as she stared at him, as if seeing nothing, or perhaps too much.

Johnnie cleared his throat. "Madame," he began awkwardly, "I'm sorry for what had to happen to your hus—"

She gave a short laugh that set the hair on Johnnie's neck atingling. "Sorry? *Sorry* about that incredible beast? Oh, dear God, how I hated him, hated him!" She spread her arms, her eyes fixed dreamily on the deck overhead. "I can't believe he's gone! For the first time in my life, I'm free. *Free!*" She looked sharply at Johnnie. "There's no possible way he could come back?"

Johnnie exhaled slowly. "No, he's gone!"

"Oh, thank God, thank God! I watched you beat and make a fool of him. It was superb! Then you picked him up like the trash he was and threw him overboard. I followed him with my eyes as long as possible. I never heard anything quite so wonderful in my life as that last scream of his! It almost paid for all the screams of the countless men he tortured. And his eyes—did you see them? They nearly puffed out of his head in terror! Oh, it was fine to see that!"

Little rivulets of sweat were coursing down Johnnie's face.

"Now, madame, he's gone, so don't think about it any more."

Her laughter rippled like brook water. "But I want to think about it!" she cried. "I feel I'll burst if I can't get it out of me! This is the first time I've ever been able to express my feelings. Sit and talk to me, sir!"

Johnnie didn't know what to say. This was an experience far beyond the ken of his imagination, yet with a sudden flash of insight, he realized that she was trying to release pent-up hates, as a surgeon might drain a boil. And though he found her intensity strangely terrifying, he felt a deep compassion. He sat down.

She continued to stare at him. "You must be very strong," she murmured. "I feared he would kill you, as I have seen him kill others. I wanted to help you, but it was as though I were chained. Now I'm released! The slave is freed! I wish I could have beaten his face like you did. It was such an ugly face, wasn't it? All sweaty and greasy! He used to rub it against mine when he lay with me. I would whimper and tremble in loathing, but he seemed to enjoy even that. He'd slobber: 'You hate me, don't you? Say you do! Say it, you bitch!' and though I loathed him, I dreaded to tell him so, for it acted as an aphrodisiac—to us both, perhaps. He craved passion, and since he couldn't get love, he'd arouse the passion of hate. So I'd tell him: 'I hate you! I hate you!' Then he'd tangle those cruel, bloated hands in my hair and hang there until his lust was spent. After that, he'd roll onto his back and pant like a floundered stallion!"

She was working herself into a passion now, and Johnnie sensed that with the proper build-up he could have her. Yet something down inside of him, a shadowy shape he refused to identify, blocked him. He rose.

"I must go, madame," he said firmly. "I'll make arrangements for you to go ashore as soon as possible. Meanwhile, you are perfectly safe."

She opened her mouth to object, but with a hurried "Good night, madame!" Johnnie backed into the passageway and closed the door.

To his embarrassment, he almost collided with Old Ames, who had just come out of the cabin, carrying a claret-colored coat of velvet over his arm. But it was the too-innocent expression on his wizened face that irked Johnnie.

"What are you doing here, ancient?"

"Why, Cap'n, I come to get this coat to tailor fer ye!"

Johnnie scowled. "Well, mark this—if you so much as breathe to anyone that you saw me—"

The old man's eyes twinkled. "May God pluck out me tongue if I e'en think o' it agin, sir!"

Johnnie grunted, and stalked past him into the cabin. His interview with the woman had disturbed him. That the ordeal had unhinged her mind, he had no doubt, and he was anxious to be rid of her. Up to now, he had always believed he enjoyed trouble, but it began to dawn on him that there were *two* kinds of trouble: the kind he was accustomed to, which could be resolved by flight or a fight, and the other to which he was a stranger that involved the lives and emotions of other people. From the latter, now that he had seized the responsibility, there was no escape. He shook his head wearily and turned to the bed.

Old Ames had laid out a nankeen nightshirt, so Johnnie stripped down and draped himself in the brownish-yellow gown. There was a fine pistol in a rack within easy reach of the bed, which he carefully re-primed. After that, he snuffed out the candle and turned in.

For a long time he lay abed, listening to the sounds of the ship, at first confused, but eventually falling into a pattern. The crescendo of the wind rose and fell, like a great elemental pulse, and the blocks groaned shrewishly. The ship was taking it easy now, and the seas ran laughingly astern. Occasionally the moon peered coyly around the clouds and winked into the cabin.

Sleep came hard. He found the deep feather mattress too soft for his liking, and, even worse, it reminded him of things he preferred to forget. But at last weariness had its way with him, and he drifted into a troubled slumber.

14

JOHNNIE WAS JERKED OUT OF THE DEEPEST SLEEP HE HAD ENJOYED in a long time to find Old Ames standing beside the bed.

"Damme, but I 'ates to wake ye, lad," muttered the old man, "but there's a storm brewin', an' it ain't weather."

Johnnie gave him a sharp glance and sprang out of bed. The sailmaker had the re-cut coat on his arm and a cutlass thrust through his belt.

"Let's hear about the storm, ancient," growled Johnnie.

Ames laid the coat on the bed and crouched down to hold the breeches for Johnnie to step into.

" 'Tis as I feared," he said gravely. " 'Tis the way o' men, for instead o' bein' satisfied wi' a fair portion o' freedom, they swings like a ruddy pendulum to the far extreme. Every bloody waister wants to be admiral, an' the talk's o' gold an' wenches."

Johnnie pulled up the breeches and began buttoning the flaps.

"The damn fools! Do they think they can get either without work?"

"They don't *think*," sighed the old man. "They on'y *feel*."

Johnnie burst out laughing. "Stab me, ancient, how did you become so hellish wise?"

Ames exhibited his solitary tooth in a crooked smile. "Well now, Cap'n, ye can't travel a long dirt road wi'out pickin' up some dust."

"I suppose not. Who *is* doing the thinking for the men?"

Old Ames was silent for a long time. He produced a pair of pointed shoes with huge silver buckles. Johnnie smoothed his stockings and slipped his feet into the shoes. The fit was fair.

"To speak true," the old man said at last, "there is no thinking. All talk at once, yet methinks big Quinn has the loudest mouth. 'E argues fer the Indies, w'ere 'e says, every man can 'ave a black 'arlot or more. But the men listen to 'im, more's the pity."

"H'mmn! That may be a good thing. I'll hoist the rogue on his own petard."

"Easy, lad, easy!" cautioned the sail-maker. "Quinn draws a deal o' water wi' the tough men for'ard."

"Go on," urged Johnnie, dressing. "How about the Mick?"

Ben Bottle was fiercely loyal at the moment, Old Ames reported; in a dazed sort of way, for Ben seemed to regard the metamorphosis of Johnnie as something almost supernatural. The rest of the men were acting like zoo-bred animals suddenly released; they didn't want to go back into captivity, but just what they did want was not clear, even to themselves. As for Quinn—well, Old Ames admitted he was baffled. Quinn appeared to be holding a middle course, yet apparently doubtful of Johnnie's ability to command.

"Blast my eyes! Does *he* want to be commander?"

Old Ames wagged his head. "Nay, nay, though 'e's a good seaman, 'e knows w'at he don't know."

Johnnie frowned thoughtfully as he tied on a cravat of foamy Mechlin. From the cabinet, he selected an old-fashioned powdered periwig, known as a "campaign wig," with large curls that hung around his shoulders. Out of the corner of his eye, he noted the old man's disapproval of his foppish choice, but gave him no opportunity to express it. He drew on the claret-colored coat which the sail-maker had altered, and it fitted to perfection. It was an exquisite piece, with wide cuffs and tails stiffened with buckram.

Even Old Ames was impressed. "Satan's backside, lad! Ye ha' the look o' a Whitehall noble, I swear!"

"Find me that Roquelaure cloak," said Johnnie, and chose himself a brace of inlaid pistols. He had just completed priming them when there was a sudden commotion on the deck overhead.

"By God! 'Tis come!" groaned the old man.

Johnnie grinned. Women he might not understand, but this sort of trouble was an old familiar enemy. He seized the cloak from the old man's shaking hands, swung it over his shoulder, and carefully selected a suitable hat.

" 'Urry, lad, 'urry!" pleaded Old Ames.

But Johnnie took his time. With exaggerated deliberation, he cocked his triangular hat at a jaunty angle, adjusted his sword, then paused for a final check in the mirror. Aye, he was *Lord Johnnie* again! After a mocking bow to his image, he grinned at the anxious old man.

"Now, old friend, we'll deal with those dogs!"

It was a turbulent scene. The mutineers were milling angrily about the waist, shouting curses and defiance at the quarter-deck, where Ben Bottle, flanked by a couple of quartermasters, stood with cocked pistols. At the foot of the ladderway below Ben, Quinn and a little knot of men were armed with cutlasses.

"B'Jesus!" Ben was shouting. "Ye put one foot on that ladder ag'in, an' so 'elp me Mither Mary, I'll gi' ye a ball physik!"

The men jeered, and Quinn roared, " 'Oo the bloody 'ell give 'e a commission? 'Oo, I arsk?"

Johnnie walked up to the rail. "*I* gave it to him, Quinn!" he said softly.

Quinn swung around, then stared open-mouthed. It was obvious that for a moment he did not recognize his erstwhile comrade-in-arms. With his inborn sense of timing, Johnnie rested one hip casually against the rail and treated himself to a pinch of snuff. Yet if his manners were those of a court fop, his eyes missed nothing. He saw that Ben Bottle was as much stunned as Quinn, and the knowledge filled him with mild contempt. "Mister Bottle! Seize that man Quinn!"

Ben blinked, like a suddenly awakened sleeper, then started down the ladder. Quinn gave ground until he felt the physical support of the men behind him, whereupon he stopped and shook his cutlass.

"Don't 'e try it!" he warned.

Watching Ben Bottle move down the ladder, Johnnie knew the Irishman was not happy about the order, but he kept going with a sort of resigned irrevocability. It was the type of chore Johnnie would have preferred to do himself, but if he was to continue as captain, he had to delegate such matters to subordinates. As Ben Bottle reached the main deck, Quinn yelled at Johnnie: "Ye can't get away wi' this stuff! We uns risked our necks to syve 'e from the yard, but we didn't get rid o' Ol' Bloody to ha' 'e bully us, damme if else! 'Oo the 'ell d'ye think 'e be?"

Johnnie opened his mouth to retort that he was captain, but the truth came from another quarter, and surprised him as much as it did the men.

"Mother o' God!" shrieked a pale youth on the fringe of the crowd. "*H'it's Johnnie Rogue! H'it's the great Lord Johnnie 'imself!*"

Had the boy claimed him the *Devil,* the silence could not have been more complete. For an instant Johnnie was taken aback, but he recovered quickly, shrewdly sensing that Fate had intervened in his favor. He favored the speaker with a condescending smile, and thus encouraged, the lad cried again: "Aye, men, h'it's 'im! 'E was in Newgate w'en I was there! H'it's Lord Johnnie 'imself, else sink me deep in forty fathoms!"

Johnnie seized his advantage. "Bring Quinn up here, Mister Bottle," he said quietly.

The magic notoriety had its effect. No one moved, save the Irishman, and though Quinn made a futile gesture with his blade, when Ben laid hands on him, he quickly surrendered.

With Quinn and Ben Bottle on the quarter-deck, Johnnie said briskly, "Turn up all hands!"

It was a token order, and he knew it, for every man on the ship was crowded on deck. But the startled boatswain went through the ritual of twittering his pipes. Then he knuckled his forelock.

"All present, sor!" he reported.

Johnnie nodded and looked down at the men. The swish of the stem cutting through the water seemed to accentuate the stillness.

"Now, what is this all about?"

The men looked guiltily at one another. The revolt had a negative quality and no one seemed willing to act as spokesman.

"Come, come, lads," Johnnie urged good-naturedly. "What's the trouble?"

Finally a man suggested: "Let Quinn talk! 'E's the cove w'at knows!"

"Very well." Johnnie turned to the prisoner. "Speak up, Quinn."

Quinn squared his shoulders, plainly unhappy to be singled out.

"It's this way," he grumbled, after a pause. "Like I said, we uns took this ship an' we're free men."

Johnnie arched his brows. "You think so?"

"Aye, so do we all! But ye jus' stepped in an' grabbed off the gravy! Now though I dislike the word, we're pirates as well as mutineers, an' 'tis the custom o' free-booters to elect a cap'n an' decide by vote w'at's to be done." He appealed to the crowd. " 'Ow about it, men?"

"So say we!" piped a hand. "We got our rights, we 'as!"

Johnnie shrugged. "I grant that is true enough," he agreed mildly. "We have stolen a vessel of His Majesty's government, and if caught, *we'll hang, every man-jack of us!*" He paused to let that sink in, then went on: "I've come twice within a hair of hanging, and that was too close for comfort. You are all aware that very shortly every navy ship in the world will be searching for us, so I, for one, would prefer to go ashore and take my chances alone, than stay on board a ship that is functioning in a state of anarchy. But, if it's a vote you want, we'll have it." He grinned at Quinn. "Do *you* want to be captain?"

Quinn's big ears turned red. "God, *no!* Only I don't see—"

Johnnie cut him short. "One thing at a time. Now—are there any other candidates for the post?" He addressed the mob. "Speak up! Are any of you qualified to navigate this ship across the ocean, or experienced enough to fight an action against a King's warship?" When he received only a sullen silence, he snarled at them.

"Then what in hell *do* you want?"

"Ye tell 'im, Quinn!" some one shouted.

Quinn threw an angry glance at the crowd, but by this time, they acted as if they had had enough. Disgusted by their lack of support, Quinn turned back to Johnnie.

"Damme, it looks like I sort o' walked the plank," he confessed candidly. "The mutiny 'appened so bloody fast, we never 'ad a chance to make plans. Since then, there's been talk, too bloody much talk, I own, but I didn't know 'e was the famous Lord Johnnie, else—" He gulped embarrassedly, "Well, speakin' strictly fer myself, I'm satisfied wi' ye fer a captain."

" 'Ere, 'ere!" yelped the youth who had first identified Johnnie. "Lord Johnnie's the lad fer us! Even the bloody King can't touch 'im!"

The men seemed only too anxious to agree, and all joined in a nervous cheer. But Johnnie wasn't satisfied.

"That's all very flattering," he told them dryly, "yet as I recall, we went through a similar session yesterday after the mutiny. There are going to be dark days ahead, and you are all seamen enough to realize that we must have discipline. Freedom is something you must cherish and fight for, but it doesn't mean license. Yet with hard work, we can succeed, and I know that for the brave, there's fame and fortune waiting out beyond the bourne, and, belike as not, the maidens such as seamen dream about."

That brought a ripple of laughter which quickly subsided when Johnnie barked brusquely: "But make up your minds right now— who do you want for captain?"

"We wants Lord Johnnie! We wants Lord Johnnie!"

Johnnie held up his hands for silence, and when he had gotten it, turned to Ben Bottle.

"Didn't you tell me the boatswain wanted to go ashore?"

"Aye, sir," acknowledged Ben. " 'E refused to jine us."

"That's his privilege," said Johnnie. "Now we'll deal with the prisoner." He stared at Quinn. "Do you want to go ashore with the non-mutineers?"

Quinn started violently. "God 'elp me, *no!* Let me st'y! I'll tyke me punishment, but let me st'y!"

"Aye, let 'im st'y, Cap'n!" pleaded the carpenter.

Johnnie stroked his chin. "H'mmn! You comprehend the need for strict discipline on this ship, Quinn?"

Quinn exhaled slowly. "Aye, aye, sir."

"And it is agreed that as captain I have the authority to punish, to promote and demote? You grant that, Quinn?"

"Aye, aye, sir!"

Johnnie hesitated as if trying to make up his mind. The men shifted uneasily, and it was apparent that Quinn had resigned himself to a thorough flogging. Ben Bottle glanced around to see where the gratings were, as if he expected the next command would call for them. Johnnie deliberately let the suspense build up before he played his hand.

"Very well," he snapped abruptly. "Quinn, I hereby appoint you boatswain of this vessel, and will hold you solely responsible for the duties of that office."

There was a long moment of incredulous silence. Quinn's eyes bugged, then went moist, and he turned disbelievingly to the Irishman for confirmation. But Ben Bottle was as surprised as he. Then the men found their voices and the tumult was deafening.

Johnnie waited calmly until it was over, then in a clear voice, ordered: "Take the deck, Mister Yew. Have all hands make sail. Shake all the reefs out. We've a long pull ahead."

15

WHILE THE AGED *Eagle* CONTINUED TO WALLOW SOUTH BEFORE A FAIR wind, Lord Johnnie had time to ponder his present predicament. He was not at all sure that he liked it. Always before in his adventurous existence, he had made it a policy never to cross bridges until he came to them; now he discovered it imperative to plan in advance.

For the present the disturbance was abated, due largely to the shock over the disclosure of his identity. The ship buzzed with it, and Ben Bottle strutted around grinning in simian ecstasy over his association with the notorious road-agent. As for Old Ames—well, Johnnie couldn't be certain how the news affected him. He had a feeling that the old man was slightly disappointed, as if, perhaps, he had expected something more of the son of his idol. Rodney Yew, of course, was as stonily aloof as ever.

As Quinn had remarked, the mutiny had happened so fast there had been no time to make plans; one moment Johnnie had been slated for the yardarm, the next, the captain of a ship. Paradoxically, though it was the very thing he had wanted, he found himself dissatisfied. A vision kept rising before his eyes to haunt him; a wraith-like face framed with black curls. Finally he surrendered to the truth: he wanted Leanna above all else. Admitting that, the decision was inevitable: he would go and find her.

For the next forty-eight hours, he pored over charts and studied all the books and records he could find in the late captain's meager collection, but it only increased his awareness of his own shortcomings. True, he had learned naval tactics under the great French admiral Richelieu, and when it came time to fight a ship, he knew he could give a good account of himself. But to navigate a ship across the broad ocean was a different matter. The only man aboard qualified to do that was Rodney Yew. To lose Yew was to court disaster. It was a cud for long chewing.

He decided to find out exactly what talent was aboard, so he sent for Ben Bottle. The burly Irishman had lost some of his jauntiness, and his red-eyed soberness afforded Johnnie the first laugh he had enjoyed in days.

"At your ease, Mick. We've some planning to do. Sometime today, we'll fetch Graciosa, and dispose of the unwilling men."

Ben nodded. "The sooner the better, b'Jesus!"

"I'm not so certain of that. How's Quinn making out?"

" 'E's makin' out fine, but damme eyes, Johnnie, 'ow come ye to nyme 'im bos'n? Why rape me fer a lubber, I'd a-swore ye meant to flog 'im, an' so did Quinn hisself!"

Johnnie sprawled on a settee. "It was the obvious thing to do," he chuckled. "The hands listen to a loud-mouth like Quinn, and if embittered, he'd be a trouble-maker. By giving him responsibility, we put him firmly on our side. Mark this, Mick, there is none such a fanatic as a fresh convert."

Ben spread his hands in resignation. "Well, Quinn's a good bos'n, to that I'll naught say nay." He squinted quizzically at Johnnie. "Jes' between friends—be ye really the famous Lord Johnnie?"

"I'm afraid so," Johnnie confessed, "though I would have preferred anonymity, Ben. However, I suppose it doesn't make much difference whether I'm hanged as Lord Johnnie, or hanged as a mutineer. Where did you hear the name, Mick?"

"Hear the name? Holy Mither! 'Tis a name as familiar as the Pope's own in Ireland—God bless 'er! A reg'lar bleedin' Robin 'Ood, ye was!" He wagged his head incredulously. "To speak true, though, 'twas a shock to meet ye in the flesh!"

"I hope to remain in the flesh," grunted Johnnie. "So rouse up Quinn and the old one. Perhaps among the three of you, I can learn something."

While Ben bustled off, Johnnie wandered onto the sternwalk. He paced back and forth along its narrow confines, wondering whether to confide to his subordinates his intention of going to New York. If they agreed, all would be well, but if not— He decided to feel them out before making the announcement.

He returned to the cabin as the others came in, all embarrassed and ill at ease. He dropped into a chair near the table, and gestured them into the others.

Quinn sat opposite him, balanced on the edge of his chair as if he found it too hot for comfort. His hairy torso bulged in a jersey of blue and white horizontal stripes, and perched on his curly black head was a low crowned tarpaulin hat blackened with tar and oil. Ben

Bottle loomed on Johnnie's right, resembling more than ever a battered ship's figurehead, with his broken nose, his woodsy coloring and his mop of bright red hair. Old Ames looked like a male witch.

Watching them, it came to Johnnie how important these men were to him, so he grinned in friendly fashion.

"Now, my hearties, the time has come for decisions. Our problem is this: we must get rid of this water-logged hulk; she's too cumbersome to maneuver and if we meet a frigate, we're lost. It's my thought that at the proper port, we might trade cargo and craft for a brigantine or snow-rigged sloop able to fight if need arise, yet fleet enough to run. For my part, I'd prefer a French-built vessel, for the French, having no love of English steel, design the fastest ships."

"Aye, that's gospel," agreed Old Ames, "but where to find one."

"That's all settled," Quinn announced bluntly. "The men voted on it last night. 'Twas agreed we'd cruise the Indies!"

Johnnie went pale with anger. "So—the *men* decided?"

"Aye," Quinn said doggedly. " 'Twas their right as gent'men rovers, as ye yersel' admitted. Belike we can find just such a ship as ye describe in some neutral port down there."

Johnnie covered his chagrin with a grunt. "Neutrality is merely another way of saying they will do as they please. The Spaniards and the Dutch are the only neutrals, and it is probable they would seize the ship for themselves under some pretext, or turn us over to the French or English—whichever seemed most advantageous. Don't lose sight of the fact that we're pirates, and everyone is against us!"

"There's still a deal o' Spanish treasure ships in the Indies," insisted Quinn, "an' maybe French as well. We can take what we desire."

"With this scow?" sneered Johnnie. "Bah! *Eagle* she may be called, but I'd as soon straddle a hen in battle!"

Old Ames had been studying Johnnie closely, and now he tried a little oil on the troubled waters.

"Avast, lads, let's not be 'asty," he urged softly. "The wise man don't go in search o' luck; 'e grabs 'er w'en she comes 'is w'y. So I s'y —sail west, an' the luck w'at's blessed us up to now won't fail us!"

The Irishman snorted. "A pox on yer wishy ideers, ol' one! Suppose there ain't no luck—w'at then?"

The old man shrugged. "W'at else kin we do, Mick? Would ye build a new ship out o' waves, an' mebbe use clouds fer syles?" He spat disgustedly. "Bah! Use yer brawn w'en the call comes, Mick, an' leave the thinkin' fer yer betters!"

Ben appealed to Johnnie. "W'at say ye, Johnnie?"

Johnnie side-stepped the issue. "We'll think about it," he temporized. "At the moment, we have to work this tub. Now let's find out what we have in the way of experience aboard. Ben—how about you?"

Ben recounted his adventures. He had made two voyages around the Cape to India, and two to Boston—the last as boatswain of a frigate. Quinn had sailed to Grenada, St. Kitts and Curaçao, and seen action off Panama. But Old Ames was the treasure, for he had served in a bewildering number of ratings, and had wound up as a gun-captain on a first-rater. Johnnie immediately appointed him to the latter position on the *Eagle*.

"Now," said Johnnie, "is there, perchance, a navigator among the hands?"

"Nary a man 'oo can so much as read 'is nyme," Quinn said flatly. "But w'at o' the lef'tenant?"

"Yew goes ashore at Graciosa."

Quinn smiled crookedly. "W'y let 'im, Cap'n? Myke 'im navigate us w'ere we will."

"Aye!" echoed Ben Bottle. "A pistol to 'is bloody skull will myke 'im see the light, b'Jesus!"

Though he didn't admit it, Johnnie had considered that possibility, but now he shook his head.

"Not Rodney Yew, lads. Neither steel nor ball can intimidate him. God knows he was well named, for like the English yew wood he does not break."

"True spoke!" chuckled Old Ames. "Yet remember the stout English archers at Cressy? Methinks a strong man can bend the yew wood to 'is bowstring, if the cord be tough!"

Johnnie frowned and stared into the watery old eyes. Then further discussion was postponed by a faraway cry from the masthead.

"*La-a-and Ho-o!*"

Steadied against the larboard bulwark, Johnnie focused his tele-scope on the small purple projection lying motionless on the horizon about eight leagues ahead. He had known the islands in the past, and memories of the little towns of Guadalupe and Santa Cruz touched off nostalgia. He collapsed his glass with a snap, and turned to the lieutenant.

"What's our speed, Mister Yew?"

"Four knots, sir."

"Very good. At seven bells, we'll heave-to and lower the cutter. You and the men should be able to row to the island in seven or eight hours."

"We'll manage, sir," Yew said stiffly.

"Have me called at seven bells," Johnnie ordered gruffly, and strode below.

As he passed Mrs. Bloodsmythe's cuddy, he remembered suddenly that she would have to go ashore with the men. He paused and knocked lightly. Though he heard movement beyond, the door remained closed. He rapped impatiently, and after a while it opened and she stared at him coolly.

He was disconcerted by her manner. "Your pardon, madame. I came to advise you we will be heaving-to at seven bells. You will be put ashore with Lieutenant Yew and the men."

"I prefer to remain with the ship."

Johnnie felt a flush creep up his neck. "That is impossible, madame. This vessel is in the hands of mutineers. We stand an excellent chance of running into a King's ship, and you comprehend what that would mean? Rodney Yew will arrange for your safe return to England."

She raised her chin slightly. "Having neither friends nor family, I have no wish to return to England, thank you."

"I'm not going to argue with you, madame!" he snapped. "Go you must. This ship is no place for a woman, especially the wife of a man like your husband, though I grant you are in no wise to blame for his conduct. Nevertheless, I cannot be responsible for your safety on board."

"You are unduly solicitous, sir!" she said haughtily. "Rest assured I'll hold you responsible for *nothing!* What I do with my life is my own affair, and since this vessel is my home, I deem it my privilege to remain!" Her lips tightened into a stubborn line. "Aside from a pittance of food, I'll ask no favors of you. So, let us consider the issue closed. Now—if you will excuse me—?"

Because he could think of nothing further to say, Johnnie bowed angrily, and tramped into his cabin.

Among the books, he found one entitled the *Compleat Modern Navigator's Tutor, or The Whole Art of Navigation,* published by one Joshua Kelly, of Broad Street Wapping near Wapping Stairs. He took it down and stretched moodily on the settee to study. But he found himself unable to concentrate on Mr. Kelly's vagaries, so he gave up and began to pace the cabin. He had to have a navigator, which meant

he had to retain Rodney Yew. It was when he recalled Old Ames'
rumination about bending a yew bow that the possible solution struck
him. He sent for Yew at once.

The lieutenant came in bristling with resistance, as if he suspected
the reason for the summons. Johnnie invited him to be seated, but
Yew shook his head.

"Thank you. I prefer to stand."

Johnnie shrugged the rebuff aside. "As you wish. You're a nigh man
with words, Rodney Yew, so I'll be equally blunt. No doubt you've
heard that the men want to take this ship to the Indies and trade her
and the cargo for a suitable craft?"

Yew's face was unrelenting. "Aye, I've heard the talk, but I'm not
interested in your nefarious schemes!"

Johnnie smiled. "You might be, Rodney Yew. Aye, you might be."
He stroked his jaw, choosing his words with slow deliberation. "On
the occasion of our last discussion, you informed me that this ship
carried much-needed supplies to our troops in America. If memory
serves me, you were troubled lest Englishmen perish for want of the
stuff?"

Yew frowned. "Your memory is superior to your ethics!"

"No doubt," Johnnie chuckled. "Nevertheless, I've been thinking
about it. Now—suppose I was to agree to deliver this cargo to the
military authorities in New York, and keep the ship for myself—would
you sail with me?"

It was the first time Lord Johnnie had ever seen surprise on the
leathery face of Rodney Yew. His eyes flew open involuntarily, then
immediately narrowed in suspicion.

"The notion's insane!" he growled. "We'd all hang!"

"The last time we discussed hanging, it was *my* hanging," Johnnie
reminded him. "You were very casual about it, being chiefly concerned
with the plight of our soldiers in the wilderness. Can it be, Mister Yew,
you value your own neck above mine?"

The lieutenant turned red to the ears. "If you are asking me to turn
pirate," he grumbled, "the answer is *no!*"

Johnnie shook his head. "Piracy is a state of mind," he argued. "You
can call Francis Drake a pirate, or a benefactor, as you will. Still, I'm
not asking you to turn pirate; I'm asking you to act as my sailing master
and navigator. In return for that, I'm offering to deliver this so-called
precious cargo to New York. Oh, I grant you, if things go wrong, as
well they may, you'll doubtless hang with the rest of us, though your

conscience may be cleaner. However, you will have gained your objective whether I do or not."

Yew heaved his shoulders in puzzlement. "I don't understand you, man! If I was fool enough to agree, we couldn't get away with it. You realize that Captain Bloodsmythe, if not popular, was well known, and we'd be clapped in irons on our arrival. There are better ways of serving England!"

"I'm not influenced by patriotism," Johnnie said dryly. "My motives are purely personal. The cargo, I grant, belongs to England, but this rotten scow is not government property but is owned by a group of scoundrelly merchants who leased her at an exhorbitant profit to themselves. I have no compunctions about depriving them of their graft."

"You'd never get out of the trap alive!" fumed Yew. "Furthermore, these mutinous dogs with you are determined to sail to the Indies. You'd not talk *them* into this foolhardy scheme!"

"I've found," grinned Johnnie, "that it is sometimes safer to thrust an arm in the lion's mouth rather than to try and run away. As for the men, they need not know. The plan, if decided upon, must remain between us, with this proviso—that you'll give me your word never to betray them!"

"And if I do not agree to sail with you?"

"If you do not," snapped Johnnie, "we'll run into a neutral port and sell ship *and* cargo for what we can get. In that event, the England you profess to love, Rodney Yew, will lose not only a carrier, but the cargo you feel so anxious about. The choice is yours alone."

Yew thrust out his jaw, and his eyes were hostile. "I repeat, sir, you're a blackguard and a scoundrel, and I'd rather hang from a yardarm than have any dealing with you!" he roared. "Yet, by the powers—!" He drew a deep breath. "For the sake of England, I accept your terms!"

He turned on his heel and stamped out of the cabin.

PART
TWO

16

DURING THE ENSUING WEEKS AT SEA, MONOTONOUS YET NEVER FREE OF tension, Lord Johnnie grew increasingly aware that he was undergoing a metamorphosis of some kind. The verve and dash which had always been such an integral part of his personality had become submerged beneath the vicissitudes of his responsibilities, which grew manifest in a new solemnity of mien, tiny furrows between the eyes, and a salting of silver among his temple hairs.

The sense of exaltation he had anticipated as captain of a ship was non-existent. The delusion had trapped him aboard a floating prison in which he was shackled to the others who shared his fate. He began to wonder if freedom actually existed anywhere, or whether it was merely an illusion dangled before the eyes of man, to make the long road of life bearable. He developed a faint, half-formed suspicion that the trouble might lie solely within himself; that his doubts and discontent were, perhaps, stowaways which he had smuggled on board in the unsounded depths of his mind. However, as self-analysis was an unfamiliar process to Johnnie, he postponed the reckoning by indulging in physical activity.

He appointed petty officers and set the men to patching up the old ship, using the argument that by so doing they could make a better deal with her. With the help of Old Ames, he trained gun crews. When the hands wearied of these pastimes, he doled out rum, for he knew that the reins of authority must be held lightly by a freebooter captain in matters of lesser importance.

Thus passed the days.

It was the nights that troubled Johnnie, and often as he lay abed, he had misgivings as to the wisdom of his course. The men, from the Irishman on down, believed they were sailing to the lush West Indies in search of treasure, and talked of little else. Johnnie wondered grimly what their reaction was going to be when they discovered he had taken them into the very womb of British sea power in America—New York.

For himself, the excessive danger was a stimulant that whetted his imagination, but now, unfortunately, he was dependent on the sagacity of even the least of his men; one false move, one thoughtless word, and all would hang.

Long ago he had learned that adversity begets strange bedfellows, so he had always traveled alone, but as the clumsy *Eagle* was no single-hander, he found it imperative to depend on, if not share the responsibility with, Rodney Yew. Their association was not compatible; it was an armed truce. Yew was frigidly acquiescent, yet efficient, and the only man aboard, except Johnnie himself, who knew the plan.

For the life of him, Johnnie could not fathom why he trusted Rodney Yew. It ran counter to his nature to place his life in the hands of another, especially those of a man who hated him. That Yew hated him, he had no doubt. Yew regarded him a mutineer, a pirate, and, even worse, a traitor. On Johnnie's part, he considered Yew a stodgy fool. How any man could have endured what Rodney Yew had suffered at the hands of arrogant bullies such as Captain Bloodsmythe, and at the same time hold such an unquestioned love for England, was more than a mystery—it was a vexation. Why Johnnie permitted it to bother him was equally obscure.

Yet bother him it did. Occasionally, during one of their conferences on strategy, their mutual antagonism would be forgotten momentarily, and at such times Johnnie felt a respect for the rock-like mariner that bordered on affection. Rodney Yew seemed to have no problem; he reminded Johnnie of a scheduled packet driving from departure to landfall without deviation. Storm and tempest were but minor happenstances which he took in stride without swerving from his predestined course. Rodney Yew lived only to serve his country; personal ambition, he had none. For that, Johnnie envied him.

Yew remained faithful to the pact they had made. It was Yew, when Johnnie ruminated that the men might grow suspicious when they encountered the cold weather off New York, who suggested they follow the warm tropical waters of the Gulf Stream up the coast. It was a brilliant solution, yet for Johnnie there remained the gnawing doubt that Rodney Yew might be playing his own game.

Also, there was the woman—potentially a fountainhead of trouble. A score of times he berated himself for not having set her ashore with the others, willing or not. Nor had she forgiven him the attempt. Though she came on deck quite frequently, and chatted amiably with Rodney Yew, whenever he drew near, she avoided him.

Meanwhile the *Eagle* made westing.

About mid-May, they entered the mighty Gulf Stream, that prodigious water-course which, after its birth in the Straits of Florida, gushes northward to expend its warmth along the coastline of North America.

Rich blue, turbulent and warm, it savored sufficiently of the tropics to deceive the men. With great cunning, Yew altered the course gradually each day until eventually the *Eagle* stood northwest. Cold weather gear was optimistically discarded, and many of the hands worked naked to the waist. The lookouts were doubled voluntarily, and the talk, invariably of gold and women, doubled too. To the men, these things seemed closer, presaged by the tropic Stream.

For Lord Johnnie, the end of the long passage augured action, and something of his old *savoir-faire* returned. Thus it was with relief one morning late in the month, that he heard the long-awaited cry of the lookout: *"Sa-ai-l Ho-o!"*

Knowing full well what the call portended, and anxious as he was to hurry topside, he remained in his cabin to dress carefully for the coming crisis. He selected the claret-colored coat and the same campaign wig that he had worn on the memorable occasion of the near-mutiny. By the time he stepped out on deck, the men were in a lather of excitement and apprehension.

Rodney Yew had just climbed down from the mizzen shrouds. He telescoped his glass with an air of finality and gave Johnnie a significant stare that was more eloquent than his simple statement of fact.

"An English frigate, sir! She's closing on us fast!"

Johnnie leaned over the rail and glanced down at the helmsman who watched him with anxious eyes. The man's body was tensed as if expecting the command to put the helm down.

"Keep her full and by!" Johnnie ordered, then turning back to the lieutenant, he lowered his voice. "What do you make of her?"

Yew tendered his glass. "I suspect she's the *Tiger,* Captain Bartlett commanding. She was on patrol off Sandy Hook on my last voyage."

"H'mmn! Then Bartlett knows Bloodsmythe?"

"Quite likely, although I wasn't with Bloodsmythe then. This is the first passage for the *Eagle* since her resurrection."

Further discussion was interrupted by the appearance of Ben Bottle who had tumbled down from above.

"Rape me!" he bellowed. "W'at in 'ell's that lime-juicer doin' in the

Indies?" He threw a nervous glance at the on-coming sail. "God A'mighty, Johnnie—w'y don't ye run? Ain't aimin' to fight *'er*, I 'ope!"

Johnnie gave him an icy stare that chilled his exuberance. "Mister Bottle, be good enough to rouse up all hands!"

Ben exhaled heavily. "Aye, aye, sir!" he gulped, and hurried away to bawl the order.

The *Eagle* was standing on the wind, but from the way in which the foresail flapped against the mast, Johnnie knew the breeze was lulling. He took the telescope from Yew and climbed atop the hammock nettings, linking his arm through the shrouds to brace himself.

Through the glass, he could see the frigate clearly. Her three masts were one, which meant that she was headed dead for the *Eagle,* and she appeared to be bringing her own wind, for she bore down on them at a spanking clip, spreading every stitch of canvas until she soared like an albatross. Johnnie sighed softly. Death she might be, yet beautiful withal. When he saw the red ensign blossom at her peak, he collapsed the glass and climbed down.

The hands had crowded into the waist, waiting in desperate anxiety for some command. The frightened steersman let her come up into the wind until Johnnie barked at him: "Get back on your course!"

The hands muttered ominously as Johnnie stepped to the quarter-deck rail above them. He stood very straight, his full mouth twisted slightly, his eyes half-laughing, half-mocking, his left hand resting casually on his sword hilt.

Unable to tolerate the suspense, an old tar blurted the question in every mind.

"Father in 'eaven, Cap'n, ain't 'e goin' to do somethin'?"

"In my own good time!" snapped Johnnie.

He knew the remark would give them no satisfaction, nor did he intend it should, for he was juggling with their fears and emotions, and the balance was delicate. Everything depended on his timing. He glanced at Rodney Yew. The lieutenant was staring off to starboard where the frigate had altered course to bear athwart their bow. With studding-sails set and royals full, she seemed to epitomize the majesty of England's sea power. Yew was watching her with eyes bright with pride, and although Lord Johnnie was reluctant to admit it, he, too, had a moment of disquiet which had nothing to do with fear.

He turned resolutely back to the men, now scared and sullen, and more dangerous because of it. A boy, more terrified than prudent, yelled, "W'y don't we run fer an island, sir?"

"There are no islands here," Johnnie announced bluntly. "We are less than six leagues off New York."

"New York!" Three score throats gasped the words in unison. At first, they stared mutely, disbelievingly at Johnny. When he volunteered no explanation, they looked at each other, first in wonder, then in fear, until at last panic possessed them. They were as dry fagots waiting for the torch which was ignited by a cry: " 'E's sold us out, the ruddy bastard! We'll 'all 'ang!"

Fanned by the winds of fear, the flames swept through them. As if viewing a play, Johnnie watched the transition from men to animals.

" 'E betrayed us! Kill 'im! Kill 'im!"

The cry was picked up and echoed back and forth. Frenzied, they seized pins from the rails and swept toward the raised quarter-deck.

Johnnie made no move, but Ben Bottle, his face pale and bewildered, edged over to take a stand beside him. Rodney Yew strode to the head of the ladderway.

"Avast, you thick-skulled fools!" he thundered in a voice that would have carried to the masthead in a gale. "By the powers, would you murder the only man with wits enough to save your treasonous necks?"

They hesitated, as befuddled cattle hesitate, but those in back, being furthest from danger, egged them on.

"Nobody can syve us now!" bleated a man. " 'E's on'y tryin' to syve 'is own bloody neck! Don't let 'im get aw'y wi' it, lads!"

The wave swelled back, larger than before, with a roar that meant blood. Johnnie began to wonder if his timing was right, and stole a quick look at the frigate. She had swung a trifle to bring a nine-pounder to bear upon the *Eagle* from her bridle-port. Johnnie held his breath. The shouting and cursing of the men deafened him. They had already started to climb the bulwarks for a concerted rush, and it required all his will power to maintain the pose of indifference.

And then it came! A white puff mushroomed from the frigate's bow-chaser, and a moment later the report reached them as the ball splashed into the sea a half-cable's length ahead.

The men froze where they stood. In the sudden silence, Johnnie called calmly to the helmsman. "Bring her up into the wind, lad! We'll heave-to." He turned back to the men.

"Courage, my hearties!" he urged. "You've heard the lion roar, now listen to the fox." He laughed to take the egotism out of his words. "Don't forget, my neck is as priceless to me as yours to you. I don't mean to strain it."

"But, Christ, Cap'n—we can't fight a thirty-two-gun frigate!" wailed an old-timer.

"Very true," Johnnie acknowledged. "But there's no need to fight. Look now, lads, you all know we require a suitable craft for our purpose, and I promise to get it for you."

"But, blime, sir—Noo Yawk!"

"Where better?" chuckled Johnnie. "You'll find more good, unpicked bones in the lion's den than in the holes of jackals! So, if we move circumspectly, we can snatch a pretty piece of meat, I'll warrant. They'll not know we seized this ship unless we tell them, and since every man's neck depends on silence, I charge you to watch your tongues, and the tongues of your fellows, and leave the talk to me. Is that agreed?"

Out of the quiet came the piping squeak of the ex-jailbird.

"Lord Johnnie'll wiggle us out o' it!"

"Thank you, lad," smiled Johnnie. Out of the corner of his eye, he saw the frigate round-to and back her topsails, with her gun-ports open and her starboard guns brought to bear. A boat was smartly lowered away and tiny figures slid into it.

"Now back to your stations," ordered Johnnie. "Show no unease, but—" His voice took on an edge. "If any man tries to betray us, *kill him!* Our lives depend upon it."

Turning to Rodney Yew, he said crisply, "They are sending over a boarding officer. When he arrives, show him down to the cabin."

"Aye, aye, sir!"

Ben Bottle was wild-eyed with excitement. Johnnie scowled at him. "Wipe that look off your face, Mick, or you'll give us away! Now make certain none of the hands has an opportunity to speak with the boarding party. Send the timid ones below. Mark me?"

"Aye, Johnnie, aye! But, Holy Mither! You ain't goin' to let '*im* meet the boardin' officer?" He jerked his head at the retreating figure of Rodney Yew.

"I only wish to God I could trust the others as much!" Johnnie growled, walking away.

At the head of the companionway, he met Mrs. Bloodsmythe coming up. Her face was flushed.

"I heard the shot!" she gasped. "Then I saw the frigate! Are we—"

"Go to your cabin," Johnnie cut her short. "And stay there!"

Her color deepened and she drew herself stiffly erect. "How dare you adopt that tone to me, sir? I go where I please!"

She made as if to pass him, but he blocked her. "You'll go to your quarters," he reiterated coldly. "If necessary, I'll have you bound and gagged!"

"You wouldn't dare!"

"*Dare*, madame? When the lives of a hundred men hang by a hair? I'd put a pistol ball through your head with my own hand before I'd let you betray us!"

She swayed against the bulkhead, her eyes searching his stern features. Finally she turned and preceded him down the passage to her cuddy. Johnnie was tempted to lock her in, but after a moment's hesitation, decided against it. He strode into his own cabin to prepare himself for the reception.

In a small brass chest was the captain's commission, made out to *Joshua Kingsley Bloodsmythe*. Johnnie sniffed. It was difficult to imagine a monster like Bloodsmythe ever having answered to the name of Joshua. Then it dawned on him that he himself had no name other than Johnnie Rogue. Something would have to be done about that. He impatiently tossed aside the vellum commission and examined the ship's documentation.

The *Eagle* was owned by a group calling themselves "The Honorable Company of Portsmouth Merchants." The charter bore an addendum to the effect that Joshua Kingsley Bloodsmythe owned a "tenth share" in the venture, and was empowered to act as the company's agent in all matters pertaining to the ship and the cargo.

Johnnie read that over again, and as he read, a smile melted the severity of his expression. When a hail outside brought him back to the present, he replaced the papers in the chest and stood up. He heard the tramp of feet in the companionway, and a moment later the door opened and Rodney Yew ushered in a young lieutenant. Johnnie caught a glimpse of a scarlet-tunicked marine posted on duty outside, then the door closed.

Yew glossed over the introduction. "Captain, this is Lieutenant Ayers, of His Majesty's ship *Tiger*."

"Glad to have you aboard," acknowledged Johnnie.

The lieutenant bowed. "Your servant, sir."

Ayers, Johnnie decided, was a bit of a fop. He wore a coat of brilliant blue with white cuffs and lapels, a quilted waistcoat, delicate white breeches and stockings to match. His sword was slung from a belt worn over his shoulder. His skin was smooth and unlined; the mouth a trifle too thin-lipped for character. Doubtless the scion of some influential lord, he was uncommonly young for his rank, and he seemed determined to compensate for this by an aggressive mien.

"Whither are you bound, Captain?" he demanded.

"New York—with a cargo of supplies for our troops."

Ayers checked this against a small book he carried.

"Now your papers, if you please, sir?"

Johnnie took the documents out of the chest and tossed them on the table.

"Won't you sit down, Lieutenant?"

"I prefer to stand," said Ayers.

He adjusted a monocle into one eye and went over the papers with meticulous precision. Johnnie caught Yew's eye and winked surreptitiously, but the other's face remained inflexible.

Ayers took an unconscionably long time to study the documents, especially the captain's commission, and although his face maintained its youthful blankness, Johnnie sensed that something had gone wrong. Twice Ayers glanced up from the vellum to stare at Johnnie, then lowered his eyes and re-read the certificate.

Johnnie decided to force the issue. "Well, Lieutenant," he growled, "what is troubling you?"

Ayers seemed a trifle unsure of himself. "Pardon me, sir, but are *you* Joshua Bloodsmythe?"

Johnnie glowered indignantly. "'Pon my soul! Do you insult me, sir?"

"No offense, sir, no offense! But it happens I recall meeting a Captain Joshua Bloodsmythe a year ago at the Duke of Gloucester's levee, and—" Ayers was getting a determined petulant note in his voice, so Johnnie banged his fist on the table.

"By the great God, sir!" he thundered. "Exactly what are you trying to say?"

Ayers reddened to the lobes of his ears. "I'll have to request that you be good enough to accompany me back to the *Tiger*, sir."

"Why, I'd see you in hell, sir, before I'd leave my ship!"

The lieutenant fingered the commission nervously. "It will embarrass me to summon the guard, sir," he said shrilly. "But I must insist. I am not satisfied with these papers, and with war impending, it is my duty to present the case to my superior. Now if you please, sir?"

Looking beyond young Ayers, Johnnie could see the *Tiger* through the open port. She showed a bristling row of teeth. Johnnie let his eyes rest speculatively on the lieutenant, whose hands toyed shakily with his monocle. Fop he might be, but there was power behind the young pup. It seemed to Johnnie his only salvation lay in trying to bluff it out.

"By God, you young whippersnapper—I *refuse!*"

Ayers pursed his lips. "You leave me no alternative, sir!" he snapped. As he turned to call the guard, Johnnie dropped his hand to the butt of his pistol. . . .

At that moment, Mrs. Bloodsmythe walked into the cabin!

Johnnie thought surely his sand had run out, but before he had time to order her away, she said, "Oh, Joshua, I wanted—" She suddenly became conscious of the visitor, and started in surprise. "Grammercy!" she cried delightedly. "Lieutenant Ayers! Of all people!"

Ayers colored, blinked stupidly and belatedly made a leg. "Your servant, my lady!"

She tripped across the room and stood by Johnnie. "La, Lieutenant, surely you haven't forgotten our meeting at the Duke's levee?"

" 'Twould be impossible to forget, my lady!" stammered Ayers.

Johnnie had been holding his breath ever since her entry. She smiled up at him, and he suspected he could read a little malice in her eyes.

"Did I interrupt, Josh?" she inquired sweetly. "You all seem so stern."

Johnnie exhaled slowly. "The lieutenant appears to doubt my credentials," he growled. "Now, my dear, if you will excuse us—?"

She laughed gaily. "I'm afraid Lieutenant Ayers has a very short memory." She said it teasingly, and Ayers' color deepened to a rich scarlet. "Yet, I presume a handsome young man meets so many people, that—" She ended in a shrug.

"Oh, no, my lady!" mumbled Ayers. "It was just that I . . . that I . . ."

"You *what*, sir?"

Ayers made a fluttering motion with his hands "I remember you, of course, my lady! 'Pon my honor, my lady! But the captain—I seemed to recall as—" He gulped and touched his forehead with a lace handkerchief.

Johnnie snorted. "You recall nothing about me!" he barked. "I was not at the levee!"

The woman gave a little squeal and clapped her hands. "La! I have it!" Her laughter trilled, bird-like. "Oh, heavens, Josh! You were at sea, and I attended the levee with your uncle." She swung on the visitor. "Why, Lieutenant Ayers—I'm furious with you! Did you think that fat old walrus was my *husband?* For shame!"

Ayers reacted as if he wished the deck would suddenly give way beneath him. "No, no, my lady! Only—"

"You *did!* You really did!"

"Forgive me!" pleaded Ayers confusedly. "I really must be getting back." He scribbled furiously across a paper and shoved it toward Johnnie. "There's your clearance, Captain. I acted hastily."

"I certainly trust you are satisfied," grumbled Johnnie.

"Quite, sir!" Ayers bowed again to Mrs. Bloodsmythe, and started backing toward the door. "And ten thousand pardons to you, my lady! I hope you will not hold it against me if I have the pleasure of seeing you in New York?"

She rested a light hand on Johnnie's arm. "But can I depend on your memory again, Lieutenant?" she harassed him.

"Oh, quite, my lady!"

"Mister Yew," rumbled Johnnie, "be good enough to accompany the lieutenant to the boarding ladder."

"Aye, aye, sir!" said Yew, and with a sidelong glance at the woman walked to the door. Ayers was only too happy to escape.

When the door had closed behind them, she withdrew her hand from his arm. Johnnie looked at her a few moments, then smiled grimly.

"By my troth, madame, you amaze me!"

"I fear you underestimated me, sir."

"Aye, I fear I did. I'm indebted—"

She stiffened her spine. "You're indebted for nothing!" she cut him off. "The debt was mine. If it is paid, then I am relieved, for I don't wish to be obligated to you further!" With that she swept out of the cabin.

17

IN A FRESHENING BREEZE, THE *Tiger* PROWLED OFF IN SEARCH OF other prey while the *Eagle* continued on toward the low, dreary shoreline of Long Island, now visible through the mists.

At the moment, Lord Johnnie was pleased with the world, which meant, of course, that he was pleased with himself. His legendary luck was holding, and the men, having survived the encounter with the *Tiger,* now believed him invincible. With land in actual sight, they had forgotten their dream of the Indies, and they lined the bulwarks and rigging, impatient as stabled stallions.

In mid-afternoon, a large convoy coming in from the North Atlantic bisected their course. Johnnie accepted it as a gift from the gods, and ordered the *Eagle* to drop astern and follow it in. The arrival of such a fleet would make the *Eagle* less conspicuous, yet by the same token it increased the danger because there was almost certain to be some officers on the ships personally acquainted with the late Captain Bloodsmythe.

But Johnnie refused to worry. Danger was a heady wine, and he was drunk with confidence. He was going in to twist the lion's tail.

The formation moved slowly. The lumbering transports huddled together like nervous sheep, while ahead and astern rode the giant seventy-fours, solid shepherds. Around the fringe of the flock swept the frigates and little sloops-of-war, watchful and eager as guardian collies. Johnnie remembered how barn-like and ugly these ships had appeared at anchor, yet here in their element, with acres of canvas billowing to the wind, and their monstrous hulls sifting through the water, they took on the attributes of grace and nobility.

Off Sandy Hook the wind slackened again, and it was ten of the clock before they worked through the Narrows with a fair tide. Finally, Johnnie bawled the welcome orders: "Stand clear of the starboard chains! . . . Let go the starboard anchor!"

The long voyage was over.

Ben Bottle was standing by the rail, staring at the sky line silhouetted by moonlight, when Johnnie joined him.

"Well, Mick, there's New York. It doesn't much resemble London, does it?"

The Irishman snorted. "Hell, there's buildin's, ain't there? An' w'ere there's buildin's there's wimmin! Rape me, 'tis better'n I 'oped fer, Johnny! I feared there'd be naught save the wigwams o' Injuns!"

"You may as well forget women for a while," Johnnie warned him. "Now find Quinn, Old Ames and Rodney Yew. I want to see you all in the cabin."

On his way down the passage, he saw a glimmer of light under Mrs. Bloodsmythe's door, so on an impulse, he knocked. After a pause, she asked who it was, and he told her.

"But I'm a-bed!" she demurred.

"Your pardon, but I'd like a word with you."

He heard her stirring about, then in a few moments the door opened. The soft candlelights touched her corn-silk hair, plaited in twin braids.

"Yes?" she prompted.

He realized then that he had been staring. "I presume you know we've reached New York?"

"Yes, I know that."

"None of the men is going to be permitted ashore. A false or careless word would get us all hanged."

She drew the front of her gown tighter. "I think I understand," she said tartly. "You are trying to tell me that I'm a prisoner."

Johnnie shook his head. "On the contrary, I came to tell you that I shall make arrangements to have you taken ashore in the morning."

She backed up and sat on the edge of her berth, her eyes searching his face. He felt uncomfortable under the scrutiny.

"Tell me—why do you trust me? Are you not afraid I may talk?"

He shrugged. "I don't quite know why," he confessed. "I suppose it is because you had an excellent chance to betray me, and didn't take it."

Her eyes misted. "You've been terribly hurt by women, haven't you, sir?" When he did not answer, she smiled wistfully. "You're a strange character. Something must have happened to throw you off your course. At times you seem worldly and courageous, at other times pathetically naive. I've been watching you all these past weeks. You play the role of a swaggering rakehell, yet beneath that false crust, you're kind and serious. Why don't you be honest with yourself, Captain?"

"I don't know what you are talking about," Johnnie snapped impatiently. "Have you gold enough to live ashore, madame?"

She smiled. "Yes, thank you. I helped myself from my late husband's supply before I gave up the cabin. I have no fears for my future."

"Then I'll bid you good night, madame, and good luck." He bowed formally, and had started for the door, when she cried: *"Johnnie!"*

As he turned in surprise at her first use of his name, she flung herself in his arms. She kissed him with a desperate urgency, then swung open the door.

"Now—please go!"

Without waiting for a reply, she pushed him into the passageway and slammed the door.

The four men were grouped around the table when Johnnie strode into the cabin. He flung his wig onto the bed, loosened his coat and dropped into a chair facing the stern windows. Seen through the openings, the bobbing anchor-lights of the fleet resembled a myriad of fluttering fireflies.

There was a period of long silence, finally broken by Ben Bottle.

"G'wan—tell 'im, Lef'tenant!"

Rodney Yew said, "Bottle refers to the convoy, sir. Some of those transports were in Portsmouth when we sailed."

Johnnie grunted. "H'mmn! They made a fast passage."

"Aye, sir," Yew agreed. "They took the nor'ard route. Bottle insisted you should be advised."

Ben seemed disappointed by Johnnie's apathy. "Holy Mither, Cap'n! Suppose we run into those other officers?"

"Suppose we do," drawled Johnnie. "If you don't shoot off your big mouth, they'll be none the wiser." He loosened his cravat and stretched his legs. "Let's not go borrowing trouble; we've a plentiful supply on hand. Now, the reason for summoning you all—first, no one is to go ashore save Lieutenant Yew, Ben Bottle and myself. Ancient, I'm placing you in charge of the boats to make sure that order is strictly carried out. Arm a gun-crew if necessary to enforce it. You, Quinn, will be responsible for the men and the ship. If any man gets away, I'll hold you accountable. Is that understood?"

Quinn massaged his neck. "Aye, sir, but they'll grouse like the devil! They've been lookin' for'ard to—"

"Let them grouse. If a hand got ashore, a flagon of ale might loosen his tongue. We can't chance it." Quinn shrugged, plainly disappointed. Johnnie looked at Rodney Yew.

"Lieutenant, you will make the customary arrangements for lighters to discharge the cargo. Be good enough to get me receipts for it."

Yew gave him a frosty stare. "You can depend on that," he said shortly.

Quinn was scowling. "To speak blunt—can we depend on *you*, Lef'tenant?"

Before Rodney Yew could retort, Johnnie cut in. "You can, Quinn. The lieutenant has given his oath that he will neither betray nor testify against any of us. Isn't that correct, sir?"

Yew bristled. "I'm not accustomed to repeating my promises," he barked, "but if necessary, here it is again: I will not betray or testify against any of you scoundrels, and may God forgive me for the dereliction!"

"Thank you, Mister Yew. Now," he told the others, "Ben and I will go ashore and sell or swap this tub for another."

Ben's eyes went round. "Holy Mither! Right 'ere in New York, man?"

"That was one of my reasons for coming here. As Rodney Yew has stated, there is a big demand for cargo carriers, and at the same time, doubtless many choice prizes taken from the French for sale. However, Ben, if you'd rather stay aboard, perhaps—"

Ben raised his hands in horror. "No, no, I'll go wi' ye to 'ell an' back! But I'm 'ere to state, Cap'n, ye're the nerviest, cold-bloodedest, ruthless cove I ever clapped eye to, s'elp me God! *Lord Johnnie!*" He made a clucking noise with his tongue.

"Well, that's another version," Johnnie remarked dryly, thinking of what Mrs. Bloodsmythe had said about him. Then he found Old Ames watching him.

"By the by, Cap'n—w'at o' the woman?"

"She goes ashore in the morning. You see to her transportation. Let her take anything she cares to out of this cabin or off the ship."

Ben gasped. "Plague take it, Johnnie! Ye can't mean it! Holy Mither, if that wench tolt w'at 'appened—"

Johnnie slapped the table with his palm. "Enough! You heard my order! She goes ashore!" He felt their silent disapproval as they rose to leave.

Old Ames managed a wry grin. "Belike by the time the cargo's unloaded we'll 'ave a fleet craft o' our own!"

"Else 'ave our bloody necks stretched!" grumbled Ben Bottle.

But hulked in the stern sheets of the jolly-boat the following morning, Ben's mood had changed, particularly in his attitude toward women. Although Lord Johnnie had outfitted him from the late captain's wardrobe, Ben still resembled a battered old pit-bear. His own fiery red mop was longer and thicker than a Ramilies wig, and his hairy wrists protruded awkwardly below the white silk cuffs of his coat. A lace cravat merely accentuated the broken nose, the ponderous lower lip, and the child-like blue eyes. He fairly quivered in anticipation.

Johnnie himself was eager, if for a slightly different reason, as he watched the town loom closer. The first building to catch his eye was Fort George at the water's edge. Beyond this clustered the houses, topped by a few church spires, and in the background the low hills and woods. It quickened his pulse to realize that somewhere in those buildings was his wife.

Prior to the last few weeks, Johnnie had considered he understood women as well as the next man; love had been as essential as food, drink and sleep. But until now, he had never known torment and yearning for one individual. It befuddled his senses and he dreaded lest it make him careless. He reminded himself that he was entering the "lion's den," and it behooved him to tread with caution. Since it was impossible to make plans, he would need all his wits to gain his objectives. He resolutely pushed Leanna out of his mind.

As the shore-boat neared the sea wall of the Battery, Ben's eyes took on the glitter of an old hound picking up a familiar spoor. Johnnie burst out laughing.

"Heave-to, Mick!" he cautioned. "If you do see a wench in your present condition, you'll land on your beam's end."

"B'Jesus!" panted Ben. "I'll run 'er to earth like a grey'ound!"

They debarked at the wall, and after instructing Old Ames to return to the same landing at four of the clock, they sauntered up Broad Street. Though it was a hot, breathless day, the streets being planted with locust and poplar trees afforded a cooling shade so that it was like walking in a garden. But the people looked strange, and never in his continental wandering had Johnnie witnessed such a heterogeneous mixture of humanity. There were rangers in greasy buckskins, Provincial soldiers in coarse blue coats and black leggings, British officers in scarlet, mountain folk in hunting shirts that reached halfway to their knobby knees; there were seamen, Indians, Negroes, a smattering of Mediterranean races, and many Dutchmen. And all of them were noisy.

Ben Bottle groaned. "Let's 'ave a drink, Johnnie." Johnnie agreed, and they went into a tavern close by. The common-room was cool and dark, and from a rear room came the pleasing click of billiard balls. As it was early in the day, they had the place to themselves.

When the gangling publican ambled over to ask what they would have, Ben snapped: *"Irish* whuskey, o' course!"

Johnnie appraised the man. "What is your best local drink, fellow?"

"Lawful heart! Ye must be strangers!" drawled the publican, looking them over. "Wall, I'll tell ye—whuskey's good enough fer a delicate stomach, but us Noo Yawkers prefer a good rum fustian." He gave his beetle brows a qualifying arch. "But 'tis a mite strong, I warn ye. The Puritans up New England way concocted it as a poison fer Injuns, an' some as claim it kilt off'n a whole tribe o' the varmints, though I'll not take me oath 'tis true."

Ben slapped the table top. "B'Jesus, if a Protestant kin drink it, *I* kin! 'Urry it along, me man!"

Johnny smiled. "What is it made of, host?"

"Oh, this an' that. We takes a bit o' gin, sherry, beer, some egg yolk, sugar, an' a pinch o' nutmeg, then mix hell out o' 'em, an' heat the blend with a red-hot loggerhead. 'Tain't exactly baby food, stranger."

Johnnie laughed heartily. "Stab me, host, you're an honest man! However, as I was weaned a few years ago, I'll chance it. But, hold a moment—will you join us? As you had the wit to see, we're strangers, and I'd like to ask some questions of the town from so discerning a man."

"Thankee kindly, sir! 'Tis allus a privilege to drink with a gentleman."

With the arrival of the rum fustians, the host sat down. Both Johnnie and Ben agreed he had understated the potency of the drink.

"Holy Mither!" sputtered Ben. "Belike them Puritans *did* murder a tribe, rape me if else!"

Johnnie ignored him and toyed with the liquor. "Tell me, man—how large is the town?"

The publican tugged on his long nose. "Wal, stranger, she's growin' by the minute. Right now, we got about sixteen thousand people an' mebbe twenty odd hundred buildin's, but I reckon in time we'll pass up Boston an' Philadelphia."

Johnnie showed amazement. "Damme! I had no idea the place was so immense! And shipping—?"

"Shippin's our strong point, stranger! Why, we got over three hundred vessels owned right here in Noo Yawk alone! Our big problem is crews. There just ain't enough men available! Prisoners don't stay in our jail long enough to be tried; they just whisks 'em away to sea."

"That 'as a familiar sound," observed Ben.

Johnnie gave him a warning scowl before continuing. "In that event, I suppose it's easy to buy and sell ships here?"

The publican glanced at him shrewdly. "I don't know w'at's behind that question, stranger," he drawled, after a pause. "And while I don't discuss politics with guests, this I'll say—'taint *easy*, not without connections, if you get w'at I mean."

"I'm afraid I don't," confessed Johnnie, smiling. "I'm just a simple mariner."

"As to that, I'll naught say," grunted the other.

Since he was manifestly disinclined to enlarge on the matter, Johnnie changed the subject.

"I marvel at your hospitality, host," he said cheerily. "With all the troops flooding in, I wonder how you handle them! Where are their wives and families billeted?"

"That's another sore spot," grumbled the publican. "Fortunately, most of the soldiers are shipped right on up to Fort Albany, but the bloody officers and their arrogant wives hang around here, sneerin' an' callin' us 'vulgar provincials,' damn their eyes!" He spat in disgust. "If it wasn't fer the menace o' the French, I'd say—ship 'em home!"

"But the French are a long way from here, man!"

The publican wagged his head. "Not the way we reckon distance in this country, stranger! Can't ever tell how them dirty Frogs will strike. They're cunnin' as Injuns. They may come boilin' down from Canady overland, or they may strike from the sea. It's the uncertainty w'ats got everybody shakin'. If we only *knowed*. The people is plain scared, fer they ain't got no confidence in the military. War here ain't fought by the rule like in Europe, but these bloody English admirals and ginerals can't see that. They figger the French is goin' to give 'em an advance invitation to the battle, like it was a King's levee!"

Three merchants waddled in, and the host left to greet them. Johnnie finished his rum fustian and stood up.

" 'Ow about another?" pleaded Ben.

Johnnie shook his head. "Business before pleasure, Mick."

"Ah, 't devil take the business. I need a woman."

"You'll either march along with me," Johnnie warned him, "or back you go aboard ship. In your present randy mood, I wouldn't trust you out of sight."

Ben sulked but followed him outside. "All right. W'at do we do now?"

"We've got to find out what that fellow meant by *connections*." Johnnie ruminated. "But the first thing I need are some decent clothes that fit me. After that, I have to locate a competent forger to alter the ship's papers, for I dare not continue to pose as Bloodsmythe any longer."

Ben started. " 'Ow the bloody 'ell ye gonna find a forger in a strange town, Johnnie?"

Johnnie smiled. "By keeping my eyes open and my mouth shut, Mick."

The Irishman sighed disconsolately. "Damme if I understan' ye. Ye been cooped up aboard that 'ell-ship fer weeks wi'out a woman, an' now that yer in a covey o' 'em, all ye want to do is find a lousy *forger*! Ain't ye 'ooman, lad?"

They spent several hours getting outfitted at the necessary establishments, but as usual, Johnnie was lucky. In a tailoring shop, he found a silk coat which fitted him to perfection: a handsome piece, of vivid scarlet trimmed with gold lace, which had been fashioned for some dandy who had had to return to England before it had been completed. Johnnie purchased a pair of scarlet breeches and a scarlet hat to match, a ruffled cambric shirt, a dimity vest, silk stockings with clocks, and a wig, which the peruke-maker called a "pigeon-winged toupee." It was an extraordinary affair, brushed off the forehead and plastered with pomatum, with large curls on either side, and gathered at the back into a huge knot which rested on the neck.

Ben howled with glee, and when Johnnie viewed his reflection in the mirror, he laughed too. But the mincing little peruke-maker swore it was the height of fashion.

"And one might as well be out of the world, m'lord, as out of the mode!" he insisted.

Johnnie took one more look at the complete ensemble before removing it and re-dressing in his old garments. Then he engaged a Negro lad to carry his purchases and strutted out.

On the street again, Ben couldn't restrain his mirth.

"B'Jesus, w'at a *Fribble* ye be, Johnnie! Wi' all that red silk on ye, they'll be callin' ye *Cap'n Scarlet!*" he jested.

Johnnie snapped his fingers. " 'Pon my honor, that's a noble suggestion, Mick! I must shed Bloodsmythe's name with his clothes, and since I've adopted scarlet in dress, why not in name? So *Captain Scarlet* it shall be, Mick! Remember that!"

From the tailor, Johnnie had learned privately that the Portsmouth transports conveying the officers' wives were debarking at Cruger Wharf, so telling Ben Bottle that he was going to look for a possible prize, they headed that way. They found the streets around Old Slip Market jammed with people who had come to stare at the women from England, and a marine guard had been posted to prevent them overrunning the already crowded wharf.

Shouldering their way to the end of the slip, Johnnie eagerly scanned the new arrivals. He found it quite easy to approximate the rank of the absent husbands by the behavior of the women. Old brass-breasted warhorses, with the toothy faces of angry mules, strutted around barking orders like generals; baby-faced youngsters, doubtless the wives of subalterns, whimpered helplessly around the fringe, while grim, middle-aged females in heavy brocades and large hoops clamored for position and recognition—wives of majors and captains, surmised Johnnie. But though he strained his eyes, he could not find the one face he sought.

Disappointed, he turned away and as it was drawing nigh to four o'clock, they started for the Battery. But on a little side street enroute, he spotted a fine Italian rapier in the window of a pawn-shop. Ordering Ben to wait outside with the Negro porter, Johnnie entered the shop to examine the blade. It was truly a treasure, fashioned of Milan steel over a century before by the famous Pietro Caino.

It took considerable haggling to secure the rapier at an equitable price, and when he returned to the sidewalk, he found that Ben had been making judicious inquiries into the subject closest to his heart.

"There's wimmen to be 'ad at a place called Johnas' Inn," Ben reported enthusiastically. "An' we kin get a good meal there, too! 'Ow about it, Johnnie b'y?"

Johnnie started to shake his head when a thought struck him. Until now, he had considered Ben's amoral hunger with impatience, but now he saw a way to twist it to his advantage. It is axiomatic to the initiated that a brothel is the best possible source of underworld information, so instead of being a mere time-consuming episode, a visit might afford him the intelligence he was seeking.

He laughed softly. "Fair enough, Mick," he acquiesced. "I'll have no peace until you're bred. We'll deliver our purchases to Old Ames, then devote the evening to your lusts."

They found the boat at the landing, and while Ben loaded the boxes aboard, Johnnie drew the old man aside.

"How goes it on the ship, ancient?"

Ames shrugged. "Middlin', sir. To speak plain, the men didn't tyke kindly to be kept aboard. They're a wild lot. I 'ope it won't be fer long, lad!"

"I hope the same thing. But this isn't London, and I've got to feel my way along. The Mick and I will stay in this evening. Pick us up here about ten of the clock."

Ames shook his head. "I wish 'e luck, laddie," he muttered grimly.

When the boat shoved off, Johnnie grinned at Ben.

"Lay the course, Mick! You're the navigator!"

In a narrow alley leading off Dock Street, they located Johnas' Inn —a dark, cavernous hole, with the smell of a fish-market.

"Johnas' is an apt name," grunted Johnnie. " 'Pon my oath, it stinks like the innards of a whale!"

They went inside and took a table facing the door, and while Ben thumped merrily for service, Johnnie looked around the place. From Ben's enthusiastic description, he had expected to find a colonial version of Madame Trull's, but this dingy hovel wasn't fit for a waister. A frowsy-looking Provincial officer dozed drunkenly on the settle beside the hearth, and in a near-by corner crouched a fox-faced character nursing a bumper of ale. Otherwise, the place was empty.

Johnnie was both disgusted and disappointed. He was about to suggest they leave, when in answer to Ben's urgent thumpings, a giggling barmaid came swaying across the sanded floor. Ben beamed with such obvious delight that Johnnie didn't have the heart to take him away. They watched her sally over, her red and white striped petticoats wiggling provocatively.

"An' w'at kin I do fer ye fine gents?" she simpered.

Ben expanded visibly. "Ho, that's the spirit, sweet'eart!" he crowed, paddling her buttocks. " 'Tis plenty ye can do, eh, Johnnie?"

Johnnie grinned. She was not a bad-looking wench. True, her hands were chapped and coarse as a chairman's, and her bodice was sweat-stained under the armpits. Yet under her funny little mop-cap, her yellow hair framed a full-lipped ruddy face and greenish eyes that held a promise of the age-old game.

" 'Tis like this," Ben went on, leering at her, "me friend 'ere an' me ain't on good terms, in a manner o' speakin'. If ye serves me, ye can't serve 'im, an' contrary-wise. Is there another lass so pert as ye in this 'ole?"

The girl giggled and switched her shoulders.

"There might be," she flirted. "Mebbe Becky will serve ye, redhead. Want I should call 'er?"

Ben reared back, "B'Jesus, 'ow d'ye like that?" he bellowed. "Mebbe Becky'll serve *me*. W'at's wrong wi' Becky servin' 'im, an' ye servin' me, sweet'eart?"

"Lydy's choice!" laughed the girl and ran across the room.

"Rape me fer a lubber!" grumbled Ben. "I should a-come alone."

Privately, Johnnie wished he had come alone. He wished it even more when the first girl came back with Becky, a dark-haired wench who looked part Indian. Both wore too much paint which was badly smeared from previous pawings, and Johnnie felt repelled. The yellow-top, who announced her name as Liza, hovered beside his bench, until Johnnie finally put his arm around her waist and drew her down.

"Now don't go get notions, mister," she cautioned, but instead of moving away, she laid her head on his shoulder, her puckered lips turned up.

Johnnie hesitated, and glanced across the table where Ben was eagerly groping at Becky's bodice while she played with his big ears. There was nothing snobbish about Ben Bottle, or his gargantuan appetites; a woman was a woman to him. Johnnie sighed softly, re-membering that someone had once said a man need never go hungry if willing to dine on turnip-tops. He didn't want to spoil the Irishman's fun, yet across his mind flashed a kaleidoscope of other days and other women—the tiny actress in Vienna, the peruke-maker's wife in Havre, the svelte inmates of Madame Trull's, Moll Coppinger—and above all, Leanna. He was suddenly depressed.

But if Lord Johnnie was hesitant, Ben was not. He made little yelp-ing noises of ecstasy that put Johnnie in mind of a hound pup on his first chase. Slightly embarrassed by this open display of lechery, Johnnie turned his head to see if they were attracting attention. They were not. The Provincial officer still dozed before the cold hearth, and the man with the fox-face was busily engaged in stealing his purse.

Being no thief-taker, Johnnie viewed the performance with cynical indifference. In the skilfully adept way the knave used his first two fingers to fork the officer's purse out of his pocket, Johnnie recognized the craftsmanship of an accomplished professional.

Liza was sighing and panting, so Johnnie was about to resume his role, when he was struck with an afterthought. He glanced up just as the thief sidled toward the street door. Johnnie unceremoniously dumped the barmaid on to the floor and sprang after him.

"Ho, Ben! *Come on!*" he commanded.

In a medley of angry feminine shrieks and masculine curses, Ben lumbered to his feet and started after Johnnie, who had already gained the door. The pickpocket was streaking toward Broad Street, but his stumpy legs were no match for Lord Johnnie's, and within a block and a half, Johnnie ran him down. He clamped an elbow around the thief's throat, and waited for Ben to catch up.

"Y're breakin' me neck!" choked the pickpocket.

"Not half what the hangman will do to it," growled Johnnie, and dragged his quarry into a secluded alleyway.

Ben was flushed and angry. "W'at in 'ell's wrong?" he demanded hotly. "God damn it, Johnnie, I 'ad me 'and on——"

"This scoundrel," Johnnie interrupted with a fine show of indignation, "stole that poor officer's purse!"

Ben blinked stupidly, but when Johnnie gave him a knowing wink, he managed to growl: "Damme! Think o' that!"

Johnnie reached his free hand into the thief's pocket and lifted out a leather sack of coins. Then he released his neck hold, and flattened the prisoner against the building with the palm of his hand.

"Belike there's a handsome reward for this knave's head!"

Ben nodded without enthusiasm. "Rape me if else!"

"Fer the luv o' God, gents, don't turn me in!" whined the little thief. "Ye have the cut o' fine fellows. Keep the poke an' lemme go!"

Johnnie hefted the purse. " 'Tis a good haul, I grant," he mused. "Still, it wouldn't be honest."

Ben sputtered, but held his peace. The thief began to sob.

" 'Ave an 'eart, gents!" he implored tearfully. "I be just a poor seaman w'at never done the like before an'——"

Johnnie straightened him with a slap across the mouth. "Don't lie to me!" he thundered. "I know a thief when I see one. It took you years to learn to scissor a poke in that fashion. I know, because I learned the trick myself!"

"Y-y-ye d-did?"

"Aye, I did!" Johnnie smiled without mirth. "What's your name, cove?"

"J-Jerry Faggot, sor!"

Johnnie reflected a long time. "Well, Jerry," he said at length, "I'll make a bargain with you. Give me one piece of honest information and I'll turn you free, with the loot to boot."

Jerry gulped. "W'at ye want to know?"

"Who is the best forger in New York capable of changing an official document?"

"Bless ye, mister, I wouldn't know wa't ye mean!"

Johnnie swung on the Irishman. "Ben, go fetch that Provincial officer!"

The fox-face took on an expression of terror. As Ben turned to obey, the thief bleated: *"Wait!"*

"Well?" demanded Johnnie.

Jerry Faggot sobbed hysterically. "It's a rum choice," he blubbered. "If I talk, I'll get me throat slit!"

"If you don't talk, you'll get it hanged!"

"Ye ain't thief-takers, be ye? 'Twould be better to dance on the gallows than 'ave me pals take revenge!"

"We're not thief-takers," Johnnie said more gently. "I'm a thief myself, and from your manner, Jerry, I recognize a professional brother. Speak the truth, and you'll go free with the poke. *But if you lie to me—!"* He shifted his grip to the knave's throat by way of emphasis. "I'll hunt you down like a dog!"

"Gawd 'elp me!" gasped the thief. "I'll tell ye true!"

Johnnie gave him enough air for voice. Jerry closed his eyes as if in silent prayer.

"'Erman Van 'Oeg is the best penman in the business," he whispered. "'E's called ''Erman the 'Og,' an' a tough cove 'e be, so 'elp me!"

"Where will I find Herman Van Hoeg?"

"'E's got a print-press down by the Exchange. God's truth! 'E lives in the back, sor!"

"Methinks the bugger lies, Johnnie!" growled Ben.

Jerry's eyes bugged. *"Lie,* sor? W'en I fyce me Maker, in a manner o' speakin'? Oh, Gawd, *no!* I swear it on me ol' mudder's sacred memory—cherish 'er, sor!"

Johnnie chuckled dryly. "Jerry's no fool, Ben," he observed, handing the purse to the thief. "He's smart enough to know that he'd never see another sunrise if he lied to me. Right, Jerry?"

"Law me, yes, sor! Kin I go now?"

For answer, Johnnie released him, and he fled out of sight like a sprung fox. Ben turned to Johnnie.

"Now, w'at's this all about?" he fumed. " 'Ere I 'ad the very thing I wanted in the palm of me 'and, an' ye jerks me away to gam wi' a lousy purse-snatcher!"

Johnnie laughed at him. "The only reason for going to that filthy hole was to make a connection with the right people. We got what we wanted, though it was from a different quarter than I expected."

"B'Jesus, I 'ad made a *connection* wi' the right people!" stormed Ben. "But I didn't get w'at *I* wanted. That Becky was the 'ottest—"

"A dirty ha'penny upright!" snorted Johnnie impatiently. "We can find all the doxies we want without trouble. Right now, we are going to visit Herman the Hog. Come along!"

Ben exhaled wearily. "Damme, 'tis plain w'y they calls ye *Lord Johnnie*," he groaned. "Well, w'ere in 'ell's the Exchange?"

18

IT WAS ALMOST DARK BY THE TIME THEY LOCATED HERMAN VAN HOEG seated on the *stoep* of an old Dutch house on Nassau Street. He was a small withered man with a curved shell-like back that gave him the look of a terrapin. He had no teeth with the result that his mouth was almost invisible because his jutting chin folded up until it nearly touched the tip of his long hooked nose. He wore rectangular spectacles with uncommonly thick lenses which magnified his eyes out of all proportion when he stared at the two visitors.

"I'd like a word with you, sir," announced Johnnie. *"Privately."*

Van Hoeg rose without reply and led the way into the narrow house. They passed through a dim-lit room, largely taken up by a cumbersome printing press, into a small office without windows. Johnnie absorbed it all with interest. The walls were covered with bookshelves, jammed ceiling-high with well-handled tomes. A flowery sofa, a chair, and a tall thin desk completed the furnishings.

The Hog took his station at the desk and gestured the visitors toward the sofa. Ben sat down nervously, but Johnnie preferred to stand. He could see better that way. The desk, he thought, was significant. Under an oil lamp was an ornate brass inkwell, containing varied colored inks, a metal holder with three goose-quill pens, and a shaker of fine sand. There was a subtle luxury about the place that didn't seem in keeping with that of a simple printer.

Too, Van Hoeg was exceptionally well dressed for a workman. Though he wore no coat, his shirt was silk, with ruffles on the front and wrists. His doublet was of cherry-colored silk covered by flowered designs, and his breeches were of dark brown broadcloth. Since entering the cool room, he had thrown a whittle about his shoulders. Up to that point, no word had passed his lips.

"I have here," began Johnnie, "a document to be *corrected*. From associates in London, I learned you were the best craftsman in the Colonies."

"I do not comprehend," muttered Van Hoeg, in a low, guttural voice that was difficult to follow. "I have no friends in England."

Johnnie stroked his chin. He found it trying to keep his gaze focused on those artificially enlarged eyes, but he managed it.

"You underestimate your fame, Herr Van Hoeg," he said, smiling. "Or—you underestimate *me*. Perhaps I had better establish myself. Did you ever hear of Lord Johnnie? Johnnie Rogue, of Whitefriars?"

Van Hoeg did not nod, but his eyelids drooped perceptibly.

"Smartest road-knight in England," he conceded. "Until caught."

Johnnie laughed. "Then you haven't heard that he escaped?"

The Hog cocked his head. "I had not heard! How was it?"

Johnnie summarized the story, while the printer sat nodding interestedly. At the conclusion, Johnnie took the ship's documents out of his pocket and dropped them on the desk.

"Lord Johnnie told me if I needed help, to look you up and use his name. I'll pay well to have these changed."

Van Hoeg moved the light a trifle closer and studied the papers. Without glancing up, he asked: "You know this Lord Johnnie well?"

"Closer than a brother!"

The Hog let that simmer as if his mind were a bake-oven in which the idea had to be carefully browned on both sides. Finally he looked up.

"Lord Johnnie has become a legend in the brotherhood," he said thoughtfully. "I'd like to oblige a friend of his."

"To be candid," admitted Johnnie, "Lord Johnnie has a finger in this pie. We took this ship from as vicious a group of scoundrels as ever starved a poor man. It is our plan to sell it here in New York."

"H'mmn!" breathed The Hog.

"I am prepared to pay for the *corrections*," Johnnie went on. "Also for information as to the best way to dispose of this ship, and the quickest to obtain a prize. I am in too great a hurry to waste time on Public Auctions, if you get what I mean."

Van Hoeg sniffed. "I get what you mean, but in New York it is not a question of the *best* or *quickest* way—there is only *one* way."

"And that?" prompted Johnnie.

The Hog took a long time in answering. "Have you ever heard of the Duchess of Tallentyre?" he asked finally.

When Johnnie admitted he had not, the old man continued: "New York is a peculiar place. In most cities I have known, the graft is controlled by corrupt politicians or gangs of thieves. Not so here. The merchants and the gentry reap the profits. They traffic with pirates, even shipping supplies to their hang-outs; they barter powder, guns and rum with the Indians, despite the laws to the contrary; they even sell supplies to the French—anything to make money. We've had more than one scandal, and Governor Fletcher was tried for dealing with pirates under the guise of privateering. The present Governor may not be in it, but the gentry are, and the Duchess—Reggie, as she is known—holds the reins now. How she cornered the business is not for me to say. Doubtless she has connections in Whitehall; certainly she has influence here. She operates a fleet of so-called privateers, and her agents, secret in the main, bid in on all prizes at the government auctions. Nobody gets a worthwhile vessel unless they purchase it later from her. Then you *pay* for it, believe me."

"Sink me!" moaned Ben Bottle. "Be she purty?"

"Pretty enough to have been a king's mistress in her day." Van Hoeg stopped short, as if perhaps he had spoken too freely. "You mentioned gold?" he prompted Johnnie.

Johnnie clanked a small pouch on the desk. The Hog seemed to weigh it with his eyes before choosing a quill pen from the stand.

"Now—the corrections you wish made on these documents?"

"The name," Johnnie told him, "should be Captain John Scarlet."

The forger scratched on a piece of paper. "It had better be spelled with two *t*s," he remarked cynically, "unless you have used the name heretofore."

"Spell it with two *t*s then," grinned Johnnie. "Further, the certification must afford me full authority to negotiate cargo or dispose of the ship in any manner I see fit."

The Hog noted that. "Anything else?"

"Aye, I shall require *letters of marque!*"

The old man peered owlishly through his spectacles. "I'm not the Governor, man!"

Johnnie laid three gold coins in a neat row on the desk-top. Van Hoeg grunted.

"All shall be ready in the morning—Captain Scarlett."

The Hog was as good as his word. The following day, Johnnie left Ben Bottle on board to assist Rodney Yew in the unloading, and came ashore dressed in his new finery. Shortly after the noon hour, he called on Herman Van Hoeg and picked up the altered documents and the false *letters of marque,* by which he expected to pass himself off as a legitimate privateer. As he was leaving, he asked the forger to direct him to the residence of the Duchess of Tallentyre.

With the information, The Hog gave him a piece of gratuitous advice.

"Tread lightly, young man," he cautioned. "Her Grace is a disarming personage, but do not forget—the closer one gets to the flame, the greater the risk of being scorched!"

Thanking him, Johnnie walked across the Commons toward the North River. Though he loved the sea and the feel of a deck underfoot, it was good to be tramping the ground again. A moderate northeast wind had swept away the humidity, leaving the air brisk. But best of all, it was a relief to be alone for the moment.

He wondered about Leanna. Had she dared to marry Laughton, knowing now that he was still alive? He doubted it. But if she had been shocked into a faint at seeing him in Portsmouth, what a surprise awaited her when she learned he had followed her to New York! He chuckled ironically. It would be a sight to see!

All too soon he arrived in front of an imposing mansion, separated from the street by a wrought-iron fence. At the north side, by the carriage porch, a pair of spanking bays pranced restlessly in the traces of an ornate four-wheeled chaise. Johnnie opened the gate and strode up to the front door.

A liveried footman answered his summons, but when Johnnie requested an audience with the Duchess of Tallentyre, the lackey shook his head.

"Her Grace is just going out, sir."

Johnnie frowned. "My business won't wait," he insisted. "Announce me to your mistress, and inform her that Captain Scarlett would fain see her at once."

The lackey demurred, and Johnnie's temper was getting short when the Duchess herself swept down the stairs behind the footman.

"Damn it, Jason!" she barked. "What's all the commotion about?"

The servant began to stammer an explanation, but Johnnie brushed past him and bowed to the woman.

"Ten thousand pardons for the intrusion, my lady!" he said placatingly. "It is imperative I speak with you at once. A matter of business, your Grace, and mutually profitable, I trust."

The Duchess cocked her head and stared at him from head to foot. Being well satisfied with the figure he made, Johnnie smilingly returned the appraisal. For the Duchess of Tallentyre was something to behold.

She had the regal, imperious look of a queen, enhanced by a green kincob gown arranged over a white satin hooped petticoat, with a 'dress apron of embroidered silk and a stomacher to match. But it was her face and eyes which intrigued Lord Johnnie, for he had never seen their equal. If the Duchess could no longer be termed beautiful, in the sense the word is applied to younger women, at least she was fascinatingly handsome. Her skin, though lined, was clear, and she retained a set of brilliant teeth. She had a too-large nose which, coupled with her direct, almost-masculine eyes, gave her face a hawk-like quality somewhat similar to Johnnie's own. Her mouth was wide and peculiarly flexible when she talked. He judged she must have been a very passionate woman in her prime, and, recalling what Van Hoeg had intimated, surmised she might still be.

"Brother God!" she exclaimed in a harsh, gravelly voice. "You're a rakish-looking scamp."

The lackey began nervously: "I tried to explain to him, your Grace, that you were just leaving—" but she interrupted with a shooing motion of her hand.

"Get out of here, Jason!" To Johnnie, she said, "Come with me, young man."

She led the way into a small, stiffly furnished room off the parlor, and after gesturing him into a chair facing the window, she seated herself so that her own face was in shadow. But no shadow could dim the bright alertness of her eyes.

"You mentioned profitable business," she prompted bluntly. "But first—tell me who you are?"

"Scarlett, your Grace. Captain John Scarlett."

She sniffed. "I'll wager you weren't born with that name. Well, Captain Scarlett, what in hell do you want? Nobody ever comes to see me unless they want something, especially handsome young cocks like you. Don't waste my time with senseless verbiage!"

Her profane directness was disconcerting, so Johnnie decided to be equally plain-spoken.

"I have obtained *letters of marque,*" he began, but she broke in with a raucous laugh.

"Faked, no doubt! You couldn't get them legitimately without my knowing about it. No matter—go on with your story."

He grinned. "You steal my wind, your Grace," he protested suavely. "I'm trying to tell you that I have a spacious East Indiaman, capable of making a deal of money as a cargo-carrier in these times, which I desire to sell or trade for a fast French-built sloop or brigantine. I was informed that you—"

She made an impatient gesture with her hand. "Yes, yes, I know—you heard that I connive to buy up all the good prizes and sell them at a profit." She chuckled shortly. "So I do. When a woman gets into her fifties, she has to use brains to get anything out of men. Where's this wonderful East Indiaman? Eaten with rot, I'll wager! Eh?"

"She may have a soft spot or two, your Grace," conceded Johnnie with a smile.

"Stop leering at me!" warned the Duchess. "Brother God, you may think I'm a worn-out old hag, but there was a time—Bah!" She sighed and stood up. "Follow me, you rakehell."

They climbed three flights of stairs to a cupola atop the roof—a sort of covered balcony—which commanded a peerless panorama of the entire waterfront. The Duchess unracked a polished brass telescope, and glanced at Johnnie.

"Point out this rotten derelict you're so anxious to swindle me with," she ordered.

Johnnie stared out over the fleet and finally directed the woman's attention to the *Eagle* swinging to her hawser astern the convoy. She was surrounded with lighters and rising high out of the water as her cargo was unloaded.

The Duchess braced herself, rested the telescope on a hook, and studied the ship a long time. Meanwhile, Johnnie studied the Duchess.

She wore no wig, not even powder in her hair, which was worn quite short and brushed upward in attractive carelessness. He was conscious of a strange magnetism about her that drew him, yet at the same time made him doubly wary.

"Practically worthless!" she snorted, and turning abruptly, collapsed and re-racked the glass. "However, I'll think about it for a while." She rested her hands on the railing behind her and eyed Johnnie speculatively. The wind rumpled her gray hair in a way that seemed to heighten its charm, and he noted with some surprise that she had a figure a girl half her age might envy.

"It's too damn bad you didn't show up a week ago," she said. "I had a beautiful French brigantine-rigged sloop-o'-war, pierced for eighteen guns, that would have delighted a young hellion like you."

Johnnie covered his disappointment. "*Had,* your Grace?"

"Yes, *had.* Hated like the devil to part with her, but since I couldn't find a tough enough young rogue to operate it for me without losing her to the first Frenchman he chanced to meet, I finally sold her to a pot-bellied Massachusetts merchant." She snorted in disgust. "A waste of a good vessel, damn my eyes! Ships are like women, young man; some are ugly drudges, born beasts of burden, such as that hulk you brought in; but others are creations of beauty and grace." She turned toward the stairs.

"My carriage is waiting," she said brusquely. "Come riding with me."

"Your Grace is very kind," murmured Johnnie. "But time is short, and I must obtain a vessel as—"

"God damn it, man! Haven't you yet learned you can't buy or sell a vessel in New York without going through me? You are a numskull!"

"But if you haven't a ship for sale, your Grace?"

"*Grace,* be damned! Stop it! I left England to get away from all that 'your Grace' and 'my lady' rot! Brother God, if I was twenty years younger, you'd be panting and pawing at me, and calling me your darlin'! Shut up—I know you would! It's quite obvious you've been around, my fine young buck. So if you hope to get a ship in New York, you had better pamper my whims!"

Chuckling, Johnnie bowed. "You overwhelm me, your loveliness!"

The Duchess laughed gaily. "That's better. You're a dear boy, really you are. But don't overdo it, or I'll remember you don't mean a word of it. Now come along."

When they had retraced their steps to the lower floor, the Duchess put on a cloak and a pert little hat, and they climbed into the chaise.

"Take a turn around the waterfront, George," she told the coachman, then settling back against the cushion, she remarked to Johnnie, "Talking with you about the *Able Lady*—that French sloop—reminded me I want to see that fat money-grabber who bought her. You don't mind?"

After a few minutes, they came to the wharves where the troops and their wives were debarking. The wharves were still piled high with trunks, boxes, portmanteaus, and crowded with querulous women and wailing children, fretful after the long voyage.

"Oh, hell!" groaned the Duchess. "I'm giving a ball for these new arrivals in a couple of days. I get so damn sick and tired of playing hostess to these cats I sometimes wish I had been born a man!" She chuckled ruefully, adding: "But then I would have missed a lot of fun!"

Johnnie made a mental note to ask the Duchess if she knew anything about Leanna—if the opportunity came up. Shortly after, she had the chaise halted by a slip.

"Would you like to have a look at the little ship, Captain?"

Johnnie agreed readily and they strolled onto the dock. His first sight of the *Able Lady* took his breath away. She was exactly what he wanted: fleet, easily maneuverable, and powerful. Dock workers were busy loading supplies, so they went aboard. The Duchess excused herself and walked back to the cabin, so Johnnie had a chance to look over the sloop. She was certainly the most beautiful model he had ever laid eyes on; smooth and clean as a smelt. He judged her length to be about fifteen fathoms and her beam a trifle under four. She would carry considerable tonnage, yet she lay so low in the water, that with a sea running, it would be difficult to see her rakish hull at any distance over a mile. Her masts were like towering coach-whips, with light and narrow yards. She had of course been designed to row in a calm.

Johnnie was so absorbed in the vessel, he was not aware the Duchess had returned until she spoke.

"Like her, Captain?"

Since he could not have her, Johnnie saw no need to dissemble. "She's perfect! With her, I could laugh at a seventy-four!"

The Duchess chuckled. "I thought you'd fall in love with her. Come, it's a beautiful day; let's drive out to the city gate." When he started to demur, she laughed at him. "I've got something in the back of my mind, so humor an old woman."

Reseated in the chaise, she barked instructions to the coachman, then turned her shrewd eyes on Johnnie.

"By the way—what was that name you gave me?"

Johnnie grinned. "Captain Scarlett, your Grace."

"Very clever! But you weren't christened *Captain!*"

"To be truthful—I wasn't christened. But my given name is John."

"That's more like it! I think we should get acquainted, Johnnie, so just for the hell of it—call me Reggie. It makes me feel frisky and flatters my vanity. You must always flatter old women when you want something from them. Now tell me about yourself. You are not a mariner by profession, and you are not a court fop. Where do you come from, Johnnie?"

He parried the question. "I've been something of a black sheep."

She cackled softly. "You intrigue me! I sense a blend of Whitehall and Whitefriars. Now don't arch your back like a tomcat—that was a compliment. No man can be completely fascinating to women without a touch of the gutter in his make-up. Tell me—why are you so determined to be a pirate? Be honest—I've a reason for asking."

He shrugged. "I don't know—wealth, I presume."

She grunted thoughtfully. "I suspect it's more than just that. Any grubbing merchant can make money. You know, Johnnie, in a paradoxical fashion, you and I are much alike; we're both after wealth, plus power and position, but seeking it from opposite directions. I've had to come down the social ladder; obviously you're going up. And neither of us is troubled with scruples. Am I right?"

"You take my breath away, Reggie!" he laughed.

"Brother God, but you're evasive!" She smiled ruefully. "I would have preferred to know you a bit better, but since you force my hand, I'll come to the point." She stared moodily into space.

The chaise was rolling out Broad Way now, and the buildings were spaced farther apart, with spacious gardens around them. Far ahead, Johnnie could see a blockhouse and the city gate. Then the Duchess started talking again.

"As you no doubt learned before we met, Johnnie, I'm in business. I own a fleet of ships and a lot of other interests that need not be gone into now. War is sure to be declared this year, and I'm readying a number of privateers. I have been able to buy everything I require save what I need most of all—men with brains and courage enough to fight these ships. How would you like to command the *Able Lady* for me?"

He frowned. "You told me she was sold!"

"She was," laughed the Duchess. "But that counting-house grub couldn't raise the final payment, so I took her back. She's completely fitted out, even to the food, water and powder. She can sail on ten minutes notice."

He was furious at being fooled. "Damn it, your Grace, I understood—"

"*Reggie*, darling!"

He laughed bitterly. "You outsmarted me," he conceded. "However, for private reasons, I cannot accept your offer. I have to get out of New York as soon as possible. Will you sell me the *Able Lady?*"

The woman shrugged. "I prefer to keep her—but here we are at the palisades. Let's look around, and we can discuss ships on the way home."

The chaise had stopped, so Johnnie stepped out and handed her down. She took his arm, and they walked along the path.

The rustic defenses interested Johnnie, for they were unlike anything he had ever seen on the Continent. The breastwork was about

four feet high and of equal width, and—so the Duchess told him—
stretched across the island from the North to the East Rivers. It had
been built in 1745 when the citizens had feared an invasion by the
French and their Indians, and had lately been reconditioned.

Nothing more was said about the previous discussion until they were
again seated in the chaise and rolling homeward. Then the Duchess
treated herself to a pinch of snuff, and relaxed.

"Johnnie, I'm not going to accept your refusal," she said meditatively. "I want you to consider it carefully for a day or so. I don't
doubt you have *private* reasons, and I won't ask what they are, but I
suspect you're skating on thin ice. Now take the advice of a seasoned
old campaigner—don't press your luck too far."

They were silent for a time, listening to the musical patter of the
horses' hooves. Finally she turned to him.

"Is there anything I can do for you in New York, Johnnie? I know
everybody in the damned town from the Governor on down."

Johnnie hesitated. "I wonder if, perchance, you know anything of
Sir Clarence Laughton, a colonel in the Scottish Highland regiment
that just came over?"

The Duchess pursed her lips. "Laughton, Laughton? The name is
familiar, but I don't believe I know him personally. However, Major-
General Sir Montague Chumbley is coming to dine with me tomorrow
night. He and his wife just arrived, and I'm sure he'll know your
colonel. Can I give him a message?"

"No, no," Johnnie said with a short laugh.

"H'mmn! From that cackle, I gather it is not the Colonel in whom
you're interested. Perhaps the Colonel's wife?"

Johnnie grinned. "Your discernment embarrasses me, Reggie."

"I thought so, you rakehell! Well, I've wallowed in intrigue most
of my life, so tell me what you want to know."

He colored slightly. "I understand the Colonel is either married, or
about to be married, to a Lady Leanna Somerset. If you could discreetly inquire—" He hesitated again.

"I'm the soul of discretion, but stop tantalizing me. Out with it,
you mooning calf!"

"I want to know where she's lodging."

"Ah, an assignation, by God!" crowed the Duchess. "Certainly I'll
do it!" She slapped her thigh. "I have it—you shall join us for dinner
tomorrow night."

"Impossible, your Grace! I have my ship to care—"

"Fiddle-faddle! There will be just the four of us, and you simply must be there to amuse me. Monty was an old beau of mine, but he's getting garrulous with age and his wife is a glum bitch who seldom opens her mouth. However, since he's in charge of feeding the army, it behooves me to entertain them. You'll be bored, of course, but I'll promise to get you the news on the Colonel's lady."

"Very well," laughed Johnnie. "I'll be there."

"I *thought* that would get you," snorted the Duchess. "To think I should live to see the day when to lure a young buck to my table I should have to use another woman for bait!" She glared at him a moment, then burst out laughing.

"Can I drop you any place, Johnnie?"

"At the Battery, if you don't mind. My boat will be waiting."

19

IN HIS ANXIETY TO GET AWAY FROM LORD JOHNNIE AND ALL HE REPRE-
sented, Rodney Yew had performed a miracle in discharging the
Eagle's cargo. Another half day would see the bottom of the holds. He
had driven the men hard, and when Johnnie came aboard, he found
them worn and irritable. Even Ben Bottle's natural exuberance was
lacking when he followed Johnnie down to the cabin, his big blue eyes
a pair of worried question marks.

"W'at luck, Johnnie?" he asked. "D'ye get us a ship?"

Johnnie shucked off his finery and sprawled wearily onto a settee.

"Not yet," he confessed. "That Duchess of Tallentyre is a tough old
harridan, Mick. I couldn't pin her down. But I'm to see her tomorrow
night—"

Ben rubbed his neck. "Tomorrow may be too late," he grumbled.
"I heerd somepin, Johnnie: the loaders was gammin' about the *Tiger;*
she's due in any day now fer supplies."

Johnnie shrugged. "What of it? Ayers is convinced I'm Bloodsmythe,
so we have no worries on that score. Getting a decent ship is my chief
concern."

"Gettin' out of New York be mine," argued Ben Bottle. "It's too
risky 'ere. One slip an'—" He paused as, after a brief knock, Rodney
Yew walked into the cabin.

"I'd like a word with you, sir," he told Johnnie.

Johnnie gestured Ben out, and invited Yew to be seated. Yew
ignored the invitation.

"The cargo will be unlightered shortly after noon tomorrow," he
said grimly. "It is my intention to leave at that time."

Johnnie sighed. "You've fulfilled your promise well, Mister Yew.
I'll be sorry to lose you."

Rodney Yew said nothing, so Johnnie added: "Is there anything
that would induce you to stay on in your present capacity?"

Yew started to bristle, then calmed down. "Under the circumstances,
that is an insult!" he said coldly. "However, this I will say; if you

were anything but a mutinous traitor and pirate, it would be a privilege to serve under you, sir!"

"Thank you!" Johnnie grinned ruefully. "To paraphrase your remark, Mister Yew; under the circumstances, that is a compliment. You're a good seaman and a good man. I wish you luck."

"I regret that I cannot wish you the same, sir!" Yew retorted stiffly, and walked out of the cabin.

Deprived of her cargo, the old *Eagle* rolled miserably and Lord Johnnie spent a sleepless night trying to decide what he should do. From whatever angle he viewed his predicament, it looked equally discouraging. If he failed to sell the rotten East Indiaman for a price sufficient to secure and outfit a suitable craft for their venture, he was in an unenviable position. He could not put out to sea again in the *Eagle*—in ballast and without water or stores—and the small amount of gold left on board by the late commander was inadequate for replenishing.

As for the Duchess—Johnnie didn't know what to think. She was uncommonly shrewd, and while he was not convinced entirely that she had things sewn up as tightly as claimed, it seemed unwise to cross her. He had no doubts that she could, if provoked, be extremely difficult.

And above all else, there was Leanna to consider. He sauntered out on the sternwalk to stare at the winking lights of New York. She was somewhere there among them, and having crossed an ocean to find her, he didn't mean to leave without her. Resolutely, he returned to the cabin and went to bed.

The following morning, after renewing his instructions to Quinn and Old Ames, Johnnie took Ben Bottle ashore with him to ascertain if the old Duchess of Tallentyre's power was as potent as reported. After a tiring day of canvassing the waterfront, making discreet inquiries of merchants and chandlers, Johnnie was forced to the bitter conclusion that he either secured a vessel from Reggie, or went without. It was close to the dinner hour when they wound up on a bench at the bowling green.

"Well, Mick, there's nothing for it but to deal with the old Duchess," Johnnie admitted.

"Aye, so it seems," grunted Ben. "D'ye mind if I stay ashore till the ancient picks ye up, Johnnie? I'd like to get me some o' that stuff the dogs an' cats fight o'er!"

Johnnie started to refuse, for he had a disturbing premonition of trouble, but the big Irishman looked so pathetically ludicrous, he laughingly agreed.

"All right, Mick, on your promise to stay sober and be at the landing not later than ten of the clock."

Ben did a jig. "S'help me, Mither! I'll be 'ere, soberer 'an a bloody judge!"

So they parted; Ben for Johnas' Inn, Johnnie for the Duchess of Tallentyre's.

He arrived to find Reggie in a twitter of excitement. She could hardly wait for him to hand his cloak and hat to a lackey before drawing him into the small room off the parlor out of hearing of the servants.

"Thank God you got here before the Chumbleys!" she cried breathlessly. "I'm bursting with news for you!"

Johnnie smiled. "I'm all ears, your Grace."

She gave an ironical sniff. "Well, your friend Laughton is not in New York; he went directly to Fort Albany with his regiment."

Johnnie tried to conceal his disappointment without success, for the Duchess cackled merrily.

"But . . . he left the little chick here! Ah—see how the rooster perks up at that crumb!"

Johnnie laughed. "You tantalize me, your Grace."

"Damn you, Johnnie! Call me Reggie, or I'll not tell you the big news!"

"Big news, Reggie?"

"You'll doubtless think so when you hear that your precious strumpet is coming here in a few minutes."

"Leanna! Coming *here?"*

"That's precisely what I said."

He laughed nervously and stroked his jaw to cover his confusion. "You're a magician, Reggie! How in the world did you manage it?"

She shrugged. "I warned you that I always get my way," she said dryly. "Well, after I deposited you at the Battery yesterday, I drove by the Prince George Inn for a chat with Minerva Chumbley. I wormed the gossip out of her, and when I learned the girl was practically a prisoner and alone, I insisted the Chumbleys bring her to dinner."

"A prisoner, you say?"

Reggie eyed him speculatively. "It is a most peculiar situation," she went on pointedly. "It seems that a mysterious and anonymous viper has wriggled into Colonel Laughton's private Garden of Eden. According to Minerva—who has the soul of a ferret for nosing into other people's business—this chit was expected to marry Sir Clarence before they sailed from England. For reasons not clear to anyone, including Sir Clarence, she postponed the marriage until they arrived in America. Strangely enough, she's still stalling, and Sir Clarence's patience, or lust, as the case may be, is ebbing. In a word, he suspects a rival!"

The Duchess arched her brows. "You wouldn't, perchance, know anything about that, I presume?"

Johnnie grinned, but sagely held his counsel. The Duchess chuckled and continued: "Sir Clarence, being a determined male, has served notice to all and sundry that he will call out the scoundrel who is distracting his bride-to-be. And parenthetically, Johnnie *Scarlett,* let me warn you—Sir Clarence is a dangerous opponent! The other officers in the contingent are afraid to be even ordinarily polite to the poor child with the result she is neglected as though she had the pox. Even Minerva Chumbley questioned me closely as to whom I was having as dinner guests because she did not want to become involved in a scandal." Duchess Reggie giggled. "I assured her the dashing Captain Scarlett was a faithful admirer of my own."

"A most worshipful admirer in all truth!" vowed Johnnie.

The arrival of a carriage interrupted their talk.

"You're a lovely liar, Johnnie!" laughed the Duchess. "But I adore it! Well, here they are, so behave yourself. I wouldn't want anything to happen to such a gallant swain!" She bustled out of the room.

Johnnie followed her into the parlor and stood by the fireplace while she received her guests in the hallway. Somewhat to his surprise, he found himself trembling. He had not prepared himself to meet Leanna tonight, and most certainly not in the presence of others. He wondered how she would react. It would be highly embarrassing if she should faint again. He kept his back to the doorway, listening to the chatter of voices. He heard the deep hearty laugh of a man, the shrill voice of an older woman, and then the low, throaty tones of Leanna quickened his pulse. Then they were moving into the parlor.

When he heard the Duchess say laughingly, "I want you all to meet my new beau!" he turned.

"Sir Montague and Lady Chumbley, may I present Captain Scarlett!"

With admirable cunning, Reggie had contrived to have the Chum-

bleys precede her, while she and Leanna brought up the rear. Johnnie
caught a glimpse of a small heart-shaped face turning pale with terror,
then he forced his attention to the Chumbleys.

"My lord!" he murmured, bowing. "And my lady!"

The Chumbleys made appropriate acknowledgments, and Sir Montague shook hands with Johnnie. Lady Chumbley was a tall, austere
female distinguished only by too much jewelry, but the General was
a jovial little man with a bald head and a paunch which in kilts made
him look to Johnnie like a pregnant woman in a shift.

"And now," trilled the Duchess, "Lady Somerset . . . Captain
Scarlett!"

Johnnie met her eyes briefly before bowing low. He saw her sway
against the Duchess who—blessedly—had her arm linked through
hers.

"Your servant, my lady!" he said softly.

Leanna couldn't reply, but the Duchess adroitly covered the pause.

"Please be seated," she urged brightly. "My dear"—turning to
Leanna—"wouldn't you like to use my dressing room? You have a
speck of soot on your lovely cheeks. New York is such a filthy hole!"

"Oh, thank you, your Grace!" murmured Leanna.

The Duchess excused herself and whisked Leanna away. Sir Montague sank heavily into a chair. "Gad! Nice place Reggie has here!"
he remarked heartily. "Didn't expect to find the like in these dashed
colonies. Been here long, Captain?"

Johnnie admitted he was a stranger. Lady Chumbley had perched
herself in a French chair, so Johnnie took another from which he
could watch the entrance. The General prattled on, making conversation out of nothing for which Johnnie was grateful. Though he nodded
politely, his thoughts were on the girl. He was haunted by the fear that
in her panic she might run away. But after what seemed to him an
interminable time, she re-entered the room with Reggie. To his relief,
her composure was flawless.

Fortunately, Reggie and the Chumbleys kept the talk going so
steadily it was not necessary for either Johnnie or Leanna to do more
than look attentive, and by the time dinner was announced, Leanna
had partially recovered from the shock. With a cheerful disregard for
protocol, the Duchess seated Leanna on her right and Johnnie on her
left. Sir Montague sat next to Leanna, and Lady Chumbley was placed
on the other side of Johnnie.

"But don't let me catch you making eyes at my captain, Minerva," chided the Duchess. "Handsome young men are scarce in New York, and I've put my mark on him!"

Sir Montague guffawed heartily, obviously amused at the thought of his hawk-faced wife stealing any man from the Duchess. Minerva's smile dripped acid.

"I fear you have had too much experience for me," she countered with sweet malice.

Reggie laughed uproariously. Sir Montague chuckled again and grinned at Johnnie.

"What's your ship, Captain?"

Johnnie could feel the Duchess' eyes on him.

"The *Eagle,* my lord."

"*Eagle?*" garrumped the General. "Ha! Thought old Bloodsmythe commanded her. Crusty old Tartar, Bloodsmythe."

"Captain Bloodsmythe did command her," conceded Johnnie, smiling. "But due to a slight mishap, I succeeded him."

"Well, well. We oldsters have to make way for you young bloods in love and in war. Eh, Reggie?" He laughed again. "How is the old rogue, Captain?"

Johnnie managed to keep a straight face. "I can't say, my lord. The last time I saw him he was alive, but sinking fast."

Reggie favored Johnnie with a flashing glance, then took over the conversation.

"Monty, you simply must give me all the gossip from London. I'm starved for scandal! Who's the King bedding these days?"

While they chatted on about the shirt-tail relations of London society, Johnnie had an opportunity to observe Leanna as she toyed morosely with her food. Once or twice she raised her long lashes for a quick look at him, but on meeting his eyes, she hurriedly veiled her own. He would have traded the *Eagle* to know what she was thinking.

Suddenly he was startled to hear Sir Montague ask, "Have you heard about the hanging match of Johnnie Rogue?"

Leanna dropped her fork with a clatter, but as the General turned to her, Reggie screamed: "No, Monty! Do tell us about it! I simply adore hangings—never missed an important one all the time I lived in London. Did the knave give a good performance?"

Sir Montague boomed heartily. " 'Pon my oath, he did! Though not what we expected, by Gad!" He glanced at Johnnie with the look of a man who doesn't want anyone to spoil a good story. "Were you there, perchance, Captain?"

Johnnie grinned. "Aye, with most of London, my lord. But since I couldn't secure seats in the boxes, no doubt your lordship had a more comfortable view of the proceedings."

"Damn it, Monty—don't keep me in suspense!" pleaded Reggie.

Satisfied that he had the limelight to himself, Sir Montague went into painful detail about the trouble he had getting a box, and the hysteria of the mob. Then he got down to the description of Johnnie Rogue.

"From the look I had of him, Reggie, he was a debonair scoundrel! Fine build, damme! They say he palmed himself off as a gentleman, and I must confess I've seen worse at Court. Made an astounding gallows' speech. I'll swear the rogue had a silver tongue!"

"The wretch should have been drawn and quartered for his treasonous utterances!" interjected Lady Chumbley. "Don't you agree, Captain Scarlett?"

"It was obvious the rogue had no love for England," admitted Johnnie.

"Oh, come now," laughed Sir Montague. "Give the devil his due. The fellow had no nerves, and I suspect he talked the way he did to further his escape."

"Brother God!" shrilled the Duchess. "You don't mean he *escaped?*"

"That he did," chortled the General. "Just as the hangman was slipping the noose over his head. Devilishly clever, what? I'll swear I never saw such excitement!"

"Oh, damn—it makes me homesick!" moaned Reggie. "We never have any sport like that here. They hang a few knaves in the Commons, but they are such a listless lot, I've quit going. Tell me—have they retaken this scamp?"

Sir Montague wagged his head. "No, and the ending is almost anticlimactic. After terrorizing the gentry of London and laughing at the King's men for five years, the villain was slain by common thief-takers two days after his dashing escape from Tyburn."

Johnnie started. "I didn't know about that, sire," he said slowly. "What happened?"

Sir Montague shrugged. "I heard the details at Portsmouth, just before we sailed. It seems that in trying to reach the Coast, the rogue stopped at a small inn. The thief-takers attempted to take him while he slept, for he was known to be a regular fiend with a sword. They shot him as he jumped out of a window. Fair blew his head off, I'm told, but he was identified by his clothing."

Johnnie risked a glance at Leanna. Her eyes were closed and she teetered faintly in her chair.

"I wonder," Johnnie remarked, "how the thief-takers could have known Johnnie Rogue would be at this inn?"

"*Cherchez la femme!*" chuckled the General. " 'Tis said some strumpet tipped them off, saying she had an assignation with him at the place."

"Brother God!" laughed the Duchess. "Isn't it always so?"

Leanna's head rocked back. Lady Chumbley started out of her chair. "My dear girl!" she cried. "Are you ill?"

Leanna straightened and managed a thin smile. "Forgive me, my lady! It's just a touch of the vapors!"

The Duchess rose majestically. "I'm not surprised—it's beastly hot in here. Let's go into the parlor." As they moved into the other room, she linked the Chumbleys on either arm. "Minerva, I must show you and Monty my marvelous view of the harbor!" Starting them toward the doorway, she gave Johnnie a knowing wink.

"Captain, I'm sure that poor girl doesn't feel up to climbing three flights of stairs. So do try to keep her amused until we return."

"I'll do my humble best, your Grace," Johnnie promised.

It was quite apparent that Lady Chumbley was not enthused over the prospect of plodding up to the roof, but the Duchess propelled her out of the room, and Johnnie found himself alone with Leanna.

She sat very straight in a green Windsor chair, staring moodily into the fire. Johnnie lounged against the mantel. Nothing was said until the footsteps had passed the first landing, then Johnnie laughed wryly.

"So—Johnnie the Rogue is dead, my lady?"

"You appear very much alive!" she muttered.

"Ah, but the spirit never dies. Especially mine."

She clenched her hands. "Johnnie, what are you doing here? Does that old crow know about—about us?"

He held up a restraining hand. "One question at a time, my dear wife! The Duchess—God bless her!—is an innocent conspirator, I assure you. As for the other, the answer is obvious. I came to see you, of course."

She colored furiously. "You gave me your word—!" she began, but he broke in.

"We made a pact, my dear, which you voided by sending lackeys to murder me." When she made no comment, he concluded: "Now we're right back where we started."

She forced her eyes to meet his. "Then what do you want now?" she cried desperately.

"*You!*"

She jerked out of her chair and crossed to the window. He waited patiently until she whirled around.

"For the love of God—haven't you tortured me sufficiently? I'm losing my mind!"

He smiled thinly. "And I have lost my heart."

"Oh, dear Lord!" she moaned, wilting into a chair. "I wish I were dead!"

"Do you prefer death to me, Leanna?"

She peered at him through brimming eyes. "Don't mock me, Johnnie! Everything is a tragic mess. Sir Clarence is furious enough to jilt me because I won't marry him at once, and I can't because of you. Won't you understand? I'm in a strange land, and penniless! I don't know which way to turn!"

Johnnie bowed. "It is quite simple. You married me to get out of one mess; now come with me and get out of this one."

"Don't be ridiculous!"

He shrugged. "I don't consider it ridiculous to want one's wife," he snapped. "And heed this—I'm not going to give you up!"

"But dear God—*why?*"

"Because I love you!" The words astonished him quite as much as they did her, for when she looked up in amazement, he grinned ruefully.

"'Pon my honor, that slipped out, my lady!" he confessed. "Though I've never spoken it before, it's true enough."

She wrung her hands. "*Love?* What does a knave like you know of love?"

"Very little, Leanna. I had always imagined it to be a pleasing headiness, like rare champagne, rather than the gnawing emptiness that has ruined sleep and haunted my waking hours. Yet unlike normal hunger, no substitute seems to appease it. Rather than starve longer, I risked my neck to follow you to New York. I'm not leaving it without you."

She was staring at him in a kind of horrified fascination when they heard the others coming down the stairs. The Duchess gave a shrill laugh that was like a warning.

"Pull yourself together," Johnnie told Leanna sharply, "or they'll surmise something is amiss. I'll arrange to see you at the inn."

"Oh, Lord, *no!*" wailed the girl in panic. "Sir Clarence is expected tomorrow!"

"In that event, I'll settle with Sir Clarence," grated Johnnie just as the others came into the room.

The Duchess took a calculating glance at Leanna, then focused attention onto Johnnie.

"What a dull blade you are! I had expected to find you two youngsters twittering like birds! This modern generation has lost the gift of gallantry! Monty, do you remember the hilarious blarney you used to give the belles?"

Sir Montague looked uncomfortable. "Now, now, Reggie! Don't exaggerate, my dear!" he protested.

Lady Chumbley sniffed. "Huh! Montague still gives the belles a lot of blarney."

The Duchess giggled maliciously, and when they were seated, channeled the conversation onto the war.

"We in New York live in dread of a surprise attack," she explained. "Where and when do you think they will strike, Monty?"

"They won't strike," Sir Montague asserted flatly. "They're just bluffing, blast them! If I had my way, we'd march up and beard them in Quebec!"

"I hope you're right, Monty. Our mariners fear a sudden attack by sea."

"Fa! Nonsense! The Frogs would never dare risk an encounter with our Grand Fleet."

"I wasn't aware our Grand Fleet was over here," Johnnie offered mildly.

On matters military, the General lost his joviality and reverted to type.

"It doesn't matter where it is!" he insisted dogmatically. "The French will only fight us by land, mark me! I know their mentality. They—" He scowled impatiently as a manservant tiptoed into the room and whispered to the Duchess.

Her brows shot up, and she looked meaningly at Johnnie.

"It's for you, Captain! A seaman. He says it is urgent!"

Johnnie hastily excused himself and hurried into the hallway where he found Old Ames nervously revolving his tarred hat. The old man had a mouse under one eye and a cut on his cheek.

Johnnie grabbed his arm. "What's wrong, Ames?"

" 'Tis the men, Cap'n!" panted the old man. "They got rum an' 'arlots aboard!" He mopped his face with his scarf. "I tried to stop it, so 'elp me, but Quinn gimme a couple of licks in the fyce. I reckoned ye'd oughta know."

"How in hell did they get 'em?" demanded Johnnie. "I told you to let no man touch the boats."

"They didn't, lad! They must 'a' made a deal wi' the loaders to bring 'em out. Quinn argied ye didn't say nuthin' agin havin' a bit of fun aboard, so—"

"I'll settle with Quinn!" raged Johnnie. "Hold, I'll be right with you." He turned and re-entered the parlor.

"Your pardon, my lord and ladies," he apologized. "I must return to my ship immediately, but"—and he looked directly at Leanna—"I hope to have the pleasure of seeing you again."

The Duchess accompanied him to the front door. "Johnnie!" she whispered. "Are you in trouble?"

He shrugged. "I'm not sure. I have to hurry—"

"Take my coach," urged the Duchess. She stepped onto the *stoep*. "George—take these gentlemen to the Battery!" To Johnnie she added softly, "I want to see you as soon as possible, young man. You've some explaining to do." Without waiting for his reply, she went back into the house.

To Johnnie's relief, when the coach deposited them at the landing, Ben was waiting. Though battered and a trifle drunk, he wore the smug look of a contented old tomcat. But when Johnnie told him about the trouble on board, he turned cold sober, and springing into the shore-boat, seized an oar.

While Ben and Ames rowed, Johnnie sat in the stern-sheets and drew his cloak around him against the damp wind. He cursed himself for having left Quinn in charge. He had a notion to pistol the man on sight. But he knew that would not undo the damage. The only thing to do now, he decided, was to confine the harlots on board until his business was settled. That would cause complications, he realized, but it seemed the lesser of two evils.

He was still a little dazed by what Sir Montague had told him: Lord Johnnie officially dead! The implications were tremendous. If he could maintain the illusion, he was free to start a new life under a new identity. But he couldn't maintain it if one of the seamen had confided the secret to a harlot. The news would spread through the underworld like wildfire!

A sudden shout from Ben Bottle jerked him out of his reverie.

"Hell an' damnation, Johnnie! A boat!"

Johnnie looked up. A small fishing smack lay alongside the *Eagle's* fore-chains, and by the light of lanthorns, Johnnie could see the seamen handing down the women.

"Head them off!" roared Johnnie. "We can't let them get away!"

As Ben and Old Ames bent to their oars, a shout went up from the *Eagle*. A moment later, the smack cast off her lines and began to edge around the ship's stem.

"Hurry, hurry!" urged Johnnie.

The little boat plowed through the chop until they were all soaked with spume, but the smack had hoisted sail and was gaining speed. Cursing, Johnnie drew his pistol, and bracing himself, stood up and sent a ball over the helmsman's head. But the smack wore around the far side of the old East Indiaman and disappeared.

Johnnie sat down heavily. "It's no use," he growled bitterly. "Head over to the ship."

The instant the boat drew alongside, Johnnie sprang into the mainchains and scrambled aboard. Quinn, followed by a half-dozen hands, came staggering across the deck.

"Didn't see 'e comin', Cap'n," he mumbled apologetically.

"You're a damn liar!" snarled Johnnie. "You've had women aboard!"

"Now, now, Cap'n," wheedled Quinn. "Ye didn't say naught again' our 'avin' a bit o'—"

Johnnie hit him so hard his shoulder blades struck the deck first. The other seamen staggered back before the blaze of his rage.

Johnnie turned to Ben who had climbed up behind him.

"Ben, weight that dog with chain and balance him on the cat-head! If any trouble comes of this, see that he's shoved overboard at the first warning. Understand?"

"Aye, aye, sir!" growled Ben. "Though I'd rather cut the vermin's throat an' 'ave done wi' 'im!"

Johnnie glared at the other men. It was his thought to rouse up all hands and explain to them the predicament their action had engendered, but a moment's reflection warned him they were too drunk to comprehend. Disgusted, he left Ben in charge and stalked aft to his quarters.

He paced back and forth across the big cabin trying to cool his rage to a point where coherent thought was possible. At last he realized the futility of self-recrimination, and tried to analyze the mess. One salient point stood out clearly—he would have to get out of New York immediately. He understood only too well the mentality of the hands to underestimate the danger; one of them, at least, would have told a harlot about the "great Lord Johnnie." That was inevitable. It was equally inevitable the wench would pass the word along until it reached the ears of some informer who would, in turn, sell the information to a thief-taker. That was common procedure, and the main reason Johnnie had always worked alone. As he had once confided to Leanna—he had learned to trust no one but himself.

In the middle of the night, he roused up Ben and Old Ames and brought them into the cabin. When he had outlined their plight, Ben shrugged.

"To 'ell wi' the dogs, I s'y," he growled. "Let's the three o' us skip out whilest the skippin's good."

Old Ames said nothing, but his watery eyes watched Johnnie quizzically. Johnnie shook his head.

"I can't abandon the poor fools, Ben. If I pulled out, they'd all hang for the crime I engineered."

Old Ames smiled. "True enough, lad. But d'ye intend to 'ang wi' 'em?"

Johnnie grimaced. "Not if I can help it." Then he told them about the Duchess of Tallentyre's offer to command the *Able Lady.*

"'Tis not a job to my liking," he concluded, "yet methinks it's the only course open. She's a fast little brigantine-rigged sloop-o'-war; and ready for sea."

"She'd better be ready," grumbled Ben. "Belike the bailiffs'll be out 'ere by sun-up."

Johnnie laughed. "Our officials don't move so fast, Ben. I'll go ashore first thing tomorrow and capitulate to her Grace. Perhaps we can get away on the afternoon tide."

"Ye're dependin' on a woman," cautioned Old Ames. "Suppose she changes 'er mind?"

Johnnie winced. "A ghastly thought, old one!" he confessed.

Ben shuddered. "B'Jesus, I'll do me beads tonight, though 'tis rusty I am at prayer."

Johnnie grinned. "It won't hurt to try, Mick. We're going to need all the blessed help we can get. Now try and catch some sleep, for I fear tomorrow is going to be a hectic day."

JOHNNIE CAME ON DECK IN THE MORNING TO FIND THE HARBOR
blanketed in fog so thick he couldn't see the jib boom from the quarter-
deck rail. Ben evolved out of the murk to comment that it would be
impossible to go ashore, but Johnnie shook his head.

"I have to go," he said grimly. "Have Ames bring the boat alongside."

He returned to his cabin and studied the harbor chart. After calculating the tide and current drifts, he worked out a course, then taking
with him a small compass, went topside again. Ben walked with him to
the chains.

"Keep a sharp lookout, Mick," he warned the Irishman. "I'll be back
as soon as possible."

Ben grinned. "God go wi' ye, lad!" he said prayerfully. "I'll 'ave
these curs sobered an' sheared like lambs afore ye return."

Johnnie dropped down into the boat and in a moment the *Eagle*
melted back into the mists. Johnnie sat with the compass on his knee,
trying to con the rowers. But the ebbing tide ran swifter than he had
anticipated, and they were carried well below the Battery. It was mid-
morning before they finally groped their way into a slip at the Fish
Market. As they tied up to the pilings, Old Ames wagged his head
admiringly.

"Satan's backside! I've seen navigatin' by sight an' by sound, but
that's the fust time I ever 'eard o' navigatin' by *smell*. Want I should
await ye 'ere lad, or pull around to the Battery landin'?"

Johnnie stepped ashore. "Don't stir from this spot," he ordered, "I
don't know how long I'll be, but be ready to shove off on a moment's
notice, for I may come with the hounds barking at my heels."

The old man chuckled. "Damme fer a lubber! Why, lad, yer daddy
spoke almost those very words to me one night when I set him ashore
in Spain. Aye, sir, I'll wait fer ye till doomsday."

To save every precious moment of time, Johnnie hired a hack to carry him to the Duchess' residence. On arrival, he bade the coachman wait, and hurried up to the front door. It seemed to take the footman an unconscionably long time to answer his urgent summons.

"Ask your mistress if she will see me at once," he barked the instant the door opened. "I am—"

The manservant bowed. "Her Grace is not at home, sire," he interrupted respectfully.

Johnnie felt a chill of apprehension play along his spine. This was something he had not foreseen.

"Not at home? Where is she?"

"She attended the races with the Governor's party, sire," explained the servant.

Johnnie tried to stem his mounting nervousness. "Can you tell me where the race is being held? It is imperative I find her Grace immediately."

The footman shrugged. "I cannot say, sire. The last was run around Beaver Pond, near Jamaica on Long Island, yet perchance this one may be run on Salisbury Plain. But, your pardon, sire, her Grace left a message if you should call."

"Well, in God's name, give it to me!" snapped Johnnie.

"She instructed me to request that you await her here, sire. She was most emphatic about it, if I may say so. Will you come in, sire?"

Johnnie hesitated. It was barely midday, and he sickened at the thought of sitting idle all afternoon. On the other hand, if he went in search of the Duchess, he might well miss her. He toyed with the idea of calling on Leanna, but that, too, might put him in further jeopardy. No, the only sensible thing to do was wait here.

With a shrug, he entered the house, and when the servant had ushered him into the small sitting room off the parlor, he bade the man dismiss his hack. After that, he tried to reconcile himself to the most difficult of all chores—being patient.

It was the longest day in Johnnie's twenty-nine years. All afternoon the fog held, damp and oppressive, sealing the house into a prison. A clock in an adjoining room tolled the passing hours as gloomily as the bell of St. Sepulchre's. A dozen times, Johnnie started for the door, unable to tolerate the suspense, but each time his reason bade him pause. Yet even reason could not stem his growing alarm.

Shortly after six o'clock, he heard the Duchess arrive. He stalked in the hallway as she was starting up the stairs.

"Your Grace, I must—"

She was dusty and tired. "Oh, hello, Johnnie!" She leaned on the balustrade and looked at him. "I didn't expect you!"

Johnnie caught a peculiar inflection in her voice, but he brushed his apprehensions away.

"I've waited all day for your Grace," he said. "I must talk to you at once."

Her eyes were not quite mocking. "Give me an hour," she suggested. "I'm positively filthy. After I bathe and—"

Johnnie tried to keep the irritation out of his voice. "I beg your Grace's indulgence," he wheedled. "But I cannot spare another hour!"

She frowned. "You are impertinent, young man!" she snapped. "If your business is so damned important, you can talk while I bathe. Come with me."

Every nerve in Johnnie's body warned him that something had gone wrong. The old Duchess was stalling. As he followed her up the stairs to her bedroom, he attempted to interpret her changed manner. Had she learned his identity from Leanna? Not that he suspected Leanna had talked, but the Duchess of Tallentyre was no fool. Quite possibly she had read between the lines. He damned himself for having confided to her his interest in the girl.

Apparently the Duchess had ordered her bath in advance, for by the time they reached the bedroom, servants were pouring hot water into the tub. Screens were placed around it, and while Johnnie settled himself in a lolling-chair, the Duchess retired behind the screens.

"Now, Johnnie," she called, "what's your difficulty?"

Being unable to see her face, Johnnie felt at a disadvantage. He was also disturbed by the absence of her amiable profanity. It didn't augur well.

"For personal reasons, I must leave New York at once," he explained. "If you will buy the *Eagle* from me, I'll accept command of the *Able Lady*."

"H'mmn! How much do you want for the old scow?"

"I wanted three thousand pounds but, under the circumstances, I'll take two."

She laughed sardonically. "Brother God! I wouldn't give you over five hundred."

Johnnie gasped. "Five hundred? Damn it, you'd make double that on *one* voyage!" he protested.

"No doubt. However, I'm not anxious to buy her, so perhaps you'd prefer to keep her."

At the moment, Johnnie was grateful she couldn't see his face. He was furious.

"You know I can't keep her," he said slowly in an effort to hide his temper. "I have no choice save to accept the pittance."

"I don't consider it a bargain," the Duchess retorted. "She's probably stolen."

Johnnie laughed bitterly. "At five hundred pounds your Grace is stealing her."

Her cackle made Johnnie think of a female Shylock. He sat flexing his long fingers until she finished her bath. In a few moments, she walked around the end of the screen dressed in a green silk negligee. She stood looking down at him a little while, then with a short laugh, dropped into a chair near by.

"So—you've changed your mind about working for me, eh?"

He shrugged. "Circumstances have changed my mind," he conceded. "Now, if your Grace will permit, I'd like to leave on the tide."

She studied him through lazy-lidded eyes. "My heavens, you're sure of yourself!"

"If your Grace please!" began Johnnie, when he was interrupted by a commotion below. There was the sound of cursing, shouts and blows.

"What the hell—?" cried the Duchess, rising.

Johnnie had sprung to his feet like a trapped panther. More by instinct than direction, his eyes searched the room for some avenue of escape. Then he heard a familiar voice bellow: *"Johnnie! Johnnie!"*

He shot out of the room and down the stairs with the Duchess behind him. In the hallway below, he saw Ben Bottle fighting with three lackeys who clung to him like mastiffs to a baited bull.

Johnnie was among them in an instant, flinging them aside. When he got Ben free, the big Irishman sank wearily onto the lower step and held his head in his hands.

"God damn it—what's this mean?" demanded the Duchess, who had paused halfway down the stairs.

Johnnie glanced up. "This is my officer," he told her. Then he turned his attention back to Ben.

The man was badly battered. His red hair was dripping water and his body was covered in the rags of a farmhand. He raised tearful eyes and looked at Johnnie.

"They've taken the ship, lad!" he moaned, and dropped his face into his hands again.

Johnnie paled. He took in the three angry lackeys and the Duchess leaning forward on the stairs. She seemed to grasp the situation, for she barked at the servants.

"Go back to your quarters at once! Say nothing of this to anyone. Now—begone!"

When the trio had disappeared, she told Johnnie: "Take your man into the sitting room. You'll have privacy there. When you're through, join me upstairs." She turned abruptly and went back to her bedroom.

The Irishman was exhausted, so Johnnie assisted him into the small room and deposited him in a chair. Then he locked the door and waited for Ben to recover his wind.

"Damme, b'y, I'm sorry!" sobbed the big man. "I kept a sharp lookout like ye warned me, but—"

"Never mind that," cut in Johnnie. "Tell me what happened?"

"Two cutters loaded wi' marines snuck up on either side o' us in the fog," Ben panted. "We didn't see 'em until they was mountin' the chains. Then 'twas too late. I tried to reach that bastard Quinn to dump him o'erboard, but they caught me."

"Caught you? How did you get away?"

Ben grimaced. "They asked for ye by nyme. 'W'ere's this Lord Johnnie?' they s'ys. 'In the cabin,' I tells 'em, 'waitin' wi' a loaded pistol fer ye bloody bastards!' So they makes me walk a'ead o' 'em like a shield. At the door o' the cabin, I shouts, 'Don't shoot, Lord Johnnie!' That mykes the curs back up a step, so I leaps into the cabin, slams the door in their fyces, an' dives off the sternwalk."

Johnnie whistled. "You *swam* in, Mick?"

"Aye, an' a bloody long swim 'twas! I clung to a log an' the flood tide carried me up the North River before I could fetch land. I sought to trade me fine garments to a yokel, but 'e was stubborn, so I 'ad to clout 'im to get 'is rags." Ben groaned heavily. "It 'appened afore noon, lad. I been all day gettin' 'ere!"

Johnnie took a couple of nervous turns around the room. The blow had fallen so swiftly he had difficulty grasping the full implications.

"The men were all taken, of course?"

"Every mither's son o' 'em," growled Ben. "Save the ancient and 'is oarsman. They'll be combin' the town fer ye, lad."

Johnnie thought furiously. Paradoxically enough, his brain worked clearer under the stress of certainty than it had when tortured by suspense.

"We'll have to save the men," he mused aloud. "After that—"

"To 'ell wi' the scum!" Ben protested hotly. "The bastards brought

it on themselves! Let's git out our ownsel's whilest the gitten' 's good."
He looked anxiously into Johnnie's eyes.

"Did ye sell the ship, b'y?"

Johnnie chuckled mirthlessly. "Perhaps it is fortunate I didn't." He
braced his shoulders. "You stay here and catch your wind, Mick. I'll be
back."

He went out and closed the door, then slowly mounted the stairs to
the bedroom. When he entered, he found the Duchess reclining in the
lolling-chair. He wasted a moment trying to read her expression, then
shrugged his shoulders.

"I'm afraid our deal about the *Eagle* is off, your Grace," he said
grimly. "The authorities have seized her."

To his astonishment, she burst into laughter. "Why, Johnnie, you
were really innocent! I thought you were trying to gull me!"

He frowned. "You knew about it?"

"Certainly! I told you nothing happens in this town that I don't
know about! The news reached the Governor's party by mid-afternoon.
Sit down, Johnnie."

He demurred. "I'd better leave, your Grace."

"*Sit down!*" she reiterated firmly. When he complied, she studied his
face. "Now let's stop this silly fencing, *Johnnie Rogue!*"

He started in consternation, but she motioned him back with a wave
of her hand.

"Don't lie to me, Johnnie! I suspected your identity when Monty
was telling about the hanging. What I can't understand, is why the
little chit took it so hard. Would you care to enlighten me on that
score?"

Johnnie shook his head. "I'd rather not," he said.

"As you wish. However, it was obvious she knows who you are." She
sniffed ironically, and continued: "I checked the records on the *Eagle*
as a matter of curiosity, and discovered that she left Portsmouth under
the command of Captain Joshua Bloodsmythe."

"Your Grace is extremely perspicacious."

"Perspicacious be damned! You can't operate a business such as mine
and be a gullible simpleton. I'm a shrewd old bitch, Johnnie."

Privately he was inclined to agree with her self-appraisal, but he
only smiled.

She watched him narrowly. "Lord Eden, the Governor, is very
anxious to make your acquaintance, *Lord* Johnnie," she observed.
"He'll pay well for the privilege."

Johnnie's nerves sounded the alarm which seemed to delight the old woman.

"Don't worry, my pet," she mocked him. "You're worth much more to me than mere blood-money. The remarkable thing about you, Johnnie, is the way you inspire loyalty. Brother God, how I envy you the trait!"

"Your Grace honors me," he countered warily.

"Do you know who betrayed you?"

He spread his hands. "The men had some harlots on board unbeknownst to me. I suppose—"

"What of Rodney Yew, Johnnie?"

He shot out of his chair as though she had touched a hidden spring, his self-control gone. It was incredible that Rodney Yew could have betrayed them, yet the very fact that this old harridan knew the name condemned him. The raucous laughter of the woman only added to his distress.

"Sit down, you fool!" she commanded dryly. "Yew hasn't talked, if that's what is troubling you. I mentioned him to illustrate my point about loyalty. The *Eagle's* log book, seized in the raid, showed that Yew had no part in the mutiny. Since he is a well-known and respected mariner, he was found and questioned. To the amazement of all concerned, he refused to talk, with the result that he has been imprisoned with the others."

Johnnie sank into his chair. "I regret that more than I can tell you," he murmured.

"I'm sure you do. The important thing now is—what are you going to do?"

He shook his head. "I don't know," he confessed.

"I like you, Johnnie—for God's sake don't ask me why! I want to help you. I could smuggle you and your man through the city gates in my carriage and perhaps you could make your way north. I have certain contacts in Canada—"

"I won't leave my men!" he interrupted.

"Brother God! What can you do about them? They're doomed!"

He collected his scattered wits. "Will you give me command of the *Able Lady,* your Grace?"

Her brows shot up. "That's impossible! You have no crew, Johnnie!"

"I'll supply the crew if your Grace will trust me with the vessel."

She pursed her lips, studying him quizzically. "Damn it, I'd like to help you," she repeated after a long pause, "but giving you my ship would be too risky, Johnnie. I cannot afford to involve myself in an actual crime."

"You needn't be involved," Johnnie argued desperately. "I can *steal* the vessel."

"H'mmn! I suppose you could steal it anyhow."

He managed a wry grin. "Not without your private consent."

"My Lord! What a bundle of contradictions!"

"The prime question is—will you trust me to play fair?"

Her breast rose and fell with excitement. "Hell's flame!" she gasped. "It never entered my head to doubt you!" She rose from her chair and crossed to the window. For a long time she stared into the darkness. Finally she swung around.

"All right, Johnnie—you can take her!" When he started to thank her, she held up her hand. "The onus shall be on your shoulders. If anything goes wrong, I'll swear you stole her."

"Agreed!"

She threw herself onto the chair. "You take my breath away, you devil!" she laughed. "How I wish I were thirty years younger! I'd go with you! Tell me—how will you manage it?"

He smiled. "That will have to be worked out, but it's better if you don't know, your Grace. I'll ask just one more favor. Can you have her moved out of the slip and anchored in the roadstead?"

"Surely. Where do you want her?"

"Astern of the *Eagle*."

"She'll go there on the next tide," promised the Duchess. Her eyes gleamed with mounting enthusiasm. "She's victualed and watered for a nine months' cruise."

Johnnie stood up. "Now to see his Excellency at the Fort."

"The Governor?" she gasped. "Have you lost your wits, man?"

He grinned. "I've been informed his Excellency empties the jails on occasion to supply crews for enterprising mariners."

The Duchess collapsed into hysterical laughter. "Oh, dear God!" she shrieked. "What colossal gall! Johnnie, Johnnie—haven't you a nerve in your body? Going to the Governor to get a crew—*you*, the most sought-after rogue of two continents!"

"At least his Excellency won't expect me," reasoned Johnnie with a smile.

"Brother God! I'll say he won't!" She became grave for a moment. "Are you serious about this insane move?"

"Never more serious, your Grace."

She chortled gleefully. "Then I shan't miss it! I shan't! You'll do the deed right here in my home, Johnnie!"

He didn't understand, and said so. But enlightenment had to wait until her spasm of laughter was over.

"Lord Eden is coming to a frolic I'm giving two days hence for the newly arrived officers and their wives. You shall attend and beard him here."

Johnnie frowned. "Your Grace's kindness is only exceeded by your recklessness, but the risk is too great and—"

"—and I wouldn't miss it for the world, you scamp," she cut in. "No, no, you can't refuse me! The Chumbleys have left for Fort Albany, and no one at the party will dream that the gallant Captain Scarlett is none other than the notorious Johnnie Rogue! Oh, Lord—what a scandal it will be!"

"I wasn't thinking of myself," protested Johnnie. "It is *you*, your Grace!"

"Pshaw! Don't worry, I'll denounce you fast enough if you're discovered! I always temper affection with expedience, Johnnie. So—it is settled. In the meantime, you and your man—"

"*Men*," he interrupted. "I have two even now waiting for me at the waterfront."

He admired the quickness of her grasp. "Excellent!" she agreed. "I'll dispatch a lackey to round them up. They can help move the *Able Lady* to her anchorage and stay aboard her."

Johnnie winced. "Suppose your servants talk?"

"They don't," she cackled sardonically. "I never take a man into my employ unless I have something on him, Johnnie."

He couldn't suppress a smile. "Was that why you offered *me* a command, your Grace?"

She shrugged. "Possibly. It is a sure way of securing loyalty. Not as good as your method, I confess, but the best I can manage." She rose to her feet. "Well, I'll get things started now, and later, you and I can discuss terms."

He tried to read her meaning, but she was already moving out of the room.

21

WHATEVER HER METHODS, THE DUCHESS OF TALLENTYRE WAS EXPE-
ditious. Ben Bottle was whisked into the harness room of the coach-
house where a lackey measured him for garments to be purchased in
the morning; while one servant hurried away with orders to the agent
for the shifting of the *Able Lady,* another carried a note of instructions
from Johnnie to Old Ames. Even the weather seemed to favor the adventure, for a light breeze sprang out of the west and swept the fog
out to sea.

About ten o'clock, when the tide was at maximum ebb, Johnnie and
the Duchess went up onto the roof to watch the moving of the sloop.
Although Johnnie was in no mood for beauty, he was awed by the
majesty of the night. He had the reverent sense of standing in a great
cathedral. In the central dome of sky, the stars shone with such brilliance he felt he could almost reach out and pluck one, while along
the western fringe, a cavalcade of rain clouds marshaled their forces.

Through the telescope, he watched the little craft edge out into the
stream. Her canvas blossomed like a night-blooming flower and she
slipped along as graceful as a swan. How the name fitted, he thought:
a *lady* to the core, and *able* too! He followed her course until she
rounded daintily into the wind abaft the clumsy *Eagle,* and dropped
her hook. She seemed to curtsy to him as her sails were furled, and
Johnnie bowed in return. Then he collapsed his glass, and turned to
the Duchess.

She was leaning back on her arms, staring at him. In the soft star-
light, with the wind caressing her hair, she looked breathtakingly
beautiful. Though he felt completely *en rapport* with her, he was
touched with melancholy. He saw in her the tragedy of successful
failure; a reflection, perhaps, of himself.

She reached out and took his hand. "Let's go down below, Johnnie,"
she suggested gently.

In silence they went down to her bedroom. She insisted on seating him in the lolling-chair, then she gave him a pipe. After that she curled up on a sofa, and waited for him to light up.

"Now," she said, with an attempt of lightness, "what are your plans?"

"Predicated on the winds of chance, your Grace. I'll doubtless start for the Indies."

She handed him a small black book. "This contains a list of my agents," she told him. "You can turn over your prizes, or at least my share, to these men. Keep a careful account and make them sign a receipt in duplicate. Send a copy to me and hold the other. I'll want fifty percent of the gross."

"Under the circumstances, that's very fair, your Grace."

"It's not fair; it's customary robbery. I'm an unscrupulous old vulture, Johnnie, yet I can't change, even toward you."

"There's no reason why you should," he countered.

She closed her eyes and leaned her head back against the cushions. "I'm afraid there is," she whispered. "Dear Lord, what a rotten thing life is! We come all ignorant and unprepared to the fork in the road so early, and by the time we have sense enough to realize the folly, we have galloped too far to turn back."

"But you've had a full life!"

She shook her head quickly. "Full enough to leave me aching with regrets." She sat up abruptly. "Johnnie—that day we met, you told me you were seeking wealth. That's too vague a term. Can't you visualize your goal?"

He turned the question over in his mind. "I thought I could," he admitted slowly. "Now I'm not so sure."

"And what did you think it was?" she urged.

He found himself embarrassed. "It sounds inane, Reggie, yet my objective seemed to be summed up in the word *gentleman*."

She laughed without mirth. "Like Monty Chumbley and his ilk, perhaps? Good God, Johnnie, even Monty envies *you*. Yes, he does; it showed unwittingly in the way he talked about your conduct at Tyburn. Laddie, you're chasing an illusion; you remind me of a wolf wanting to be a lap-dog. Can't you realize how bored our wolf would be if he were deprived of adventure and forced to lie idle on a silk cushion, expected to do cute tricks for some pampered female?"

He forced a smile. "What you mean is—once a rogue, always a rogue?"

"That is only a half-truth, an over-simplification," she said with a trace of impatience. "The road of life leaves as strong an imprint on the man as the man leaves on the road, Johnnie. We are all the fruits of our experiences. You can't change that."

"A bitter truth," he agreed.

She studied him a long while in silence. "That girl has altered your outlook, hasn't she?"

"Let's say she clarified it, your Grace."

"Clarified be damned! You're sick with desire. The point is—what are you going to do about her?"

"I don't know."

"Well, for heaven's sake, make up your mind!" she cried, rising. "Now get out of my sight! I don't mind telling you, the little bitch makes me jealous as hell! I wish I hadn't invited her to the frolic!"

The Tallentyre mansion was a glittering beacon toward which a light chaise was drawn by two spirited bays down the carriage-lined street on the night of the ball. A casual glance would have indicated nothing unusual about the equipage, save, perhaps, the ludicrous appearance of the red-headed giant in the coachman's box, who in borrowed livery resembled a dressed-up gorilla, and the fact that the horses were unnecessarily fast and powerful for so light a rig. Even the slightly bored-looking gentleman, garbed in flaming scarlet, languishing among the cushions, appeared conventional enough.

However, a closer inspection would have aroused the beholder's curiosity, if not alarm. The battered weather-beaten features of the driver wore an expression blended of desperation and consternation, and beneath his coat, his belt bristled with pistols. By way of contrast, the sharp face of the modish gentleman reflected sardonic amusement. Yet even he carried primed pistols under his scarlet coat.

As they came within sight of their destination, the giant in the box turned around for one last appeal to reason.

"B'Jesus, Johnnie, 'tis madness!" he groaned. "Let's turn back afore 'tis too late?"

The young gentleman flicked a lawn kerchief at his driver.

"Tut, tut, my good fellow!" he drawled. "Be good enough to stay in character."

The Irishman sighed. "Me knees are rattlin' like dice in a box."

Lord Johnnie grinned in anticipation. The old Duchess was looking forward to a scandal, was she? Well, he'd give her one never to be forgotten. Since he had not seen her all day, he had told her nothing of his plans. He had left in mid-afternoon, having deemed it advisable to put in a belated appearance as a chance guest rather than risk compromising his hostess by being on hand when the first visitors arrived. He suspected that by now she would have decided that he had lost his nerve and fled. He laughed softly.

Ben brought the equipage to a pause before the house and lumbered down from his box to assist Johnnie. Johnnie tucked his kerchief up his sleeve and glanced around him. Through the open windows he could see the guests milling about, and hear the music of a stringed quartet.

"Holy Mither!" groaned Ben. "I'd fight a regiment o' King's Guardsmen wi' tooth an' claw afore I'd go in there, rape me if else!"

"Every man to his taste," grinned Johnnie. "Now, look you, Mick—stand alert. Are your pistols primed?"

"Aye, Johnnie!"

"Good, but don't be premature. If I come a-running, flight may be preferable to fight."

"Me very thought," grumbled Ben. "I'd take me flight now an' me fight anon."

Johnnie laughed grimly and strutted up the walk. Peculiarly enough, he felt little reluctance to enter the house. Only one qualm disturbed him—he had been informed that the frigate *Tiger* had come into the harbor for revictualing and rewatering, and a meeting now with young Lieutenant Ayers would be awkward. But it was a chance he had to take, and Lord Johnnie was accustomed to taking chances.

The course was studded with liveried lackeys as he mounted the circular staircase to deposit his cloak, hat and cane. From the landing, the lower floor, crowded with guests in a dazzling panoply of blue and scarlet uniforms and vari-colored silks, was brilliant as a bed of pansies. For just a transient moment, he had a twinge of nervousness. Johnnie Rogue of Whitefriars was not habituated to fraternizing with titled lords, save behind a mask and pistol on lonely heaths. Yet when he paused before a French mirror to adjust his cravat and periwig, the image satisfied him and his jauntiness returned.

Retracing his steps to the lower floor, he sauntered into the drawing room. A serving man came up with a tray of refreshments, then the Duchess herself floated across the floor toward him.

She was radiant! Her gown was of pale blue lutestring, trimmed with lace in festooned falbalas and edged with gimp. She had powdered and restrained her wind-blown hair with strings of pearls. Only her eyes remained as wild and untamed as always.

"Where have you been, you fiend?" she hissed out of the corner of her mouth, then loudly: "So sweet of you to come, Captain Scarlett!"

He realized abruptly he was staring, so he bent over her hand in the French fashion, and touched it with his lips.

"Your *Majesty!*" he murmured. "You blind me!"

Her eyes sparkled mischievously. "I'll rape you if you give me any more of that blarney!" she whispered. "Brother God, you're handsome enough to cozen a queen. I feared lest you had deserted me."

"Your servant, Madonna!"

She brushed him with her fan. "Enough of that, sir! Now bestir yourself and titillate some of these bored bitches, but if you attempt to leave the room with one of them I'll . . . I'll . . ." She burst into laughter. "Oh, hell, I'll come after you!"

"'Pon my honor, your Grace, 'twould be deserting the sun for a candle!" he swore gallantly. Then, softly aside: "Where will I find his Excellency?"

She shook her head. "Lord Eden is in the other room, but don't hurry things, you fool! I'll present you at the first opportunity. Do be careful Johnnie! Your name is on everyone's lips, and my old heart is pounding like a wornout pump!" She favored him with a bantering smile, and glided away to greet another arrival.

Johnnie looked about him. Most of the guests had lately arrived from England, and it was highly probable that some of them had attended his near-hanging at Tyburn, as had General Chumbley. In the hubbub of conversation, he heard the names of the *Eagle* and Johnnie Rogue bandied around several times, which merely tickled his sense of the dramatic. He found the women staring at him, but their glances were admiring rather than suspicious. But as he scrutinized the other young fops fluttering and strutting amongst the ladies, he suffered a sense of depression. Was this to what he had aspired? Bitterly he recalled the Duchess's analogy of the wolf and the lap-dog, and recognized its truth. These vain little peacocks impressed Johnnie as being vapid and callow, and left him with a disillusionment that bordered on regret. As Reggie had so adroitly phrased it, he had been carried too far along the wrong road for turning.

Now the stringed quartette struck up a waltz, and he was about to ask a girl to dance, when Reggie appeared at his elbow.

"Now, God help you!" she whispered. "I'm going to present you to his Excellency!"

Lord Chauncey Eden wore his rank without ostentation. A tall bony

man, seeming even more so by virtue of an exceeding slenderness, he
was to Johnnie the epitome of elegance. He was dressed in white silk,
laced with gold braid, and with his white tie wig and pale visaged
face, appeared strangely ethereal. His was a remarkable countenance.
A splendid forehead sloped gracefully to bushy gray brows which
shadowed a pair of somber blue eyes. The nose, in harmony with the
rest of him, was excessively long, while beneath it was a wide generous
mouth with a protruding nether-lip which made him appear perpetu-
ally thoughtful. He had reached the age when it was no longer necessary to assume a supercilious imperiousness to establish his position, so
his demeanor was one of gentle melancholy. Johnnie was impressed.

After the formal presentation, he smiled at Johnnie and inquired
if he had come over with the convoy.

Johnnie glanced briefly at the men surrounding the Governor, then
shook his head.

"No, your Grace. I left my ship in Philadelphia and journeyed overland to seek an old shipmate who I believed to be in New York. I was
advised to lay my case before her Grace"—he smiled at the Duchess
who was staring at him apprehensively—"who is so well acquainted
here, but alas, she had never heard of Rodney Yew."

Lord Eden's eyes kindled with interest. "Rodney Yew!" he said.
"Might I ask what business you had with him?"

Johnnie bowed. "Your servant, my lord. This doughty mariner is a
peerless navigator and as I heard he might be available, I came to offer
him a first lieutenancy on my ship. Would it be presumptuous to inquire if your Grace perchance knows where he can be found?"

The Governor grunted. "You can find him in prison," he said
moodily.

Johnnie gasped unbelievingly.

"Your Grace jests!" he dared. "Else it cannot be the same man! Why,
my lord, the Rodney Yew of whom I speak is a model all English seamen would do well to emulate! May I ask the charge against the man?"

Lord Eden rested his chin on his tapering fingers.

"Yew was involved in a mutiny—" he began, but Johnnie interrupted with laughter.

" 'Pon my honor, your Grace had me worried for the nonce, but 'tis
plain we speak not of the same Rodney Yew. My friend, who was on
the East Indiaman *Eagle,* would have cut off his arm rather than go
against his King!"

Johnnie heard the gasps and resentful mutterings of his audience at

mention of the *Eagle*. The Duchess had paled perceptibly, but Lord
Eden's face remained imperturbable. If he found Johnnie's brashness
offensive, he gave no sign.

"Rodney Yew himself took no part in the mutiny," he told Johnnie.
"It was engineered and executed by a notorious scoundrel from London
known as Johnnie the Rogue. But for reasons quite unfathomable,
Yew refuses to give testimony against the mutineers."

Johnnie arched his brows and turned to the Duchess. Her features
were a study in consternation.

"Do you hear that, your Grace?" he appealed to her. "Did not Sir
Montague swear the rogue had been slain?"

The Duchess fluttered her fan before her face. "He said something
of the kind," she managed breathlessly.

"So goes the rumor," admitted the Governor. "Yet the prisoners
apparently believe their leader to be the infamous scoundrel. The
guards report having overheard them say that Lord Johnnie would
liberate them. I must confess a morbid curiosity to meet the knave."

"From your Grace's remarks, I gather the dog has not been appre-
hended?"

Lord Eden smiled wryly. "Our dog-catchers have not proved efficient."

Johnnie bowed. "A thousand pardons, your Grace, for my imperti-
nence," he apologized. "My concern for a valued friend made me forget myself. I only wish I might be of service to your Grace, if in part
for selfish reasons, for I am loath to abandon such a loyal mariner
when His Majesty so sorely needs his like." He made a leg. "Your
humble servant, my lord."

He proffered his arm to the Duchess and retired. The instant they
were out of hearing, she turned on him.

"You damned hellion!" she raged. "Are you trying to commit
suicide? Brother God, I came nigh to fainting at your gall!"

"Faintness becomes your Grace," grinned Johnnie.

"Dear Lord!" she gasped. "What did you hope to gain by that display of impudence?"

Johnnie laughed softly. "I planted a seed in fallow ground. Soon I
shall pluck the fruit."

Her face showed real distress. "Johnnie, in heaven's name, take care!
Eden is no fool! He'll have you dangling in the Commons if you slip."

"*If* I slip. Has your Grace lost confidence in her captain?"

The Duchess bit her lip. "No, damn you, your cockiness is contagious. But I warn you, Johnnie—if you're unmasked, I can do nothing for you!"

Johnnie bowed again. "I'm so deeply in your debt already, I could ask no more."

When she left him, he strolled casually about the rooms, admiring the ladies and taking measure of the men. He classified the latter into three groupings: innocuous, uncertain, and dangerous. He was hovering within sight of the hallway when, about eleven of the clock, Leanna arrived with Sir Clarence Laughton. Johnnie heaved a long sigh of relief. It was time to act.

As Leanna and Laughton started up the stairs, Johnnie walked quickly into the room where Lord Eden was chatting with friends. He approached boldly, and bowed.

"Your Grace," he begged, "could I have a word of utmost importance with you?"

The Governor frowned, and for one awful moment, Johnnie feared a rebuff. But he excused himself, and stepped aside with Johnnie.

"Well, young man?"

Johnnie appeared to hesitate. "My lord, being but a blunt-spoken mariner, I find myself at a loss to express my sentiments with proper address. I know naught of legal procedure, yet I make bold to claim a knowledge of men. If this Rodney Yew is the man I seek, then I'm positive I can learn from him what he knows of this Johnnie Rogue!"

Lord Eden fingered his gaunt cheeks. "You have something in mind, Captain?"

"Only this, sire—with your Grace's permission, I beg leave to reason with him."

"To what purpose?"

"If I understood your Grace's meaning," Johnnie said, "Rodney Yew himself is guilty of no crime, save that of silence. I but hope—" He paused, as if afraid to continue.

"Go on, young man," the Governor urged kindly.

" 'Tis my thought, sire, that if, perchance, Rodney Yew could inform us where this Johnnie Rogue is hiding, you might release Yew to me. My need for a navigator is desperate enough to risk your Grace's displeasure by my suggestion."

Lord Eden smiled thinly. "My displeasure is not so easily incurred, young man. I have no objection to your talking with Yew. As for his release—I'd gladly trade a dozen like him for a meeting with this elusive rogue."

"Your promise gives me heart, my lord!"

"It's worth a try," grunted the Governor, starting to turn away. "See me at the Fort tomorrow."

Johnnie's face showed dismay. "Tomorrow!" he gasped, so strickenly that Eden paused. "My lord, that is impossible! I must leave at sun-up by horse to reach Philadelphia in time to sail in convoy!" Johnnie's voice turned pleading. "If your Grace would but give me a note to the gaoler, I could see Yew at once, and possibly put the finger on Johnnie Rogue tonight!"

Eden scowled, while Johnnie held his breath, then burst out laughing.

" 'Od's blood, sir," he chuckled. "You're an impetuous young man! However, if you're willing to abandon so much pulchritude to visit a prison, I'll not gainsay you. If I can tear my aide-de-camp away from the ladies—" He looked around for that officer.

This was something Johnnie had not foreseen, and it left him speechless with chagrin. But not for long.

"If your Grace please," he protested hastily, "there is no need to disturb your aide. Under the circumstances, I should prefer to make my visit as private and unobtrusive as possible."

Lord Eden shrugged in a manner that indicated his patience was running out. "As you wish," he said shortly, "but I cannot tarry longer. My friends—"

Johnnie dared one more interruption. "Her Grace has quill and paper in the study, my lord—" He edged toward the small room adjoining.

The Governor stalked inside. Johnnie whisked a square of the Duchess of Tallentyre's crested stationery on the desk before his Excellency was seated. With a grunt, the Governor scrawled a brief note granting "Captain Scarlett" permission to interrogate "the prisoner Rodney Yew" in private, and signed it "Eden" in bold strokes.

While he was thus engaged, Lord Johnnie surreptitiously slipped several blank sheets of the same stationery into his pocket.

22

WHEN HERMAN VAN HOEG UNLOCKED HIS DOOR IN ANSWER TO THE urgent poundings, he was startled to find Johnnie standing on the *stoep*. Before he could open his mouth, Johnnie brushed past him into the print shop and closed the door.

"Herr Hoeg—I have a job for you!"

The Hog blinked behind his spectacles and slowly withdrew his turtle's head into the shell of his back. The wavering candle in his hand made him appear more inhuman than ever. He wore no wig, and a nightcap stood perched on his bald head.

"The hour is late—!" he objected gutturally.

But Johnnie was already moving into the small rear office so The Hog padded after him, and lighted the oil lamp. When he had seated himself at the desk, Johnnie laid the Governor's note before him, with four blank sheets of crested stationery.

In emphatic yet lucid language, Johnnie explained what he wanted. The Hog crouched over and peered at the handwriting, then settled back.

"*Impossible!*" he croaked.

Johnnie's smile was sinister. "And why so?" he asked softly.

Van Hoeg spread his hands. "God's death, man, it would be worth my neck to have a share in this business! 'Tis the rankest folly, and certain disaster!"

"In which event it will be my neck, not yours."

The Hog wagged his head. "I won't touch it," he insisted, drawing back from the papers. "The whole town is seething with rumor and spies. Every catch-poll and thief-taker is after the blood-money offered, for 'tis said Johnnie the Rogue himself is in New York. Nay, nay— I'll have no part in it!"

Johnnie dropped his hand to his pocket. "Not for gold?" he queried gently.

"Not for gold!" echoed the forger.

Johnnie leaned over the desk and pointed a pistol at the old man's head.

"If this won't change your mind," he urged quietly, "at least it will *open* it!"

The Hog blinked owlishly at the weapon, then raised his eyes to his visitor. Lighted from below, Johnnie's face appeared that of a bird of prey. As Van Hoeg stared, what color there was drained out of his features.

"Mein Gott in himmel!" he choked. *"You* are Johnnie Rogue!"

"Time is short, Herr Hoeg," smiled Johnnie. "Both your time and mine."

"It's suicide if I do it!" groaned Van Hoeg.

"There is some doubt about that if you do," Johnnie conceded. "None, if you don't. Now have at it, maestro. *Quickly!"*

The Hog's hands trembled as he reached for a quill, but under Johnnie's calm dictation, he steadied down. Even so, it was a long time before the order was faked to Lord Johnnie's satisfaction.

On his return to the chaise, Johnnie found that Ben Bottle had changed from his coachman's livery to the garb of a mariner. In a fine blue coat and cocked hat, and his mop of red hair smothered under a black wig, he characterized the typical swaggering sea-dog.

"Very impressive," approved Johnnie. "Now for the Fort."

Ben grimaced. "Damme, Johnnie, I've bats flappin' aroun' in me belly till me bladder aches!"

"You'll lose that when we get to sea, Mick."

Ben cackled without mirth. *"If* we get to sea," he amended, and climbed into his box.

At this hour, New York had the appearance of a deserted town. Save for the croaking of frogs and the clump of the horses' hooves, they moved through a vacuum of silence toward Fort George. Johnnie relaxed in his seat, swaying effortlessly with the motion of the chaise. He gave no thought to the coming encounter but concerned himself solely with the weather. Therein lay the only danger over which he had no control. At the moment, the wind came lightly out of the northwest, but if it died—? Johnnie shrugged.

A couple of startled soldiers tumbled out of the sentry-box as Ben brought the chaise to a halt before the main gate. Johnnie lolled indolently among the cushions, and commanded them in the Governor's name to summon the captain of the guard. As one of the sentries bustled off on this errand, Ben climbed off his perch and leaned against the carriage.

In a remarkably short time, the officer appeared. He was a brisk little Irishman named O'Regan, and he read the note Johnnie handed him with frank amazement. As he raised his eyes, Johnnie held up a restraining hand.

"Be so good as to remove your men from hearing," he said sternly. "As the note cautions you, Captain, this business is extremely *sub rosa!*"

O'Regan was impressed. He motioned his men away, and turned back.

" 'Tis astounding, sir!" he stammered. "I had such emphatic orders only this afternoon that—"

"By the powers, Captain, do you question his Excellency's discretion?" flared Johnnie, straightening belligerently.

"Not so!" protested O'Regan. "I'm . . . I'm merely flabbergasted!"

Johnnie sprang out of the chaise with a laugh. "Aye, and you've a right to be, Captain," he said pleasantly. "Your incredulity augurs well for our enterprise." He dropped his voice to a confidential level. "More important people than you are going to be amazed at this night's work. If you but knew the full import of it—!" He dropped one eye in a knowing wink. "Come now—attend me personally, for the fewer ears that hear about it, the fewer mouths will talk. When the whole truth is divulged, I promise 'twill be a story your grandchildren will whisper about."

"That be the God's own trufe!" offered Ben fervently.

O'Regan guided them into the prison—a stone square with cells on three sides above which ran a cat-walk for the guards. Standing in the entrance, Johnnie surveyed it critically before turning to O'Regan.

"Have the men assembled in the square," he told the officer. "I shall address them from the rail overhead."

"They're a surly lot!" O'Regan muttered.

Johnnie snorted. "I'll take that out of them, never doubt!"

O'Regan shook his head admiringly and gave the orders. By the time he had led Ben and Johnnie up to the cat-walk, the men were stumbling sleepily in the square below. Johnnie rested his hands on the wrought-iron railing and stared at them, then beckoned O'Regan to bring the lanthorn close enough to illuminate his figure.

"Now, men," Johnnie began quietly, "I am going to—"

To his dismay, he was interrupted by a wild shout from one of the men.

"Gawd A'mighty! I tolt ye all Lord Johnnie—!"

"*Silence!*" thundered Johnnie in a voice that brought instant quiet. "I'll hang the next man who breathes that dog's name!" He leaned over the rail, and dropped his voice to a sinister sternness. "Now I'm here to offer you scoundrels an opportunity you don't deserve. I sail this night on a dangerous mission and need a crew. Your choice is this: you can stay here and hang with your Johnnie Rogue, when they catch him, or"—he paused to lend emphasis to his words—"*you can ship at once with Captain Scarlett!*"

There came a startled gasp, then an old tar called facetiously, "We'll sail wi' 'e, Captain Scarlett!"

Johnnie frowned at the speaker. "By God, you'll change that tone, my man!" he retorted sharply. "I'm a lamb of kindness if you behave yourselves. But give me any insolence, and, by God, you'll find me a *rogue!*"

Even Ben gasped at this direct quotation from Bloodsmythe's declamation. O'Regan obviously mistook the reaction, and nodded approvingly. Johnnie casually turned his back on the crowd.

"Now, Captain," he said clearly, "if you'll be so kind as to herd these cattle into boats, as his Grace has ordered, I'll be on my way."

"Won't you require guards, sir?" gasped O'Regan.

Johnnie chuckled. "Only to the landing. Once aboard ship, my shepherds will care for the flock."

O'Regan sighed and lighted the way below. Johnnie lounged in the doorway as the men were marched past him. Their expressions ran the gamut from shocked bewilderment to smirking satisfaction. In order to keep O'Regan diverted, Johnnie kept up a running fire of comment.

"Scurvy dogs!" he grumbled haughtily. "God's life, Eden spoke more highly of them. Bah! They'd hardly give a good show on the gallows! What think you, Mister Murphy?" This to Ben.

"Scurvy ain't the word for 'em, yer ludship," snorted the Irishman, adding, with a twinkle in his eye: "They'll sing a different turn w'en we gets 'em aboard, I vow."

Johnnie smiled. "There's a bucko for you, Captain," he remarked to O'Regan. "Mark him well, for I doubt not you'll hear more of him."

Ben's face purpled, and O'Regan laughed. "Aye, sir, Mister Murphy looks very capable."

The twisting queue of men, flanked by soldiers, coiled off into the shadows of the parade ground. Johnnie turned to see how many were yet to come when he found himself face to face with Rodney Yew.

Yew stopped so short the following man bumped against him. A soldier lowered his musket to prod him along, but Johnnie gestured him away. Johnnie stared into the steel-gray eyes, now bleak with hostility.

"Stab me!" he exclaimed. "This is no common seaman!" He looked to O'Regan for some explanation.

The captain nodded. "He was the navigator of the *Eagle,* sir. If you don't desire him, I can—"

"Oh, I'll take him," said Johnnie. "It would be foolish to leave him here to face the music while the others go free. Yet methinks I'll mention his case to his Excellency." He jerked his head for Yew to continue his march. "I'll talk with you later, my man."

Yew gave him a cold stare and strode after the others.

When the last man had passed through the gates, Johnnie, Ben and O'Regan followed them to the landing. The guards were already loading the first arrivals into a government cutter lying alongside the quay. Johnnie stood apart from the others, brooding thoughtfully, then turned to O'Regan.

"Be good enough to have that navigator called aside," he requested. "I'd like a word with him privately."

Yew was brought over, and Johnnie took him out of hearing.

"I deeply regret—" began Johnnie quietly, but Yew cut him short.

"Belay that gab!" he growled. " 'Tis my just deserts for having any truck with a damned scoundrel like you!"

"Hear me," urged Johnnie. "Scoundrel I may be, yet no innocent man has ever suffered for my crimes. Nor will you. Look now—get the men aboard and have the brigantine readied for sea. Instruct Old Ames to meet me instanter at the usual landing. Then you are at liberty to go ashore. Meanwhile, I'll go back and clear you with the Governor."

Yew glared at him. "*You'll* clear me? By the powers, his Excellency would give a deal to see you, sir!"

"His very words," grinned Johnnie. "I have his promise that if he can set eyes on Johnnie Rogue, Rodney Yew goes free. You have mine, Mister Yew." He left Yew glaring at him, and returned to the two Irishmen.

After pointing out the position of the *Able Lady* to the coxswain of the cutter, he thanked O'Regan for his timely assistance, then nodded to Ben Bottle.

"Now, Mister Murphy, we shall return to her Grace's."

Ben, having started for the boat, swung on him in alarm.

"Holy Mither! Ye ain't serious—"

"*Mister Murphy!* You forget yourself!" roared Johnnie. "By God, sir, another such outburst and I'll revoke your commission!"

Ben quaked. "But, Cap'n," he implored, casting a nervous glance at the astonished O'Regan, "time be short an'—"

"Time is never too short for the amenities," Johnnie snapped. "I have not yet taken leave of her Grace, nor have I advised my Lord Eden of Captain O'Regan's magnificent cooperation."

O'Regan flushed with pleasure. "Oh, thank you, sir! 'Twill be an honor to be brought to his Grace's attention."

Ben glowered. "B'Jesus, ye'll be brought to 'is attention, never fear!"

Muttering ominously, he followed Johnnie and O'Regan back to the chaise and climbed onto his perch. When Johnnie had seated himself luxuriously, O'Regan gave him a brisk salute.

"May I wish you luck on your venture, sire, whatever it may be?" he offered.

Johnnie merely smiled, but Ben snarled: "Aye, an' 'tis bloody certain we'll be needin' it!" He slapped the horses with the reins and they started off.

Once out of sight of the Fort, however, he slowed and swung around.

"Fer the luv o' 'eaven, lad—"

Johnnie laughed at him. "Mick, you lack imagination!"

"The 'ell I do! I can only too bloody well imagine w'at the Governor'll do w'en he learns 'ow ye gulled 'im!"

Johnnie waved a languid hand. "And would you deprive me of the pleasure, man? Tut-tut—drive along! We've less than an hour before turn of tide."

Leaving his cloak and hat in the chaise, Johnnie entered the house. The party seemed much as he had left it earlier. As he started into the parlor, he was disconcerted to find Colonel Laughton standing with his back to the doorway. Johnnie beat a hasty retreat and continued down the hallway toward the dining room—just in time to encounter the Duchess herself.

She gasped at sight of him. "Brother God, Johnnie! What's happened? I thought you had gone for good!"

"Without taking leave of your Grace?"

She glanced apprehensively around to see if they had been observed,

then shoved Johnnie into a pantry opposite the dining room and
closed the door.

"Have you lost your wits?" she cried distraughtly. "Eden told me you
had gone to the prison!"

He bowed. "I did, your Grace. My crew is even now aboard the *Able
Lady,* readying her for sea."

"Then in God's name—why did you return here, of all places?"

"To bid your Grace good-bye."

She gave that impatient snort he had come to know so well.

"Then for God's sake, do it like a man, not a lick-spittle! Here—!"
She moved toward him, and he took her into his arms. Her full soft
mouth had a flexibility that sent his head a-reeling.

She swayed away from him and massaged her forehead with her
fingers.

"What now, Johnnie?" she whispered weakly.

Johnnie collected his scattered senses. "I'll entice his Excellency
into your study. When you see us enter, come in alone. Leave the
talking to me."

He slipped into the hallway and cut through the dining room. Lord
Eden was chatting with three dowagers when Johnnie came up. Eden
looked at him, and smiled.

"Well, Captain, what fortune?"

Johnnie bowed.

"Excellent, my lord! Could I beg your Grace's indulgence to speak
with me privily? I dare hope your Grace will be pleasantly amazed at
my success!"

Lord Eden took his leave of the ladies, and strode into the study.
Johnnie followed and shut the door.

The Governor showed a trace of impatience. "Have you learned the
whereabouts of Johnnie Rogue?"

"Aye, your Excellency, yet—" He paused as the Duchess swept into
the room.

She backed up a step at the look on Lord Eden's face, but Johnnie
moved swiftly behind her and closed the door again.

"Do join us, your Grace," he said. "I have news of import which
your Grace should hear, though I trust it will go no further for the
nonce."

Eden glanced at the woman. "This remarkable young man claims
to have located the infamous Johnnie Rogue, Reggie."

"Brother God!" breathed the Duchess, staring at Johnnie in horror.

Johnnie bowed slightly. "'Pon my honor," he acknowledged. "Yet I am constrained to beg two favors of your Excellency. The first concerns Rodney Yew. He took no part—"

"I have already told you I'd release Yew if you produced Johnnie Rogue," Eden cut in shortly.

"For which I thank your Grace," Johnnie continued blandly. "However, that is in the nature of a pardon, and is therefore inadequate. Rodney Yew persuaded the so-called Johnnie Rogue to abandon a plan to sell the cargo on the grounds it was sorely needed in America. It was for this reason Yew stayed with the ship instead of escaping with the other loyal men. He should be honored, not pardoned!"

Eden drummed his fingers on the desk. "I presume you received that version from Yew?" he said dryly.

"On the contrary, your Grace, it comes from the lips of Johnnie Rogue."

Lord Eden half rose from his chair. "You've actually *seen* the knave!" he exclaimed.

"One moment, my lord!" Johnnie said so calmly that the Governor sank back. "There is a second consideration. Aye, I've seen Johnnie Rogue. Yet this man's reputation being what it is, my very life would be forfeit if I did not take measures to protect myself."

"'Od's blood!" snapped Eden. "You shall have my protection!"

"That alleviates my anxiety, in part," said Johnnie. "However, as I suspect the rogue has friends in this very house, for our mutual safety, I ask your promise not to leave this room until five minutes after I do."

"Damn your impudence!" blazed Eden, rising.

"Do you realize what you're doing?" gasped the Duchess.

"Perfectly, your Grace," smiled Johnnie imperturbably. "It is a small thing to ask in return for such vital information."

"All right, all right!" fumed the Governor. "You have my word. Now, in God's name—where is the dog!"

Johnnie slipped his hand in the front of his coat and bowed low. "Standing humbly before your Grace," he murmured.

His quiet manner as much as the announcement itself shocked Lord Eden speechless. The Duchess of Tallentyre whispered, "Oh, my God!" and sagged limply into a chair.

Eden recovered his voice. "By heaven, I'll—" He made a move for the door—to find himself staring into the business end of a pistol held in Johnnie's competent hand.

"Need I remind your Grace of your promise?" he said gently. "It would embarrass me to be forced to shoot so esteemed a noble."

Eden appeared on the verge of strangling with fury, then unexpectedly blew his wind in a brittle laugh and backed onto a settee.

"Checkmated, by God!" he grunted ruefully. He stared at the other with growing interest. "So you are really Johnnie the Rogue?"

"I confess that doubtful honor, your Grace."

Lord Eden proved he had a sense of humor by a dry smile. "For unmitigated temerity, this beats anything I've ever witnessed! You realize, of course, you cannot escape?"

Johnnie returned the smile. "A moot question, my lord." He glanced at the clock. "Much as I would enjoy debating the matter with your Grace, time passes and I must take my leave." He bowed to the astounded Duchess.

"Your Grace," he told her softly, "I beg your forgiveness for the ill manner in which I have presumed on your hospitality. I came to you a total stranger and you accepted me on the strength of false references. I deeply regret the necessity of the deception."

"You had better go!" she managed faintly.

Johnnie backed over to the door. "My lord! My lady!" he murmured, and backed out of the room.

For a moment Johnnie paused with his back against the closed door. Outwardly, his demeanor was unruffled, and if his heart beat slightly faster than usual, his gun was in his pocket. He was reasonably confident that Eden would keep his word, yet there was a possibility, aye, even a probability, that one of his courtiers would enter the study in search of him. Johnnie smiled grimly, and looked around for Leanna.

He saw her finally through a break in the crowd—standing near the arch to the hallway. He pushed his way to her side.

"Leanna—!"

She swung around in terror. Laughton was but a few feet away, chatting with another officer. Leanna's face was chalky.

"Please don't talk to me!" she whispered. "If Sir Clarence sees you—!" The very thought froze her tongue.

"Unfortunately there isn't time for considering Sir Clarence, my lady. The Governor has just learned my identity, so I must leave slightly faster than expected. I'm taking you with me."

Her eyes widened. "*No!*"

Laughton turned. When he saw Johnnie, his pendulous cheeks crimsoned with anger. He stalked over, glaring.

"What's this?" he demanded hotly.

"You are laboring under a misapprehension, my lord," Johnnie said quietly. "I was not addressing you."

Sir Clarence's eyes blazed. "I' faith, who is this man, Leanna?" he bellowed, loud enough to make them the cynosure of every eye in the parlor.

Panic-stricken, Leanna laid a restraining hand on his arm.

"Please, Clarence!" she sobbed. "Not here—!"

Laughton shook off her hand. "I repeat—who is this scoundrel?"

The answer came from a most unexpected quarter.

" 'Slife! He's the knave who seized the *Eagle!* It's *Johnnie Rogue!*"

In the sudden hush that followed this proclamation, Lieutenant Ayers shoved his way through the startled guests. Leanna uttered a frightened bleat and sagged in a faint.

Johnnie caught her with one hand and produced his pistol in the other.

"Stand where you are!" he cautioned.

The deliberate softness of his voice was more menacing than the weapon. Ayers stumbled back a step, while Laughton seemed rooted to the floor.

"Out of respect for her Grace," Johnnie went on, smiling, "I would regret the necessity of killing one of you here." He raised his voice: *"Mick!"*

The front door banged open and footsteps pounded up the hallway. Then the gargantuan figure of Ben Bottle loomed in the archway, two cocked pistols in his hairy paws.

"Aye, Johnnie!" he roared. "Who d'ye want shot fust?"

Johnnie chuckled delightedly. Anticipation might reduce the brawny Irishman to terror, but action was his meat.

"This lady requires fresh air," he told Ben. "Carry her tenderly, on your life!"

Ben hesitated but an instant, then belting one pistol, he lifted Leanna gently into his arms. Sir Clarence choked an oath, but Johnnie relieved Ben of the other pistol, and warned him back.

"On your way out, Mick, put the door key on the outside."

As Ben moved away with the girl, Laughton found his voice.

"By God, you damned blackguard, I'll—" he blustered, but Johnnie prodded him in the stomach with the muzzle of one weapon.

"I suggest you all concern yourselves with the condition of his Excellency and her Grace. I left them in the study."

The implication impelled every eye toward the closed door behind them. When they turned back—Lord Johnnie had vanished.

23

THAT MAD DASH THROUGH THE DESERTED STREETS OF NEW YORK RE-
minded Johnnie of his flight from Tyburn. A different town, a different girl at his side, but the same old thrill. Braced against the wild
rolling of the coach, steadying the limp body of Leanna in his arms,
he decided this was the very quintessence of living. He had been a fool
heretofore, but that was over now. No more futile dreams of being a
gentleman, no more posing. From this point on, he was going to concentrate on being Johnnie the Rogue.

The spontaneously formed pursuit was soon immunized by Ben
Bottle's masterly driving, and before the girl had fully recovered consciousness, he had fought the lathered horses to a halt at the Battery
landing. As Johnnie sprang to the ground, Old Ames appeared out
of the darkness with a hooded hurricane-lamp. Johnnie favored him
with a grin and carried the girl into the waiting boat while Ben lashed
the horses on their way. Seconds later, the boat shoved off.

Johnnie gauged the wind, and sighed with satisfaction. His fabled
luck was holding. The unexpected appearance of young Ayers had
temporarily disconcerted him; it meant the *Tiger* would soon be
alerted. But he reasoned it would take considerable time for the authorities to learn what ship he was on, after which Lieutenant Ayers would
have to be rowed out to the frigate and communicate the intelligence
to his captain. By the time all that could be accomplished, Johnnie and
the *Able Lady* would be bowling through the Narrows.

A stirring of the girl warned Johnnie she was recovering her senses.
He chuckled and adjusted the cloak which he had hastily thrown
around her shoulders.

She straightened abruptly and stared about her. On the thwart
facing her, Ben and Old Ames, grinning like gargoyles, drew lustily on
their oars. Behind them sat an equally villainous-looking pair of
seamen, and beyond—nothing but the empty gloaming of the harbor.

With a little wail, she swung on Johnnie. She eyed him in a silence broken only by the grunts of the oarsmen, the retch of the tholepins, and the sibilant swish of the boat through the chop.

"Merciful God—what have you done?" she cried.

"Kept my promise," Johnnie told her softly. "I warned you I would not leave New York without you."

Her eyes widened in horror. "Oh, you *couldn't!*"

A quizzical arching of brows was his only answer. Somewhere on shore, a bell began to toll feverishly.

Ben hooted in derision. "The 'ounds be givin' tongue, Johnnie!" he panted.

Johnnie laughed. "Aye, and they'll soon be giving chase. Hale and draw, my hearties."

" 'Tis a fair wind fer the Indies!" cackled Old Ames.

The thunder of three cannon booming in quick succession from the Fort wiped the smile from Johnnie's face. Puzzled, he jerked around and looked behind.

"The fools can't 'it us in this light!" jeered Ben.

Johnnie frowned. He saw the winking lamps clustered around the landing, then suddenly a vertical string of lights appeared atop the southwest bastion of the Fort. It did not require a code-book to tell Johnnie it was a signal to the *Tiger* and other frigates in the harbor.

In a trice, he realized his mistake. He had completely ignored the possible use of night signals, and had overlooked the fact that the coxswain who had ferried out the crew would immediately report the sloop's position. Now, instead of an hour's grace or more, the *Tiger* doubtless would be under weigh before he reached the *Able Lady*.

"Faster, faster!" he urged the men. "They're warning the frigate!"

Cursing, the men quickened their strokes until all were drenched by flying spray. Leanna started to rise in terrror, but Johnnie yanked her back.

"Behave yourself!" he barked. "We've played your game long enough. From now on, we'll play mine!"

In the uncertain light, she searched his face.

"Good God, you're not kidnapping me?"

"It's not *kidnapping* to take one's wife from another man."

She shrank from him. "Did . . . did you tell them *that?*"

"I told them nothing," he said tartly. "The explanation, when it comes, will come from you."

She crouched in a listless coma until the boat hove alongside the sloop, when she began to scream and fight hysterically. Without a word, Johnnie heaved her across his shoulder and sprang into the chains.

The men gave him a rousing ovation as his head appeared over the bulwarks, but when he landed on deck with the struggling girl in his arms, the cheers died in mid-air. Johnnie seized the sudden hush to bellow an order to Ben Bottle.

"Rouse all hands! Man the bars and weigh anchor!" Then commanding Old Ames to follow him, he carried Leanna, shrieking and kicking, into the cabin aft and dumped her unceremoniously on the bed.

"Guard her!" he told the embarrassed old man. "Use force if necessary, but see that she stays here!"

As he shucked off his sodden wig and coat, he glanced about the cabin. After the spacious quarters of the *Eagle,* it seemed like a cell. The head-room was an even fathom between the deck beams, and Johnnie was forced to move with a stoop. There was no sternwalk, but there was a padded settle under the glazed windows, and if small, the cabin was comparatively new and luxurious. Bright tapestries testified to the Sybaritic tendencies of her former master, and Johnnie noted with more than passing interest an excellent pair of matched rapiers in a rack on the forward bulkhead.

He was starting for the door when there came a wild shout from the deck, then a shot thundered across the water. With an oath, Johnnie jerked open the door and dashed for the companionway. Before he reached the deck, there was a crash forward and the ship's head fell off the wind.

When he appeared on deck, Ben excitedly called his attention to a large frigate silhouetted against the paling sky and bearing down on them under easy canvas.

"Holy Mither!" he yelped. " 'Tis the *Tiger!*"

"I have eyes," snapped Johnnie. "You'll be kicking from her yards if you waste time in senseless conversation. Is the anchor—"

Yew came striding out of the half-light to answer that.

"I took the liberty of slipping our cable, sir," he reported. "The *Tiger* laid a warning shot athwart our hawse."

Johnnie stared at him in astonishment. "What in hell are you doing here? I told you to go ashore!"

"I prefer this to prison," Yew returned coldly.

"But, you stubborn fool, I risked my neck to clear you! Take the shore-boat and escape!"

Yew snorted and pointed to the boat bobbing off to leeward with two men at the oars and one crouched in the sternsheets.

"Quinn and two other cowards," he explained brusquely. "Now— may I remind you we are adrift? What are your orders, sir?"

Johnnie curbed his temper. "Make all sail. Dress her in every rag she'll carry." He turned on the Irishman. "Mick, tell Ames to lock the woman in the cabin, then he's to run out the guns." When Ben hesitated, Johnnie thundered: "Jump when you hear an order! Else, by God, you'll go back to the fo'c'sle where you belong!"

Yew was bawling his commands. "*Topmen, aloft! . . . Man the tops'l sheets and halliards! . . . Lay out! Loose! . . . Let fall! Sheet home! . . . Hoist away the tops'ls!*"

With incredible speed, the gaskets were off and the sails fluttered from the yards. When the sheets were home, the sails hoisted and trimmed, the *Able Lady* trembled with eagerness and began to run.

Johnnie exhaled relievedly and glanced at the sky. Night still lingered in the west where the dark purple strip was studded with stars, but eastward the upper lobe of the sun was peeking over the horizon. The northwest breeze was light, yet gusty.

He took another look at the thirty-two-gun frigate. The *Tiger's* captain had hauled his wind on the same tack so as to prevent Johnnie from coming about.

Johnnie's choice was not a pleasant one. To starboard lay the tip of Manhattan Island and the guns of Fort George; to port, the anchored convoy. With the *Tiger* coming up rapidly astern, his only opening was the North River. Yet to flee up the river was at best delay, not escape. When he put the glass on the frigate, he could see her gun-crew laboring to bring a nine-pounder to bear through her bridle-port.

Shaking his head, Johnnie turned back to his own ship. Under Rodney Yew's competent direction, every sail was drawing. Johnnie swore under his breath. He had sprung this trap in an effort to save Yew, and now the obdurate fool was caught in it with the rest of them.

"Bring her up a point!" he growled to the steersman at the tiller.

The man echoed his order and brought her closer to the wind. The topsails began to quiver, but she stood it. The *Tiger* immediately attempted the same maneuver, but was forced to fall off. Johnnie grinned. At least the little sloop could outpoint her.

However, it was of small consequence, and from the stately progress of the frigate on her former course, it was apparent her commander was not worried about the outcome.

Yew came aft and took a look at their pursuer.

"She seems to be gaining," Johnnie observed grimly.

"Aye, so she does, sir," agreed Yew.

"Fortunately she can't loose a broadside without endangering the convoy."

Yew grunted noncommittally. "True, yet we'll soon put the convoy astern. And then—"

It was not necessary to enlarge on their predicament. Once started up the river they would be bottled securely. To offer the powerful frigate action would be suicide.

"Be good enough to take the deck, Mister Yew," said Johnnie, then shoving the glass into his pocket, he swung into the shrouds. He climbed to the cross-trees from which he commanded an excellent— if discouraging—view of the situation.

In the wan light, he could see the frigate's men running out her larboard guns. Realizing that she was going to come about for a broadside as soon as he cleared the convoy, Johnnie made a megaphone of his hands.

"Ahoy the deck! Put her about, Mister Yew! Run in close to that merchantman!"

The crisp commands echoed up to him. *"Ready about! . . . Ease down the helm! . . . Rise tacks and sheets! . . . Haul taut!"* The rest was drowned in the squeal of blocks as the *Able Lady* danced handily on her new tack. With the wind on her beam, she tore straight for a monstrous old cargo ship as if to ram her, then veered up sufficiently to clear the hawse. They were in the open now, with nothing ahead but the river.

Steadying himself, Johnnie looked aft. The *Tiger* had gleefully duplicated the maneuver. Now that she had her quarry in the clear, she could soon open fire. Johnnie sighed and cast wistful eyes on the convoy. From his elevated station, he could look down on the cumbersome ships spaced systematically, like checkers on an unplayed board; each in its place, riding to its anchor hawse, with just enough room to swing in unison to the change of tidal current. He hated to see them fall astern. His position was analogous to that of a fox who, having placed himself between the hunter and a flock of sheep, was safe from the gun so long as he stayed there.

Abruptly an idea came to Johnnie, so reckless that he discarded it at first. When it persisted, he shielded his eyes from the rising sun, and speculated on his chances. If he could double back and run through the convoy—?

Manifestly, the odds were heavily against success. There was scant space for maneuvering between the ships, and with the wind so flighty, if he got himself becalmed under the lee of one of those towering merchantmen, he would be helpless. Also, it was highly probable that one of the ships might not have swung with the others, for the tide had barely turned. On the other hand, slim as it might be, it offered hope, whereas to continue their present course would be fatal.

"Mister Yew!" he shouted down to the deck.

"Sir?"

"Stand by to wear ship! Put her before the wind!"

He could see the consternation on Ben Bottle's upturned face, and Yew's astonishment. He smiled grimly. Certainly it was an evolution the big frigate would not dare attempt in such close quarters.

"We'll go through the convoy!" Johnnie roared. "I'll con you from here!"

"Aye, aye, sir!"

Johnnie set himself against what he knew was coming. Far below he heard the calls: *"Haul taut . . . Up helm! . . . Clear away the bo'lines!"* Under a gust of wind, the *Able Lady* heeled sharply and he had the sensation of falling into the sea. *"Brace in the after yards!"* Then the sloop rose to an even keel and charged into the opening between the nearest ships like an eager terrier.

"Steady as she goes!" bawled Johnnie.

Now that he had committed himself, the gap looked woefully small. Glancing aft, he could see the uncertainty of the *Tiger's* commander registered in her actions. The frigate had boiled past the front end of the convoy, and unwilling to be caught in a trap had hauled her wind and was coming about in orthodox fashion. But the maneuver was costing time.

Johnnie was too busy to concern himself with the *Tiger,* for the sloop was headed straight for the larboard beam of an anchored merchantman. Below him, Yew stood stolidly by the steersman, his head cocked for the expected command. Johnnie was able to imagine how hopeless it must appear from the deck, yet from his vantage on the cross-trees, he was better able to note their chances. The *Able Lady* was traveling at a speed that made her smart to handle, so he waited until the last possible moment before shouting: "Hard a-port!"

The helm was put down before the words were fully out of his mouth, and the sloop reeled around with the wind on the opposite quarter, passing the merchantman with less than a fathom to spare.

"Very good!" yelled Johnnie. "Keep her at that!"

"Aye, aye, sir!"

Yew seemed as calm as if running before a trade wind in mid-ocean, but the Irishman was wagging his head disconsolately. Johnnie chuckled and stole a hasty look at the frigate. Her captain had obviously decided on discretion—since the chase was taking place within full view of the entire harbor—and had doubled back along the outside of the convoy. He could well afford to play a conservative game, for the *Able Lady* was like a rabbit loose in a kennel of hounds, and unless she discovered a hole in the fence, she was doomed. Johnnie concentrated on finding that hole.

A lugger suddenly loomed up dead ahead, so he bellowed to have her wore about. They shaved the lugger too close for comfort, and for the next half-hour, zigzagged their tortuous course through the anchorage. Meanwhile a land mist drifted out from the Jersey shore, and by shortening visibility made the run more hazardous than ever. But while it increased the danger, it helped in a perverse fashion by hiding their wild gyrations from the frigate.

Johnnie seized the opportunity to slip out the opposite side of the convoy and try for a clear run to the open sea. Unfortunately, the mist was not consistent, but hung in tenuous streamers, like tufts of wool bandied about by the vagaries of the wind. It was, in all truth, a game of hide-and-seek.

As he was no longer needed aloft, he slid down to the deck to find Ben doing a jig of jubilation.

"Rape me, Johnnie b'y—we made it!"

Johnnie grunted. "Aye, from the frying pan into the fire."

Ben's face lengthened. "But she sails like a bitch, lad, an'—"

"She's still a small craft, Mick. In light airs we can glide along faster than a heavy ship, but if the breeze freshens, the *Tiger* will run us down."

Yew was staring thoughtfully at the fore-topgallants. Sensing he had something on his mind, Johnnie asked: "What think you, Mister Yew?"

The first officer took careful appraisal of the sky.

" 'Tis my opinion this wind will die within the glass."

Ben groaned. "Well, me grandaddy was 'ung too."

For a while it seemed as if Rodney Yew was mistaken in his prognosis. The wind veered a couple of points, but held steady to carry them around the stern end of the convoy. There, however, the mists had risen, and to Johnnie's chagrin, he discovered the *Tiger* standing on a converging course less than a mile to larboard. She had the wind broad on the beam, not her best point of sailing, yet with everything flying, she was ploughing through the water with a kind of grim irrevocability. A big second-rater wallowed behind her.

"See if you can't coax a little more speed, Mister Yew."

At Yew's direction the yards were trimmed afresh, the tacks hauled closer out, and the halliards sweated up until the yards pressed hard against the sheaves. All this effort added about a half-knot to the sloop's speed, but it was not enough.

Johnnie shrugged and stared ahead. The foot of the foresail had been drawn up slightly by the bunt slab-line, and he could see the Narrows, almost shrouded now in a low haze. Silently he cursed his luck. If only the Fates had permitted him to reach that fog bank ahead of the *Tiger*—

"Beg pardon, sir," Yew said. "The frigate is losing the wind."

Johnnie swung around. It was true! The *Tiger's* studding-sails were still full, as were her topgallants, but the rest of her canvas flapped impotently.

"'Pon my oath!" crowed Johnnie. "We'll make it after all!"

The hands witnessed the phenomenon, and a roar of elation swept the sloop. But hardly had the echo died away before their own foresail plopped slowly against the mast, and the triple row of reef-points rattled along the topsails—a certain symptom of approaching calm. Soon the happy rush of water past the stem slowed to a weary gurgle.

The frigate still had sufficient steerageway to answer her helm, so she altered course to bring her forward guns to bear. Watching, Johnnie saw a white mushroom of smoke blossom from the muzzle of a nine-pounder, and seconds later the ball dropped close astern the sloop.

Johnnie looked along his own deck. The recent merriment of his men had turned to grim foreboding. Johnnie grinned ruefully and raised his voice.

"Come, lads, don't lose heart!" he told them. "We've all been in tighter spots than this. They haven't caught us yet."

"They'll sink us, Cap'n!" wailed a boy.

"Damme," jeered an old hand, "I'd as soon drown as swing!"

Johnnie laughed. "'Tis not my intention to do either, lads. Now obey orders smartly, and I'll get you out of this." He turned to the first officer. "Mister Yew, have the sweeps broken out!"

"Aye, aye, sir!" Yew returned with something akin to enthusiasm, and gave the order.

The men cheered and rushed to the task. Johnnie looked at Ben. "Mick—pass the world to Old Ames to secure his guns."

Ben chuckled. "Aye, aye, *Lord Johnnie!*"

The guns were hauled inboard and secured. Meanwhile, Yew had gotten the sweeps out—huge oars requiring the exertions of five men to each. Johnnie kept his glass on the frigate. The wind had died completely and the *Tiger,* unable to use her helm and too large to carry sweeps, was having difficulty keeping her forecastle guns to bear. But the shots were drawing uncomfortably close. If the tide swung her around for a broadside, the sloop was doomed.

With the sweeps in the water, Johnnie's hopes picked up. The men plied the gigantic oars with a will born of desperation. Once again Johnnie had cause to bless Rodney Yew, for Yew had united the looms of the sweeps with a hawser stretched fore and aft so they worked in perfect unison.

"Good work, my hearties!" Johnnie cheered the sweating men. "We'll show the bullies a clean wake, or I'm a lubber!"

But privately, he knew they were not out of danger. Through the glass, he could see the *Tiger's* crew slewing around a long eighteen-pounder on her upper deck. If she managed to place a ball among the sweeps, half of Johnnie's crew would be sent spinning about the decks.

"Heave, heave!" he encouraged them.

The men strained and yo-hoed, and the sloop made slightly more than a knot through the water. Slow as it was, the gap between the vessels widened perceptibly. Anxiously, Johnnie studied their progress. The ebb tide was carrying both ships toward the Narrows.

Suddenly, he thought he detected little cats-paws far ahead—heralds of wind. He called Yew to his side and pointed.

"By the powers!" exclaimed Yew. "There *is* a breeze coming from the nor'east!"

Johnnie exhaled slowly; he discovered he had been holding his breath.

"Hoist the jib, Mister Yew. Shift over the head-sheets and brace up the after-yards. We'll be ready to welcome it."

"Aye, aye, sir!"

The *Tiger* was firing intermittently, but most of her shots were short. Johnnie kept his eyes on the fog which was now rolling slowly into the harbor with the wind. The *Able Lady* would get the breeze ahead of the frigate.

Then a lucky shot from the frigate struck the fore-topgallant mast, and the crash threw the men out of stroke.

"Steady!" roared Johnnie. "Mick—take a gang aloft and clear the wreckage."

As Ben Bottle led a squad up the rigging, another ball stove in the bulwarks near the larboard quarter. From the cursing and shouting, Johnnie knew no one was injured. But a minute later, the water began to ripple around them and the sails cracked full.

"Ship sweeps!" thundered Johnnie.

The great oars were hauled inboard as the sloop heeled to the breeze. Through his telescope, Johnnie could see the frustration manifest aboard the *Tiger*. Still becalmed, she was helpless to prevent the escape of her victim. Like her namesake, she loosed an angry roar of defiance in the form of a broadside. But as she wasn't broad off, it was a futile gesture. Only one ball, ricocheting off the water, struck the sloop, staving in a plank, but as it was well above the waterline, the damage was negligible. Meanwhile, the *Able Lady* seemed to hoist her skirts like a hoyden and went kiting for the Narrows. By the time the frigate got the wind, the mists had closed around them. They were safe.

Johnnie stood between Rodney Yew and Ben Bottle.

"Well, lads, our troubles are over!" he exulted.

"You are to be congratulated, sir!" Yew said stiffly, and walked away.

Johnnie bit his lip and turned to Ben who was mopping perspiration from his face.

Ben gave him a sly glance.

"W'at o' the woman?"

Johnnie winced. "By God, I had forgotten her! Where is she?"

"Locked in the cabin," grumbled Ben. "By yer own blisterin' order!"

"Did I say our troubles were over?" grinned Johnnie, and started below.

The key was on the outside of the door, so Johnnie unlocked it and entered the cabin. He found Leanna curled up on the settle, staring moodily at the white mist. He shut the door, and when she did not turn, coughed gently.

"Your servant, my lady."

She rose with all the majesty of her diminutive person. Anger heightened her color and the slant of her snapping eyes was more pronounced than ever.

"You low-born beast!" she raged at him. "Where are you taking me?"

Johnnie heaved his shoulders. "Where fortune wills."

"Dear God! What do you hope to gain by this?"

"A wife," laughed Johnnie.

She stared at him a long time, then sat down calmly and folded her hands in her lap.

"You'll have a wife," she echoed, "but only in name. Once you were able to force your will on me, Johnnie Rogue, because you held my future in your hands."

"May I remind you—I still hold it!"

She laughed mirthlessly. "Oh *no* you don't! You destroyed completely whatever future I hoped for. The tables are turned now. Instead of fear, I have only the utmost contempt for you!"

Johnnie frowned. Rage he had prepared for, but this cold hostility caught him unawares. He could only shrug.

"That's your privilege," he conceded. "Yet it doesn't alter your marital status."

"It may when I set foot on shore. If I talk, they'll rid me of you at a rope's end."

Johnnie felt his temper soar. "Hold your tongue! Are you not afraid I'll drop you out that window?"

"*Afraid?*" she mocked him. "Why, I'd almost welcome it to see the last of you! No, Johnnie, I'll never be afraid of you again!"

Shaking with anger, he jerked open the door.

"*Mister Bottle!*"

Ben came tumbling down the companionway, pop-eyed with curiosity. Johnnie glared at him.

"Mister Bottle, you will usher this woman into the second's cuddy!"

"But, Jo—" Ben caught himself. "But, sir—!"

Johnnie cut him short. "You will bunk somewhere else, Mister Bottle!" He glanced at Leanna and realized that she had only the evening gown on her back. "Find her some clothes in the slop-chest or elsewhere."

"Holy Mither! There ain't no lydy's gear aboard, sir!"

"She'll have to get along with what we have," snapped Johnnie.

"When you get her settled, ask Mister Yew to step down here. That's all!"

Leanna marched across the cabin with her chin high. Ben gulped and moved aside as she stalked past him. He gave Johnnie an injured look.

"Damn me eyes!" he mumbled grumpily. "Fust 'tis Bloodsmythe's widder, now this 'un. Dooce take it, Johnnie, ain't I *never* goin' to 'ave no cabin?"

Without waiting for an answer he scuttled out and slammed the door.

Johnnie was in no mood to mince words when Rodney Yew came striding in.

"Mister Yew—*sit down!*"

Startled, Yew dropped into a chair. Johnnie leaned one hip against the table and scowled down at him.

"Be good enough to explain why you did not go ashore when I so ordered?"

"I considered it an ill-timed jest," Yew snapped.

Johnnie's smile was cold. "Jest, eh?" Then he detailed exactly what had happened between the Governor and himself relative to Yew. "Does that still strike you as a *jest*, Mister Yew?" he concluded.

Yew stared at him incredulously. "By the powers, sir, I owe you an apology!"

"That doesn't better your plight," Johnnie said dryly.

To his amazement, Rodney Yew laughed, albeit a trifle bitterly.

"Aye, true enough. 'Twould seem the jest was one of Fate's. Yet, I think you'll grant I cannot be censured for not anticipating such magnanimity from a man of your reputation, sir!"

Johnnie had to grin. "In a word—you didn't expect fairness from the Devil?"

Yew shrugged. "I repeat what I said once before, sir. You pass all understanding."

"It's impossible to put you ashore now."

"Obviously. I'll have to pay for my misjudgment."

Johnnie suppressed the impulse to smile. He dropped onto the settle and stretched his legs.

"Then you'll join our venture?"

Yew's face hardened. "Since I have no alternative, I'll sail with you, sir. But I like it not."

The smile broke through. "One man's loss is another's gain." Johnnie laughed. "Being no fault of my own, I must confess I'm delighted to have you, Mister Yew. You'll get a share—"

Yew stopped him. "I want no shares in a pirate venture," he interrupted curtly. "I'll serve you through necessity, but join you—*never!*"

"'Pon my oath, you're obdurate! You might as well have the game as the name!"

Yew shook his head. "My own conscience is the best judge of that, sir."

Johnnie spread his hands in resignation. "As you will. Now, if you'll summon all hands aft, I'll explain the deal to them. After that, be good enough to arrange the watches and organization to suit yourself. You are a better seaman than I am."

"I'm beginning to doubt that," Yew said, rising. "But I'll carry out the order." He quitted the cabin.

Johnnie tidied and donned his wig and coat, and by the time he stepped on deck, the men were waiting for him. They greeted him with a rousing cheer, then waited eagerly for his words.

As lucidly as possible, Johnnie outlined the venture. Without naming the Duchess, he told them about the deal and the percentages. They would cruise south, he said, and masqueraded as a privateer prey on shipping around the Indies and the Bahamas. Time after time they broke in with enthusiastic *huzzas,* and when he had concluded, a man shouted: "Yer pardon, sor—will ye tell us 'ow ye got us out o' prison, fer 'twas a miracle no less?"

So Johnnie related how he had beguiled the Governor into giving him a handwritten order to see Yew and how he had persuaded a forger to revise it into an order for a wholesale prison delivery. The men roared with merriment, and when the same old tar shouted: "Damme, Cap'n, we'll foller ye to 'ell an' back!" they echoed a thundering chorus.

"Aye, to 'ell an' back wi' Lord Johnnie the Rogue!"

24

ALTHOUGH THEY HAD ESCAPED THE TRAP IN NEW YORK, THEY WERE never farther from danger than the horizon, for the entire coast, from Halifax to the Bahamas, was patrolled by English warships and privateers, and an occasional French raider. At any moment, a sail might loom over the distant rim, like a white flag of danger, so the *Able Lady* was kept alerted for instantaneous action.

However, the crew now had supreme confidence in Lord Johnnie. After their recent experiences, they attributed to him almost supernatural powers. And Johnnie, on his part, had equal faith in his vessel. For her tonnage, the brigantine-rigged sloop was the equal in speed, maneuverability and armament of any vessel her size afloat. She was clean-bottomed, well found, and staunch enough for protracted cruising. Her only disadvantage was her size. In a good breeze, a larger ship could run her down, and she wasn't capable of coping with the fire power of a frigate. But even more serious was the problem of confinement. Johnnie's cabin was the only place aboard with head-room, and the crew had to endure quarters that would sicken a hog.

Paradoxically, the addition of one lone woman complicated the situation more than an extra fifty men would have done. The natural habits of rough seamen, long accustomed to a strictly masculine environment, had to be restrained. There was no privacy on a flush-decker, and Leanna could not be restricted to a cuddy barely four feet high and constantly impregnated with the stench of the bilge and the suffocating odor of fish-oil lamps.

Fortunately, good weather prevailed the first week, and only once did they sight a sail—within an hour of sunset on the second evening, and they lost her in the darkness. Meanwhile, Johnnie set a southeasterly course, standing well out to sea so as to avoid the inevitable concentration of warships which he suspected would be hovering off the Chesapeake.

Yet despite his seeming good luck, Johnnie began to question his rashness in bringing Leanna aboard against her will. When she remained below deck the first day and a half, he assumed that she was thinking things over and would bow to the inevitable. He was wrong; she had been sewing. She appeared finally in a costume which quite took his breath away. She had fashioned a long skirt of blanket material, and a pair of canvas sandals with rope soles; above the waist she wore a too-large sailor's jersey underneath a pea-coat—all of which accentuated her femininity.

His gallantry, she scorned; his attempted conversation, she ignored. She acted as if he did not exist. Johnnie was in turn furious and perplexed. As she had taunted him—the tables were turned. Instead of a source of pleasure, she became a hazard. Disappointment swelled to apprehension when he recalled her threat to betray him at the first opportunity. He tried, not too successfully, to shrug the problem aside and concentrate on his job.

He worked the men hard. Old Ames proved his worth by heckling the gun crews at practice until they were as proficient as a man-o'-war's crew. Within the week, they could clean, load, run-out and loose a broadside with amazing precision. Rodney Yew trained the hands in the finer use of cutlass and pike, and their outlook quickly changed from that of the hunted to the hunter. To a man they began to spoil for a fight.

Only Johnnie remained unaffected, and with the passage of time, grew increasingly morose. Vexed, he tried to shake it off, and baited himself with the inevitable "why?" Yet he kept remembering other days, now lost in the long, long ago, when he had dreamed of commanding a stout little ship. Now, incredibly, that vision had become an actuality. Then what was wrong?

By the simple process of elimination, he was forced to face the obvious—he was brooding over Leanna. The realization disgusted him. He considered himself an adventurer, a sea rover, and such men took their women where they found them—as a pleasure, a relaxation, or a debauch. To be crushed by the indifference of one lone female was, by Johnnie's lights, an evidence of weakness. Yet deny it he could not, for whenever Leanna walked her trim little figure down the deck, the ache in his diaphragm grew unbearable.

She spent most of her time forward with the hands, taking an interest in all things nautical, from the operation of the vessel itself to the tiny ship-models and scrimshaw the old tars fashioned in their idle time.

She mended their clothing and mothered the youngsters who occasionally grew homesick for the England they would never see again. Big, sentimental Ben came to worship her in a calf-like manner that irritated Johnnie, and even Old Ames and Rodney Yew succumbed to her friendly charm. Johnnie was dumfounded when he came unexpectedly on deck one night to find Yew explaining to her the mysteries of the stars.

He realized then that his little world stood in jeopardy, so he made his decision: if he could not win her, he'd have to be rid of her.

Because appearance and surroundings gave him confidence, he put his cabin in order and dressed meticulously in his scarlet costume. Then in the early evening, he summoned Old Ames and sent him to ask Leanna to come to his cabin. While waiting, he polished two long-stemmed wine glasses, and set them on the table. When he heard footsteps coming along the companionway, he turned to greet her.

Old Ames came in very red-faced and alone. He stood before Johnnie, nervously tonguing his lone tooth.

"Well—!" demanded Johnnie.

"Damme, Cap'n, I kin do naught but gi' ye 'er lydyship's very own words," he blurted. "If 'Is Royal 'Ighness wishes to see me—she s'ys— 'e can come to my cabin." Ames spread his hands helplessly.

Johnnie laughed ruefully and sat down. "What would you do in a predicament like this, ancient?" When the old man hesitated, he urged, "Come—speak the truth?"

"Arsk me 'ow to shoot a flea off'n a mast-head a league to wind'ard, an' I'll tell ye, lad, but wimmen I know naught. Still, if 'twere me— w'ich it ain't—I'd go. A strong man don't ha' no need to try 'is strength on females."

Johnnie winced. *"Touché,* old one. Sobeit—I'll go."

He had never been in her cuddy, and he was appalled. It put him in mind of a cave. A grimy glazed port offered a meager light which she had supplemented by a purser's glim—a cheap, thin candle. As the height between decks was about four feet, Johnnie had to scrunch down to enter. The odors almost choked him.

Yet somehow, Leanna endowed the hole with dignity. She reclined on the rough bunk with all the poise of a queen on a throne. She appeared unconscious of the squalor, nor had she changed from her customary sea-going garb.

Bent nearly double, Johnnie had trouble bowing.

"My lady," he murmured. "I bow to your command."

"You bow to the lack of head-room in this pigsty," she said with asperity. "You come through no command of mine, sir, but since you are here, pray be seated. You look extremely silly at the moment."

Nonplused, he lowered himself gingerly onto a small seat a seaman had fashioned for her out of a bucket. The contrast between his elegant costume and the surroundings defeated his purpose in dressing so carefully. He felt ridiculous and out of place. Leanna did nothing to lessen his discomfort, but waited haughtily for him to state his business and begone.

Now that he was in her presence, his determination began to wane. She had never, he thought bitterly, looked so desirable. The oversized clothing by its very coarseness heightened the delicacy of her features, and the yellow candlelight high-lighted the texture of her skin. It required all his will power to speak the words he had to say.

"Leanna," he managed finally, "I've come to make amends."

A slight raising of the eyebrows was her only answer. He went on slowly.

"There is no way of undoing what has already been done, but at least I can end the farce, and attempt restitution of a sort."

"Grammercy, what nobility of spirit! The slayer weeping over the body of his victim, no less!"

"I haven't *slain* you, my lady!" he protested.

"That would have been a kindness compared to what you have done to me!"

He flinched at that. "I doubt it. But hear me out. 'Tis my thought to give you money, and, in some fashion yet to be worked out, send you back to New York."

She laughed without mirth. "Your charity overwhelms me, sir! And after I'm bought off and shipped back, in this miraculous *fashion yet to be worked out,* pray tell me—what kind of a reception do you anticipate I would receive in New York?"

"It might be a trifle awkward, that I grant, yet no one knows of our relationship and—"

"A *trifle* awkward? Dear Lord, how you understate it! As for the relationship, as you so smugly phrase it—their presumption would be as ghastly as the truth!"

Johnnie fetched a heavy sigh. Somehow, he had expected her to jump at his offer, and her mockery disconcerted him.

"Well, it appears the only solution," he grumbled.

Her eyes flashed. "Does it now? I wouldn't depend on that!"

"And what can I depend on?"

She leaned forward and spaced her words like the stabs of a knife. "That you will have cause to regret this vicious act you have perpetrated!"

He spread his hands in resignation. "I regret it now," he confessed. "Yet though the act itself was vicious, the impulse was sincere. Aye. Ridiculous as it may sound now—I had hoped to win you."

"God in heaven!" she cried. "Your overweening temerity is insufferable! A filthy felon and a pirate—"

Johnnie stiffened in anger. "My crimes were no obstacle to our marriage, I might remind you—*wife!*"

"Must you continually bring that up?"

"I must, since they are so closely allied." He chuckled bitterly. "In the romances I have read, the wooing precedes the wedding. I can understand the advantages now. But look—let us not bicker. 'Tis agreed we both erred sadly. Do you accept my offer?"

She bit her lower lip. "How can I? You've destroyed me."

He looked her full in the eyes. "You may be embarrassed socially, my lady, but most assuredly you are not destroyed. You have never looked more lovely!"

"Hold your tongue, sir!" she flared. "I resent the unsolicited opinions of a pirate!" She made a gesture of dismissal. "Leave me—I'll send my decision when I perceive it."

Enraged, Johnnie sprang to his feet—only to crack his head against the beams so hard it drove him to his knees. Leanna laughed, in spite of herself, and his humiliation was complete. He retrieved his hat and wig, and stumbled blindly out of the cuddy.

For the first time in his life, Lord Johnnie savored the dregs of defeat. Unable to sleep, or even sit still, he kept the deck all night, pacing moodily back and forth along the weather deck until he had the steerman as nervous as himself.

His confusion swelled to a monstrous passion. *Filthy felon and pirate,* was he? By the powers, she had a fool's courage to throw that in the teeth of Johnnie Rogue! It was high time somebody taught the chit a lesson! Didn't she have the wit to know that he could rape her or throw her overboard, as he chose? He marveled that he didn't do the former and then the latter. It would serve her right!

The very beauty of the tropic night irritated him. When he glowered over the taffrail, he read mockery in the shimmering phosphorescence of the wake; when he looked forward, he saw the watch loafing contentedly on the hatches. Even the stars overhead blazed with unreal serenity. In the midst of contentment, he was discontent. Echoes haunted him—*filthy felon . . . pirate!*

When the first squall screamed down on them, shortly after midnight, he was almost pleased, for the savage fury of the elements matched his own mood. He took in the topgallants, but carried everything else with abandon until the little *Lady* reeled and complained under the shrieking gusts.

That squall had passed but an hour when they were lashed by a second, and just before dawn by still another—the worst of the three. It laid the little sloop almost on her beam's end and tore the foresail out of the bolt-ropes.

Fortunately, the very violence of the squall quickened its end. Yet the disaster they averted came not from the wind, but *with* the wind, for barely had it passed, when a frantic scream rang from the masthead.

"Sail ho! Sail ho! One point on the weather bow!"

Johnnie jumped into the weather shrouds to descry a large brig bearing down on them under easy canvas, barely out of musket-shot. If the squall had lasted a few minutes longer they would have collided.

"Up helm!" he shouted to the steersman.

As the *Able Lady* sheered off to starboard, Johnnie took another look at the stranger. She must have sighted the sloop at the same instant, for she veered a point to larboard. In the rapidly improving light, he could see that she was either a small frigate or a large sloop-o'-war.

"Beat to quarters, Mister Yew!" ordered Johnnie, dropping to the deck.

As the men scurried to their stations, Johnnie focused his glass on the stranger. Ben and Yew stood beside him, shading their eyes from the sun. It was obvious to all three that flight was impossible.

Ben summed it up in his comment: "B'Jesus, she's a big bastard to 'ave the weather-gage, Cap'n!"

Johnnie grunted. Having the *weather-gage* signified that she was to windward, and thus had the advantage of maneuverability, speed and the privilege of choosing or declining action. Conversely, standing close-hauled with a ruined foresail, Johnnie's position was unenviable.

"She hasn't shown her colors," he observed.

"May we show ours, sir?" asked Yew.

"If you wish," Johnnie agreed indifferently.

Yew's judgment seem vindicated as soon as the British ensign

fluttered aloft, for the brig immediately hoisted the same colors and
fired a warning shot across their bows to heave-to.

Johnnie sighed relievedly. "Thank God she wasn't French!" He
gave the order to put the helm down and the sloop lost way.

But his optimism wasn't shared by the others. Ben was appalled and
Yew regarded Johnnie with an ironic glance. It remained for Leanna,
who had come on deck, to phrase the thought in every mind.

"Well, Captain," she said with malice, "it appears retribution has
come earlier than expected."

Johnnie bowed. "It will no doubt disappoint you, my lady," he
mocked, "to learn that I sail under *letters of marque.*"

Her eyes went saucer-round. "*You?*"

"Aye, by the Governor's signature—though to be frank, he knows it
naught. Now I'll trouble you to go below. Mister Bottle, please convey—"

The order was not needed. Leanna turned on her heel and disappeared down the companionway hatch.

Chuckling, Johnnie went amidships to reassure the men. The brig
was closing rapidly down their larboard.

"Be of good cheer, my lads!" he told them. "We operate under
letters of marque." As they gaped in wondering admiration, he continued: "Now act naturally when the boarding—"

"*Johnnie!*" shrieked Ben Bottle. "*Oh, Mother o' Jesus—!*"

Johnnie swung around in time to see the Royal ensign hauled down
from the brig to be instantly replaced by the French colors.

It was too late to do anything; he was caught like a sitting duck.
In savage desperation, he yelled at the old gunner, "*Ames! Fire
when—*"

His words were lost in reverberating thunder. The scene vanished
in an acrid cloud of smoke as the brig fired a full broadside at point-
blank range into the *Able Lady.* She reeled from the concussion and
Johnnie was knocked off his feet. He lay stunned, trying to separate
the noises. The shrieks, curses and screams of a hundred men fused with
the ear-splitting crash of breaking timbers and the peculiar whistling
wail of passing shot. The deck beneath him buckled and shuddered
under each blow, yet he could see nothing. A spar cracked somewhere
above him and came tumbling down in a mass of rigging.

As the wind carried the powder-fog away, he staggered to his feet.
The Frenchman was off the lee quarter, weaving about to deal the
coup de grâce with her starboard guns. Raging, Johnnie roared at

Ames to give her a broadside. It seemed a futile gesture, for the brig presented only her stern to them.

Johnnie stumbled aft to find Rodney Yew on all fours, blood gushing from a head wound. Johnnie moved to aid him when he saw the young steersman step away from the tiller and collapse—the stump of his left wrist spurting blood.

"Another steersman aft!" he bawled and leapt to stay the weaving bar. He felt the roar as his own guns gave feeble answer, then Ben—black with smoke—came charging aft.

"She hulled us!" he cursed.

Yew had hauled himself erect and was clinging to the bulwarks.

"The damned treacherous devil!" he panted. "He hulled us deliberately. He means to sink, not take us!"

"He's coming about," began Johnnie, when a yelp from Ben stopped him.

"Holy Mither! Look at 'er!"

Johnnie could hardly believe his eyes. Instead of wearing around, the brig was yawing uncontrollably. Rodney Yew was the first to realize the import.

"By the powers!" he roared. "We must have sheared her tiller ropes! She's helpless for the moment!"

Ben swore. "Bad cess to 'er! But it can't 'elp us, fer at the rate we're makin' water, we won't last the glass!"

"By God, it will!" shouted Johnnie. "We'll board him!" He put the tiller up.

"Gad A'mighty, b'y!" protested Ben. "She out-numbers us two to one!"

"I'm not drowning alone!" snapped Johnnie. "Mister Yew, call all hands for boarding. Have lashers and grapplings ready. Mick—pass the word for Ames to come here."

Another helmsman ran aft, so Johnnie turned the tiller over to him. Though the topmasts had been shot away and the sails riddled, the sloop still had steerageway.

"Lay her alongside!" Johnnie ordered, then started below to summon Leanna. To his surprise, he found her on deck, working over the stricken steersman. She had tied a tourniquet around the stump and the youngster was clinging to her in terror.

"You shouldn't be—" Johnnie began, but she gave him such a look of fury, he never completed the sentence.

"Go on with your butchery and leave me alone!"

While he hesitated, Ben returned with Ames. The old man was hopping mad. Johnnie forced a bitter smile.

"Excellent shooting, ancient!"

"Satan's backside!" he piped. "If I'd only known in time, I'd ha' given 'im somethin'—"

"You can, you can," Johnnie interrupted. "Hear me, for we'll be alongside shortly. Can you make up a couple of bombs by filling two kegs with powder and lighting them with fuses?"

Ames squinted at him. "Aye, quicker'n a flash. Big ones?"

"Not too big to hoist to the end of the yards," Johnnie told him. "When they're ready, send two of your best men out on the larboard end of the foreyard with one keg, and you and another take the main. Use short fuses to explode them as they hit the deck."

The old man grasped the plan at once.

"Jesus wept!" he crowed. "Yer the spit o' yer pa!" And he scuttled off to obey.

Leaving Yew and Ben to bring her alongside the Frenchman, Johnnie ducked below. He pocketed his forged *letters of marque,* chose a freshly primed pistol and his favorite rapier.

When he stepped on deck, he was startled to find they were already sliding along the brig's starboard quarter. Her decks were packed with jeering seamen ready to repel boarders. Johnnie glanced aloft. Two men balanced a cask on the end of the foreyard that would soon be over the Frenchmen's deck.

"Mick, pass the word quietly not to board until I give the order!" cautioned Johnnie.

He took a final appraisal of his own deck. Two or three dead men lay twisted in grotesque positions, but the wounded had been hauled behind the dubious shelter of the pumps. A starboard gun had been blown upside down, pinning a red mass under it, not recognizable as human. Ben was moving among the crouching boarders, who, knowing it was a case of win or die, were recklessly eager. Dressed only in trousers, their bodies blackened with smoke, they looked like deputies of Satan.

As they drew abreast, the Frenchman loosed another broadside. The *Able Lady* staggered under the impact and began to settle by the head. Once more smoke blotted out the scene.

"Helm hard a-starboard!" bawled Johnnie, and in a grinding crash, the vessels collided.

Drawing his sword, he sprang into the rigging. Through the murk, he saw the grapnels heaved aboard the brig. The French seamen tried to break them loose, but the Englishmen had secured their ends to the bitts and the sinking of the *Lady* embedded the prongs in a death grip.

Then the bombs fell, exploding with terrible execution on the teeming deck. When he could make himself heard above the screams and confusion, Johnnie bellowed: *"Boarders away! Enter! Enter!"* and made a flying leap for the brig's shrouds.

He clung there an instant to orient himself. His own lads were swarming over the bulwarks, shrieking like savages. Then choosing an opening, he dropped into the melee.

Though long accustomed to hand-to-hand fighting, Johnnie had never witnessed carnage comparable to this. Over two hundred men jammed chest to chest, emptying pistols at a range of inches, and without room to swing a cutlass. So they beat and hacked and drove the hilts of their cutlasses into their opponents' teeth while the smoke settled down to make identification impossible.

As Johnnie dropped to the deck, a Frenchman slashed at him with a cutlass. Johnnie skewered the man through the breastbone, parried another's cut, and fought his way aft to the small raised quarter-deck. Of the two officers there, one had been shot through the sword arm, but the other—a mountainous figure, topped by a black wig, and balanced on spindly legs—engaged him viciously.

Johnnie let him carry the fight. He parried, making his thrusts deliberately weak, and inviting a riposte. After the third disengage, he lunged his blade through the Frenchman's shoulder muscles. As the man swayed back, his sword clattering across the deck, Johnnie laid the point against his throat.

"Command your men to lay down their arms!"

The Frenchman steadied himself against the bulwark.

"Hold! I surrender!" he stammered in execrable English, then turning to his wounded officer, he gave the order in French.

"Monsieur Cartier, call off the men! Strike the colors! We are undone!"

As Cartier staggered to the rail, Rodney Yew climbed onto the quarter-deck. With clothes in tatters and his face a red mask of blood, he little resembled the solid navigator he was.

"They have struck," Johnnie told him shortly. "Have the Frenchmen driven below hatches, then look to Lady Somerset."

"She's already aboard," retorted Yew. "Caring for the wounded."

Between Yew and Cartier, the fighting was finally halted, though not without difficulty, for Johnnie's men felt they had been treacherously served. But when it was over, Cartier stumbled back.

"It is as you commanded, *M. le Capitaine!*" he murmured tearfully.

M. le Capitaine accepted the situation with philosophic calmness. He gave a shrug that in the true Frenchman achieves the acme of eloquence. Bowing to Johnnie, he introduced himself in French.

"I have the honor to be M. Antoine de Gounod, Captain of His Most Christian Majesty's sloop-of-war *Beausejour.*"

"Speak English, if you please!" snapped Johnnie.

After a slight raising of the eyebrows, de Gounod repeated himself in English.

Johnnie returned the bow. "And I am Captain Scarlett of the sloop *Able Lady.*"

"The *late* sloop," growled Yew, "thanks to his dirty treachery!"

De Gounod spread his fat hands in a deprecating gesture. "Ah, monsieur, as you English say it—all is fair in love and war."

Johnnie laughed. "Aye, Mister Yew, *M. le Capitaine* is correct. *Fas est et ab hoste de-ce'ri;* it is right to be taught even by an enemy. 'Tis a good trick to remember."

Yew glowered, but de Gounod smiled blandly. In repose, his face was merely repulsive, mirth made it revolting. It was deeply pitted by pox scars, with heavy dewlaps and a flabby, liver-colored lower-lip. His eyes resembled two small-shot holes in a melon, and his nose, where not vein-streaked, was covered with warts. Now he turned his head and glanced at the stricken Cartier.

"My compliments to le Chevalier de Maurin," he drawled in French. "Inform him we have surrendered. He will know what to do."

Johnnie frowned. "What was that order, *M. le Capitaine?*" he demanded.

De Gounod fluttered a lace handkerchief. "I merely told my officer to reassure our passenger," he explained casually in English. "He might be worried."

"He might have reason to be," Johnnie retorted. He gave Yew a significant glance. "I think I shall accompany M. Cartier, Mister Yew."

De Gounod started to expostulate, but Yew clapped the muzzle of a pistol to his head and he relaxed with a shrug.

Johnnie hurried after Cartier who had disappeared down the companionway hatch. The latter hesitated before the door of the main cabin when he saw Johnnie, but Johnnie pricked him with the point of his rapier, and Cartier opened the door.

Standing on the far side of a table was a tall, slender Frenchman, busily engaged in weighting a leather portfolio with two heavy pistols tied together. A long sword lay naked on the board beside him.

He looked up in startled anger at the intrusion. Cartier was plainly terrified by the message he had to convey, and his voice cracked painfully as he stammered in French.

"*M. le Capitaine's* compliments, *M. le Comte!* We have surrendered!"

The Chevalier de Maurin seemed momentarily stunned. He was a strikingly handsome man, with a large head set disdainfully on a pair of splendid shoulders. He stared at Johnnie, now entering the cabin, with the haughty eyes of an aristocrat.

"*Diable!* Surrender? Never, never!"

Before Johnnie could prevent it, he seized the weighted portfolio and hurled it at the stern windows. The pistols smashed the glass, but the container caught against the frame and tumbled back into the cabin.

With a cry, the Chevalier leaped toward it, but Johnnie was before him. Jostling the Frenchman aside, Johnnie snatched up the portfolio. As he straightened, he saw de Maurin coming at him with his sword.

Johnnie parried the thrust, but the force of it jarred him from wrist to elbow.

"Give it here, give it here!" shrilled de Maurin.

Johnnie disengaged and tried to back away. "Stop, you fool!" he shouted in French. "The ship is ours!"

"*Mon Dieu!*" cried de Maurin. "You shall not have it!"

He lunged forward with such suicidal ferocity that Johnnie had to give ground. It took but a few counters to convince Johnnie that he was up against a seasoned swordsman of the old school, and that he would have to fight as he had never had to fight before. In the close confines the most he could hope was to guard and parry, and so quick was the Chevalier, it seemed to Johnnie as if he were opposing a veritable octopus with eight swords. He cautiously retreated through the companionway to the deck.

As they emerged into the open, Ben and three tars charged forward with cutlasses to cut the Frenchman down, but Johnnie shouted them back.

"Keep out of this! Give us room!" He tossed the portfolio to Ben, and sprang clear of a hatch.

For a moment, it seemed as though de Maurin would follow his precious portfolio, but when Johnnie engaged him again, he returned to his task—of killing Johnnie.

Startled and awed, the men climbed into the rigging to watch the spectacle. Yew and Gounod gripped the quarter-deck rail, staring in breathless silence, now broken only by the ringing steel and the restless crunch of rubbing ships. There was still another audience—the dead. They slumped in rows along the bulwarks, their heads bobbing indifferently with each roll of the brig.

As a nobleman, the Chevalier had been all but born with a sword in his hand, and he seemed tireless. If his emotions had run away with him, they merely aggravated his physical coolness. He steadied down and fought like a chess-player planning his game in advance. His weaving blade became an impregnable wall of steel.

Johnnie gave ground slowly, studying the timing. De Maurin was fighting with a rhythm—cut and thrust; *quarte, sixte, septime* . . . Parrying tightly, Johnnie sensed that he was attempting to establish a false tempo deliberately to provoke an attack that would draw the Englishman's blade into a line which must open him to an irresistible lunge.

They fought up to the foremast and back down the larboard side before Johnnie caught an imperceptible change in pace. He gave no sign he was aware of it. He tried a series of double and triple feints, and de Maurin backed away. They engaged in tierce, and Johnnie led in with a straightening of the arm. The Chevalier followed with the *demi-contre,* which Johnnie countered by a thrust in *quinte.*

Then it came—after a series of disengages, de Maurin stretched almost to the deck in a dazzling upward lunge. . . .

Though precisely what Johnnie had been expecting, the execution was so brilliant it was impossible to parry. As he felt the steel enter his left shoulder, he jerked back and countered mechanically with the evolution already prepared in his mind. De Maurin had staked his life on his lunge, and now too far forward to recover his balance, he took Johnnie's point through the throat.

As Johnnie stumbled back, Ben ran forward to assist him.

"Johnnie b'y, Johnnie! Be ye bad 'urt?"

Johnnie shook his head. "I'm all right, Mick," he gasped.

Assured of his safety, the men broke into a wild tumult of cheering and swarmed over the deck. Johnnie waved them away.

"Protect the Chevalier's body, Mick," he commanded, and walked painfully back to the quarter-deck.

He eyed de Gounod bleakly. "Enough of your lies, you shifty black-guard!" he warned the man in French. "Who was the Chevalier?"

De Gounod made a gesture of resignation. "A King's courier, monsieur, with a *lettre de cachet* for Canada. More than this I do not know."

Johnnie grunted. "Was it for that reason you tried to sink us without stopping?"

The Frenchman shrugged. "I but obey orders, monsieur, you will understand."

Johnnie crossed to the bulwarks and surveyed the *Able Lady*. Her decks were awash and she seemed supported solely by the heavy grappling lines. With a sigh, he turned back to Rodney Yew.

"Salvage what you can, then cut her adrift, Mister Yew," he said glumly, "though I hate to see her go."

"Aye, sir, in that I agree."

"Then repair this charnel house and get under weigh."

"One moment, monsieur," interposed de Gounod. "My carpenter has spare tiller ropes, and is familiar with the task. Meanwhile, permit me the courtesy of inviting you to a drink."

Yew was bristling in anger, but Johnnie sensed something behind de Gounod's offer that intrigued him.

"*M. le Capitaine,* you are a credit to France," Johnnie said with subtle irony. "However, since your men are comfortable where they are, we shall not disturb them."

"You decline my hospitality, monsieur?" pouted de Gounod.

"Quite the contrary, *mon capitaine,*" returned Johnnie. "If you will precede me to the cabin—?"

As de Gounod ambled down the hatch, Johnnie winked at Rodney Yew.

"This Frog's up to some deviltry," he told Yew. "Have the new cable rove as soon as possible."

Yew scowled. "You're not going down there with him alone, sir?"

Johnnie laughed. "Certainly. That great toad—" A sudden pain flashed through his shoulder and made him wince.

Yew beckoned Ben over. "Mister Bottle," he said sharply, "accompany your captain!"

"Aye, aye, sir!" growled Ben.

De Gounod had already seated himself in a chair facing the shattered stern windows when Johnnie came in, flanked by the Irishman. Johnnie dropped onto a settee and took the portfolio from Ben. As he started to break the seal, de Gounod interrupted.

"One moment, monsieur. We have not yet discussed the terms of surrender."

"*Terms?* What a delightful wit you are, *mon capitaine!*"

"But, monsieur," insisted de Gounod. "It is customary. We are not at war! This ship was on a diplomatic mission when you boarded us!"

Johnnie straightened with a bitter laugh. "'Pon my honor, you amaze me! Who started this fracas, I'd like to remind you?"

"*Started?*" De Gounod shrugged. "Ah, who can say, monsieur? Your first actions were suspicious. An impartial court, perhaps—"

"In this case—*I* am the court!" snapped Johnnie, and ripped open the portfolio.

Once again, de Gounod protested. "Monsieur, I beg you! Those documents are protected by diplomatic immunity! I repeat—we are not at war."

Johnnie looked at Ben. "Mick, induce Captain Gounod to hold his tongue."

"B'Jesus, will I!" growled Ben Bottle whose patience had long since been exhausted by the flow of French.

With Ben's pistol to his head, de Gounod relapsed into a sullen quiet. Johnnie began to read the fine French script. He was reading it a second time when Leanna came in.

"Mister Yew requested me to look at your wound," she told Johnnie impersonally.

Johnnie smiled. "That is extremely considerate—of Mister Yew. However, I'm sure there are others more deserving—"

Leanna closed the door. "They have been cared for. Now if you will remove your coat, please!"

He was about to refuse, but her aloofness piqued him so he tossed the letters at her. He knew their contents would startle her.

Puzzled, she glanced at the first page. Then she sank onto the far end of the settee under the windows. He saw the blood drain out of her face, and when she raised her eyes to his, her hands shook.

"Merciful God, Johnnie—where did you get this?" Her tense voice was pitched for his ears alone.

"De Maurin was conveying it to the French high command in Canada."

De Gounod had been watching them anxiously. "Monsieur—I protest!" he wailed. "This is unethical—!" His argument ended abruptly as Ben rapped him over the head with the pistol barrel.

"B'Jesus, do I 'ave to waste powder on ye?" growled the Irishman.

Leanna looked at the Frenchman. "Does *he* know?" she whispered.

Johnnie attempted a shrug, but the pain prevented it. "Apparently not," he said.

"Oh, it's terrible, unspeakable! What are you going to do about it, Johnnie?"

"*Do?* What affair is it of mine?" He paused, conscious of de Gounod's stare.

Leanna was regarding him with a mixture of dismay and impatience. "Does Rodney Yew know of this . . . this catastrophe?"

"No one knows but you."

"And *you*, Johnnie!" Before he could grasp her implication, she rose to her feet. "I'm going to tell Yew!"

Johnnie grinned. "As you wish. There's nothing he can do about—" But she was passing through the door before he finished.

The pain in his shoulder was increasing and he began to regret that he had prevented her from dressing the wound, yet the pride that had interposed on that occasion now kept him from attending to it himself in front of de Gounod, who, by a quirk of fate, had been wounded in almost the same place.

While he was musing this, Leanna returned with Rodney Yew. The Englishman looked puzzled and testy at being hauled so precipitously from his labors.

"Here's Mister Yew, Johnnie! Tell him!"

Both Ben Bottle and Yew started in surprise, both at the peremptoriness of her tone and the use of Johnnie's given name. On Johnnie's part, he was a trifle surprised that she had left the telling to him. Yet though it amused him, it didn't dull his caution.

"Mick, usher the captain on deck. I'm sure he needs the air."

"Take heed, monsieur!" de Guonod said ominously. "You may live to regret this indiscretion!"

Johnnie inclined his head toward the door. Ben took the hint, and placing his bare foot on de Gounod's excessive counter, precipitated him violently into the companionway. Leanna shut the door and, with Yew, stood facing Johnnie.

He waved a hand to the papers on the table before him. "Well,

Mister Yew, I've discovered why de Gounod tried to sink us in that first broadside instead of attempting capture, and by the same token, why de Maurin preferred death to surrender. The Chevalier was a King's courier carrying secret orders to Canada relative to an unheralded naval attack on New York, timed to coincide simultaneously with a formal declaration of war to be made next month."

Yew's ruddy face paled slightly. "May I see the papers?" he asked.

"Help yourself," grunted Johnnie indifferently.

When Yew had scanned the contents, he folded the document carefully and laid it down.

"If this be put into effect," he said, "they'll catch New York unprepared, in the same fashion Drake caught the Spaniards napping at Cadiz!"

Johnnie chuckled sardonically. "Aye, and certain to succeed, for though surprise is the basic element of all military tactics, the English never seem to comprehend it."

"Dear Lord above!" cried Leanna. "Must you discuss it as a chess game already lost? There'll be no *surprise* if you warn the authorities!"

"If *I* warn—?" Johnnie burst into laughter. "'Pon my soul, you have a sense of humor, my dear!"

"I have a sense of *honor!*" She looked at him with dismay. "You can't mean that you will just sit here and do nothing while the French amass a fleet to ravish your own country! Can't you understand, Johnnie? England is in danger!"

"A very dramatic performance, my lady," he applauded dryly. "You speak feelingly of 'my country,' forgetting, I fear, that I have no country. In your own words—I am a thief and a pirate."

"God's love! Can't you stop thinking about yourself! What of those unfortunate people in New York?"

"Sir Clarence, perhaps?"

She went white with rage, then caught herself and gripped the edge of the table. "Mister Yew!" she appealed. "What would you do?"

"Need you ask, my lady?" Yew said shortly.

Johnnie frowned momentarily, then his mouth twisted into a sarcastic smile.

"But *I* need ask, Mister Yew. I'm curious."

Yew regarded him coldly. "We've been over this same ground before, sir. I believe I made myself clear at the time."

"You did, and I let myself in for a lively time because of it. I'll make myself equally clear, I'll not tempt fate twice with the same mistake.

I was a fool to have disclosed this business to her ladyship, but that's the end of it."

"No, Johnnie, *no!*" Leanna cried. "If you won't go back like a—" She caught herself, then plunged on: "Find some way to warn them! At least be *that* human!"

Johnnie was cordially sick of the whole argument. "Perhaps you would like to take the long-boat and row to New York?"

"You could put me ashore and I could—"

Yew put a kindly hand on her arm. "Please, my lady," he urged. "That would be futile. The question of time—"

He was interrupted by Ben Bottle who burst unceremoniously into the cabin.

"Johnnie!" panted the Irishman. "There's two sail bearin' down on us!"

Johnnie sprang to his feet and led the rush to the deck. Using his one good arm, he hauled himself part way up the weather rigging. The on-coming vessels were already hull up—due to the press of work, no lookouts had been stationed—and he could see that they were ship-rigged. More menacing than their size, however, was the fact that they approached from opposing angles of which he was at the apex, thus cutting off escape save by heading shoreward.

"Mister Yew," he called down. "How soon before that rudder will be ready?"

"Another hour—at least, sir!"

Johnnie climbed painfully down to the deck. One look at the triumphant leer on de Gounod's face was sufficient to confirm a grim suspicion.

"So, *mon capitaine,* it becomes obvious why you were so anxious to delay. You did not sail alone?"

De Gounod waved one hand airily. "Hardly—in these English-infested waters, monsieur! I had the honor to be convoyed by two of the fastest and most powerful frigates of our Most Christian Majesty's navy."

When Johnnie digested that in silence, the Frenchman laughed heartily. "Come, monsieur," he chided. "It is but the fortunes of war. I will accept your surrender, if you please."

Johnnie stiffened, then his shoulders sagged dejectedly. "We cannot run away, and it would be futile to fight so overwhelming a force."

Leanna, Ben and Yew stared at him unbelievingly. De Gounod applauded his acceptance of the obvious.

"Quite futile," he agreed. "*Mon Dieu!* Even if this little sloop was in repair, those greyhounds could run you down in a trice. Come, monsieur, as an officer and a gentleman, I beg of you to waste no lives on heroics!"

Johnnie pondered. "How can I be sure the frigate captains will honor a surrender to you, *M. le Capitaine?* What if they—"

"Bah!" scoffed de Gounod. "They are under my command."

"H'mmn! That puts a different light on the matter. However, they may shoot first and question later?"

"That is why I insist on your immediate compliance to my demand for surrender," barked de Gounod officiously. "They look to me for signals! If they are not forthcoming—" His scowl was significant.

"In that case," murmured Johnnie, "there is but one thing to do."

Leanna ran across the deck and grasped his arm.

"*Don't!*" she pleaded. "Don't! Better we all be killed than let them recover those plans. In God's name, don't surrender!"

Johnnie glanced down at her in mock amazement. "*Surrender?* Why, my lady, after the bitter lesson I learned at your hands, I'll never surrender again!"

She swayed back as if he had struck her. De Gounod glowered fiercely.

"You make the joke, monsieur?" he demanded.

"Aye, *mon capitaine,* I make the joke." Johnnie smiled so pleasantly de Gounod broke into a loud guffaw.

"Be pleased to give the order for the release of my men," he said at the conclusion of his merriment. "My compatriots will be looking for a signal within the glass."

"So I see," admitted Johnnie. He stepped out of hearing and beckoned the wide-eyed Irishman to his side.

"Holy Mither!" moaned Ben. "I bloody well 'ates to—"

"Be quiet and listen," snapped Johnnie. He gave his instructions in a low voice, and when Ben had scuttled forward, he rejoined the others. Leanna turned her back on him, but de Gounod was offensively jovial.

"As a matter of curiosity, *M. le Capitaine,*" asked Johnnie, "how did you get separated from your consorts?"

"Ah, the squalls, monsieur. By night we run without lights." He shrugged. "But all has turned out for the best."

Johnnie sniffed. "I see you have a penchant for platitudes. We have another you should learn: He who laughs last laughs best."

De Gounod slapped his thigh and roared with mirth.

"*Mon Dieu!* That is good. And I laugh now, eh?"

"As the occasion merits," conceded Johnnie.

At that moment, Ben returned to the quarter-deck carrying a cane-bottomed chair. He was accompanied by Old Ames who toted an iron pot of liquid in one hand and a yard-long length of wicking in the other.

Without a word, they walked aft. Ames placed the pot amidships and stepped back so that Ben could set the chair astride it, facing the taffrail, after which the Irishman cut a circular hole in the cane seat with his knife. When completed, the contrivance resembled a chamber-pot.

All this had been viewed with astonishment by those present. Johnnie bowed formally to the scowling Frenchman.

"To the victor belongs the spoils, *mon capitaine,*" he offered smilingly. "Pray be seated."

"Name of a name!" roared de Gounod. "What madness is this?"

"Consideration for your comfort, my dear captain," Johnnie assured him. "The pot is filled with lamp-oil, which in event of necessity will be lighted by my chief gunner to warm your nether parts. I ask you to sit down."

"*Canaille!*" choked the Frenchman. "I refuse!"

"I expected as much," sighed Johnnie, and nodded to his men.

They seized de Gounod and banged him into the chair. A few turns of marlin and he was secured. While Old Ames stood behind him, blowing on the end of his lye-soaked wick to nourish the flame, Johnnie addressed himself to the French captain.

"Since you enjoy a good joke, *mon capitaine,* you will appreciate this one. You will sit here and watch for signals from your frigates, which you will interpret for us and suggest the appropriate return. Mister Bottle, with whom you are already acquainted, will serve you as aide. You will be very comfortable—so long as all goes well. I know the thought of treachery would never enter your mind, but it might be fair to remark in passing that if so much as a *single* shot is fired upon us, M. Bottle will ignite the oil beneath you."

"*Dieu mon Dieu!*" burst out de Gounod. "They will not go away even if I signal!"

Johnnie laughed. "I have no objection to sailing under such distinguished protection. However, monsieur, don't trouble your head about inconsequentials. As you so aptly remarked—all is fair in love and war."

De Gounod stared around at the grim faces in consternation.

"Monsieur!" he appealed to Johnnie. "Consider your honor! This is not the act of an English naval officer—it is the act of a *pirate!*"

"Exactly!" smiled Johnnie, bowing. "But then, *mon capitaine—I am a pirate.*"

On that note, Johnnie went below.

25

ALONE IN THE CABIN, JOHNNIE FELL PREY TO REACTION, BOTH PHYSICAL and emotional. He slumped in a chair and stared moodily out the windows at the blue rollers building up astern in the increasing wind. Intellectually, he knew his victory had been brilliant, but the cost in men had robbed him of any sense of exultation. Even his mawkish humor with Captain de Gounod disgusted him; he should have hanged the treacherous scoundrel out of hand. He cursed the impulse which had induced him to show the dispatches to Leanna. If anything had been needed to definitely alienate him from Rodney Yew—that had done it.

But most of all, for some obscure reason beyond his understanding, he was depressed over the death of de Maurin. He despised the French nobility as a matter of course, and he was prone to attribute the Chevalier's suicidal refusal to accept surrender as the characteristic arrogance of his class. Yet he couldn't quite convince himself. De Maurin had chosen death before what he had considered dishonor, and in his present condition, Johnnie was forced to a grudging admiration for the man. It was the sort of heroics Rodney Yew would perform under similar circumstances.

When he felt the brig move under him, he knew he should go on deck, but he was overcome with a strange lassitude that seemed to emanate from his wounded shoulder. He was still sitting there when Old Ames came in to report the rudder repaired.

"And the frigates, ancient?"

The old man grinned. "They made signals, an' Gounod made a speech about dyin' fer France, but w'en the Mick blew on 'is match, the coward changed his mind. We made the proper answers, but they be keepin' close company. Seems like we be ridin' the bear's tail."

"Better than riding in his mouth," Johnnie said with forced humor. "Tell me—how bad were our losses?"

Ames shook his head. "Heavy, sir. Nigh a third o' the lads slipped their cables."

Johnnie sighed. "Ask Mister Yew to step down here, old one."

Ames scuttled out of the cabin in that peculiar crab-wise way of his, and Johnnie crossed to the stern windows. He could see one of the frigates now, jogging within cannon-shot off the larboard quarter. Her topgallants were reefed to slow her down to the speed of the brig, and he could well imagine how fast she would be with everything drawing. The knowledge did nothing to lighten his dispondency.

Yet when Yew stalked in, Johnnie greeted him with a smile.

"Well, Mister Yew, it appears the fox is running with the hounds?"

Yew snorted. "For the nonce, aye, but it can't last. Sooner or later—"

"It doesn't need to last," Johnnie interrupted. "When darkness falls, we'll wear around and lose them."

Yew nodded approvingly. "Aye, it might work, if the wind holds, which I think it will." He looked steadily at Johnnie. "And then, sir?"

"Why then we'll be where we were before—with a better ship under us, though I dislike to admit it."

Yew shook his head. "Not exactly where we were before, sir—there are those dispatches."

Johnnie bit his lip. As he had expected, those damn dispatches were going to cause a breach.

"Confound it," he said impatiently, "it should be obvious to a seaman of your experience that there is nothing I can do about it!"

Yew leaned his knuckles on the table. "What is obvious," he rumbled bitterly, "is the hopelessness of appealing to your patriotism. So though it galls me, I'm going to ask a favor for myself. You know I have not joined your venture; that was understood. In New York, you offered me a boat to go ashore. I chose to remain."

"For which I'm grateful," confessed Johnnie.

"Thank you, sir," Yew said dryly. "I trust your gratitude, as you choose to term it, will take a practical form."

"Come to your point."

Yew reddened. "Very well, sir—I ask that you permit me to take a boat and try for the coast."

Johnnie whistled. "We're a hundred miles off shore, man!"

"We're about a hundred and fifty miles from Charleston," amended Yew. "But if you turn westward in the night and run southwest, which would be the most practical maneuver from your point of view, I can make it without too much difficulty. I should be able to find an English squadron there."

"Very likely," sniffed Johnnie. "And doubtless they've been warned about us, and would promptly hang you for your pains."

"If I may say so, sir—that need not concern you."

Johnnie turned to the stern windows and rested his knee on the settee. The whole left side of his body was growing numb and he had difficulty keeping his mind from wandering. His common sense bade him refuse the request, for he could ill afford to lose the services of Yew. But fatigue weakened his powers of resistance and he was getting heartily sick of the tension.

"All right," he growled, swinging around. "On one condition." A sudden dizziness made him pause, and he dropped onto the settee.

"If you fear I will betray you," the other filled in the silence, "you can be sure—"

"No, no, I wasn't thinking of that," Johnnie said abruptly. "I want you to take Lady Somerset with you."

Yew's eyes widened in surprise. "By the powers, sir, an open boat—"

"There'll be no danger!" Johnnie cut in grimly. "I'll run you close inshore and drop you with a fair wind for Charleston. You should pick up an English ship on station before sunset tomorrow night."

Yew stared at him as if about to ask a question, then seeming to think better of it, straightened.

"Very good, sir. I'll inform her ladyship of your wishes."

Johnnie smiled tiredly. "It's your wish, not mine, Rodney Yew."

"Thank you, sir!"

"Cover the dead with tarpaulins," Johnnie ordered. "We can't risk a sea burial in the daylight with those damned frigates so close. Meanwhile, I'll get a bit of rest. Call me at sunset."

Johnnie kept to his feet until the door closed behind Yew, then he stretched out on the settee. His wound was beginning to throb, and he knew he should do something about it, but to exert the necessary effort was beyond him.

Sometime later, he heard a knock on the door. To his surprise, it was Leanna. He attempted to rise, but when he found the pain too great, he stayed where he was. He preferred to have her think him rude rather than know the truth.

"Rodney Yew told me of your plan, Johnnie," she said eagerly. "I want to thank you."

"If Yew told you it was my plan—he lied," Johnnie said stiffly. "It was entirely his own."

"Including my accompanying him?"

"I merely anticipated you in that, my lady."

She colored and he could see her struggling to control her temper. Finally she said in a low tone, "I'll never forgive you for dragging me aboard against my will, Johnnie, but if Rodney Yew can get those dispatches to the government in time to prevent disaster, at least it may have accomplished something."

"Rodney Yew is an obstinate fool," snapped Johnnie, "and so am I. I wish you luck, my lady, both with the dispatches, and . . . with Sir Clarence."

Her lips tightened into a bitter line. "Oh, I wish that Frenchman had killed you!" she cried, and ran out of the cabin.

Shortly afterwards, he heard the ship's bell clang five times. He was surprised it was so late. He closed his eyes. . . .

He woke to see the early sunrise streaming into the cabin. Startled, he propped himself up on one elbow and looked out the windows. To his consternation, he saw the frigates still within gun-shot on either quarter. He tried to rise to his feet, only to find his legs would not support him. In something akin to panic, he crawled back onto the couch.

"*Ames!*" he bellowed. "*Mick!*"

A moment later, Ames scuttled into the cabin followed by Rodney Yew. Johnnie stared at him in amazement.

"Blood and fury!" he raged. "Didn't I order you to put about in the darkness? Now I see those damn frigates—"

"Begging your pardon, sir," interrupted Yew, "but there was no *darkness*. Last night's full moon was as clear as daylight. The frigates hung close aboard and escape was impossible."

Johnnie gaped. That was a factor he had not foreseen.

"'Tis the bloody trufe, sir!" put in Ames, mistaking his silence for disbelief.

Johnnie laughed half hysterically. "'Pon my soul, Mister Yew, it appears the Fates have prevented you becoming the savior of your country!"

Yew ignored the sarcasm. "Not necessarily, sir," he retorted. "We're running that much closer to New York. Perchance tonight—"

"Bah!" snorted Johnnie. "If the wind dies, one of those damned

Frenchmen will put a boat over for a visit. Then there won't be any *tonight* for us."

"I doubt the wind will die, sir. We're in for a blow, if I mistake not the signs."

Johnnie grunted and made a motion for dismissal. "Go get some sleep. I'll take the deck."

As Yew quit the cabin, Johnnie beckoned Ames to his side.

"Help me to my feet, ancient," he growled. "I'm a trifle stiff."

He put his arm around the old man's shoulder and again pushed himself clear of the couch—only to fall against the table and slide to his knees.

Ames cursed and scurried to the door. *"Mick!"* he shouted. "Mick, ye carrot-topped devil!"

Almost immediately, Ben came pounding into the cabin. He took one look at Johnnie on his knees, then with a startled "Holy Mither Mary!" he sprang to his side. Between the two of them, they lifted Johnnie onto the bed. The old one opened his coat sufficiently to note the angry wound, and trumpeted in rage.

"Satan's backside, ye damned younker! W'at in 'ell d'ye mean leavin' it that way?"

Johnnie managed a sickly grin. "Come, ancient, assist me on deck before I log you both for mutiny."

"Mutiny me arse! Ye'll lay hove-to where ye be, else I'll 'ave the Mick sit on ye. Mutiny, is it, with two frigates ridin' our tails an' the only man who can syve us tryin' to kill hisself? Ye can talk o' mutiny w'en yer able to do some'at about it. Until then, ye'll be'ave yersel'! Watch 'im, Mick, whilest I get some 'ot water."

As he scrabbled out of the cabin, Ben came close and leaned over Johnnie. His wide eyes were moist.

"God A'mighty, b'y, why didn't ye tell us ye was bad 'urt?"

"Hell and damnation!" fumed Johnnie. "Am I to be nursed by you two sentimental old women every time I get a scratch?" He tried to struggle to a sitting position, but Ben gently forced him back.

" 'Azy, b'y, 'azy! Y're balmy in the crumpet!"

Further argument was precluded by the return of Ames. He bustled in officiously with a bucket of hot water and at once took charge. He cut Johnnie's coat away—despite the latter's violent protestations that it was his only garment—and bared the wound. Unfortunately, it had not bled sufficiently to cleanse itself.

The old man cursed bitterly. "Ye ought to get the cat fer neglectin' it!" he stormed, crawling onto the edge of the bunk like an angry spider. "Now, by God, I'll 'ave to open it again! 'Tis full o' poisons!"

"Open and be damned!" said Johnnie. "I've got to get on deck!"

Ames dipped his knife in the scalding water. "Now, Mick, 'old 'im —this be goin' to 'urt, I fear."

But Lord Johnnie didn't feel the pain—for at the first stroke of the knife, he passed out. . . .

Then followed the fever, and Johnnie found himself chained to a stake in the middle of raging flames which transformed his body into a pillar of sentient fire. He screamed and struggled until at last his freed spirit soared into the past, and he landed back in the little private academy in France, once more a tall, gangling boy of twelve.

He found himself in the midst of an almost forgotten quarrel. An older boy was berating him for being a bastard.

"We don't want you here," the boy was telling him. "Your father is unknown and your mother nothing but a English whore—!"

Johnnie knocked him down and caught him by the throat.

"I'll kill you for that!" he shrieked, and was suiting the action to the word when strong arms bore him away.

"Fer God's sake, Johnnie!" pleaded a faraway voice. "Take it 'azy!"

Johnnie was astounded to hear that voice in this little French school. He opened his eyes. Through shimmering heat waves, he distinguished the worried countenance of Ben Bottle. There were other faces, too vague to recognize.

"What are you doing here, Mick?" he asked.

"'Tis all right, b'y, I ain't lef' ye!"

But the flames began again to consume him, so Johnnie escaped once more—to a small grove in the Bois de Boulogne near Paris. For a moment, he couldn't orient himself. He was standing in his stockinged feet, with a dueling sword in his hand. On the ground in front of him lay a dead man, a doctor bending over him. Johnnie looked around in surprise and saw the lieutenant of a French ship on which he had served standing beside him, holding his coat.

"You had better run for it," the lieutenant advised anxiously. "You have killed him!"

"But I killed him fairly!" Johnnie protested. "And with provocation. He insulted my mother's memory!"

"I know, I know," muttered the officer. "But, *mon Dieu*, he was a marquis, and you—" The speaker hesitated.

"I am nothing, eh?" filled in Johnnie. When he received no reply, he cried out: "Then if I have no legal status, I'll have another of a kind!"

The doctor and the marquis' second tried to prevent him from leaving, but Johnnie fought them off with his sword and sprang onto his horse. As he galloped away, the flames caught up with him and sucked him back to his stake.

After that, his visions grew fragmentary, dipping here and there, without regard for chronology, into those incidents of his past which illuminated the theme of his unrest. He dropped in at the home of the Duchess of Tallentyre, to find Sir Montague discussing his hanging.

". . . he was a debonair scoundrel," the General was laughing. "Fine build, damme! They say he palmed himself off as a gentleman, and I must confess I've seen worse at Court!"

Then as Johnnie leaned forward to hear the rest of it, he discovered the scene had shifted to Moll Coppinger's room in Whitefriars. Moll was screaming at him:

" 'E got big notions o' bein' a gent'man an' risin' out o' yer class . . . but y're just a low-born common bastard like the rest o' us—!"

Johnnie turned his back on her and came face to face with Rodney Yew. The navigator was shaking his head.

"I can't understand you, sir. You have the appearance of a gentleman, yet—"

Always that qualification! Johnnie tried to escape, only to find Leanna before him.

"Why did you become a thief, Johnnie?" she demanded wistfully. "You could pass for a gentleman! That name—John Ballantyne! Why, it's a noble-sounding name, Johnnie! I almost wish . . . Oh, I hate you, I hate you!"

But Moll caught his arm. "She must love 'e out of all reason," she hissed, pointing at Leanna, "for only a woman deeply in love would be so wrought-up as to want 'e dead!"

"Love does not enter into the question," Leanna retorted. "Once upon a time I had ideals and romantic dreams, but that's all over."

"A man's conscience is the best judge," broke in Rodney Yew. "An Englishman's duty is to his King and his country. There are worse things than death!"

"*Mon Dieu!*" cried the voice of the Chevalier de Maurin from the background. "Death before dishonor!"

Suddenly all faded away but Leanna. As she began to grow dim, Johnnie grabbed her in an agony of desperation.

"Don't go!" he begged her. "Can't you see how it has been for me? I love you, Leanna."

But she was already dissolving in his arms, and he could see only darkness beyond her.

"It's passing strange," she whispered sadly. "I find myself wishing . . ." And then she was gone.

The fire came licking through the darkness to claim him and from the shadows he heard the Duchess say: "That girl has altered your outlook, hasn't she?"

"She's clarified it, your Grace!"

"What a rotten thing life is!" came the dimming voice. "We come all ignorant and unprepared to the fork in the road so early that by the time we have sense enough to realize the folly, we have galloped too far to turn back."

Johnnie shouted: "Wait for me! Wait for me!" and began to crawl ahead of the flames. Slowly, tediously, he widened the gap. The terrible heat lessened and at long last he fought out into a cool plain. . . .

"Ancient! Ancient!" roared Ben Bottle. " 'E's comin' awake!"

A door slammed, and Johnnie opened his eyes. The Irishman was bending over him, and Old Ames came scuttling across the cabin.

"Bless ye, younker!" panted the old man. " 'Tis a relief to see ye out o' it!"

Johnnie smiled. He couldn't remember when he had ever felt so relaxed and rested.

" 'Pon my soul!" he chuckled. "I must have fallen asleep. Did you get the wound bled, old one? It feels better, I admit."

Ben blinked his surprise, but Ames said quickly, "Aye, lad, the worst is o'er."

"An' thank God fer it!" groaned Ben. "Another two days o' yer buckin' an' 'ollerin' an' we'd all be in bed, rape me if else."

Johnnie started to laugh, then stopped short.

"Two days!" he said sharply. "What are you talking about?"

Ames sat down on the edge of the bunk beside him.

"Now don't gi' us any more trouble, laddie," he urged. "Ye been out o' yer 'ead wi' fever these past two days. But fer the skill o' Mister Yew an' the blessed ministrations o' 'er ladyship—"

"My God!" gasped Johnnie. "Are they still here?"

Ames looked puzzled. "Still 'ere? W'y 'er ladyship rarely left the cabin!"

Johnnie groaned and closed his eyes. "And the French frigates—?"

"Right w'ere they was, damn 'em," admitted Ames.

He stood up abruptly, and Johnnie raised his lids to see Leanna moving toward him.

" 'E's awake!" crowed Ben.

She gave him a tired smile. "So I see. Now you two boys go get some rest. I'll stay with him awhile."

"Thank 'e, ma'am," said Ben. "But w'at if 'e starts 'oopin' an' 'ollerin' again?"

She laughed lightly. "He won't, Ben. The delirium has passed with the fever."

Johnnie kept his eyes closed until he was certain Ben and Ames had quit the cabin, then he stole a furtive glance at her. She had seated herself near by and was sewing on a skirt. The dark circles under her eyes gave evidence of sleeplessness.

"Leanna!"

She started in surprise. When she met his eyes, she quickly composed herself.

"Yes?"

"I just wanted to make sure you were real," he confessed. "They tell me I owe you my life."

"That is not true," she said. "I've merely taken my turn sitting here. If you owe it to anyone, it's to Rodney Yew."

"You mean for keeping the deck—?"

"I mean for applying the poultice of mould and spider-webs to draw the poisons from your wound. The rest of us had given you up for dead."

"Rodney Yew did that!" gasped Johnnie. "I can scarce believe it!"

"Please lie quiet," she ordered brusquely. "You must be very weak."

But Johnnie didn't feel weak. He started to throw off the covers. Then, realizing he was naked, he begged her to send for Yew. At first she refused, but when he threatened to go on deck as he was she hurried out and shortly afterwards Yew walked in.

From the bluffness of his manner, Johnnie deduced he was embarrassed.

"You desired to see me, sir?" he said, as if nothing had happened.

Johnnie smiled. "Aye—to thank you for saving my life!"

"It is hardly *saved*, sir," grunted the other, nodding toward the stern windows. "The Frenchmen may claim it."

"Damme! Apparently none of you wants to assume the responsibility for pulling me through!" When Yew reddened under the thrust, Johnnie chuckled.

"Well, more of that anon. How come we haven't lost our consorts?"

"For the same reason we didn't lose them the first night: the moonlight has been too brilliant."

"And our present position?"

"Approximately twenty-five leagues due east of Cape Charles."

Johnnie turned that over in his mind, but found it difficult to adjust himself to the fact that two full days had been blotted from his consciousness. At his request, Yew spread a chart out on the bunk and indicated their position.

"We're steering a nor'-nor'east course to clear the station of the New York guard ship," he added. "The wind has been fresh from the sou'east for the past three days."

"That's providential," grunted Johnnie.

Yew shrugged. "It appears Providence is playing with us, rather. True the wind holds fair, but the moonlight keeps us chained to the frigates. 'Tis a sorry mess, I wean."

"What have you decided, Mister Yew?"

Yew frowned. "Now that you have recovered, sir, the decision—"

"Since my recovery is obviously a surprise, you must have considered the alternative. I'd like to hear your own solution."

Watching the mariner's embarrassment, Johnnie began to understand him better. Yew's talents were manifold, but imagination was not one of them. His very single-mindedness of purpose limited his grasp of intangible ideas.

"Well, sir," he stammered, "there's naught to do but put our trust in God!"

"Captain de Gounod is doubtless doing the same thing," Johnnie commented dryly. "That's expecting undue partiality from the Lord."

Yew flushed angrily. "I don't run counter to His laws!"

"Very laudable!" laughed Johnnie. "Yet if I remember my Bible, it contains a bit of potent advice to the effect that—God helps those who help themselves."

"A quotation which has been used by self-seeking scoundrels to cover a multitude of sins, if I may say so."

"You may," chuckled Johnnie, "and very apt it is. Leave the chart here, Mister Yew. I'll see if I can find some way of cooperating with the Lord."

But when Yew left him, Johnnie stared hopelessly at the chart. The problem appeared insoluble; it was a question of which came first—a dark night or a calm. If the former, the brig had a fair chance of escape, but in the event of the latter, they were sure to be discovered. Johnnie knew their fate if taken.

He brushed the chart onto the floor and lay back against the pillow. The gliding motion of the brig was easy, and under different circumstances, he would have been delighted with her. At the moment, however, he was merely restless. The tortuous visions conjured up in his delirium had left their mark on him, and, albeit somewhat unconsciously, he found himself coupling the delivery of the French dispatches to the British with his own escape. His mind had conceived an idea in the wanderings of fever but it was still too vague to be termed a plan.

He threw back the cover and slid to the floor. His legs were weak, but he managed to totter over to the window seat. The sight of the French frigate, riding so arrogantly a mile to seaward, stimulated him. He made his way to the door and shouted for Ames.

The old man flew into a tantrum on seeing him out of bed. But Johnnie silenced him.

"That's enough of your womanish temper, ancient! Mind your tongue, or by God, you'll taste the cat!"

Ames looked startled a moment, then broke into clucking laughter. "Aye, y're better, Cap'n!" he chortled.

Johnnie grinned. "So, you old termagant, rustle me up some clothes!"

Ames darted to a locker and lifted out a fine suit of black silk. Johnnie whistled admiringly.

" 'Tis a gift o' yer sword, lad!" explained the old man. "Belike the Chevalier won't be needin' it no more."

Johnnie winced, but as he had no clothing of his own, he donned the suit without comment. He felt much better dressed, yet when he saw the effect in the mirror, he was dismayed by the appearance of his face. The skin under a three-day growth of beard was pasty, and the eyes sunken. Ames offered to shave him, but Johnnie shook his head.

"I must take the deck," he insisted. "Rodney Yew needs a rest."

Although he had to call on the old man to help him up the companionway ladder, once on deck the clear cool air wrought miracles. The watch broke into a cheering welcome, and when Johnnie settled him-

self in a chair brought up by Ames, he felt as good as ever. He ordered
Yew below, and looked over the ship.

The dead had been disposed of and the decks cleaned until no
evidence remained of the carnage so shortly past. Yew had listed the
commonest signals flown by the frigates so that de Gounod was only
brought on deck when occasion warranted. Leanna, Ames told him,
was catching up on her sleep.

With the brig running free on the starboard tack, Johnnie had
nothing to do save work on the problem. As the embryonic idea developed into a recognizable form, he began to wonder whether it was
a child of his fever or his brain. Nevertheless, he decided to accept it.

"What's your course?" he asked the steersman.

"Nor'nor'east, sir!"

"Make it north then."

"North she be, sir!"

As the brig veered on the new course, a series of flags fluttered up
the signal halliard of the inshore frigate.

"What's he say?" Johnnie asked Ames.

The old man stroked his chin. "Burn me, sir, that's a new 'un!"

Johnnie grinned. "I can guess, but send for de Gounod."

When the French captain was brought up, he took one look at
the signals, then glared at Johnnie.

"My *confrères* are alarmed that we stand so close to the coast," he
decoded the message.

Johnnie raised his eyebrows. "Do they now? I wasn't aware that
naval officers—and *gentlemen*—challenged their superiors."

"But what is the purpose?" protested de Gounod. "Unless you keep
well off to sea, there is the danger of running into the accursed
English ship on guard station!"

"We can discuss that at leisure, *mon capitaine*," Johnnie retorted.
"But for the present, be so good as to signal your compatriots to follow
you without question."

De Gounod swelled dramatically. "*Mon Dieu!* My honor will not
permit—" he protested, but Johnnie turned to Ames.

"Ancient, where are your manners? Bring Captain de Gounod's chair
at once, and don't forget the *warming pan!*"

The Frenchman wilted. "No, monsieur, no!" He tearfully supplied
the proper return to make, and the frigates soon shifted to the same
course as the brig.

"Thank you, *mon capitaine*," said Johnnie. "That will be all."

But de Gounod hesitated. He looked uneasily from Johnnie to Ames and then back to Johnnie.

"Could I speak with you privately, monsieur?" he pleaded.

Ames began to bristle, but Johnnie waved him out of hearing. The Frenchman took a nervous turn around the quarter-deck, then came to a halt close to Johnnie.

"Monsieur," he whispered. "Is it true you are a . . . a *freebooter?*"

"*Pirate* is the commoner term," admitted Johnnie.

De Gounod's smile was sickly. "In that event, you have more interest in profit than in England, monsieur?"

"As a pirate that would be obvious."

De Gounod rubbed his hands. "Ah! Then perchance we might come to terms?"

Ordinarily, Lord Johnnie would have been amused, if not actually interested, yet now for some reason beyond his comprehension, he felt overwhelmed with rage. Without pausing to analyze the reaction, he bellowed for Ames.

"Take this cur out of my sight before I slit his throat!" he thundered. Then as if to add insult to injury, he snapped at the steersman: "Another point to larboard!"

"Larboard a point!" echoed the helmsman.

Stunned, de Gounod permitted himself to be led away without protest.

26

FOR THE FOURTH CONSECUTIVE NIGHT, THE MOON BEAMED ON THEM with malicious generosity, to the bitter disappointment of the crew, but Lord Johnnie was indifferent, having become enamored with his new scheme. True, it was not escape; rather a shifting of the dilemma from the busy hands of Providence onto the broad shoulders of Johnnie Rogue.

Yet while willing to accept the responsibility, Johnnie was not quite certain what motivated him, for he hardly recognized himself as the parent of so alien a stratagem. He was not trying to usurp the just prerogatives of the Almighty, but he reasoned the French had just as valid a claim to Providential assistance as the English, and he preferred to stand or fall by his own mistakes. So exploring the compulsion no further, he held to his altered course until after midnight when exhaustion forced him to summon Rodney Yew.

When that doughty mariner came on deck, Johnnie cautioned him to maintain lookouts aloft, and with no mention of the change in heading, went below.

Shortly after eight bells in the morning watch, he was awakened by Ben Bottle with the news that a sail had been sighted off the larboard bow. Johnnie slipped into his clothing and went on deck.

The French frigates had also made out the stranger and were signaling frantically, but as Yew had gone to the masthead with his glass, the signals remained unanswered.

"Shall I bring up the Frog, Cap'n?" asked Ames.

Johnnie shook his head. "That won't be necessary. Make the same reply you used yesterday—*follow my lead.*"

As the old man hastened to obey, Johnnie turned to Ben.

"Now, Mister Bottle," he said, "when Mister Yew comes down from aloft, tell him my orders are to close with the stranger. Is that clear?"

Ben nodded. "Aye, aye, sir!"

Ames, having returned from his signaling, was taken below to act as barber. About an hour later, shaved, bathed and meticulously garbed,

Johnnie stepped on deck again to find the stranger hull-up, closed-hauled on the starboard tack. Rodney Yew was studying her through his glass with a mixture of puzzlement and anxiety.

"What do you make of her?" asked Johnnie.

Yew frowned. "Damme, I fear she's an English frigate, sir. Same class as the *Tiger*."

"I suspect she is the *Tiger*."

"Then, by the powers!—what's she doing away out here?"

Johnnie smiled. "We are not 'away out here,' Mister Yew. I altered our course yesterday to make westing. I imagine she's right on station."

Yew's mouth sagged open in amazement. "By God, sir, do you mean you've deliberately sought her out?"

"Precisely!"

Yew stared at Ben and Ames, but their astonishment was as great as his own.

"When do you estimate she'll be in range, Mister Yew?"

"Before noon," gasped Yew, then his face darkened. "But, as Heaven is my witness, if you mean to fight her, I'll—"

Johnnie laughed. "Oh, it shouldn't be necessary to fight her, Mister Yew," he interrupted. "These fine French mastiffs will keep her busy enough, I'm certain."

Ben slapped his thigh delightedly. "B'Jesus, I ken ye!" he roared. "While the dogs is fightin', the fox slips away! Eh, Johnnie?"

"A possibility," admitted Johnnie noncommittally. "Ames, bring up de Gounod."

" 'Tis the act of a coward!" spat Yew, and turned on his heel.

Johnnie flushed, but let him go. The crews of all three ships had climbed into the rigging to watch the approach of the stranger. Johnnie's men appeared apprehensive and sullen. Then Captain de Gounod mounted the quarter-deck, and Johnnie turned his attention to him.

"Well, *mon capitaine*, I've been thinking of our little discussion of yesterday. How is this for cooperation?" He pointed to the on-rushing frigate.

"*Ventre-dieu!*" swore the Frenchman. "Is it English?"

"Aye, a thirty-two-gun frigate—a gift for your greyhounds of war."

De Gounod gripped the rail and stared at Johnnie without comprehension.

"Come now, *mon capitaine*," laughed Johnnie, "I confess I expected more enthusiasm from you. Isn't it probable that your Most

Christian Majesty would regard the exchange of this miserable little brig for a fine English frigate a profitable deal?"

De Gounod's expression changed swiftly from suspicion to avarice, without increasing his charm.

"Ah! I begin to understand, monsieur!"

"I trusted you would," said Johnnie, smiling. "It must be irksome for a mariner of your obvious talents to be temporarily without a command. If God favors your cause, that may be rectified."

De Gounod leaned close and examined Johnnie's face for some indication of irony, but on finding none, he asked tentatively, "What is your plan, monsieur?"

Johnnie shrugged. "That's for you to say, *mon capitaine*. If I were in your shoes, I should desire my consorts to take her with as little damage as possible—nothing that could not be repaired at sea and quickly."

De Gounod took his ponderous lower lip between his forefinger and thumb and tugged it thoughtfully.

"The accursed English captains fight to the last man!" he grumbled.

"True, yet three to one appears on the surface a singular advantage. The very stubbornness of the English may be utilized in your favor. Suppose, for instance, your frigates formed a V, with this brig at the small end. If they hold their fire, the Englishman with undoubtedly sail into the trap, and could be boarded from both sides, with only superficial damage."

De Gounod cackled delightedly. *"Mon Dieu,* you have a talent for warfare, monsieur! This plan is worthy of a Frenchman!"

Johnnie bowed. "I have learned a lot from the French, *mon capitaine,* as you will see before we part. Now the signals, *mon capitaine—?"*

De Gounod supplied the code with enthusiasm, and Johnnie issued the necessary instructions to Ames. The signals were promptly acknowledged, and for a moment or two, Johnnie held his breath. This was the weakest link in his stratagem, for he had to depend on de Gounod's credulity. If the Frenchman had given the wrong signals, Johnnie was undone. He had already sensed the treachery behind that pox-pitted mask, but aware of the fear inherent among the French navy of British warships, he was gambling that de Gounod would decide to wait until the English frigate was subdued before turning on the brig.

To his relief, he saw the French frigates draw apart to form a flying trap. He ordered Yew to back the topsails to let them in the van, then taking a position behind and between the two, swept on to meet the *Tiger*.

De Gounod was voluble in his delight. *"Dieu mon Dieu!* Is it not a beautiful sight, monsieur!" he crowed loudly, waving his arms.

Johnnie was watching the *Tiger* charging like a terrier against what she must feel to be overwhelming odds.

"A cause for just pride," he agreed.

De Gounod's antics had not been lost on the seamen, and if they couldn't understand his language, at least his meaning was obvious. They began to collect amidships in little groups, and at last moved aft in a body.

"Cap'n!" called an old tar. "We uns want to know w'at ye intend?"

Ben and Old Ames edged over to support Johnnie, but he ignored them and sauntered to the rail overlooking the men.

" 'Pon my soul!" he said mockingly. "Are you all blind? That's our old enemy the *Tiger!*"

"Aye, sir, so we see!" returned the spokesman. "But we uns want to know if ye mean to fight 'er?"

"And why not?" challenged Johnnie. "You were willing enough to fight her a few weeks ago! Have you lost your stomachs for battle, lads?"

The men muttered among themselves a moment before the old hand once more addressed himself to Johnnie.

"That was a family fight, sir, in a manner o' speakin', to save our very lives! But, sink me, sir, if we want to jine wi' these murderin' French curs to jump 'er w'en she's outnumbered!"

"God bless me!" jeered Johnnie. "Haven't you the wit to see your lives are still in jeopardy? Have you forgotten we're pirates?"

Above the rumble of resentment rang the old tar's retort: "By God, sir, we ain't forgot we're still Englishmen!"

Johnnie raised his eyebrows and glanced toward the stern, unrelenting figure of his navigator.

"D'ye mark that, Mister Yew?"

"Aye, I do, and I'm proud o' them!" snapped Yew.

Johnnie laughed ruefully. "By my troth, this hardly seems a vote of confidence, yet it is my thought to save our necks without much fighting. So come now, my hearties, keep your faith in Lord Johnnie and go back to your stations. If you obey orders smartly, I doubt not we'll all see tomorrow's sunrise." He beckoned Old Ames. "Mister Ames, I want the guns run out in case of need."

The seamen hesitated in the face of this casual dismissal, but when Ames bustled down among them bellowing orders, they moved in obedience. Ignoring Yew's challenging stare, Johnnie sauntered to the weather rail to view the spectacle.

As Captain de Gounod had observed—it was a beautiful sight. Broad off both bows, their great white sails stretched like wings, the proud hawks of France swooped on their prey. Straight toward them charged the indomitable British lion, her bluff bows tossing the seas aside in contempt. With gun-ports raised and teeth bared, she was the incarnation of old England. Suddenly the Royal ensign blossomed defiantly from her masthead.

Johnnie glanced over his shoulder. "Mister Bottle, hoist the French colors!"

With a grimace of distaste, Ben did as he was bid. Before the flag had reached the truck, the French frigates followed suit. This brought a challenging roar from the *Tiger's* bow guns, which the French answered in kind.

Johnnie swung himself into the rigging. The trap was closing. The French frigates were backing their topsails, and forming a V, into which the *Tiger* was plunging. At the moment, the brig was at the lower end of this triangle—directly in the path of the *Tiger*. If the latter fought through the two frigates, which was barely possible, she'd be at the brig's throat.

"Mister Yew," called Johnnie, "we're not needed here. Bear away to larboard and run in close behind the in-shore frigate, if you please."

Sourly, Yew issued the necessary instructions, and the brig pulled out of danger and began to move up toward the big French frigate, putting her between them and the *Tiger*.

Satisfied, Johnnie dropped to the deck, where Yew, de Gounod and Ben Bottle formed a moody group.

"Well, *mon capitaine*," Johnnie said cheerfully, "what think you now?"

De Gounod leered. *"Mon Dieu,* I should like to be in the battle myself!"

Johnnie roared with laughter. "If that be your wish, monsieur, then, by God, I'll oblige. Ames! *Ames!"*

The old man scuttled onto the quarter-deck. "Aye, sir?"

"Ancient, Captain de Gounod desires to take part in the action. I want you to point your guns as low as possible to hull her below the waterline."

"*Bon Dieu,* not below the waterline!" protested de Gounod. "We do not want to sink the Englishman!"

Johnnie feigned surprise. "*Englishman, mon capitaine?* Who said anything about the Englishman? 'Tis the *Frenchman* I'm referring to!"

De Gounod's eyes started out of his head.

"Monsieur—?" he choked.

"Now, now," mocked Johnnie. "To quote your own words, *mon capitaine*—'tis but the fortunes of war." He looked into the astounded face of Rodney Yew.

"Mister Yew, we'll try the lesson we learned from good Captain de Gounod. Lay close aboard the frigate, and when our bowsprit draws level with her main-chains, haul down that damn ensign and run up the Royal colors!"

Yew's face exploded into a knowing smile. "Aye, aye, sir!"

Cackling like an old hen, Ames scampered forward to lay his eggs. Only then did complete understanding dawn on Captain de Gounod.

"*Maldito labrón!*" he screamed. "Accursed thief! I am betrayed!" Before Johnnie could reach him, he sprang backwards and jerked a pistol from under his coat.

There was a loud report as Johnnie ducked. He straightened and started for de Gounod, only to see the man crumple before him. Then Ben Bottle strode over with a smoking pistol in his hand.

"B'Jesus, I never trust a Frenchman!" he spat. "I been expectin' 'im to try that."

"Johnnie sighed. "He was a treacherous dog," he agreed grimly, "though I'm sorry you had to kill him. I wanted him alive."

Ben's retort was lost in the thunder of guns.

Johnnie turned back to the problem at hand. The *Tiger* had slewed around sufficiently to pour a broadside into the off-shore frigate and was coming about to deal a like dose to her consort. If she was concerned with the odds, she gave no evidence of it.

Johnnie sprang onto the bulwarks to gauge his distances. Sailing large before the wind, the brig was fast drawing under the French frigate's counter. Both ships were rolling heavily in the swells, and Johnnie knew that it was safer to loose his broadside on the up-roll in such a sea, for if the brig rolled her open gun-ports under, she might well founder. On the other hand, if he fired on the down-roll, trusting to the skill of his men to close the ports in time, his shots would strike lower where the Frenchman was most vulnerable.

"Mister Ames!" he called. "Fire on the down-roll as your guns come to bear!"

Ames touched his forelock. "Aye, aye, sir!" he bawled cheerily. As he moved among his men, Johnnie could hear his comments.

"Easy, me 'earties, easy does it! Keep yer matches glowin' and don't forget to draw back smartly so the 'uff won't burn ye!"

Rodney Yew had stationed a hand at the flag halliard, with the Royal ensign draped over his arm. Yew himself was standing by the steersman, waiting for orders.

"A trifle closer, Mister Yew."

Yew acknowledged the order stoically.

There was enough of the poet in Lord Johnnie to let him savor the full flavor of the drama about to unfold. It was a study in contrasts. The day was unsurpassingly beautiful, with sharply defined cumulus clouds decorating the azure sky. The lithe hull of the brig plunged through the royal blue water with the joyousness of a porpoise, while the three frigates circled like gliding gulls.

Johnnie nodded at the man with the flag. In a trice the French ensign was hauled and the Royal colors swept aloft.

The reaction on the frigate was instantaneous. So close she was, Johnnie could hear the frantic commands being shouted, and see the crew diving for the larboard guns. But before they could more than raise the ports, the brig was abreast.

"Let her have it, Ames!" Johnnie shouted.

In one reverberating crash, the beauty was destroyed. The brig heeled recklessly, and smoke blotted out the vision. Johnnie clung desperately to the rigging as they tore past the frigate and waited for the fog to lift.

When it did, the sight that met his eyes was, if less poetic, much more satisfactory. The frigate was listed heavily to larboard as water poured into the gaping holes along her waterline, and her starboard guns, which a few moments before had been trained on the *Tiger* were canted impotently skyward. The confusion aboard was manifest. Her crew was wildly jettisoning her larboard guns to keep her afloat.

The *Tiger* did not pause to question this gift of Providence, but had turned to lay aboard the other enemy.

"Bring her about, Mister Yew," shouted Johnnie. "We'll give him a dose of our larb'd curative."

"Aye, aye, sir!" returned Yew with uncharacteristic enthusiasm. "We've whittled him down to our size."

The French frigate, unable to use her guns because of her list, was crowding on sail to escape. But Lord Johnnie had a remedy for that.

"Mister Ames—aim high to dismast her!"

Cutting across her bows, they ran up to a point-blank range and dealt the *coup de grâce*. When the smoke and thunder rolled away, the hawk of France had lost its wings. The brig slid past, but before she could come about another time, the frigate hoisted English colors from the stump of her mainmast—a token of submission.

The crew went wild with elation, and even Rodney Yew deigned to smile.

"By the powers, sir—that was well handled!"

Johnnie chuckled without mirth. "De Gounod gave us a lesson in artifice."

"That he did, and you've repaid him with interest."

Johnnie shrugged and crossed to the rail. A half-mile off their larboard quarter, the *Tiger* was closing on the surviving Frenchman.

"Put her on the starb'd tack, Mister Yew," said Johnnie. "We'll stand by for the finish."

"Ahoy, the deck!" roared down Ben from the cross-trees where he had gone to watch the battle. "The Frog's struck 'er colors to the *Tiger!*"

Yew snorted. He had the average Englishman's inherent contempt for their perennial enemy.

"Aye! They don't like the game unless the odds favor 'em!"

"We'll heave-to, Mister Yew," said Johnnie.

Ben swung down out of the rigging too late to hear the last command.

"B'Jesus, b'y, we'd best be gettin' the 'ell out o' 'ere w'ilest the gettin's good."

Johnnie shook his head. "No, Mick, our work here is not finished."

The brig, meanwhile, had come up into the wind and was plunging in the swells like a restless horse. Ben's eyes widened in bewilderment.

"But, God A'mighty! That's the *Tiger,* man!"

"I'm equally aware of that, Mick."

As Ben gaped, open-mouthed, Leanna appeared beside them. The Irishman turned to her in desperation.

"Yer lydyship—fer God's sake myke 'im lissen to reason. 'E won't run!"

Leanna gave Johnnie a curious glance. "My influence over the captain is negligible, Ben."

Johnnie was about to retort when Yew broke in: "Beg pardon, sir—the *Tiger* is sending over a boat!"

Johnnie glanced over his shoulder. "So she is, Mister Yew. So she is."

Ben groaned. "An' no doubt yer precious friend Ayers'll be in 'er!"

"I'm certainly counting on that fact," Johnnie conceded dryly. His manner turned brisk. "Mister Yew, I'll manage to detain Lieutenant Ayers here while you and Lady Somerset go aboard the *Tiger*."

"But, sir—!" began Yew.

"No argument, if you please," Johnnie interrupted. "You can tell Captain Bartlett enough of the truth to satisfy your impeccable conscience—that you and her ladyship were abducted by that archscoundrel, Johnnie Rogue; that the *Able Lady* was sunk by de Gounod, but the brig was finally carried by the survivors. If your conscience will permit, you may imply that I am among the missing—I shortly will be in a different sense if my luck holds. I'm quite certain the French dispatches which you give him will more than cover any discrepancies in your story. Is that clear?"

Yew met his eyes. "The credit belongs to you, sir!"

"*Credit?* On the larb'd end of the foreyard! No thank you, Mister Yew."

Leanna touched his arm. "Johnnie, please! Mister Yew speaks the truth! This is your opportunity to—"

"Holy Mither!" shouted Ben. " 'Tis the cap'n's own gig w'at's comin'!"

Johnnie moved to the bulwarks. It was true—the ornate barge moving toward them was the captain's personal boat. Johnnie took his glass and focused on it. To his relief, he made out the slight figure of a dapper young officer in the sternsheets.

He laughed relievedly. "You gave me a bad start, Mick," he chuckled ruefully. "But I think I recognize young Ayers."

"The scheme is madness!" protested Yew "Bartlett will ask about Ayers—"

"You can explain he met with a slight mishap—which I'll guarantee will be the truth—and that he'll be sent over later; also true." He turned to Leanna. "You'd best make ready for the trip, my lady!"

She looked at him a long time, then a flush spread over her features, and she turned slowly away. Johnnie sighed softly.

"Ancient—Lieutenant Ayers hasn't the pleasure of your acquaintance," he told Old Ames. "Greet him when he comes aboard and usher him into the cabin. Mister Yew, Mick and I will receive him there."

"Rape me fer a lubber!" moaned the Irishman as he lumbered after Lord Johnnie. "I never seen a man w'at liked to stick 'is neck into so many nooses, damme if else!"

In the cabin, Johnnie placed a pair of pistols on the table, and sat down. He took the priceless dispatches from his pocket, hefted them tentatively in his hand, then passed them over to Rodney Yew.

"I wish you luck, Mister Yew."

Yew accepted the package. "This time, sir, I wish you the same in all sincerity," he said solemnly. "England lost a great captain, sir, when you—" He paused in embarrassment.

Johnnie laughed. "England can afford to lose me much better than I can afford to lose you, sir." The conversation was taking a turn which Johnnie didn't like. "There is only one thing I charge you, Mister Yew—make it extremely plain that Lady Somerset was dragged aboard *against her will*. Of all the crimes I've committed—and they have been many—that is the one of which I'm most thoroughly ashamed. Also, if you feel kindly enough, you might visit the Duchess of Tallentyre. Explain that though I lost the *Able Lady*, I've gained another craft and will recompense her for the loss. Will you do that?"

"Gladly, sir!"

They heard footsteps coming down the companionway, so Johnnie made a motion of farewell. Then the door opened and a young naval officer came in followed by Old Ames.

Johnnie's sardonic expression changed to dismay.

"Cap'n!" Ames announced with a trace of grimness. "This 'ere's Leftenant Troubridge!"

Lieutenant Troubridge was a brisk, ruddy-faced young man flushed from the excitement of battle and irritatingly effusive.

"Captain Bartlett's compliments, sir!" he gushed, striding into the center of the cabin. "Your timely assistance turned a nasty show into a glorious victory. On behalf of—"

Johnnie recovered his wits. "Excuse me," he cut in. "Where is Lieutenant Ayers?"

"Oh, you know Ayers, sir? Why, he's aboard—" Johnnie's spirits took a nose dive, then recovered slightly as Troubridge added, "But I regret to say he was wounded in the action. Now, sir, Captain Bartlett requests the pleasure of your company so he may thank you in person. As a special mark of his esteem, he sent his own barge—"

Lord Johnnie was no longer listening. Of all the contingencies which had passed through his mind, this was one he had not foreseen.

"How badly was Ayers wounded!" he interrupted.

Troubridge smiled. "Not seriously, I'm happy to report. A splinter in the arm. But he was in the cockpit getting patched up and Captain Bartlett was anxious to see you, sir, so—"

Johnnie rose wearily to his feet. "Very well, Lieutenant, I'll accompany you."

Ben gasped. "Holy Mither, b'y—!" he began, but Johnnie motioned him silent and looked at the old man.

"Mister Ames, be good enough to show Lieutenant Troubridge around the ship while I make ready. Now, if you will excuse me, Lieutenant, I'll join you in a moment."

As Ames and Troubridge quit the cabin, Johnnie turned on the astounded Yew with a bitter laugh.

"There's irony for you, Mister Yew."

"Need it alter your plan, sir?"

"Obviously! As captain, I can't very well send another in my place. Bartlett would be affronted, and worse, he'd be suspicious."

"But, God A'mighty, Johnnie!" argued Ben hotly. "What'll 'appen to ye? Yer commission reads *Cap'n Scarlett,* and Bartlett knows Cap'n Scarlett commanded the *Able Lady* w'at made such a fool out o' 'im!"

"Bottle's correct, sir!" put in Rodney Yew. "But if that wasn't bad enough, there's young Ayers to denounce you! Let me go, sir! I'll make some excuse for your absence—"

Johnnie grinned. "You forget that Ayers knows you, too! You'd be promptly clapped in irons, Mister Yew."

"I'm willing to chance that, sir!"

Johnnie reached for his hat. "Well, I'm not. Now I'll trouble you for those dispatches, Mister Yew."

Yew handed them over reluctantly. He was not accustomed to arguing with captains, but he made another attempt.

"Sir!" he pleaded. "Heretofore, I've obeyed your commands whether I liked them or not. I think you will grant me that."

"Aye, that you have, Mister Yew, and I'm grateful."

"Then in God's name let me go to the *Tiger!* At least my fate won't be the yardarm, as is almost certain to be yours. Bartlett won't be unreasonable with me, and with at least one French prize he isn't likely to chase you if you flee now. It's your only chance, I submit."

Johnnie shook his head. "Though it may surprise you, Mister Yew,

I, too, have a conscience of a kind—one that doesn't permit me to let another man suffer for my mistakes. I thank you kindly for your offer, but I think we're anticipating trouble. I feel quite confident I can handle the situation. When I return, I'll send you and Lady Somerset. If I don't come back, I suggest you get away as best you can."

Johnnie did not see Leanna before he left the brig. In a sense, he was relieved, for it made the parting easier. Having sampled the irrevocability of English justice, he bore no false optimism. Yet if his emotions were raw, his outward appearance was as jaunty as usual. Ignoring Rodney Yew's impulsively thrust-out hand, he waved cheerily to the awed group, and climbed down into the barge.

During the long haul, Troubridge recounted his impressions of the battle. When the *Tiger's* officers had seen the three ships flying the French colors, they had felt sure their sands had run out; their only course but to make a good fight out of it.

"Then, sir, imagine our delight to see you hoist the Royal ensign and hull that Frenchman almost in the same breath! Perish me, sir, it brought tears to my eyes! How was it possible, sir?"

Johnnie shrugged. "It's a long story," he said.

"Oh, of course, sir! I didn't mean to presume! By the way, sir, I didn't catch your name?"

Johnnie was caught off guard. "Why . . . Ballantyne, sir," he said curtly.

"Thank you, sir," murmured Troubridge.

They were drawing close to the *Tiger* and Johnnie could see a prize-crew pulling over to the Frenchman. He offered up a silent prayer that Lieutenant Ayers had gone on that duty. Then a few moments later the barge bumped alongside the *Tiger,* and Troubridge was inviting him to mount the ladder.

It was plain the *Tiger* had been roughly handled in the engagement, but despite the turmoil aboard, a squad of marines was drawn up as a mark of honor. As they snapped to attention, Johnnie's humor gained the ascendancy. What a situation—naval honors for Johnnie the Rogue! Chuckling softly, he permitted Troubridge to lead him proudly to the quarter-deck where a group of officers awaited them.

To Johnnie's intense relief, Ayers was not among them. Then Troubridge was presenting him.

"Captain Bartlett, sir, I have the honor of presenting our gallant compatriot, Captain Ballantyne!"

Bartlett reminded Johnnie of a Rodney Yew who had been submitted to the hands of a cultural lapidary. Beneath the polish and poise, he recognized the same qualities of stolidness, inflexibility and single-mindedness of purpose.

"Captain Ballantyne, I am delighted to have you aboard, sir, so I can thank you personally, and on behalf of England and my officers, for your brilliant assistance!"

Johnnie bowed. "Your servant, sir. Your arrival was equally providential, for I was in effect a prisoner of the French."

"Incredible, sir!"

"Not nearly so incredible as the news I bring you, sir," added Johnnie. "Without disrespect to your officers, this matter is of sufficient moment to request a discussion in private."

"Certainly, certainly!" agreed Bartlett. "Excuse me, gentlemen, I'll introduce you later. Come, sir, we'll repair to my cabin."

He took Johnnie by the arm and steered him toward the companionway hatch, only to meet Lieutenant Ayers coming out of it.

Ayers stopped so abruptly they almost collided with him. His eyes appeared to start out of his head, and though his left arm was in a sling, and his face bloody, his voice was unimpaired.

"God in heaven!" he gasped. "You blackguard!"

Bartlett swore in amazement. "What in blazes—! How dare you, Ayers? Blast me, what effrontery to Captain Ballantyne! I'll have you—"

"*Ballantyne!*" cried Ayers hysterically. "He's *Johnnie the Rogue,* sir! The scoundrel who commanded the *Able Lady* when we chased her in New York."

"You're out of your mind!"

"As God's my witness, it's him, sir! I dare him to deny it!"

Bartlett turned apologetic, if wondering, eyes on Johnnie.

"I'faith, sir, this indignity shall not go unpunished, I promise you," he barked firmly. "If you'll give it the lie for the record—"

Johnnie smiled. "The young man's vehemence is pardonable," he said quietly. "I'm afraid I've taken advantage of his naïveté."

"You see, sir!" shrieked Ayers. "He admits it!"

"Stop bellowing on my deck!" snapped Bartlett. "He's admitted nothing. Now, sir"—he turned to Johnnie—"do you care to explain your remarks?"

Johnnie shrugged. "With your permission, may we do it in the privacy of the cabin."

Bartlett nodded, his stern face frozen. He gestured for Johnnie to precede him, then scowled at Ayers.

"May God help you," he warned grimly, "if you can't give an account of yourself!"

In the cabin, Bartlett invited Johnnie to be seated, then he himself sat down. Ayers was left standing in the center of the carpet.

"Now, genlemen," growled Bartlett, "this affair is unprecedented in my experience. To have such a heinous accusation hurled against a gallant fighter and an honored guest is reprehensible. I warn you, Mister Ayers, that at the moment you stand in danger of arrest. Now proceed at your peril."

Ayers was shaken. His lip trembled and he seemed on the verge of tears. Johnnie chuckled ruefully.

"Captain Bartlett, perhaps we'll save time if I concede young Ayers' charge."

Bartlett half rose from his chair, then sank down in astonishment. "You mean to say you are an impostor!"

"On the contrary, I'm anything but an *impostor*. Ballantyne is my name, though on occasion I'm known as Johnnie Rogue."

Ayers gave a little bleat of elation, but Bartlett motioned him silent. "And you're the pirate who stole the *Able Lady?*"

"I commanded her when we were so fortunate as to elude you in the harbor."

"He also kidnapped the bride-to-be of Sir Clarence Laughton!" put in Ayers hotly.

"A matter which is no concern of yours," Johnnie retorted. "But for your information, Lady Somerset is well and safe aboard the brig."

Bartlett leaned back and stared incredulously at Johnnie. "I'faith I can't believe it!" he gasped. "On my oath, I can't! How could you dare come aboard my vessel posing as an honest seaman?"

Johnnie arched his brows. "*Pose,* sir? I *posed* as nothing. And may I remind you, I came abroad at your invitation."

Bartlett blinked. "So you did, so you did. But God's life, *why?*"

"I confess that requires some explanation," Johnnie said wryly. He told them about his encounter with the brig *Beausejour,* of his duel with de Maurin, and the subsequent discovery that he was a King's courier.

"Those *lettres de cachet* are of the utmost importance to England, Captain Bartlett, so Lady Somerset and Rodney Yew—both prisoners, in a sense, aboard my vessel—convinced me I should deliver them to the authorities."

"Preposterous!" cried Ayers. "If all that took place a week ago, why were you running along so blithely with the French frigates?" He appealed to Bartlett. "It's all a pack of lies, sir, to—"

"Talk when you're spoken to, not otherwise!" Bartlett roared at him. He continued to stare at Johnnie.

"This doesn't make sense—none of it!" he growled. "What were the frigates doing when all this alleged melodrama was taking place?"

Johnnie grinned. He recounted their chagrin on discovering the frigates soon after the fight, and the stratagem he used to make Captain de Gounod cooperate with him. Bartlett did not smile, but he seemed slightly relieved when he said, "Ah, then this de Gounod can support your wild tale?"

"Unfortunately, Captain de Gounod was the sole casualty in this last encounter," Johnnie admitted. "However, I should think my presence on the scene should be sufficient *support,* as you choose to term it, and the dispatches will prove my intent." He tossed the envelope on the table between them.

As Johnnie had surmised, Bartlett had a single-track mind. It was obvious he did not intend to take up a separate problem before disposing of the one on hand. He did not touch the papers.

"Assuming these dispatches are of moment," he went on after a judicious pause, "I'm confounded if I can see why you came to *me,* as you claim!"

Johnnie laughed shortly. "There you have a point, sir. But having to choose between you and eventual discovery by the frigates, I considered you the lesser of two evils."

"By God, you're a cheeky rascal!" marveled Bartlett. "After making a fool of me in front of New York, have you the gall to expect leniency? I'faith, sir, had I been in your shoes, I would have preferred to take my chance with the French!"

"Not if you had read those dispatches," said Johnnie.

Bartlett frowned, and without another word, opened the letters. He read them slowly, with no show of emotion, then calmly put them back in the envelope.

Johnnie's heart sank. Was the obdurate fool going to disregard them? With something like panic, he recalled the Chevalier's frantic attempt to destroy these very papers which Bartlett now viewed with so little concern.

"Mister Ayers," Bartlett said sternly, "be good enough to ascertain the condition of our prize, and whether she's capable of sailing into New York. Tell Mister Dudley to prepare to get under weigh as soon as possible. That is all."

"Aye, aye, sir!" stammered Ayers. "But the brig—"

"*That is all!*" thundered Bartlett.

When Ayers had scurried out of the cabin, he rapped the envelope on the edge of the table.

"This borders on the embarrassing," he grumbled. "When you out-smarted me in the harbor—and a damn fine piece of seamanship it was, sir—I swore I'd have the pleasure of hanging you. Then, by God, you show up when I could use the help of even a pirate. For that, scoundrel or no, I'm grateful, damned if I'm not. That is personally, mind you! Officially, I'm in command of a King's ship of war, and you're a sorely wanted criminal. Do I make myself plain?"

"Unmistakably," smiled Johnnie. "But before your enthusiasm for hanging carries you too far, may I remind you that my so-called crimes are all of a civil nature, and not within the jurisdiction of the navy?"

Bartlett blew his wind. "After that display in New York—" he began, but Johnnie interrupted him.

"I didn't fire on you, sir. I merely declined your somewhat vehement request to heave-to."

"Damn, what difference does it make who hangs you?" he snorted. "The point I make is—if you expect me to let you go, you're mistaken, sir. It would cost me my commission!"

"I haven't asked for my release."

Bartlett rose in exasperation. "Then, by God, what *do* you want? No sane man, crooked or not, walks into a noose for nothing! Come to the point!"

"Don't you credit those dispatches?"

"I don't know what to think of them!" growled Bartlett. "It is in-credible the French would have the temerity to attack us in that fashion. Naturally, I'll place the matter before the proper authorities, but—"

"That's all I ask of you for myself," Johnnie agreed. "However, for my men who are guilty of no crimes, I ask that you permit them to go free with the brig."

Bartlett shook his head. "I can't do that. They broke jail, and—"

"They did nothing of the kind!" Johnnie shouted angrily. "*I* took them out under armed guard!" When Bartlett's eyes widened in disbelief, Johnnie bluntly told him the truth about the forged release.

"So you see," he concluded, "what crime there was was mine! Are you going to penalize them for disabling a frigate that was at your throat? Is that a sample of naval justice?"

Bartlett took a slow turn around the cabin.

"Justice is a slow process," he reflected moodily. "My task is the enforcement of law, not the administration of it. No—the brig will have to go into New York. I'll remove Lady Somerset and put a prize crew aboard."

"That," said Johnnie bitterly, "makes me regret bringing you the dispatches!"

Bartlett appraised him speculatively. "I doubt that statement, sir!" he barked gruffly. "I don't profess to understand you or your motives. From what I've *heard* already of your escapades, I'd say you were an unregenerate scoundrel, but from what I've *seen* of your nerve and seamanship, I'd say you deserved a better fate than a rope's end. As somebody once remarked about Hawkins and Drake—you seem to have the qualities of a burglar and the ideals of a bishop." He started for the companionway. "We'll see what Eden has to say about the matter."

27

LORD EDEN HAD NOTHING TO SAY WHEN JOHNNIE WAS BROUGHT BY Captain Bartlett into his richly wainscotted office the following day. It was a solemn conclave. Seated around a great table were the commanders of both services: Vice Admiral Belloc-Mason of the New York naval squadron, and Major General Sir Humphrey Scott of the army. A Major Laporte, acting in the double capacity of interpreter and notary, sat next to Eden.

Johnnie and Bartlett were motioned into places at the far end of the table, and Major Laporte began reading aloud a translation of the French dispatches. As Johnnie watched the reactions of the others, he saw nothing to encourage him. Eden slumped in his chair, his long bony fingers pyramided in front of his mouth, his pale ascetic features hauntingly melancholy. Belloc-Mason was a stout, beefy-faced man who snorted continually through the reading as if troubled with a catarrhal condition. He was obviously anxious to terminate the ordeal and he kept shifting impatiently in his chair. Sir Humphrey endured it all with cold disdain. Only Captain Bartlett exhibited any spirited interest as he glanced shrewdly from one face to another.

When the translation was concluded, Eden raised his lazy-lidded eyes.

"Well, gentlemen, you have heard the alleged dispatches. What is your opinion?"

"Damnable nonsense!" the Admiral exploded. *"Vox, et praeterea nihil!*—sound without sense! Why, curse me, my lord, it's preposterous on the face of it! The French would not dare attack New York!"

"It is doubtless a forgery planted for a motive!" offered General Scott.

Lord Eden's eyes kindled at the word *forgery*. He let his glance rest speculatively on Johnnie. Johnnie felt his features redden.

"If your Grace please!" he burst out. "The Admiral's words have a too familiar ring. Down through history, admirals have insisted the enemy would never *dare* attack them in their lairs. The Spanish admiral wouldn't believe that Drake would *dare* attack their fleet in Cadiz, but he sailed into the harbor and did it. I doubt not that future admirals will make the same stupid blunder, but I pray not this time! If Latin quotations are your guide, then I submit one more apt: *Verbum sat sapienti*—a word to the wise is sufficient!"

Eden arched his eyebrows quizzically, but Belloc-Mason sprang to his feet.

"You damned impudent hound!" he roared. "I'll have you—"

"Gentlemen! Gentlemen!" interposed Eden, languidly waving the admiral back into his chair. "This is a conference, not a tavern brawl."

Johnnie stood up. In his black brocaded coat, with the black Ramilies wig framing his sharp, wind-burned features, he had the look of an indignant hawk.

"Your Excellency—may I be heard?"

" 'Od's fish! We've heard too much from a bloody pirate!" stormed Belloc-Mason.

Lord Eden, however, bobbed his head, so Johnnie continued: "Whether I am a pirate or not has no bearing on this matter. If you could have seen the way in which the French courier fought to protect his *lettre de cachet,* you would give it more heed. It was because of their conduct, from the vicious attempt to sink us to the reckless fight of the Chevalier de Maurin, that I was convinced of its authenticity. It was then we decided to get this information into your hands."

"You're a bloody mutineer!" the Admiral reminded him hotly.

"To that I'll not say nay," returned Johnnie. "But I understood this was a conference to consider the dispatches, not a court-martial to try *me!* I reiterate, I'm asking nothing for myself, but if this information proves of value to you, then I beg clemency for my men. They became mutineers—as you choose to label them—through circumstances, not from choice. It was *I* who seized the *Eagle* because I was about to hang."

"You're still *about to hang!*" shot back the Admiral.

Johnnie's temper broke loose. "Hang and be damned to you! But don't let your pig-headedness blind you to the truth!"

Lord Eden quieted the tempest, then sternly warned against any further outbursts. When the uproar had subsided, he looked bleakly at Johnnie.

"Your record hardly justifies confidence," he observed dryly. "Have you any credible witnesses to support your remarkable contentions, young man?"

Johnnie gasped. "But, my lord, those dispatches themselves—" he began, but Eden smiled.

"As someone remarked—they might be forged," he interjected. "I believe you are familiar with the process?"

Johnnie colored. "I have no witness save Captain Bartlett," he muttered.

Bartlett started in astonishment. "*Me?* Great Gadfry, I know nothing of the fellow, save that he gave me a merry chase through the harbor, damn me if he didn't! Embarrassing, by God!" He *harumped* a couple of times, then chuckled without mirth. "To give the devil his due, however, I'll admit he hulled that frigate in fine fashion, and afterwards, boarded the *Tiger* of his own volition, but as to the truth of these dispatches—" He spread his hands in a gesture of indifference.

"But there were two frigates convoying the brig, you say?" drawled Eden.

"Aye, your Grace. One sank, but we have the other a prize. Yet though we questioned the officers, none knew of these alleged *lettres de cachet.*"

Belloc-Mason lumbered to his feet. "Pshaw! I can't fiddle around all day!" he growled. "Come, have over with this nonsense. Throw the blackguard in irons, Bartlett, and if the French fleet comes, I'll teach them a lesson. By God, I will!"

"I agree," said Scott.

Bartlett rose and touched Johnnie's arm, but Eden motioned him away.

"I'm not entirely satisfied with all this," he mused. "In any event, I'll have the sheriff confine the prisoner in the Fort with the rest of his men."

"But, my lord, he's a naval prisoner!" protested Belloc-Mason.

Eden smiled wearily. "We have several prior claims. Colonel Laughton has already filed civil charges against him for abducting Lady Somerset, and there's the matter of forgery, prison delivery, assault—"

"Oh, damn it, I care little who does the hanging so long as the blackguard hangs!" fumed the Admiral impatiently. "He's the Devil's Advocate!"

Lord Eden laughed softly and tugged a bell-cord. An instant later, a burly man strode into the office.

"Sheriff, I remand Captain Scarlett into your custody," ordered the Governor. "He is to be held incommunicado for the present."

As he saw the sheriff move toward him, Johnnie felt a touch of panic.

"Your Excellency!" he cried. "Won't you take heed of this warning?"

Eden treated himself to a pinch of snuff. "We'll see, we'll see," he drawled with a yawn.

"My good God!" groaned Johnnie. "I understand now why on the Continent they call the English bull-headed!"

Later, as Lord Johnnie was marched by the sheriff down the gloomy corridors of the jail, he saw some of his men in the cells. They watched in hushed expectancy, but he merely smiled and touched his hat in salutation. When he was finally ushered into a cell, he found Ben Bottle waiting for him.

Ben took one look at Johnnie's face, and groaned: "B'Jesus, it didn't go so good, eh?"

Johnnie stretched tiredly on the lower shelf. "I'm afraid not, Mick. They wouldn't even credit the dispatches. The admiral accused me of forgery."

Ben spat in disgust. " 'Tis the English in 'im, b'y! Once a Britisher gets an ideer, or e'en he don't get one, wild 'orses can't budge 'im! Ah, t'ell wi' it. W'en do we 'ang?"

"They couldn't even make up their minds about *that*," grunted Johnnie. "Tell me, Mick—what happened to her ladyship?"

"Oh, she was met in proper style!" Ben snorted. "That pregnant-lookin' colonel wi' the skirt met 'er in a barge an' carried 'er off."

Johnnie sighed. "Did he seem angry with her, Mick?"

"Angry? Why the fat bastard was a-simperin' like a cream-fed tom-cat!"

"Well, I'm glad, very glad. And what of the men—are they bitter toward me, Mick?"

"To speak true—they ain't. W'en ye went off to the *Tiger*, Rodney Yew piped all 'ands aft an' tolt 'em about the dispatches an' w'y ye led us to the *Tiger*." Ben hesitated and his expression grew puzzled. "Damme, Johnnie, the crazy bastards gi' ye a cheer, rape me if else!"

Johnnie felt an unfamiliar catch in his throat, but his eyes twinkled as he glanced at Ben.

"I gather you didn't share their feeling, Mick?"

Ben squirmed. "Ye know 'ow it be wi' me, Johnnie—I don't 'old fer yer bloody England. But a fren's a fren' to Benjamin Bottle o' Belfast, Ireland, an' we sinks or swims together." He cackled mirthlessly. "An' that goes fer 'angin', too!"

A crash of thunder cut off the conversation, for which Johnnie was grateful. The strain was beginning to tell on him, and he dreaded lest his emotions get out of hand. Then the rain came, and after the summer squall had passed, it settled into a steady drizzle. Johnnie stood under the small, high window, breathing in the smell of earth and flowers flushed up by the rain. Though weary and disappointed, he knew a kind of peace. He was sorry for Ben and the others, very sorry, but for himself almost relieved. When the sun dropped over the harbor, he climbed onto his shelf and fell into a dreamless sleep.

With the dawn came doubt. When the turnkey brought their breakfast, Johnnie tried to question him. Had the fleet moved? Were they making preparations? What of the army? But the jailer knew nothing.

Time after time during the day, the sheriff came to the prison and took away some of the men in pairs. Johnnie's heart sank. Were they hanging them so soon? About noon, Rodney Yew and Old Ames were led out, chained together. The old man waved a cheery hand as they passed Johnnie's cell, but Yew never turned his head.

Seeing this, Ben broke into a torrent of curses. "I tolt ye, Johnnie, s'elp me God, I tolt ye! That bloody bastard's waited to get 'is revenge!"

Johnnie said nothing, but he had been hurt.

In the late afternoon, the sheriff came for Ben Bottle. The Irishman was defiant and angry to go without Johnnie, and it took three men to drag him forth. As they hauled him down the corridor, he shouted farewell to Johnnie.

"An' don't ye fret, b'y! These ruddy catch-polls'll get naught from me, I promise ye!"

Alone now, Johnnie paced the cell. The shadows lengthened until the sunset tinted the cubicle scarlet. Still they did not come for him, and suspense began to raise a torment of its own. Finally even the sun left him, and the cell grew dark and foreboding. The distant laughter of people on the streets accentuated his aloneness. He remembered the nights on the *Able Lady;* the shimmer of phosphorescence on the blue-black water and the murmur of the drowsy watch. Had he done the wrong thing? *Nay,* whispered the small voice, it had been inevitable, yet he couldn't help a shudder at the fate of his men. They who had followed him so faithfully, even into disaster. And they had even cheered him, according to Ben.

Yes, it had all been inevitable. Only his death could release Leanna. He winced to think of her in Laughton's arms, but that, too, was what she wanted. So be it. He forced himself to lie down and eventually sleep claimed him.

He was awakened by the High Sheriff, who looked uncommonly surly as though he, too, had spent a troubled night.

"Come on, *you!*" he growed. " 'Is h'Excellency's ready to dispose o' you!"

"Well, thank God he's made up his mind to something," grunted Johnnie, and began to dress.

Lord Eden was alone when Johnnie was led into the office. In the early sunlight, the great office seemed harsh and austere. The Governor lay sprawled in his chair, his legs spread apart, his sleepy eyes fixed meditatively on the ceiling. He did not look at the visitors as they entered, so the sheriff pushed Johnnie into a chair placed at the far end of the long table, and stood beside him.

In vain, Johnnie scrutinized the Governor's bony face for some hint of his fate. After an uncomfortably long time, Eden brought his eyes down to the visitors.

"Be kind enough to wait outside, Sheriff," he ordered.

That worthy shuffled out with obvious reluctance. As he closed the door, he favored Johnnie with a baleful scowl. When he was gone, Eden smiled a twisted smile.

"The good sheriff holds a lurking suspicion that you are the infamous London road-agent," he remarked offhandedly, "despite that we have learned on unimpeachable authority that the real Johnnie Rogue was slain by thief-takers."

Johnnie looked for some sign of mockery, then shrugged his shoulders.

"It matters little who I am, your Grace. You have more than enough charges against me already."

Eden pouted out his lower lip. "Including a threat against my own life, eh?"

Johnnie flushed. He found the Governor's unwinking stare extremely disconcerting.

"I can hardly deny it, your Grace," he conceded.

"Hardly. I don't mind confessing to you privily, young man, that in my long and not-uneventful career, I've never encountered a more fabulous character!"

Johnnie said nothing and Eden drummed his taloned fingers on the table.

"For my personal satisfaction, I'd like to know your history. We questioned your men separately without much success. Most of them knew nothing, except that toothless old man—Ames, I believe is his name—who was reluctant to talk about you. It required something close to bribery to loosen his tongue."

Johnnie colored angrily, but Eden only chuckled. "But your friend Rodney Yew talked freely. I gather he did not want to join your little . . . ah . . . venture on the *Eagle?*"

"I told you that before!" Johnnie snapped. "Rodney Yew took no part in that, even when a gun was put to his—"

"Hold a moment!" commanded the Governor. "I warn you to make no incriminating statements!"

"Incriminating, be damned, sir! Yew is not involved in any of it. He was taken out of prison by your own guards and forced onto the *Able Lady*. He couldn't help himself! Please believe me in that!"

"You'll convict yourself if you're not careful," sighed Eden. "And there's the matter of your *letters of marque*. Damned clever forgery, I declare. I thought it was my own signature! Would you tell me who accomplished that devilish piece of artistry?"

"That must remain my secret, sir."

Lord Eden seemed indifferent. "I wonder, young man, why you did not petition me for genuine *letters of marque?*"

Johnnie was startled. He laughed hollowly. "That should be self-evident, sir! You would have thrown me in irons!"

Eden nodded his head. "Very likely, though the way you twisted me around your finger at the Duchess of Tallentyre's, you might as easily talked me into granting you a commission. God knows England needs all the clever seamen she can get! Belloc-Mason still refuses to believe you seized the brig the way it is reported."

"Your pardon, my lord, but Admiral Belloc-Mason is a fool!"

The Governor chuckled. "Tut, tut, lad—not a fool. Stubborn, perhaps, but a valiant sea-dog of the old school."

"Yet he's going to sit here on his fat hams and let the French fleet surprise him!" flared Johnnie.

Eden made a neat adjustment of his fingers. "Cool down, young man, I'll get to my point in my own good time. You're not going to leave as precipitously as you did during our last little chat. That, I know. Now about Belloc-Mason—he's a methodical man, and you must realize that neither you nor your men can be deemed credible witnesses since you are all, technically, conspirators. It therefore was necessary to get the truth from unbiased sources."

"But, damn it, your Grace—we're the only ones who know the facts!"

"On the contrary," Eden contradicted him, "we have discovered witnesses above repute."

"Then the French officers—!" began Johnnie, but Eden cut him short.

"It suffices to say we know the story is true, and when the French come, I promise you they'll be well received. Belloc-Mason is smarting under his previous doubting, and he'll take his revenge on them."

Johnnie heaved a great sigh and sat back. When he met Eden's searching glance, he grinned.

"That's almost more than I hoped for," he confessed.

His Excellency took a pinch of snuff, toyed with the jewel-encrusted case a few moments, then leaned sternly on his elbows.

"With that disposed of," he proceeded briskly, "the question now remains—what is to be done with you?"

"Is that complicated, my lord?"

"It grows so," said Eden. "You were held on a charge of abduction. Now, out of a clear sky, Laughton has withdrawn his complaint without explanation, so of course, the Crown cannot prosecute on that charge."

Johnnie whistled in amazement. "I'll be damned!"

"H'mmn! And so will I, sir! I'm not anxious to testify in open court how you hoodwinked me in the matter of liberating your men; it would make me the laughingstock of the Colonies. And as to the mutiny— we have recovered the *Eagle* and Rodney Yew has convinced us that Captain Bloodsmythe was criminally insane. I almost regret that he *jumped* overboard—a brute like that should be court-martialed!"

Johnnie held his breath. Though Eden was not smiling, there was a ghost of a twinkle in his eye. Yet Johnnie dared not let himself hope.

"The upshot of the matter," Lord Eden said at last, "is that I find myself in a very embarrassing position. We have a prisoner on our hands, but no legitimate charges against him. To complicate it further, I discover that he had powerful and influential friends here in the city to back him."

For the first time in his life, Lord Johnnie was thoroughly and completely flabbergasted.

"I . . . I don't understand, sir!"

" 'Pon my soul, for an obviously clever man, you certainly have a blind side," snorted Eden. "Why did you not tell me you were the son of Lord Ballantyne?"

Johnnie went white. "I regret you learned that, my lord!"

His Excellency shook his head. "You should be extremely proud of the fact. John Ballantyne was a gallant gentleman. It was my privilege to know him well." He became conscious of Johnnie's acute discomfiture, so he rose and circled the table.

"I won't prolong this, lad," he said kindly. "This is a new world where we must judge men by their deeds, not by their past. You risked your life as surely as your father did in the service of your country, and she is indebted to you. Despite that, however, I cannot let you go scot-free, for England needs every ship and fighter she can get. But I have a proposition for you, Captain." He forced an envelope into Johnnie's rigid hands. "Here are *letters of marque*—unforged this time. If you will accept them, we'll consider the case closed."

Johnnie swayed to his feet, unable to believe his ears. He stared hard at Lord Eden until he realized the smile he saw was as genuine as it was kindly.

"But my men, your Grace?"

". . . are already aboard the *Beausejour*, watering and victualing her for sea. Oddly enough, Rodney Yew insisted on serving under you, although I offered him a command of his own. So, you have a full complement, and with a large French fleet on the way over, I fancy there'll be plenty of stragglers that will net a tidy fortune to an interprising young privateersman. How about it, Captain Ballantyne?"

Johnnie's eyes blurred until he could hardly see the long white hand held out to him. He grasped it shakily and tried to express in his grip the feelings his voice refused to convey.

Lord Eden draped a friendly arm about his shoulder and walked him to a door leading into an adjoining room. With his free hand on the knob, Eden paused briefly.

"Good-bye and God speed you, John. Your father would have been very proud of you, as I am." He opened the door and steered Johnnie through it. "I imagine you are anxious to get back to your ship, but you had better spare the time and take leave of your friends." He gave Johnnie a gentle push, and closed the door.

"Brother God!" rasped a familiar voice. "You act like you've been pole-axed! What in hell's the matter with you, Johnnie?"

Johnnie pulled himself together. There before him stood the Duchess of Tallentyre, and, more miraculously—Leanna. He managed to bow, but when he tried to speak, his voice broke.

"Your Grace! My lady!"

Leanna was pale and trembling, but the old woman broke into a merry cackle.

"Bless him—he's in a trance!" she remarked to the girl. "Since it's not over me, I'm damned certain, it must needs be over you. Can't you do something to revive the poor oaf?"

"What can I do, your Grace?"

"God damn it, child, do I have to give you lessons? Bah, there's plenty you can do, I'll warrant! Well, it's plain he's not capable of talking business with me, so I'll leave you the field."

Leanna leaned forward impulsively and kissed her cheek.

"God bless you, dear Reggie! I thank you from the bottom of my heart!"

The Duchess of Tallentyre reared back and gave her a frosty stare.

"You've nothing to thank me for, my pretty wench!" she snapped. "Just count yourself lucky I'm a decrepit old hag, for to speak plain, if I was thirty years younger, I'd be clawing your eyes over this handsome buck, believe me!"

She whirled around and offered her hand to Johnnie. "Here's luck, you rakehell! With this gorgeous chit breathing down my neck, I know I can't expect more than a handshake—damn her lovely eyes!"

Johnnie knelt and raised her hand to his lips.

"I owe you more than I can ever hope to repay, your Grace," he murmured.

"Oh, twaddle!" sniffed the Duchess. "I told you I was a business woman. You'll *repay,* all right—count on it! Chauncey and I didn't put up the bond for your commission just for the hell of it, my buck!"

"Chauncey? You mean *Eden—?*"

"Naturally!" laughed the Duchess. "Although it's off the record. He's been after me for some time to cut him in on a paying venture that was legitimate, so we decided to take a chance on you together."

She saw Johnnie was too stunned to say more, so with a brief "Good luck, both of you!" she sailed majestically out of the room.

Johnnie turned slowly to Leanna.

"She's a wonderful, wonderful woman!" breathed the girl.

Johnnie bit his lip. "I'm beginning to see through the fog, Leanna. It was *you* who convinced Eden the dispatches were genuine!"

"Rodney Yew backed me in that, Johnnie."

"But you should not have involved yourself! Suppose Sir Clarence hears—"

"He has heard, Johnnie! I told him the truth!"

Johnnie gasped. "You told him about *us?*"

"The whole truth. He was very understanding, and offered to get me a divorce." She saw the sudden pain on Johnnie's face, and she laughed softly.

"But I assured him I loved you, darling, and only you, so he went to Eden, like the gentleman he is, and withdrew the charges."

Johnnie sank limply in a chair and covered his face with his hands. "My God!" he said. "I can't believe it!"

She put a hand on his shoulder. "It's simple enough, my darling—you are free. Free to start all over again. Johnnie the Rogue is dead, and John Ballantyne has emerged."

He raised his eyes to her face. "Did I hear a-right, Leanna? Did you say—?" He held his breath.

She went down on her knees before him. "You said some wonderful things in your delirium, Johnnie—about loving me. Can you say them again in your right mind?"

He touched her cheek tenderly. "I'm not in my right mind now, sweetheart, but I'll try."

Somewhere in the distance the noon gun thundered, but John Ballantyne did not hear it.